NIGHT SUN

A NOVEL

NIGHT SUN

──── A NOVEL BY ────

DAN VINING

VIREO/RARE BIRD · LOS ANGELES, CALIF.

THIS IS A GENUINE VIREO/RARE BIRD BOOK

A Vireo Book | Rare Bird Books
453 South Spring Street, Suite 302
Los Angeles, CA 90013
rarebirdbooks.com

FIRST HARDCOVER EDITION

This is a work of fiction, all of the characters and events in this story are imagined.

Set in Dante
Printed in the United States

Book Design by Robert Schlofferman

10 9 8 7 6 5 4 3 2 1

Publisher's Cataloging-in-Publication data
Names: Vining, Dan, author.
Title: NightSun : a novel / by Dan Vining.
Description: First Hardcover Edition | A Genuine Vireo Book | New York, NY;
Los Angeles, CA: 2018.
Identifiers: ISBN 9781945572647
Subjects: LCSH Private investigators—Fiction. | Los Angeles (Calif.)—Fiction. |
Dystopias—Fiction. | Science fiction. | Noir fiction. | BISAC FICTION / Noir | FICTION
/ Science Fiction / Apocalyptic & Post-Apocalyptic.
Classification: LCC PS3622.I56 N54 2018 | DDC 813.6—dc23

Chapter One

Roy Orbison's "Oh, Pretty Woman" played over the thin Echoflex speakers sunk into the black ceiling joists. Coming out onto the runway from behind purple curtains, a bit hesitantly, was the next pretty thing, dressed as a secretary, or at least some tired old man's idea of one from back when they still called them that, when the song was still young.

"She isn't a woman, but isn't she pretty?" the MC said. Only his eyes were visible through the inch-wide slit in the painted-out window of the DJ booth.

The club had a name but it kept changing so nobody bothered to remember it anymore. The space had last been a theater, before regular people stopped going out to the movies. The reconstructors had ripped out the seats and flattened the floor and converted the black hole into a "gentlemen's club." It could hold a hundred people, but this Tuesday night there were just eight or nine men in the joint. And one woman who stayed in the deeper shadows at a table for one.

"Call her... 'Jane,'" the MC said.

Two men clapped in response. Two or three others set down their drinks and joined in, thinking Jane would like it, that somehow it would buy them something with her. She walked that one-foot-in-front-of-the-other walk out to the end of the runway and stopped as the music faded, replaced by ambient tones from a machine. She just stood there. It was like a fashion show, only she wasn't selling anything. Yet she wore "business attire," sixties vintage, a tight gray skirt that ended below her knees, a white blouse, and a gray jacket over the skirt. Hose, heels, probably a garter belt. She took a step forward, went right up to the edge of the stage, and looked out into the red-and-white glare, projecting *alone*. It was as if she were looking out her office window before she started work, as if it were morning and she were the first one in and already needed to see what she was missing, cooped up inside like this. She was good at her job.

She let them get a long look at her—let them start filling in the blanks in their own heads, let them make her *theirs*—before she turned her back on them. As she walked toward the purple curtain, an old-style curved-corner gray metal desk, a roll-around armless chair, and a black obelisk of a file cabinet glided out to meet her, as soundless as any dream, a slick bit of stagecraft. The desk came to an at-rest position just as she reached it.

She took off her suit jacket, folded it, and put it over her chair, smoothed out her skirt, and sat down. She straightened a stack of papers in the "out" basket, whipped away the gray cover for the IBM Selectric, folded it, and slid it into the top drawer of the desk. The set was on the diagonal so they could see the leading edge of her shape as she sat there. But this wasn't about her legs or her hips or her breasts, though her body was exhibition quality. They'd all already seen as much skin as they were going to see: a V of flesh at the collar, her bare arms, her knees and calves. And that beautiful, unsatisfied face. There wasn't a sound—there weren't any sound effects—but the phone "rang" and lit up. She looked down at it and sighed and waited another long second and then picked it up, pretending to answer. She smiled ever so slightly.

Who was calling? *You.*

It was a story bar. Some called them "fiction clubs" or "vignette joints." They'd come along in LA in 2017 or '18, the next thing after the last bleak permutation of the strip bar had been exhausted, after women had offered every inch of themselves and skin—just skin—had grown hard to market. What do you sell of a woman when you have sold every inch of her? Her story. A secretary, a nurse, a waitress. A checkout girl at the grocery store. A bank teller. A teacher in a classroom between classes, looking out the window. (Why were they always looking out windows?) What was her story? What was she thinking of? You. Coming home to you, running away from it all with *you,* counting the slow minutes until she could be in your arms. Most men weren't good enough at lying to themselves to buy into the story if these little dramas had been set in the here and now, in the present. Things being the way they were now, there was no place to find this kind of fantasy but the past. Fantasy was probably too pretty a word. Whatever you wanted to call it.

Human hunger. That's what Nate Cole called it, with a mixture of his own longing and a general disgust at the ways of man. He was something of an expert on the subject of what men wanted, what drove them to do what they do, what fires burned inside them, burned them right down to the ground sometimes. He was a cop. If they had story bars for women with *men* in poses and vignettes, and if Nate had somehow come to be on one of those stages, he would have been billed as The Protector. Hard on the outside but soft inside. That fantasy.

Nate Cole was a White—big, good-looking—a standout even before he opened his mouth. He looked as if he'd played high school ball out in the Valley, but he hadn't. He was almost tall enough and good-looking enough to require him to go into show business. It was 2025 and most of the other CROs—the cops on the beat—were small now, certainly smaller than cops had been in the old days when half of the LA force was made up of White former high school linebackers, meaty Catholics, or strapping Born Agains, the other half Latin or Black or mixed-race former running backs or point guards, in a ratio determined by whether an African-American or a Latino was mayor. LA had long since forgotten how or why to get a White mayor elected. These days, governance seemed to be about keeping people of color happy—or keeping them down, depending on which way the riot smoke was blowing.

Nate fiddled with a bullet as he watched Jane, turned it end over end, wearing down the lead another fraction of a millimeter. He always needed something to do with his hands. The bullet was an old .38 Special, round with a flat head, a range load, and a wad-cutter that weighed as much as ten regulation rounds now. Thirty-eight hollow-points were what they issued to the men and women in blue back in the olden days, back when they still wore blue and hardly ever had to shoot anybody. Then, even one round fired meant a week's worth of paperwork and straight-faced debriefings on hard chairs. And that was if nobody died. Nowadays, all Internal Affairs really cared about was whether a cop coming in off a shift dumped his "brass" in the recycling bin. (They still called it brass though the casings were polymer. The slugs themselves were tempered glass.)

Jane produced another phony smile as she spoke into the phony phone. Nate was almost falling for it and was annoyed with himself because of it.

"I didn't know you were into drama," a dark voice said, standing over him. A female voice. "I took you for an old school skin-and-gin type."

Nate raised his glass. "I'm as liberal as the next guy."

Ava Monica was a cop, too, but private. Tonight she wore a dripping black raincoat. She took it off, draped it over the empty chair.

"You call that rain?" Nate said.

"Anytime it even drizzles now," Ava said. "I think it's going to be the last we ever see."

She was dressed in her signature outfit, a cat suit with a tight hood that fit like a helmet and went right up under her chin and over her ears, an outfit made out of some kind of knit that would make anyone who'd ever read a book think of a knight's chainmail. The suit was dark gray and tighter than it needed to be.

"Hey," Nate said, "I just noticed: you're a woman." She was still standing.

"And pretty," she said.

"Where do you hide your gun in that get-up?" Nate said.

"My mind is my weapon," she said.

"Yeah. Me, too," Nate said. "That and all my, you know, weapons."

She sat down before he could tell her to. The two of them watched Jane for a long moment. "This goes right over my head," Ava said.

"*Young Mom Washing the Dishes* is next I think," Nate said.

"Nothing sexier than that."

"I'm not sure it's about sex anymore," Nate said and looked across the table. It had been a couple of months since he'd seen Ava. He'd forgotten how good-looking she was. He wondered what that meant, that he'd forgotten. With Nate, every thought had a follow-up. "You guys threw in your cards on that a while ago," he said.

"*You* guys?" Ava said. "I haven't played for years. I'm out here all by my lonesome."

Nate said, "I know a gunner, works nights just like you. I'll hook you two up. You can go out for brunch in the Marina." Nate drained his club soda. "You want a drink?"

Ava shook her head. Her eyes kept returning to Jane. "So if she's not a woman, what is she?"

"It's complicated," Nate said.

"She's not mechanical, right?"

"They don't have robos this real," Nate said. "But I guess they keep trying. They got a sex doll out now with a heater in it. And a cat that gives a shit."

Ava pried her eyes away from the stage. "I don't even want to know," she said.

"Like I said, it's complicated."

Ava didn't like it when men blew her off. "Complicated how?" she said.

Nate said, "They start with Thai or Islander boys, sixteen or seventeen. Bleach the skin, fix the eyes, make a few cuts, start the augmentation…"

Ava held up her hand to stop him. He stopped.

The stage lights went out. When they came on again, Jane and her stage set were gone. There wasn't much applause. The lone woman in the shadows at the back of the club stared into her untouched red wine.

Ava broke the silence. "I forget, are you giving me money this time or the other way around?"

Nate dug an envelope out of the chest pocket of his RefCord armored jumpsuit and tossed it onto the table. "Or maybe you want food stamps," he said. "I think I got a block of soy in the trunk of the rig."

"I tell you what, I'd take a cheeseburger. A hundred-dollar cheeseburger."

"The TV said no beef until the end of the month. I forget which month."

"I don't get it," Ava said. "How do you run out of cows?"

Nate pushed the envelope toward her. "Thanks," he said, and meant it.

"So he was there."

"Wearing an XXL Rams shirt and a stupid little twenty-five-caliber auto in his sock, a steak knife in his back pocket. His brother was in the other room, too high to get involved. Just like you said, pill-crushers one and all."

Ava said, "So you took him alive?"

"I didn't say that."

"I'll sleep just fine," Ava said. "He was a brute. He made his little boy go fetch the baseball bat he beat her with." She took the envelope of cash and made it disappear into the folds of her slinky suit.

She looked him in the eye. Nate Cole. She was thinking, *Hey, I could have a drink with him... Where's the harm in that?* Across the street was a real bar with a singer/piano player with a long memory. She could admit she was lonely. She was way downtown tonight, in more ways than one.

She got up, pulled the raincoat over her shoulders, and flipped the hood over her knit headpiece. "The night calls," she said.

"I always forget how tall you are," Nate said.

"I always forget how bad you are with women," Ava said.

Nate watched as she walked out. The crowd just sat there in the dark, deader than dead, watching the empty stage, waiting for the next fake thing to happen. None of them even looked at Ava, a real woman in the here and now. As she reached the padded leatherette door to the outside, it opened by itself, letting in the hiss of the rain, like a sound effect, like some kind of cheap cue for melancholy, and she was gone into the night.

Chapter Two

The CRO cops—it stood for Civic Reconnaissance Officers, as if all they did was *look*—had given up the ground game and gone to the air. There weren't fifty rubber-tire patrol cars left in the Los Angeles Police Department. Cops still walked a beat or rode bicycles, but most of the real LAPD manpower was in the air. Everything was in the air: EMT rigs, fire trucks, bomb squads, SWAT. It wasn't by choice. The streets now were all but useless, for people in cars and trucks anyway. Getting from downtown to Century City or Westwood or Long Beach in a car took longer than getting from LA to Santa Barbara.

The gridlock was the result of the immutable Law of Unintended Consequences. In 2018, California had built twenty-two new mini-nukes—called Schwarzeneggers for their squat shape and brute power—fired them up before the mud was dry, lit up the state. The juice in the grid was so cheap now it wasn't even metered. The gridlock problem blew up a year after the nukes came along, in 2019, when the government introduced a stripped-down rubber-floor-mat one-speed one-color electric car called a Federal. Built in China. A busboy working half-shifts could pay off a Fed in six months, if the government hadn't already given him one outright when he got a vasectomy. From Oxnard to Anaheim, the lights in the 'burbs were blazing, but nobody was home. Overnight, all eighteen million Angelenos hit the dusty trail in their Feds, nose to tail, elbow to elbow on the 10 freeway, on the 405, on the 60, on the 90, and on every cross-town surface street, creeping along, covering a half mile every two hours, happy idiots listening to their music players. (Federals didn't have radios.)

After a few months, the smart people caught onto the obvious and started leaving their cars home in the driveway—walking, biking, skating, or riding the Metro trains—but most Angelenos somehow had never figured it out. Or maybe they just liked driving. Or "driving." By now the population was up to twenty million, even after subtracting the three million Mexican nationals who moved back to Mexico in 2024. Freeways were clogged, big streets were clogged. Some smaller streets were halfway open for part of the day, except for the intersections. Street cops wrote thousands of $384 tickets for "Abandonment of a Working Vehicle on an Operative Thoroughfare." The city bus system had all but died. Who wanted to sit with other people crawling along when you could sit alone crawling along? City buses turned into diners with a nostalgia theme. At least there weren't any hit-and-run accidents anymore.

The cops flew lightweight two-person helos not much bigger than Jet Skis. They had an official name made up of letters and numbers, but everyone just called them Crows, like the cops who piloted them. A CRO in a Crow, man and machine become one. The stubby sky-cruisers were black on the bottom and white over the cockpit, which meant that from below they were all but invisible. From above, you could see them from miles away. The white paint was photoluminescent. From on high, LA at night looked like a reef thick with prowling fish.

The CRO rigs were the product of another big-dollar rushed government engineering job, but they were rock-solid and fast as a Ferrari. The super-efficient engine was internal combustion, aluminum, ran on hundred-and-one-octane race fuel nobody could get just for fun anymore. Lift came from a pair of six-foot rotors side by side above the cockpit, control from stabilizers on the tail. Some engineering trick made the birds almost silent. The city had pulled down all above-ground wiring. No telephone poles, no wires to impede the CROs in their Crows. Every building three stories or higher was required to clear a space for a landing pad. *"Always There..."* was the LAPD slogan painted on the door now—complete with the ellipsis—replacing *"To Protect and To Serve."*

Every CRO had an armed-up bodyguard to watch his back and get him downstairs and through the crowds on the sidewalks. They were called "gunners." Or, impolitely, "killers." Nate Cole had been through five gunners in the past year, three killed on the job, one who never showed for his second day—even though the job paid more than what a high school teacher made—and a fifth who lasted a month before he put in for psych disability. Gunners weren't CROs. They weren't even like street cops or bike cops, who were a big step down in power and prestige from the cops in the air. Gunners were hired guns. Bodyguards. Meat. Gunsels.

They were there to look fierce and identify targets and shoot straight, skills most of them brought to the job from the street. Or video games.

A Long Beach Samoan, Isaako Tauiliili, was Nate's gunner now, though Nate had a rule that he never learned their names until a month or two in. So he just called him "Gunner," or "you big dumb mother-humper," a term of endearment in Isaako's case. In spite of himself, Nate was growing prematurely attached to this one. Isaako had been with him three weeks and hadn't made a bad move yet. And there he was, standing in the weak drizzle beside the rig, fully alert, a fat finger resting on the trigger guard of the full-auto rifle in his hands. A short-barreled Streetsweeper shotgun hung off his shoulder, upside down on his back, making him look like a Sicilian mob guard in an old movie. Nate had set down the bird on the roof of a brick apartment building next door to the story bar.

"You don't have a hat?"

Isaako grunted some kind of answer.

"It's not like anybody is going to jack the Crow," Nate said. "It hasn't gotten that bad yet."

Nate slapped a remote control switch sewn into the left sleeve of his jumpsuit. The helo's engine started, the side-by-sides began rotating, and the cockpit hatches came up automatically, gull-wing style. Nate wasn't in any hurry to go anywhere. He stood under the upturned hatch, using it as a porch, and looked out across the grayed city. He liked the rain—even a pitiful little squirt like this—liked the look of it and the smell of it, liked to fly in it, liked to look at it out the window when he was home, liked to walk rainy streets. Truth be told, he liked to splash through puddles in his oiled Doc Martens when no was around to see. He put his palm out, thinking maybe he'd catch the last raindrop to fall on LA. Maybe he'd put it in a bottle, donate it to The Museum of Rain.

Isaako started to walk the perimeter of the craft, a by-the-book security routine.

"Forget it, get in," Nate said.

The Crows had the cop/pilot up front and the gunner behind them in a slightly elevated second seat, stowed like luggage. Gunners had nothing much to do as long as they were up in the air. Some took catnaps on the short hops across the city or just stared at the floor when they were cruising looking for trouble. The designers hadn't put a window in back. A gunner had to lean forward for a view of the rooftop as they were landing to see what they were getting into.

Nate flew out of DTLA toward South Central, staying above the all-but-stalled traffic on the 10. Below, the freeway was a river of white on one side and red on the other. The red side looked like slow-flowing lava.

"They have volcanoes in Samoa?" Nate said to the back seat.

"Vailulu'u," Isaako said.

"What?"

"Vailulu'u. Near where my father was from."

"I'd like to buy eleven vowels," Nate said.

"What?" Isaako said.

"You never saw that show, when you were a kid? *Wheel of Fortune?*"

"No."

"How old are you?"

"Nineteen," Isaako said.

There was a number Nate was now wishing he didn't know. He pivoted and dove down, slowing as he moved over the tops of the creeping cars. In the air, behind the stick, was the only place Nate was anything near this graceful. He hovered, the down-tilted nose of the rig just twenty feet above the traffic, the spotlight hung from the undercarriage shining right in the motorists' eyes.

"Hey, Killer," Nate said. "You know what they used to call the inside lane?"

"What?"

"The fast lane, swear to God."

Isaako grunted a laugh and leaned forward to see what Nate was seeing.

"Look at them," Nate said. "Happy as pigs in shit."

A dozen cars crept along underneath, like embarrassed house pets slinking away from an "accident." But Nate was right, the drivers were all smiling.

"I don't get it," Nate said.

Then one guy, eyeball to eyeball with Nate—a guy in a business suit with the tie pulled to one side—flipped him off.

"There you go," Nate said. He pulled up and killed the NightSun, kicked the Crow into a hard turn, and headed off toward Hollywood on the diag.

After ten blocks, the screen in the heads-up display came to life, a blue-eyed beauty with black hair in a cut that was all zigzags. She didn't really exist. How could she? She was there all shifts, seven days a week. She didn't exist, but they called her "Carrie" and treated her as if she did. She was as much of a steady girl as most of the CROs had.

"One down, Nate Cole," Carrie said. "South Central. No CVA." She spoke out an address as it was printed across the screen. "No CVA" meant *No Continuing Violent Activity*. "Down," of course, meant *dead*.

◆ ◆ ◆

EIGHTY-EIGHT.

Six minutes later, Nate was standing over a dead boy laid out in his momma's bed. He'd been shot somewhere else, brought home by friends. Nate guessed he was still officially a boy. He looked thirteen or fourteen. He was dressed like a boy, but a boy pretending to be a man who still dressed like a boy. He was sure enough dead, a hot one right through the head, back to front: not the most attractive way to do it. The bedroom was crowded with mourners. There were two aunts and three cousins, including a little girl with her backpack still on who'd probably started the day in a classroom. They were all Blacks. The women and girls looked alike—strong genes. They looked like decent people. Family. The womenfolk had put the boy on his back in the bed, a pillow under his fouled head, on top of a patchwork quilt, the kind nobody made anymore.

"How old?" Nate said to the woman standing closest to the bed.

"Thirteen," she said, not lifting her eyes from the body. She was the only woman in the place who wasn't bawling her eyes out. It would turn out that she was the boy's mother.

Nate let her be, stepped away a couple of feet. They were in a ten-by-ten front bedroom. The house at 5163 South St. Andrews Place was a neat, kept-up, one-story Craftsman bungalow with a little patch of mowed grass between the porch and street, in a neighborhood of similar homes. It wasn't what most people pictured when they heard "South Central" on the news. Gawkers were on the lawn outside the iron-barred bedroom window, peeking in, as if they were watching a scene on TV. Nate looked over at them, about to shoo them away, but thought better of it. Some of them were crying too, and it wasn't because it was a good show. It was their neighborhood, not his.

"What's his name?"

Nate didn't get an answer because in the next second something happened that made his whole body rock back involuntarily, a plot point, a turn of events there was no way for a man to be prepared for, even a man who'd been in rooms like this time and again.

The dead boy came through the bedroom doorway. Fast. With a gun in his hand. Same face, same clothes, same body. Same boy—or so it seemed.

"Samuel, no!" the mother said.

Isaako was right behind the boy, trying to get a hold of his gun hand. Nate dropped into a crouch with a hand over his head as if the ceiling were falling in on them and went for his service pistol, deciding without deciding that he'd figure out who was who and what was what later. Probably after he shot somebody.

"*Samuel!*" the mother screamed again. The boy looked her in the eyes, then looked at himself on the bed, then at Nate the CRO on the floor with the gun in his hand.

The boy's gun hand started to come up. Isaako dove at the back of the kid's knees.

In his mind, Nate had already fired the gun in his own hand.

Next, quick, all in the same crowded moment, the looky-loos outside started screaming and saying, "Oh no!" ducking and diving, turning, looking up the street, in the direction of a sound, a motorcycle sound.

Nate turned. "What the—"

A heartbeat later, bullets started coming through the bedroom windows and walls. The sound caught up with the visuals, the sputtering of machine-pistol fire and a shattering, splintering noise on top of the swelling motorcycle racket. Getting louder. Was there a second motorcycle? The answer came immediately and along with it a *new* sound, a pounding, like somebody beating on a steel door with a hammer.

Nate was about to put a name to it when he took one in the calf. He was still only halfway to the floor. His gun was ready to go in his hand but there was no place to point it. Isaako dropped, shot, two or three rounds in the chest plus one more punching a hole in his throat, which was already blowing out blood. Other bodies started falling, aunts and cousins. One skinny woman—no more than a teenager—was blown against the dresser, breaking her spine so that she was left draped over it backward.

Nate landed on the brown carpet, right in Isaako's face, eye to eye.

Somehow the boys' mother was untouched. She hadn't moved from where she stood when she'd answered Nate's first question. It was as if she were in a steel bubble.

Then it was quiet again, save a dying moan or two.

Nate stood up, the useless gun still wrapped up in his white, bloodless fingers. He didn't put it away for another three or four minutes.

Chapter Three

Eighty-eight. Eighty-nine. Ninety. Ninety-one. Ninety-two. Ninety-three. Four CRO units showed up. An EMT wagon, an ambulance—they were called Dittbenners for a reason lost to time—landed in the street and the techs went in to fetch the surviving twin. The second boy, Samuel, wasn't badly hurt. With all of the old-school lead flying in the bedroom, it didn't make any sense that he hadn't been killed, but there it was. A minute after the techs went into the house, they came out with the boy snugged in a hold-suit and strapped onto a gurney. They clamped the gurney onto the skid of the ambulance, jumped in, and lifted off for KingMem. A coroner's rig dropped in as soon as the Ditt was out of the way. The coroner's office techs—they were almost all women, so the CROs called them *coronettes*—stepped over a body or two in the front yard and went into the little box of a house. They would bag up Isaako first, before the women and girls inside or the three men killed outside. Professional courtesy, even for a gunner.

The murder room got too crowded for Nate, so he went into the kitchen and found a beer in the fridge and stepped out onto the front porch, using the toe of his boot to open the screen door. He took in a deep breath. The nothing rain was long gone. In LA it was always a little cool after any rain, cool in a way that made you feel a bit more alive, as if you'd survived something, as stupid as that was. It likely had something to do with Los Angeles being in the middle of a desert. Over on the grass, someone was pushing on the chest of one of the dropped spectators, but the young man was way gone, Nate could tell from twenty feet away. The other dead spectator was an old man, his gray head resting on the younger man's leg, as if he were taking a nap at a picnic, leaning against his son.

Ninety-four. Ninety-five.

"Shit," Nate said, standing there on the porch. He meant it in an amazed way. He never twisted off the cap of the beer.

He had blood all over his arms, most of it Isaako's. He bent down and turned on the garden hose. With the miser valve the water only came on for ten seconds and then shut itself off for a full minute, so it took a while to clean up.

"Sir," a voice said in front of him.

Nate just waited, squatting in the grass, head down. He knew from the shape standing over him who it was and what the kid was going to say next.

"Sir, I'm your new gunner. My name is—"

Nate said, "I'm just going to go on home. You too. Tomorrow."

"But, sir," the kid began.

Nate stood. He wiped his wet hands on the kid's shirt. "Tomorrow. Go. Go away. Come back ten years older."

"I understand," the new gunner said.

Nate thought about shooting him. The kid retreated just in time.

Nate went back inside, did what he had to do at the scene, his part of the wrap-up. The mother had already been hustled out the back door by one of her people. She wasn't going to talk to the police anyway, Nate knew. He scanned the dead boy's fingers, the one in the bed, pulled prints, stuck a DNA straw up the boy's nostril and inserted it into the scanner for quick read. It came back: *Nathanial Wallace, DOB: 07/16/2012.*

Nathanial Wallace. The kid's name was Nate. It always added something when you shared a name with one of the dead. He stepped back and played dumb when the CSI team came on scene. He left it up to them to come up with the official, ordinary version of what had happened, leaving out the poetry. Nate had a bad attitude about forensics. He'd been a cop a long time—twelve years, a lifetime in cop years—and knew that most of the time it wasn't about science or cells or DNA or fingerprints. The *why* was human nature, the ways of the beast. It was anthropology, if you wanted science. You "solved" murders one way: by leaning on murderers and the people who knew murderers, got them to blurt out something, some unfiltered something.

Nate walked down the middle of South St. Andrews Place, heading back to his rig. He'd parked it on the pitcher's mound on a homemade ball field the neighbors had built on a vacant lot. He hit the button on his upper sleeve and the doors lifted and he got in; he was up and out of there, almost before the tach and roto-gauge went green for go.

He circled the murder house and clicked on his fake sun. Three cops in the backyard, who were shining their silly little flashlights at an illegal barbecue grill for some reason—probably because they were thinking of getting one like it—looked up at him. One of the men was a cop on the gang squad—the GU— whom Nate had some history with, a Black named Whitey. He looked up at Nate and put his hands together in front of his face in the yoga prayer pose and bowed, like an asshole.

Gang members were gathering in front of the house, wearing white tees and black rags on their heads, a crew called the Twenties. The Twenties were a multiracial group: Blacks, Latins, Islanders, Mixers, even a few Armenians. The Twenties were supposed to be defunct now but here they were, big as hell. They were standing atop some fresh/fast street art, apparently left by the shooters; a ten-foot drawing of a hooked-beak eagle, under it the word "Inca," in case anybody didn't get it. The Incas had been around since Nixon, too, like the Twenties. In the old days, the Incas had been mostly Mexican. Now they were from every other Latin American country, including Blacks from Cuba and Haiti and the Dominican Republic.

Nate circled the gangsters for another look. Something about this wasn't right. Who was the dead kid, and what did he have to do with a gang that everyone had said was dead and gone? Out in the street in front of the house was the beginning of an army, and it had come out of nowhere, while the bodies inside were still warm. Why had Whitey and the GU shown up right away? Why did the dead boy in the bed matter? Why had he been killed? Who were the motorcycle shooters? This was so…2015. In the old days there would always be retribution for a drive-by, but it usually came later rather than sooner. But that was then. Gangs didn't bang anymore. Now they were self-regulated criminal enterprises combined with social clubs. A few more Twenties showed up, nodding greetings to the others in the street, older men. Tribal elders?

As one, they glared up at Nate in his sculpted seat behind the plexi of the cockpit. He doused the spotlight and steered east toward downtown.

◆ ◆ ◆

NATE COULD SMELL ISAAKO'S scent in the cockpit, probably some kind of sports-themed "body wash." He said Isaako's name out loud, not because he was sentimental or grieving—he was long since past that, or thought he was—but just because the name had an interesting sound. *Isaako.* Rest in peace, you big dumb mother-humper.

Carrie came on the screen. "Are you going home?" she said with surprising warmth and familiarity. Concern. Empathy. Nate wondered for the thousandth time who had programmed her this way and why. Not that he was complaining. He needed a friend about then, even one that didn't actually exist.

"Where did my wounded single go?" Nate said.

"King Memorial," Carrie said. "First name, Samuel. Last name, Wallace. Date-of-birth: zero seven sixteen, two thousand twelve. Twin of deceased. Tissue damage. The projectile exited clean. He is about to go into an OR. He is not fully cooperative, asked to be released multiple times, third-level agitated."

"I like your hair," Nate said. "It's shorter."

"No one else noticed," she said, putting her hand behind her head, lifting her 'do. "I did it a week ago."

They both let a moment go by, a moment and ten blocks. She sat up a little straighter. It was the middle of the night and they had it all to themselves.

"So he was *agitated*," Nate said. "Agitated how?" Now he was flying over USC and what was left of the Coliseum.

Carrie said, "He wanted out of there. He thought his wounds could be treated by himself or by others. He twice said he was prepared to decline protective custody, if the custodial officer would release him."

"Why? He wanted revenge? He wanted to see his mother? He wanted to bury his brother? He was hungry?"

"He thought our involvement was either insufficient or improper."

"I'm starting to like this kid," Nate said. "I'm glad I didn't kill him."

He said bye and she disappeared and he punched the gas. He'd been in this situation more than a few times, when he'd had his hands on Death. Or it'd had its hands on him. He'd long ago given up beating himself up for feeling a little exhilarated.

Nate set down the Crow on the roof of King Memorial Hospital, on a secondary pad apart from the four round landing grids used by the air ambulances. The round landing pads were called the "skillets," as in, out of the frying pan…

"We had to knock him out," an ER doctor told Nate in a white hallway on the top floor. "He was not happy to be here."

"I heard," Nate said. "You guys still working on him?"

"He's out of the OR. It was straight through the shoulder, an easy fix." The doctor dug his finger into the soft flesh in Nate's shoulder. "Best place to be shot, if you have to be shot, as long as it misses the artery or doesn't hit a bone and start bouncing around. He's in recov, bed ninety-nine, down the way, but he won't come around for another hour at least. One of your guys is sitting out front babysitting him."

"Thanks," Nate said and started away.

"You want me to do anything about your calf?" the doctor said.

"No. Thanks." Nate actually hadn't thought about it since he'd been shot. It wasn't the first time he'd been nicked. He had a kit at home to dress it. His mother was a nurse.

"You want some pills?" the doctor said.

"I got all I need."

No sign of a babysitting cop in the hallway, but in the recovery room a nurse was with Samuel Wallace. Knocked out like this—sleeping on his back, his mouth open—the boy didn't look thirteen, more like eight.

The nurse tending to him was a guy in his thirties with tattooed arms and thick biceps, which meant there was plenty of skin to write on. He looked like the kind of inner-city deep-shit critical care nurse who liked his job, mostly because it wasn't spreading hot tar on a roof out in Pacoima all day. With this job you got to work at night and they gave you the best speed in the world, whether you needed it or not. When Nate came through the curtains, the nurse was adjusting one of the monitors, holding the boy's right hand as he did it, a gesture that, in spite of everything that had happened that night, looked tender to Nate, a little picture of wholly unearned kindness. What was it they said? The test of a man's character is what he does when he thinks no one is watching. The nurse looked up and tipped up his head to say hello.

"You're probably going to have to tie him down when he comes around," Nate said.

"Eh, I'll talk to him," the nurse said. "Sometimes they just hate cops."

"Sometimes?"

"He can probably go home in two to three hours, in the morning anyway. Or go somewhere."

As it turned out, that wasn't going to happen because behind them the curtain opened again, and the next act on tonight's bill appeared: a grizzled-looking gangbanger on the dark side of fifty, a blue do-rag tied around his head and a gun in his hand. A silenced gun. At Do-Rag's side was another gangbanger, a kid not much older than the boy in the bed. It was either on-the-job training, or the second gangster was there to hand the oldster another gun if the first one jammed. What anybody would remember about the standby kid—besides how young he was—was that he had a cross tattooed on his left cheek, presumably the cheek Christ would want him to offer up after he had been smote on the right.

Nothing was said. The OG looked Nate in the eye. The young gangster looked dangerously skittish, first-timey. Not that he didn't also look murderous. The nurse was already backing away from the bed and raising his hands, eyes on the floor, almost as if this happened all the time. Protocol. Nate shook his head slowly at how dumb and predictable the whole thing was, but he did what the nurse did, backing off, holding his hands out from his body. Only he didn't look at the floor. When Nate and the nurse were out of the way, the shooter shot. It was low caliber, probably a .25. Barely a *pffft!* It didn't even move the boy's head much when the round went in, right on the bridge of young Master Wallace's nose. A second round punched in a little higher. A sigh escaped from the boy's mouth when the rest of his body got the bad news.

With the hand that wasn't his gun hand, the old shooter tossed a copper Inca coin onto the bed. The man was missing two fingers on that hand, his index finger and the middle finger, giving him a lobster claw. The younger gangster was already halfway gone through the curtains. The OG walked out, not fast, not slow. No eye contact.

Nate went after them, quicker than was prudent, his gun coming into his hand. He'd already decided to shoot both of them in the back, just because he could. The exit door to the stairwell was five feet away and just now it was closing with a sigh of its own. The gangsters must have propped it open or had a third man waiting—the babysitter cop, in on it?—because Nate hadn't heard a thing before the two men came in. He almost got off a shot at the top of the young gangster's head but there was a civilian in the stairwell, a nurse coming up. And then they were gone.

Ninety-six.

◆ ◆ ◆

NATE COLE LIVED IN a house in the Hollywood Hills that was almost all glass, slab to flat roof, curvy, the kind of Moderne house built in the sixties that they used to say "looked like a spaceship" before people actually saw real spaceships. Standing in his living room, looking out, was a lot like being in the cockpit of the Crow, with the traffic of the Cahuenga Pass slinking along below.

Eight hours ago, he'd started his shift flying across LA with Isaako quiet in the back, the sun a smudge of color behind the improbable rain clouds out over the ocean. He'd landed on the roof of a twelve-story Deco apartment building in Pacific Palisades, left Isaako with the rig, took the stairs down, alone, with a bottle in his hand, "Going to see a man about a thing..." A few minutes later, he was back behind the stick, lifting off into the new night, hoping it wouldn't be too quiet a shift. Now, home, he unwrapped what looked like a piece of bulbous jewelry, about eight inches tall, clear shiny glass with a polished brass base, curly wires inside so delicate it was hard to imagine how it had been made. By hand, certainly, years ago. For some reason, nothing delicate got made anymore. Or so it seemed to Nate. He polished it with the brown tissue paper it came in. He'd had to wait six weeks for it to turn up, putting the word out on the electronic gear underground. It cost $300 and a bottle of 2012 George Dickel Rye.

He pushed the vacuum tube down into the socket in his low-power transmitter, then used a square of soft black cloth to wipe off his single fingerprint. He was in the interior of the house, in the second bedroom, a room he'd converted into a radio room, a studio. He stepped away from the console and closed the heavy drapes. He sat down at the control board again, flipped the main switch, and the transmitter came to life, just like it was supposed to. A pair of cherrywood vintage speakers, Altec Lansings—a name out of the past that meant something to collectors—thumped and then emitted a warm hum that matched the pulsing glow coming from the tubes. He had two turntables and a microphone, a mic that one of his collector pals had sworn on a stack of *Rolling Stones* had been used to record vocals on The Beach Boys's *Pet Sounds*.

Nate broadcast when he felt like it, four or five nights a week, usually those hours between the end of a shift and dawn. He never said his name. "The All-Night Man," he sometimes called himself, when he was feeling pretentious. He played nothing but vinyl, most of it from the sixties and seventies, mostly his dad's old records. Nights when the atmospheric conditions were on his side, the range of his little radio station was twenty miles or so, all of it toward the south and west. It was completely illegal, unregistered, unapproved, pirate.

Most nights when he fired it up, he talked for two or three minutes to kick things off—just whatever he was thinking—but tonight he didn't much feel like talking so he looked for a particular record on the rack on the wall, found it, rolled the disk out of the sleeve, blew off the dust, and cued it up.

"I've been gone awhile, but I'm back," he said into the mic. He had a good voice, rich and real. "Here's some Nick Lowe," he said.

He had slip-cued the record—the second cut in—and let it go. After a little hiss and pop, the diamond stylus found the vocal, which began a beat before the first spare guitar notes. The voice was clean, naked, the words unrhymed and ragged…

> *The beast in me is caged by frail and fragile bonds,*
> *Restless by day and, by night, rants and rages at the stars.*
> *God help the beast in me.*

Nate leaned back in the swivel chair and lit a cigar, one more thing that was illegal now. He couldn't stop thinking about the faces, the black bandanas, the white shirts—out there on the street in front of the murder house, standing atop their old enemies' trademark—the eyes looking up at him, full of hate. Defiant, intent. But intent on what? Almost every night when his shift ended there'd be one image that stayed in his head, no matter what he did to chase it out, no matter what tricks he employed to try to replace it with something of his own choosing. Tonight the image in his brainpan was the gathering gang, the Twenties. The younger of their number had their arms folded across their chests, the way boys in men's bodies will do when they're scared and don't want to show it. The older ones had their arms at their sides, like jacked-up fighters between rounds, impatient, twitching, single-minded, and not nearly smart enough.

Chapter Four

It was a little after midnight. The rain hadn't amounted to much, barely enough to wash the lottery tickets and dusty bear shit out of the gutters; still Westwood looked almost fresh, almost clean, as if LA had been given a makeover, maybe even a do-over.

Take two.

Westwood Village was between the Hills of Beverly and the sprawl of the Veterans Cemetery, that expanse of row after row after row of white headstones, identical except for the names of the fallen and the crosses and Stars of David. And a few crescents. On the top edge of the boneyard were even the graves of a dozen Wiccan vets under headstones with pentangles. Westwood was the first edge of The Westside but a place unto itself, almost as if it had a wall around it. LA had become even more sectionalized over time, more feudal, another change that might be blamed on the traffic. The Village was home to the University of California, Los Angeles, which, in the last twenty-five years, had come to look like a sprawling manufacturing plant for some essential, prosaic product. In the 1930s, Westwood was home to the big movie houses, thousand-seat "palaces" with velvet seats and gilded curlicues going crazy across the absurdly high ceilings. Deep carpet made the vast rooms quieter than churches, at least until the picture started, which is what they called a movie then. The big theaters were still there, kept alive for red carpet premieres.

Ava Monica's office was in a three-story building on the corner of Gayley Avenue and Weyburn Avenue in a brick building that looked as if it were out of another time the day it was built. Her heels clicked on the sidewalk as she walked away from her car, a land-yacht, a fat, bulbous resto-mod 1956 Hudson Hornet with chamois seats and an electric engine. Black. (Or maybe it was dark green. It was hardly ever out in the full sun.) Ava was just coming back to the office to check her messages. Plus, she wasn't much good at sleeping. Midnight for her was like the middle of the morning for everybody else.

"There's a man," the security guard at the desk inside the front door said. "He looked all right and he was crying, so I let him go on up."

And there he was, sitting in one of the chairs in the hallway outside her office door.

"Hello," he said when Ava's clicking heels got close.

"Handsome" was a poor word for what he was, with all he had going on. Even in the dimness Ava could see the steely blue eyes, the salt-and-pepper hair, the cut of his $10,000 silver-gray suit. Just sitting there in the hallway, he was like an ad for something you've wanted your whole life, probably in secret. He smiled and stood. He had stopped crying.

"Hello," Ava said back to him, trying to keep it from sounding like, Hel-*lo*...

His name was Beck. "I know it's late," he said.

"My watch stopped in nineteen fifty-six," Ava said.

She let the two of them into her office. As she closed the door, the words on the glass office door—"AVA MONICA" and "INVESTIGATIONS"—crawled up his pant leg. She went straight to her desk. And straight to a bottle in the bottom drawer.

"Forgive me," she said, "I've been out on the frontiers of fashion and my throat is a little dry."

He sat across from her. She poured two drinks, pushed one across the wooden desk.

"It's real," Beck said when he'd had a taste.

"Uh-huh," Ava said, swiveling absently in her wooden swivel chair.

She really hoped he was sitting there before her because he owned a big box store and the boys down on the loading dock were ripping him off and he needed a month or two or three of professional undercover surveillance. With a lot of "meetings"..."updates."

"I'm looking for someone, a woman," Beck began, disappointingly.

"No!" Ava said with mock sympathy.

"I don't know her full name. I don't know what she does for a living or where she lives, for that matter. She would never tell me. We always just met at places of her choosing. I don't know where she's from. I don't know how old she is. She's about your height and build—her breasts are a little fuller..."

Ava took a slug of bourbon.

"She's blonde, very blonde," Beck said. He stopped. "I'm sorry, is this how it's done? I've never looked for anyone before."

I bet, Ava thought. "Go on, you're doing swell," she said.

"You have to understand something," he said. "I'm in business, an importer/exporter. I've been everywhere. I've been places most people only dream of. I'm a man of experience. I've been loved, and I have loved in return, but I have never experienced what I experienced with Cali."

"Cali?" She asked him to spell it. He spelled it.

"I have this," Beck said. "I don't know if it will help or not." From his suit pocket he took an elegant women's high-heeled shoe. Red. He set it on the desk between them.

Ava looked it and then at Beck. "This 'Cali' have any wicked stepsisters?"

Beck didn't get the reference. "Not that I know of," he said. "She was so beautiful, so pure, so perfect, so much a part of this place. She'd been so long at the beach she even tasted like the sun. And when she laughed…it was magical. She was the purest, most sympathetic and loving soul I've ever encountered."

"Got it."

"Sorry, it's just that—"

"It always is. How long have you known her?"

"A week," Beck said. "An eternity."

"It would help if you didn't say things like that," Ava said.

"Sorry."

"When was the last time you saw her?"

"We were on the beach at Malibu three nights ago."

Ava put her finger to her chin and conjectured, "You had a bottle of wine, a blanket? You watched the moon rise while the warm breezes lifted her hair? Maybe you recited a little verse?"

"Everything but the poetry," Beck said, hopelessly serious. "That was implicit in the moment."

"What did I just say?"

"Sorry."

"So where'd you meet her?"

"On the street. Downtown. Hill and Third. At one eleven on a Wednesday afternoon. The wind blew her hat off. I caught it."

Ava felt something turn over in her chest, a sweet hurt, a longing, the kind that hooch can't heal, despite all the advertising. "So what happened?" she said. "How in the world could something so perfect go wrong?"

Again, Beck missed her tone. "We argued," he said. "I was supposed to leave this morning for Alabama on the Trans-Electro. Montgomery. I wanted her to come with me. I believed we would be together forever. I *believe* we will be together forever. Present tense. She was sad about something—before we argued, I mean. Maybe I pressed too hard, spoke too honestly, said too much, asked for too much from her. She always seemed…unsettled, restless. We argued and she pulled away from me and—"

Ava was still holding the fancy red shoe. "She wore these to the beach?"

"We had been out to dinner. At The Rings of Saturn. It was her favorite place."

"What'd you have? I've never been there but I've heard good things."

"The mock starfish," Beck said.

"Mmmm, mock," Ava said. "Go on. Rings of Saturn. Starfish. Malibu. Sad. Unsettled. Alabama. You argued. She pulled away."

"She swam into the ocean, crying," Beck said. "She just kept going."

Ava set the shoe on her desk, now that she saw where this was headed. Lust only distracts a girl up to a point.

"She just disappeared," Beck said, looking at his hands. "I swam after her but she was too fast. I waited and searched the shoreline but…"

"Did you go to the cops?"

"I don't deal with the world that way," he looked up and said.

"So, if she's shark bait…pardon me, but what's the point?" Ava said, "I mean, what do you want me to find out?"

"She's not dead!" he said and slapped the desk-top. "She's not dead. I would know. You don't understand. Between us there was a kind of communication that would preclude any possibility of—"

"What's your name?" Ava threw back the last of the Old Grand-Dad.

"Beck."

Ava pushed a paper pad across the desk. "Give me your numbers. I get two thousand a day plus bribes. Let's say ten thousand now, the rest later."

She was about to tell him how to zap the money to her when he went to his pocket and came out with a clip of bills. He dealt off $10,000.

"You have a picture of her?" Ava said. "Maybe a candy snap, something from the photo booth at the Ninety-Nine Cent Store?"

"Only this," he said. He held out a heart-shaped gold locket.

Ava took it. It was warm. Of course it was, he'd been clutching it all along. She popped it open. It was one of those new jobbers with a microchip in it, a little screen. There she was, Cali, a shimmering image, a talking head that mouthed the words, *I love you...* over and over. She had soft, magical blonde hair, like Veronica Lake, over one eye like Veronica Lake, and each time she said, *I love you...*she brushed her hair back off her face.

"Can I keep this?" Ava said.

"No, please," Beck said and snatched it back. "It's all I have now."

"How's about I just download it, then?" Ava said. She was half past tired of him and the lovesick horse he rode in on.

But she took his money, scooped it right up, the way they do in the casinos, quick, before it sinks in that you're a sap.

◆◆◆

SHE DROVE THE HUDSON out of Westwood. It being late and with the rain and all, the traffic was light. She steered down Gayley to Wilshire. Ava Monica was one of the last of the free-drivers, Queen of Surface Streets. When she spotted a slowdown ahead or when a monitor on the dash alerted her of a looming dead-stop jam—what the locals called a "Sig Alert" for some reason—she would crank the wheel and power down a side street, blowing past stuck traffic until she found herself an escape route, a "surface street" somehow undiscovered and clear. Sometimes she would drive twenty circuitous miles to go three miles across the city, three miles as the crow flies. The light was red at the corner of Gayley and Wilshire, so she squeezed around a couple of Feds, law-abiders, and turned left, heading up the wrong side of Wilshire Boulevard through the grand canyon of high-rise condos where the Saudis and undead old movie stars lived. When she met some traffic, she ducked over into the alleyways behind the towers then cut across onto Little Santa Monica, into West Hollywood.

Where was everybody? Maybe another bomb had gone off.

Cali was on the monitor on Ava's dash. *"I love you, I love you, I love you…"* Cali said and brushed, brushed, brushed her hair off of her face.

"I love you, too, honey," Ava said.

She punched a button and another face replaced Cali's on the screen.

"Hey," Penny said a second after she appeared. She was behind a panel of switches and wires and old-style monitors, filing her nails, her legs crossed. Penny looked to be in her low twenties with a waist in the same range, straight blue-black hair, bangs. In the background were other girls behind other switchboards, a room full of them, wearing headsets. Maybe. Ava didn't know if Penny was real or not, had never been face-to-face with her without some electronics between them. It didn't much matter anymore, if Penny was real or not. Funny thing about progress, take it far enough and it's people who get cheap. If Penny was human, she worked a twenty-hour-a-day shift. She was never not there and perpetually as bright and chirpy as a bird. If there was one thing the world had perfected, it was manufactured attentiveness. Her real name was Penelope, after her mother's favorite movie star. Or so she said. Her last name was Lane, which only confused things further, but interestingly so.

"Got any messages for me?" Ava said.

"What were you just watching?" Penny said.

"New case. Missing love of his life."

"OK," Penny said, confessionally. "I was listening in when you were back in the office. You left the service monitor on. I heard it all. Beck & Cali. Malibu. Sorry. You know, Ava, I was thinking—"

"You got any messages for me, Penny?"

"Roland Turnbull, twenty ten," Penny read. "WCB. Your Auntie Eve, twenty sixteen. She loves you, wants to borrow some money. Roland Turnbull, twenty twenty, twenty twenty-five, twenty twenty-eight…"

"Put him up," Ava said.

A man appeared on Ava's dashboard screen, a middle-aged man with a flushed face, blood red with frustration. A graphic overlay showed his rising BP. Little jets of steam coming from his ears would have been fitting.

"Yikes," Ava said. "Get him off."

Roland Turnbull went away and Penny came back on the screen. "Who is he?" Penny asked.

"Domestic surveillance job from six months back. His girlfriend skipped away with a prep chef. Ol' Roland just *had* to know. She was nineteen. These guys kill me. Reality clears its throat and they get mad at *me*."

"You know what?" Penny stopped filing her nails and said, "I bet she was terminally ill and couldn't bear for him to know."

Ava said, "I'll show you the pics. She was nineteen. And acting all nineteen-ish."

"No, I meant Cali," Penny said. "She couldn't bear to see how it would hurt Beck, that she was dying and all."

Ava said, "I love how everyone just acts like 'Cali' is a reasonable name for a woman in twenty twenty-five. I can't wait to find out what her last name is."

Penny continued, "She wouldn't/couldn't allow her personal health problems to weigh on him so she chose to harbor her secret alone, deep within, bear that burden in secret, right to the end. It's so romantic."

"What I'm trying to figure out is how to drag it out over another week. This guy's rich as sin. The jerk."

"*She'd been so long at the beach she even tasted like the sun...*" Penny repeated and sighed.

"Yeah, right."

"That's so beautiful," Penny said. "Of course Beck stole it from that Rod McKuen spoken-word album that won a Grammy in nineteen sixty-eight. Still, I've never had a man steal from a best-selling spoken-word album to describe me. And I don't believe you have either."

"No," Ava said, trying to sound sarcastic but coming off wistful.

"You know what I think it is about this one, Ava?" Penny said. "What it is about it that gets us where we live? It's our dream. The slavish devotion of a top-notch guy..."

"He had beautiful hands," Ava said, mostly to herself.

With just three more detours she'd already made it to her destination, West Hollywood, Santa Monica Boulevard, a strip of shops and fussy restaurants and bars. With the rain gone and the chill after the rain gone too, the gay bars were all fired up, the guys out on the sidewalk, having more fun than anybody else in LA. Or at least trying to make it look that way. The Hudson took itself over to the curb. "Eighty-eight seventeen Santa Monica Boulevard, West Hollywood," the car's voice said, a man's voice. A chick voice had come stock with the nav system. Ava put up with it for a day or two but then took it back in for an after-market retrofit. This voice *sounded* like a Hudson Hornet. He was real—a real man—a burned-out actor from the nineties most people thought was dead.

"I'm there, Penny," Ava said. "Don't wait up for me."

"I guess," Penny said absently, sounding sweetly sad now. "Ava…" she said.

"Yeah?"

"Let him down easy, if you can. So he won't be busted for the next girl."

As Ava got out of the car, a flying wedge of eight Crows cruised softly overhead, headed due south toward downtown, big trouble somewhere.

Chapter Five

On the north side of Santa Monica Boulevard was a candy store, the windows dark. Ava rang the doorbell using the toe of the shoe she'd pried out of Beck's hands before she pushed him out the door. While she waited for somebody to answer, she leaned against the doorjamb and tried it on. Too tight. Ouch. After a moment, a speakeasy window slid open, revealing the face of the Candy Lady. A sour face it was, too.

"Closed," she said, darkness behind her.

"Oh, I bet that's why all the lights are out," Ava said.

"What do you want?"

"Not candy," Ava said. "Starts with an S…"

"Shoes?"

"That's it."

"Do you know the word?"

"You mean besides, 'shoes'?"

"You have to know the word," the Candy Lady said.

"Money?" Ava said.

"That's not the word," Candy Lady said. Ava could hear someone grumbling in the background, a man.

"Lotsa money?" Ava said. "No, that's two words. Let me think…"

The door opened. Ava stepped in. Candy Lady, who was seventy-ish, moved to one side with a practiced the-customer-is-always-right smile. It was dark inside but there were countertops covered with candy, some of it obscene. The air was all sugary. A door stood open in the back of the store, a wedge of light thrown onto the floor, and a spry older man was moving into a back room, looking over his shoulder to make sure Ava was following. A four-foot-long lizard crawled across the floor and disappeared down an aisle, unremarked upon by any of the principals in the scene.

Once they were back in the workshop, Ava handed him the red shoe.

"You wish a…replacement?" the Shoemaker said. He examined the shoe, but not for long. He knew what he knew and he wasn't much of an actor.

"Did I come to the right place?" Ava said. "I saw the mark, on the inside of the heel."

The Candy Lady had followed Ava into the back room. "We don't know you," she said. "This is real animal skin. It's—"

"Illegal," Ava said. "Look, if I was an animal lover, I would have gone to Walmart. Hey, even my underwear is leather. I don't want shoes, I want information. I know you made the shoe. I want to know who you made it for."

Ava put one of Beck's new hundred-dollar bills on the work bench. The lizard made another appearance, stood its ground below Ava, looking from face to face.

"How do we know you're not a Regulator?" the woman said.

"Because I speak in complete sentences and I don't have my hand in your pocket?" Ava said. "Because I have a hundred dollars?"

The Shoemaker turned the shoe over and over in his hand. He licked the tip of his finger and touched it to the toe to wipe away some stain. He started, "I think it was—"

The Candy Lady interrupted, "He's proud of his work. To a fault, given the times we live in." She slid the hundred off of the workbench. "We didn't use names," she said. "Names are never used."

"A beachy blonde?" Ava said. "About my size? Maybe a little fuller up top."

"A little younger, too," the Candy Lady said, too quickly.

"Her Hobarts or the whole package?" Ava said. "Never mind. How'd she pay?"

"Same as you," the Candy Lady said. "Hardware."

"Wait, let me guess," Ava said. "She didn't tell you her name, didn't give you an address. No digits, no diggity. She came back to pick them up herself in the dead of night. No paper trail."

The Shoemaker said, "We have to be very careful."

"Very," the Candy Lady said.

"So you don't know anything else about her," Ava said, not really a question.

The two had nothing to say. The lizard shook its head wearily and went under the workbench. The Candy Lady shoved the C-note deeper into her pocket.

Ava took the shoe and started back out through the store, the couple right behind her, as if they thought she might swipe one of the penis lollipops. She stopped at the front door. "You don't have any chocolate, do you?"

The Candy Lady said, a little less guarded than before, "Nobody does. The heat is on again."

Ava put her hand on the knob. "They're always afraid somebody somewhere is having a good time…"

She was halfway out the door when the Shoemaker said, "She wasn't alone. She came in with that star. The crazy one, the singer-slash-actress."

"She only *looked* like her," the Candy Lady said, sharp. "And not very."

"It was her," the old man said to his wife. "The crazy one."

"Oh, go to hell, Leo," the Candy Lady said and disappeared back into the workshop.

When they were alone, the man said, "Vivid. She came in with Vivid."

"Really?" Ava said. "Vivid. She *is* crazy. I like that one song though…"

The Shoemaker looked back at the workshop, made sure his wife was beyond hearing. "I made her a pair two months ago, Vivid herself. It was right after that business in Milan and just before the bed fire at The Cliff House. My wife never knew about it. A pair of open-toes. Gold-colored. She was very pleased. And the next time, she brought your girl back with her. For the red ones."

"You're sure it was Vivid?"

"I had a dance band," the Shoemaker said. "In the seventies. We cut a few records, toured with Sylvester and The Gap Band." He stood with his feet apart, pointed with one hand toward the ceiling and put the other hand on his hip, a pose that apparently had meant something once.

"You know, Vivid's fans like to dress up like her," Ava said, gently. "She could have been an imposter."

He held up a wait-here finger. He went back into the workshop, there was the sound of a drawer opening and closing, and he returned with a picture clipped from a magazine. There she was, Vivid, on stage somewhere wearing what anyone not in the fashion trade would call a one-piece bathing suit. And a pair of high-heeled, open-toed gold shoes.

"She was crying the whole time, your girl, Blondie," the Shoemaker said. "I guess Vivid was trying to cheer her up, buy her some custom kicks, like hers."

◆ ◆ ◆

THE SHINOLA SUPPER CLUB overlooked the ocean at Santa Monica where San Vicente dead-ended. Off to the left was The Pier, to the right the curving stream of headlights and taillights that was Pacific Coast Highway. Like all of the best places, The Shinola wasn't open to the public and had no signage other than the noise of the bands and the sound of people laughing and honking and calling out to each other when they left drunk. You had to know somebody to get in. Ava knew everybody, everybody knew Ava—at least among the up-all-night monied crowd—so she didn't even slow down as she pulled past the guard tower. It had taken her the better part of an hour to zigzag across the Westside from the candy shop in West Hollywood, so by then it was bumping on 3:00 a.m., not that the night was anything like over. The parking lot was packed. The bulbous Hudson stopped right at the head of the silver red carpet and a valet guy snapped to and opened her door.

"Hey, Ava. You want a hand wash?" he said.

Ava got out. "Oh. You mean the car," she said. "Why not?"

Ten feet away, a pimp named Action Man was just then shoving four girls into the back of an idling stretch limo helo, his clients a couple of out-of-towners wearing the short-sleeved business suits that had been in style a few years ago.

"I'm happy, hope you're happy, too," Action Man said, loud enough for everyone to hear. It was his catch-phrase. He was the sort of lowlife who thought it important to have one, a catchphrase. He closed the limo door and turned his back and the helo rose behind him.

He glanced at Ava as she went into the club. They didn't like each other. How could they?

A lithe Black in a black tux stood on the stage in a shaft of blue light so intense it reminded one of a transporter beam in a science fiction show.

What he was singing was…

> When Sunny gets blue, her eyes get gray and cloudy
> Then the rain begins to fall, pitter-patter, pitter-patter
> Love is gone, what can matter?
> No sweet lover man comes to call…

The room was round, the small stage across the way through a grove of chrome palm trees. There was no curtain for the stage, just the open windows with the glassy ocean as a backdrop. A light sea breeze moved everything dreamily. A crowd of a hundred or so late-nighters seemed pleased with themselves for being there. A half moon cracked a smile out over the water.

Ava took a stool at the bar, her back to the singer and the room and the moon. The bartender was a war vet missing a hand, Tommy Cairo. "What'll it be, Ava?" he said.

"Surprise me," Ava said.

The bony manager of the place, Silky Valentine, was three stools down. "Use my bottle," he said to his bartender.

"I'm surprised already," Ava said.

Valentine wore a slick white dinner jacket. "Silky, you're looking deceptively handsome tonight," Ava said, without looking at him. Valentine ignored the modifier, heard it only as a compliment. He made a double clicking sound with one side of his mouth, his patented way of acknowledging things. Ava's drink came across the bar. She lifted it, took a sniff and then a sip. It tasted like very expensive cotton candy.

She spun on the stool and turned her attention to the Johnny Mathis on stage. Or was it supposed to be Nat "King" Cole?

"I like him," Ava said. "He seems sincere."

Valentine and Cairo exchanged a look. "I'll tell him you said so," Valentine said. "Who are you looking for, Ava?"

"The man of my dreams," Ava said, eyes still on the singer on stage. "Or maybe my mother's dreams."

"Seriously," Valentine said. He hated not knowing everything, or what he had convinced himself was everything.

"Who said I was looking for somebody?"

"You don't talk to me unless you are," Valentine said.

"A blonde. With a funny name, even funnier than normal," Ava said. "Cali." She tossed him a little dub-player with the *"I love you…"* loop.

Valentine glanced at the screen, handed it back to her. "Nope, no blondes here," he said. Half of the women in the room were blondes. He double-clicked again and laughed at his joke, all out of proportion.

"Is Vivid coming in tonight?" Ava said fast, offhanded, hoping for a fast, honest answer.

"We never know," Valentine said, just as fast.

Everyone knew Vivid owned The Shinola. She tended to buy any place she went to if there was a wait to get in. (She also owned The Rings of Saturn supper club down the beach.) Without warning, sometimes on a Sunday night—everyone knows how lonely Sunday nights are—Vivid would dance through the front door with two or three or four or five girlfriends, stopping The Shinola's patrons midsentence, suspending cocktails on their way to lips. *It's her!* Some of those nights she'd just sit in the dark in her booth in the back with her posse eating skinny fries with truffle oil. Sometimes, she'd stay ten minutes and then blow. But other times she'd hang around and take the stage and sing and the crowd would be mesmerized, barely breathing, feeling unspeakably lucky. She'd sing for hours, as if she were afraid to go home. She'd burn through every song in her catalogue of hits. And then some. Vivid was addicted to lying. She'd lost any sense of the difference between what was true and what she wished were true. And of course no one would call her out on anything. She'd sit up there on the stool under her signature pink lights and take a drink of water and say something like, "This is new. I just wrote it. I just wanted to try it out on you guys. It's just what I've been feeling a lot lately." Then she'd nod to her keyboard man and sing some songwriter's song her management firm or a producer had pushed on her that afternoon. And she'd make it *hers*, which is what stars do.

Vivid also was known for fans who cut their hair or bought wigs like hers, girls (and a few boys) who dressed like her, who spoke like her, who said "just" a lot, too. Who lied a lot, too. They followed her around, tried to guess where she'd show up next, read everything there was to read about her, watched everything there was to watch, bought the most expensive tickets down front at the Hollywood Bowl or the ObamArena and sat together, shoulder to shoulder, singing along to the songs. Even the covers, which Vivid would also intro as her own, even when it was an old Madonna hit or John Lennon's "In My Life." When one of them started to cry, happily, the others would pat the crier on the knee, and then they'd all be crying, crying and singing, happily. They didn't have a complicated name. They were just "Vivids."

Tonight, three of them sat at a table just below the stage drinking some blue drink in a square glass Vivid had been seen drinking a week ago at a bar down in Poodle Springs. It wasn't hard to look like Vivid. All it took was a lot of black around the eyes, a mole or spot over the lip on the left, bright perfect teeth behind purposefully smeared lipstick. It was a bruised look, a *rehab-in-progress* look, a *not-there-yet* look. As for the hair, it was ever-changing, often shock-pink or banana-yellow or silver-silver, sometimes snow-white then shoeshine-black an hour later. These three Vivids wore silver wigs, which meant they matched the chrome frond-heads of The Shinola's palm trees. They didn't seem to be much digging the Black crooner on stage right in front of them, since they were talking among themselves.

Ava was watching them. Beck's Cali didn't seem to be a Vivid, a superfan, at least not from the pic Ava had. Vivid always looked like what was new or what was next while Cali looked more than a little like what had been, a classic California beach girl. But maybe, Ava was thinking, Cali had started out as a fan, then had somehow managed to get close to Vivid for real. At least close enough to walk a mile in her shoes.

Across the club from the three Vivids, staring at them, a tall man sat alone in a black suit and a pink tie, a man with a gun tucked under his armpit. Any fool could tell about the gun by the way he left his suit coat unbuttoned, the way he kept shrugging his shoulders, as if the holster wasn't comfortable. Or maybe he had just picked up the shrug watching old movies. But then the pimp Action Man came over to him with a nasty grin and a whispered message, which meant the skinny gunsel was for sure up to no good.

The lithe Black on stage sang the last sad word of his last sad song and then said, "Goodnight," bowed at the waist, and stepped off stage left.

The crowd made a little noise.

A disembodied *basso profondo* voice, an MC, said in pearly tones, "Johnny Blue. *For remembrance…*" He let the ceiling fans rotate a couple of orbits—so they all could continue to pretend they were in a movie—and then said, "Now *for the mind…*The Duke."

A young White in a creamy suit stepped to the microphone from stage right. The spotlight went to icy white. He had no props, not even a fake cigarette. Just words and a rich, dramatic voice. His eyes were fixed somewhere over their heads.

He wasn't just another singer. He was a reciter. He opened his set with…

When you are old and grey and full of sleep
And nodding by the fire, take down this book
And slowly read, and dream of the soft look
Your eyes had once and of their shadows deep...

The crowd went back to their drinks and chatter. The three Vivids picked now to head to the powder room.

Ava stood. "Thanks for the toot, Silk," she said.

Valentine nodded. He watched Ava follow the Vivids toward the door marked *Damas*. "I'll be on the roof," Valentine said to the one-handed bartender and stepped away. On his way through the club, he nodded and click-clicked to a few customers but walked right past the young woman alone at a table next to the mirrored wall, unsteady, drunk or stoned or just too blue for words. Her lipstick was bright red and smeared in the Vivid fashion. She had black hair and every few seconds she brushed it off her face.

This as The Duke spoke the next verse...

How many loved your moments of glad grace,
And loved your beauty false or true.
But one man loved the pilgrim soul in you
And loved the sorrows of your changing face.

Not that Cali heard him or had any thought that it was about her.

◆ ◆ ◆

TWO OF THE THREE Vivids were leaning into the ladies' room mirror, smearing their lipstick. The other was in a toilet stall.

"Love your shoes," Ava said to the girl closest to her, the one wearing open-toe knock-off heels like the gold pair the Shoemaker had made for Vivid but in silver.

"Thanks?" the girl asked.

The girls at the mirror looked at each other, stuck as to what to say next. Ava wasn't much past thirty but to the Vivids talking to her was like talking to their moms. Or stepmoms. They fidgeted, rolled their eyes, fluffed their silver hair, sighed. The toilet whisper-flushed and the third girl came out. Up close, this one almost looked enough like the real Vivid to pass. She washed her hands like a good girl and then went to work on her lips in the mirror.

"What's your name?" Ava said to her.

"Vivid," the girl said.

"I mean in the daytime."

"Laurel," the Vividest Vivid said, somehow projecting bored and angry at the same time. It surprised Ava that she gave up on the *I am Vivid* thing so quickly. The two other girls looked both hurt and annoyed in a way that said this had happened before, Laurel getting special attention because she looked the most like the real Vivid.

"My name is Katy," the girl in the copycat shoes said, without being asked.

"Wow," Ava said to all of them, "Vivid has been all over the tube lately, huh?"

"It's so unfair," the nameless third girl said, fluffing up her silver wig. "Why won't they just leave her alone?"

"They can't," Katy said.

"Think how it must hurt her, what they're saying," Laurel said to the face in the mirror.

"It's none of their business!" Katy said.

"I hate them so much, all the snoopy-snoops, the reporters, and the news-readers," the third girl said. Now it was as if Ava wasn't there and they were just talking the way they just talked every day and night.

"It's not 'news' if it hurts someone," Laurel said.

"Really," Katy confirmed.

"Hey, do you guys know Cali?" Ava whipped out her little dub-screen again, the *I love you*...loop. They barely looked at it. It was clear they knew who Cali was. They traded some looks, thinking they weren't revealing a thing.

"Who *are* you?" Laurel said.

"Her hair is so pretty," the third girl said, still looking at the little Cali movie on the screen. "Is this old? She doesn't look as much like Vivid in this."

"Yeah," Katy said. "Who *are* you?"

"A friend. Of Cali's. From high school."

"That's a big fat lie," the third said, flaring. "Number one, she's young. Number two, she wasn't from here. What, you got on a plane and came all the way out here from Florida just to find her?"

"What we do is our business!" Laurel said, glaring at Ava as if she was Mom. She looked away.

It was then that Ava saw the scars under the line of Laurel's jaw and at the hairline, evidence of some recent cut-and-paste, a stitch job, and not the kind the stars get in the secret clinics out in Two-Bunch Palms. This was a cruder makeover, perhaps with a more desperate purpose than trying to ease aging. Laurel was too young for that. She must have wanted something else, wanted to be some*one* else, leave herself behind, cut away herself.

"Leave us alone, lady," Laurel said and grabbed her clutch purse. She yanked open the door and looked back at Katy and the third girl until they grabbed their bags and followed her out, like you're supposed to when you're in a gang.

"Who does the work on you guys?" Ava asked. Too late. They were gone.

Had she really called Ava "lady"?

◆ ◆ ◆

OUT IN THE PARKING lot, Action Man had Cali by the arm, leading her toward a boxy Bentley from the late nineties. It was the color of tarnished silver. The tall gunman in the black suit and pink tie from the club stood beside the open back door.

Ava came out of club just in time to hear Cali say, drunkenly, "Please, I'm no good to you now."

"Let her go," Ava said.

"She works for me," Action Man said. "Stay out of it, Ava."

"Let her go," Ava said. She said it in the tone of voice people use when they have a gun in their hand. The skinny man by the Bentley looked as if he was a second away from going for *his* gun, but he didn't. He shrugged his tough guy shoulders instead.

"Let her go," Ava said.

Action Man turned loose Cali's arm and Cali fell to the ground. "There, I let her go," Action Man said.

Ava knelt beside her. "Are you all right?"

"Who are you?"

"We can talk about that."

"Just leave me alone," Cali said and pulled away from Ava, ran toward a taxi cruiser across the lot, a low-slung four-passenger helo.

"Wait," Ava said. "Beck sent me."

At the sound of Beck's name, Cali stopped. She turned and looked at Ava with a face that seemed about to break into pieces. "I can't," she said. "Tell him."

The tall man beside the Bentley had seen enough. He slid behind the wheel of the big cruiser and fired it up and sped away, blowing out a white cloud of old school stink, burning dinosaur bones. Ava stood there, watching it go, breathing in the perfume of the exhaust cloud. Nostalgia was going to get her killed some day.

There was no tag on the back of the car, just a plate with the initials DL.

"Down Low?" Ava said to nobody.

The air taxi lifted. Cali looked down out the window and brushed her black hair off her face, so sad and lost, as the bemused moon slid away off the glass.

Chapter Six

Ava drove away from The Shinola.

"Let me take the wheel," the Hudson's voice said. "You're blowing a point-oh-nine."

"I had one drink."

"Tell it to the judge."

"Fine!" Ava said and lifted her hands from the wheel.

"Where are we going?" the car voice said.

"I thought you knew everything," Ava said.

The car voice laughed warmly.

"You know," Ava said, "you're getting way too familiar."

"How about I take you home?"

"Penny!" Ava said.

Penny came on screen. "I was hoping you'd check in," she said. "What happened with Cali? Did you find her?"

"Sort of. Ask me in the morning," Ava said. "Get me Chang."

Life had gotten cheap and information had gotten dirt cheap. Not much was considered private anymore. What do you want to know? Who was a crusher, an addict? Who was dying of some shameful fourth-world virus? Who was diddling whom? Who was suicidal and calling the hotline? Who was in jail? Who was in church on his knees? Who was crying her eyes out in the back of a helo-cab?

Edward Chang appeared on screen. "What do you need?" Chang said. "Ten dollars."

A woman was shouting in Chinese in the background, unseen. Ava had always guessed that Edward Chang was thirty-something, but maybe she was wrong, maybe he was a teenager, still living at home. He'd let slip once that he lived over a restaurant in Chinatown.

"What do you need?" Chang said again. "Ten dollars."

"Yellow AirCab three-oh-eight-C." Ava made a C with her finger and thumb. "Ten dollars."

"Nine dollars? I'm not paying you eight dollars!"

Edward Chang had never stopped typing since he'd come onto the screen. Who knew how many ten-dollar jobs he was juggling at the moment. He said, "Yellow AirCab three-oh-eight-C, Destination: Twenty/Four/Seven Admiralty Way, Marina Del Rey. Ten dollars."

"I'm sorry, how much do you charge?" Ava said. She slapped the button on the dash before he could answer.

"Did you get that, Mr. Nosey Car?" she said.

"Nine minutes," the Hudson voice said. "We'll be there by four ten."

And so Ava rolled south on Lincoln Boulevard. This time of night, the traffic was almost free-flowing traffic, the hours between the night people dragging home their spent selves and the rest of LA getting up and heading off to their cubicles or the unemployment office. It was smooth sailing, except for having to dodge four or five abandoned cars every block.

Penny returned on the screen. "Beck has called like nine thousand times. We talked for fifty-two minutes. He was so…"

"Yeah, yeah, yeah. Not tonight," Ava said and punched Penny's lights out.

Beck. Her client. The job. Ava didn't know what she was going to do when she was face-to-face with Cali again, without pimps and Bentleys and gunsels around, assuming she could find her at the address. A little woman-to-woman talk? In person, Cali looked about nineteen, no older than the girls in the ladies' room. Beck didn't see fit to mention that, did he? The cradle-robbing, lovesick jerk. A woman-to-*girl* talk? Ava wasn't thinking that far ahead. All night— all *day*—she'd had just been putting one foot in front of the other. She wondered if everyone's life was like hers. Improv. Reactive. Impulsive?

The autopilot slalomed around two Feds parked side by side in the middle of Lincoln, a couple standing between them, waving their arms, flailing around, fighting. Or maybe they were dancing. No, there was no music.

It had been a long day, a day that had started two hours too early for her taste with a call from her mother, who wasn't doing well, her mother who had lost something that just had to be there somewhere in the house, but she couldn't find it. Ava had crisscrossed the city in the Hudson four times that day, first from her apartment in Hollywood across to Pasadena and the family house, then downtown to see the CRO Nate Cole. Then, while she'd been in the neighborhood, she'd scarfed down a $100 steak at The Original Pantry—What beef shortage?—then drove out to the office in Westwood, then to the candy shop and then back west to The Shinola. She was tired, tired of the miles, tired of the traffic, tired of the stop-and-go. Tired of people she had to see, tired of the people she couldn't find, tired of the people she had already found, tired—if the truth be told—of the glib bullshit she'd heard herself say all day long. What else? Oh yeah, she also was tired of the way she looked when she'd caught sight of herself in the blue mirror behind the bar at The Shinola, tired of everything being lost, or on the way to lost.

She slapped herself to snap out of it. "Ouch," she said.

And Ava couldn't forget that one of the Vivids had called her *lady*. Laurel. Laurel was also the Vivid who'd said, *It's not "news" if it hurts someone!* The girl had gotten it precisely back-assward in that way only the young can. Vivid herself wouldn't be news if she *wasn't* coming apart on a daily basis, if she wasn't hurt, if she wasn't hurting the ones who cared about her. Cali wasn't famous like Vivid, but she wouldn't be news either if she wasn't publicly coming apart. Ava wouldn't be looking for her if Cali was healthy and happy and whole, if she wasn't lost, if she wasn't bad news.

The Hudson parked itself on Admiralty Way. Ava got out, looked up. Twenty/Four/Seven was a twenty-story residential tower that overlooked the boat slips and the bight beyond, built in the shady eighties, probably with cocaine for mortar. Huge fake elms held forth out front and the whole scene was bathed in the ugly orange of the anticrime streetlights. Down here the ocean-adjacent air was always misty. At least there was that. Ava stood beside the car and huffed a lung full of it. It smelled good, salty, a little sour, but alive. Like her.

She used a Pik-Lok to get in the lobby door. Cali's apartment was on the seventeenth floor, three floors down from the penthouse: 1717. There were no names on the backlit lobby directory, just faces, little moving digital images, all of them smiling—except for the old people, most of whom looked like they'd just been awakened from a nap. Here was yet another version of Cali. Big surprise. This Cali on the lobby directory didn't look like a teenager; she looked late twenties. Her hair was light brown and shorter and she was smiling and tilting her head to one side at the end of the loop, an endearing gesture.

Better days? Maybe it was just better acting. At least she wasn't mouthing, *I love you…* over and over without even being able to see the person she was talking to.

With any luck, she'd be asleep in bed. If so, Ava wasn't going to wake her. *Sleep, baby, it'll all be good in the morning, you'll see.* That lie. She'd just tuck her in and make sure she wasn't choking on her own vomit and leave a note. Or if Cali was awake—watching the tube or something or staring at the wall, crying some more—Ava would just tell her to call Beck, tell her that's what big girls did when they wanted to break up with a guy, not pretend to drown themselves in the shore break.

She stepped into the elevator. There were no buttons to push. "Uh… seventeenth floor?" she said to the ceiling. "Cali? About five five, blonde? Or jet black? Or…light brownish? Young? Pretty? Cries a lot?"

It was one of the new whisper-quiet lifts—the doors closed, the doors opened, and you were there—a little creepy. The door to 1717 was standing open an inch. Not a good sign. Maybe it was just carelessness on Cali's part, upset, distracted, tired, forgot to close the door behind her?

"Yeah, keep telling yourself that," Ava said out loud.

She pushed open the door. The sprawling flat felt empty. Half dark, too quiet. The only light came from outside, the orange glow from seventeen floors down. There was a balcony, the vertical blinds open, the sliding doors parted.

"Honey Pie?" Ava said. "Cali?"

The living room was dark except for the pink blush from a little night-light made out of a real seashell, down near the floor in the entryway. A souvenir of Florida? The girl in the loo at The Shinola had said something about Cali coming from Florida. There was another shell night-light in the one bedroom, under the nightstand beside the king bed. The bed was empty except for a red satin heart-shaped pillow. The pillow had *Beck* and *Santa Monica Pier* written all over it, though not literally. There was something else on the bed: a black wig, curled up like a cat.

On the floor was a large suitcase. Ava lifted it. Empty.

The light was on in the open walk-in closet. Three sad limp filmy bright pretty dresses hung on wire hangers on the rod on the right side. Three *identical* sad limp filmy bright pretty dresses. The same print. So there was that. The rest of the closet was empty. The top shelf above it was cleared. Was that where the suitcase had been stowed? There was room for it and maybe another one.

A smaller, absent one? Had Cali figured out she only needed the one small bag where she was going so she left the other one behind? The shoe rack held a few pairs of shoes—practical and impractical—including one, an orphan, that was the companion to Beck's keepsake.

"That's what you call *detective* work," Ava said to no one.

A dresser drawer was open. Underwear, all of it white. So Cali hadn't taken everything with her. Or maybe she hadn't taken anything, maybe she'd come in, whipped off the black wig, looked at that silk pillow on that king bed, turned around and run back out the door. Maybe she'd just come back to change into some comfortable shoes. Running shoes. But running *to* Beck or *from* him?

In the master bathroom were two more seashell night-lights—these imprinted with the name *Gulf Shores*—and the usual array of girlie stuff on the stone countertop. Cali had left without her lip gloss? A used hand towel hung beside one of the sinks. She'd washed her hands and face, then split? Ava turned back toward the bedroom. She stared at the empty suitcase again. It was cheap, used, dirty white, regular people's luggage, almost the only thing in the room that wasn't new, the only thing in the apartment that seemed to have any real history. That and maybe the little shell night-lights from Gulf Shore, Florida. The suitcase seemed terribly sad for some reason, for all it said about coming to Hollywood, about trading *there* for *here*. Then for now. Known for unknown.

Once Ava sussed out that she was alone, she went into the kitchen and poured herself a blast from the bottle of vodka she found in the freezer. She walked the drink back out into the living room. This was the kind of thing she did all the time for work, breaking and entering to try to figure out the truth— it *was* the work—but something about this go-around was creeping her out. She turned on a lamp. And then another. Then one more. She plopped down in a chair, took stock of things. What do we have? A kitchen, a living room, a half bath, a dining room with a table and six chairs in which no person had ever sat, the Xanadu-size bedroom and master bath. Fresh flowers on the coffee table. White roses. Another dry bunch in the kitchen, upside-down in the trashcan. Was Beck sending her roses every day? No, he'd said in Ava's office he didn't have an address for Cali. So someone else had sent them, someone who did know where she lived. And maybe was paying for the apartment? Vivid? One of Action Man's johns? The Shoemaker? Or maybe Beck was a big fat liar and he knew exactly where Cali lived and what her last name was and everything else.

And what did Cali mean when she'd said in the lot of The Shinola to tell Beck she just couldn't? Couldn't what?

No TVs on the walls, no screens anywhere. Not any pictures, moving or still, personal or general. Against one wall was a bookcase that didn't hold any books, just row after row of Russian nesting dolls, unpacked, side by side. Over the couch, nicely framed (and hand-signed?) was a red-white-and-blue poster of a big-toothed politician. Block type, all caps, sans serif—a bit Stalinist for Ava's taste—spelled out his name across the top, **JOHN TERN**. Along the bottom of the frame was the word, **EMPATHY**. Actually, **EMPATHY!** Ava hadn't heard of him, which didn't mean much. She'd long ago surrendered her citizenship, in her mind at least. Voting was for voters, the suckers.

"Politically active, idealistic," Ava said to the empty living room. "Perfect."

The poster was the only art in the place, if that's what you wanted to call it.

No, there was something else: a postcard-size print on the bookshelf, leaning against one of the nesting dolls. It was an odd image: a lighthouse alone on a rocky point on a brilliant blue day, gulls banking, waves breaking. The artistic style was similar to a subset of advertising illustration called "California Orange Crate Art." What that meant was bright colors and lots of light—a childlike sensibility, which wasn't the same as childish. What made the little print on the bookshelf odd, what caught the eye, were the two cones of black coming out of the lens atop the lighthouse, where beams of light would be in nighttime.

"Hmmph," Ava said, judgmentally.

So which version of *gone* was Cali? Gone out of her last known address? Out of LA? Out of the country? Or just out of her mind? Ava started thinking about what she could report to her client. Something vague enough to drag out the case another ten grand but not *too* vague. Maybe she'd just tell Beck that she hadn't been able to find Cali, that his dream lover was almost certainly dead, drowned, even if there wasn't a body. She could lie and let him get on the train to The Gump, get back to his exportin'/importin' so that in time he could fall in love again with another too-perfect woman. Maybe she'd even type up a *paper* report, to make it realer than it was. Lovesick clients liked that, clutched the report in their little lovesick paws, something tangible in a world of intangibles.

"*This is all I have now,*" Ava said, in a mocking voice. Being a smart ass was something else that was going to catch up with her someday.

Then she saw it.

At eye level was an envelope stuck to the half-open sliding glass door that led onto the balcony. She put down her drink. The envelope had no name on it, just the word *Happy*. Ava turned and looked back toward the apartment's front door. Line of sight. Beck would have seen it when he walked in, if he did know where she lived and he'd walked in. Or did Cali guess that it would be Ava who found it? Happy. Happy? She pulled it off the glass, half-expecting it to be stuck there with bubblegum. It was unsealed.

The note didn't say much, just: *I'm really sorry. I just couldn't go backward.*

It wasn't signed. Ava was about to lift the stationery to her nose for a sniff to see if it was perfumed when she saw the white legs, out on the balcony, on a chaise.

Chapter Seven

Cali was sho'nuff dead. A goner.

"Perfect," Ava said, standing over the body, trying to sound way tougher than she was. Or maybe trying to convince herself she'd seen this coming. She was waiting for the ladies from the coroner's office to show. For some reason, she couldn't bring herself to turn her back on the girl. Cali, *her* Cali. So now she was Ava's Cali. The night was quiet, even quieter now, the same soft misty breeze off the Pacific. Ava listened for a siren but she'd told the HotCall operator this one was real dead so maybe there wouldn't be a siren. It had been thirty minutes since she'd called it in. It felt like two hours. The coronettes had probably stopped for a malted milk somewhere or were banging a cop. No rush. After all, they didn't get paid by the body.

Cali's right hand was stiff against the left side of her face, that brush-back-the-hair gesture one last time. Her blonde hair—her *real* hair?—was pinned up. She'd cleaned off all her makeup. That would be what she'd used the hand towel in the bathroom for. Her eyes were closed. She didn't look "at peace" or asleep. She looked dead. Gone. On the little teak table beside her were six plastic pill bottles, in a sad straight line as if they were game pieces on a board. Ava picked up the littlest bottle, figuring correctly it would be the most powerful of the drugs. It was a painkiller called Hark. (The pharmaceutical companies had given up on the multisyllabic, made-up, Greek-root drug names. They'd gone simple. And fricative.) Hark, 0.5 mg, quantity thirty. They should have named it *Hark!* Hark the herald angels sang. The bottle was only half empty.

Ava hadn't really looked at the body yet, really looked. Now she looked. Cali's lipstick—so red, so vivid out in front of The Shinola—was gone. Her uncolored lips made her look more like a person, like somebody's daughter instead of somebody's piece of ass. Her lips were parted a bit, just enough for a last breath. Or maybe she'd whispered a name. Something told Ava it wasn't Beck.

It would surprise most of Ava's friends and clients to learn that she had only seen three dead bodies in her whole life. She liked to project an *I've-seen-it-all* attitude, but in a moment like this Ava was less a cop and more…somebody's daughter, a young woman who talked a good line but who—like most of the rest of the populace—knew blessedly little about death and dying. She had seen her father's body at Forrest Lawn in Glendale, before it was dressed, because her mother was out of town—*conveniently* out of town, Ava had thought at the time—but she was just a teenager then and almost everything she said or thought about her mother was bitter and preemptive. That was the first body she'd seen. Her grandmother she'd seen in a coffin on the bema of a Pentecostal Holiness Tabernacle in Glendale. Two. Ava's third moment of grim witness came when she'd come upon an accident on Little Santa Monica Boulevard. It had been the middle of the afternoon on a Thursday, a bent bicycle and a girl who never got to be thirteen, never got to say bad teenager things about her mother. Ava had pulled over and stopped and got out. No one had covered the girl's body. It was summer and it was LA, nobody had coats, much less long coats to put over a body. Ava just stood there in the street until the CROs and EMTs came on scene. God bless The Interveners, Ava thought then. How many of these have *they* seen? And at what cost to them?

The crew from the coroner's office didn't knock or ring the bell, just walked right on in, three of them, two proper coronettes and a guy, a tagalong, an EMT, Emergency Medical Tech. All of a sudden they were standing behind Ava, one more thing she didn't see coming. Or *hear* coming. They would have arrived in a helo, probably landed on the roof. Those things really were quiet.

"Hey," the EMT guy said. Generally speaking, he was as loose as a pair of board shorts, even blonder than Cali and dangerously tanned. These days most EMTs were med school bounce-outs, usually because they had thrown themselves a bit too eagerly into the drug training. Or else they were former firefighters, fed up with dying on the job. "What we got?" the surfer EMT said. He liked his work. You could just tell.

Ava pocketed the Hark—why, she didn't know.

The two twenty-something coronettes pushed the EMT and Ava aside and kneeled beside Cali, started working their way down the checklist. A carotid reader confirmed what everyone already knew. One girl called out a number from the readout on the meter—presumed time of death, 3:55 a.m., almost an hour ago—and the other coronette tapped it into the form on a tablet.

"Epic," surfer boy said.

He pulled a big fat windup watch on a chain out of his right pants pocket and stole a look at it. The second coronette slid back the sliding glass door to give them more room on the balcony and snapped open a rubber-tire gurney while the other coroner's assistant bent to scoop the five remaining pill bottles into a purple plastic bag.

The EMT stopped the pill-scooper. "Wait. Let me see, Carlotta," he said and started looking at the labels on the pill bottles.

They all wore latex gloves, DayGlo green, glow-in-the-dark gloves. Ava had never seen them in use before. The glow-gloves gave the whole grim, matter-of-fact bagging-up-the-body routine a clownish feel, like the least funny circus bit ever.

The other coronette was digging through her go-kit. "We don't have an eighty-eight," she said. The first girl cursed. The EMT guy said, quickly, "I got a box of seventy-sixes up top," and pointed at the ceiling. "Same thing."

"I don't even know what they look like," the first coronette said.

"I could go with you," the EMT said. "Or not." They exchanged a look that would make more sense in a minute.

The first coronette followed the other young woman off the balcony, but not before she snatched a pill vial out of the EMT's hands, put it with the other dope in the purple dope bag, zipped it and locked it. The lock beeped twice.

So then it was just Ava and the EMT. And the deceased Cali.

"You aren't a big sister," the beach-boy EMT said to Ava. "Or a neighbor or a friend. And no way you're her mom." The coronettes had just gone out the front door, headed for the roof, so now Ava and the EMT were really alone. "You're a fixer, aren't you?"

"I'm a private cop. What we used to call a *detective*. I go around detecting."

"What did you pocket?"

Ava wasn't up for a fight. She pulled out the bottle of Hark.

"Cool," he said.

Ava put it back in her pocket.

The EMT had good eye-contact skills, like every other hustling salesman. He looked Ava right in the eye and kept nodding yes. Little yesses. The setup. Then he looked away from her to let his eyes fall on Cali's face and body and for a while both of them just considered her. Cali hadn't changed out of the white dress she'd worn to the club, a white dress with a full, pleated skirt. The wind off the marina had blown the skirt up, like Marilyn Monroe standing over the manhole cover, baring those white legs, only this time there was nothing fun about it and no one with a heart would take a picture of it.

The EMT shook his head slowly. Was he actually, legitimately, ever so slightly sad?

"She's hot," the EMT said. So much for the empathy.

"What's your name?" Ava said.

"Whoa. Why?"

"What's your name?" she said again, with less threat in it.

"Sean. But some people call me Shawn. I gave up on trying to correct people."

"Everybody gives up on a lot of things," Ava said.

"That's heavy," he said. "Actually, my actual name is Everett."

She wanted to like him, one human being to another. It was just the two of them, standing out there in the sea breeze in the thinning night over a dead body. What could make you want human contact more than that? It was almost five o'clock in the morning. It was an hour for forgiveness, an hour for letting things slide.

Ava was about to say something genuine and not smart-ass when Sean or Shawn or Everett said, "Cold boot."

Cold boot. Was it that obvious that she had a stack of hundreds in her pocket?

"Do you know what I'm talking about?" he said.

So much for forgiveness, so much for almost liking the surfer boy. Ava had an exit line with a bad word in the middle of it but she didn't use it. While she hesitated, he pulled out that watch-on-a-chain again, like The Stage Manager in *Our Town*. He looked at it, put it away.

"How much?" Ava said. Apparently, she had left her better judgment in her other pants.

"We have to hurry," the kid said.

"How much?"

"Three grand."

"You can do it?"

"Not five minutes from now," the EMT said, blustering.

The front door opened, the coronettes returning. "What about them?" Ava said.

"They're hella cool." He started to reach for his watch again.

"Yeah, I know, time flies," Ava said and went into her pocket and came out with her bankroll. She dealt off thirty hundreds. He stuck the bills in with his pocket watch. He was good at making money disappear too.

He went right to work, unpacking his goodie bag—four vials of something red that wasn't blood, a syringe the size of a turkey baster, and a chunk of electro gear that appeared to be homemade. He ripped open Cali's dress. Her breasts looked like they were made out of wax. With just his finger, he drew an X over Cali's naked heart, a target. The gesture seemed almost religious. First rites?

"You're gonna freak," he said enthusiastically, without looking up, loading the syringe.

"No, I'm not," Ava said, turning away.

As he plunged in the big needle, the EMT said to Ava's back, "You know where we're taking her, right? The Garden of Allah. They'll watch her a few days. It's for her sake. Some of them have a little trouble believing it."

"Yeah, yeah, yeah," Ava said. She made it out the door without looking either one of the coronettes in the eye. Or looking in the mirror in the foyer.

Cold boot.

◆ ◆ ◆

As Ava drove away, the coroner's helo-hearse lifted off on the roof behind her and slid north, catching an edge of dawn light on its belly. She made it a half block before she encountered Action Man, arriving too late in an electric Jag.

Chapter Eight

Twin chain-link fences ringed the place, twelve feet high. The day was so clear and bright the curled razor-wire atop them looked like jewelry. Cheap jewelry. Lompoc Prison was about sixty miles on up the coast from Santa Barbara, a quarter of the way to San Francisco, off California 1. It was a *prison,* not a *correctional institution,* as these facilities had been called in the touchy-feely years when they'd painted the cages calming colors and pretended they were engaged in taming the beasts within. *Prison* sounded more brutal, and brutality had become useful again. The cons said "Lompoc" was the Chumash word for "screwed," as in, *You're Lompocked now, friend.* Still, it was a medium security lockup, one of the safer, easier places to do time, and must have seemed to some of them kinder than home.

A man walked out the front door, free, or at least not in prison anymore. He was Black, in his forties, wore crisp get-out clothes and too-white sneakers. Under his arm was a package that looked like a present, except the wrapping paper was grocery-sack brown. In his left hand, unwrapped, was a white Bible the size of a cake box. The hem of the new khakis broke over the heels in a way that made him look shorter than he was. He was right at six foot, lean but not muscled up. He hadn't been the kind of convict who'd bulked up in prison, who lifted weights obsessively or ran wind sprints in that frantic, all-out way that must give pause to the guards. He hadn't put on weight or lost weight. He'd used up his hours on the yard walking, alone, trying to find peace, staying to himself, internal. Or maybe plotting revenge, all up in himself. His sentence had been like four years of a silent retreat, only here the monks had rifles.

He was Derrick Wallace—"Zap," some of them called him, or had in his life before.

The sky was blue and blank and wall to wall in a way that would've stirred the soul of even the freest man, who'd never been caged, but as Wallace walked across the parking lot he showed no emotion. He didn't look back, didn't look up at the sky, didn't take a deep breath with his arms outstretched. He didn't smile, didn't cry. He just walked, with a steady stride that didn't say anything, even if you knew him. Had he changed? He was clean-shaven, as before. He'd come in without a tattoo on his body, and he was leaving the same way. He had reading glasses now, in the shirt pocket. The most that could be said about any change to his exterior self over those four years plus six days—he had made parole because of overcrowding—was that his cropped hair had gone gray at the temples.

It was a Thursday. The big visitor parking lot was mostly empty, just a few dinky Federals and two or three real cars. A candy-apple red 2020 Cadillac was parked hogging the single patch of shade at the edge of the lot. The Cadillac started up politely and glided toward Wallace. An ugly skin-and-bones gangster, another Black, slouched behind the wheel, tipped to one side that way they do. Wallace kept walking, ignored the sparkly Caddy as it rolled up behind him, tailing him at one mile an hour. He could hear the music from the car. As if he hadn't gotten enough of that noise inside. At the far edge of the lot another car waited, a ten-year-old silver Lexus sedan with the windows down, a woman behind the wheel staring straight ahead. Wallace kept walking toward it, toward the second car.

But then he stopped. He walked back to the Caddy. The gangster driver braked, smiled. He had a cigarette in his hand out the window.

"Zap," the man said.

"What were you thinking," Wallace put his eyes on him and said, "coming up here in this?"

"Nix thought—"

"Nix. You got a 'ho and a forty in the back for me too?"

The gangster was about to offer a literal answer to the rhetorical question but before he could, Wallace turned his back on him and went on toward the Lexus. The skinny, confused driver watched him go with no idea what to do. He had sense enough not to follow him.

Wallace opened the passenger side door of the Lexus and tossed the paper-wrapped package and the Bible into the backseat. The way he did it made both the package and the holy book seem incidental, like props some stage director had handed him just before he walked out on stage. He sat on the passenger side. He was wound too tight to talk. He tried to slow his breathing. Without looking at the woman behind the wheel, he untied the prison-issue sneakers and tossed them out his window. He pulled off the cheap white socks. A pair of worn, broken-in loafers waited on the floor mat in front of him. He slipped them onto his bare feet.

"Sorry," he said to the woman behind the wheel and looked at her for the first time.

She was the mother of the dead twin boys. Her name was Jewel.

When he saw her face, he said, "What?"

◆ ◆ ◆

NATE WOKE UP THAT afternoon, 2:30 p.m. With the felt blackout drapes it might as well have been four in the morning. The house was quiet in that way that houses can be for those who live alone long-term, unpeacefully quiet, as if the Cosmos is about to lean close and tell you that thing it keeps meaning to tell you, that thing you're pretty sure you don't want to know. He opened his eyes but didn't lift his head off the pillow. For the thousandth "morning," he stared up at brown water stain in the corner of the ceiling. It had been there when he'd bought the place, and it hadn't spread, so he hadn't done anything about it other than fixate on it every time he woke up. It was like an old friend now. Or nemesis. Some days he thought the shape looked like Florida, all the way down to the dribble of The Keys. *Key West.* Was there any place that could be farther away from this, from the here and now, LA? As snapshots of Key West express-trained through his head, he realized he hadn't been out of town in a year. For a second or two he wished he had someone to go somewhere with—go back to The Keys with— someone to tell that story to about the sea turtle trying to make its way up onto the public beach crowded with drunks at 3:00 a.m. to lay her eggs. Someone to share this glass box of a house with, to wake up to, someone to watch cross the room through half-open eyes, someone elsewhere in the house in the morning making predictable, familiar, reassuring noise, brewing something or cleaning up, or even pissing in the bathroom.

But then the idea evaporated, as most ideas do, and Nate got up. He tapped a switch on the floor beside the nightstand and the drapes opened. The wall behind the bed was floor-to-ceiling glass. He walked toward his reflection. High white cottony clouds painted a heaven behind the old rugged cross on the hilltop across Cahuenga Pass. The 101 freeway wasn't moving, not a bit. At two in the afternoon on a Thursday. He looked south, to the right. A quarter mile this side of the Sunset Boulevard off-ramp, a truck was wheels up and burning atop a couple of Feds, with a pair of Crows circling. He could feel the cops' boredom from here, could see it in the way they flew. A Fire Department tanker was flying in from the south, redder than red.

Nate turned his back on the catastrophe and went into the bathroom and brushed his teeth, went into the shower, and came out of the shower in two minutes, two seconds before the miser valve shut it off. He dried his face with a towel, ran a comb through his hair. He went into the kitchen, slid a breakfast tray into the oven and ate a cold hotdog from the fridge while he waited for it. The coffee machine sighed a tiny cloud of steam.

The Wallace twins were looking down on him from the screen on the wall in the dining room. Headshots, their yearbook video from middle school. Seven dead in and around the house on South St. Andrews Place and one more at King Memorial, a big enough number to make it into heavy rotation on the local news. *The News.* That meant something…*new* now. Newspapers were no more. There was nothing black and white waiting on your doorstep each morning to tell you what was what, what was important in some generalized way. How could *they* know? *You* knew what was important, important to you. Now the news was targeted at you, like almost everything else shooting through the air. Your wants, your needs, even the wants and needs you didn't know you had until they told you. The news feed came to your screens endlessly, if you wanted it that way.

There were ten News Zones. Someone or something somewhere determined what you wanted to hear about and gave it to you, according to your priorities. The News Zones…

1. *Within a mile of where you are*
2. *Within ten miles of where you are*
3. *Your city*
4. *Your county*
5. *You subregion*

6. *Your state*

7. *Your region*

8. *Your country*

9. *Your continent*

10. *The world*

Most days, Nate checked the screen when he woke up, and, if his official departmental picture wasn't on it, he went on about his business.

He tapped the vid-phone on the counter beside the toaster and said a name out loud, and after a second a face appeared on the screen. It was a tough face, an old, Brown, acne-scarred face. They could fix those scars now—the government even paid for it, citizen or not—so the way this one looked said this was the way he wanted to look. It was the face of a Mexican, a certified national, which meant he could have gone back to Mexico with all the others if he wanted. For some reason, for him it made sense to stay in LA, with his face just exactly the way it was.

"Damn, you naked?" Johnny Santo asked.

Nate looked down. "I have on white socks," he said.

"It's two thirty, Cole."

"I work nights. Like you." He poured the coffee into a clear glass cup. He took a sip, then blew little waves across the surface to cool it. "Where do you get those shirts?" he said.

"What's that supposed to mean?"

"Where do you get those shirts?"

"Downtown," Santo said, not sure that Nate was mocking him.

"I'm going to get me one of those," Nate said. On the front of Santo's polyester shirt was a rendering of a Mexican man with a mustache in a white shirt and necktie. "Jesus Malverde, right?" Nate said.

"You know it," Santo said. "The Saint."

"You think Jesus Malverde watches over cops too, or just narco bandits?"

"Careful, man."

Nate drank about half the coffee, slowly.

"I guess I know what you want," Santo said, squirmy. "I don't know nothing about it."

"Yeah, but you know what *it* is."

"The house in South Central. Last night. Shoot 'em up."

"I thought that kind of gang shit didn't happen anymore."

"Everybody's talking about it, on the whatchacallit, grapevine," Santo said and stopped, trying to leave it at that. Wherever he was, he kept looking around, as if someone might hear him.

"I should probably be talking to somebody who knows something," Nate said, turning his back on Santo, something he'd never do if the two were in the same room. Or in an alleyway.

"Lompoc," Santo said. "Somebody getting out. Today. It has something to do with that."

Nate looked him in the cold, pixelated eye. "Who?"

"Somebody getting out."

"Who?"

"Somebody big."

"I should pay you by the word. Now we're up to, what, eight dollars?"

"Zap Wallace." Another nervous look over his shoulder and the screen went white. No bye, nothing.

And just as the huevos rancheros dinged and slid out of the oven.

"Johnny Santo!" Nate said, just because he liked the sound of it.

Chapter Nine

Eucalyptus trees always made Nate think of scrolls, the way the bark peeled off in curling sheets, like trees made out of parchment. Whenever LA went into a hard drought, like now, the already dry eucalyptuses were the first things to fall apart. But somehow they were still there when it was over. They were tall, taller than any other trees in LA, usually planted in windbreak rows—framing what once had been a farm or a walnut orchard, or hiding a freeway or fencing off Dodger Stadium—and permanently bent by any prevailing winds. They were all over the city. They dug in easily and grew fast. Government landscape regulators hated them because they weren't indigenous, as if anybody in California had any right to rag about *that* anymore. Or even notice. Gardeners hated them because they made a hellacious mess. They always looked as if they'd had a fight with something in the night. When it got *really* dry and the Santa Ana winds came calling, branches broke off, branches as big around as trash barrels, and smashed parked cars. The leaves were pale green, dusty, long, and pointed at both ends like some kind of Aboriginal throwing-knives. And eucalyptus trees had a strong, primitive smell, especially when it was raining. Everybody complained about it. A famous writer said that eucalyptus trees "had that tom-cat smell." But Nate liked the way they smelled. He didn't have any idea how to describe it, but he liked it. He suspected the trees would be left long after all the people were gone. They smelled like that.

He wished he'd brought a cigar. It would have given him an excuse for dawdling like this on an iron bench, under the eucalyptus trees, looking across the grass at Building D of the Police Sunset Home. He'd been hanging out—procrastinating—a half hour already. His Crow was parked out on the far end of the nearly empty lot. The "ranch-style" cop retirement home and convalescent hospital were across the street from Blue Field, the cop cemetery. When an LA cop died, they cleared the road out front for a pokey motorcade: a hearse, a dozen vintage Harley-Davidson motorcycles, a V of Crows overhead. And a half mile of "brothers in blue" on foot delivering "one of our own" to "that final shift." Most of the marching cops would rather think about the cemetery than the rest home so they tended to keep their eyes straight ahead as the procession went by.

A pair of orderlies had walked past Nate's bench a couple of times and a few others like himself, visiting family members, or delaying it, walking in circles. Or collecting themselves after the visit, before they got behind the wheel. Some of them, the other sons and daughters and wives of cops, brought flowers, as if a beat-up old cop wanted a dying purple hydrangea to stare at. Or sometimes family or friends smuggled in something greasy and beloved out of the past—a Philly cheesesteak, a Tommy burger, or a bucket of tamales—contraband, playing a childish game they hoped said *I love you* in some way they couldn't say otherwise. Or was it *I'm sorry*? Nate was almost always empty-handed.

The wind rattled the leaves over his head. He got up.

The floor nurse lifted her head as Nate came toward her down the hallway. She started to say something, give a report, but apparently the look on his face or the way he walked made her think better of it.

"Hey," Nate said to her, self-conscious about always being such a sullen crank when he came to call. She smiled, almost certainly used to about everything by now.

Nate assumed his father would be asleep. It was late afternoon and hot. Maybe that was why he'd hung out on the bench under the eucalyptuses, hoping the old man would be asleep. But Bodie Cole was awake. He'd gotten himself out of bed and into a metal chair by the window. He never asked the nurses and orderlies for help. He was sitting there with his back to the doorway. Nate tried figure the angle of the view out the window, wondering if his father had seen him on the bench, running out the clock.

Nate had the rush of thoughts and feelings he always had at first sight of his father, standing at this spot. *Who is that? Did I get the wrong room? That's my father. How could it be that he's still alive in 2025?* Then the second wave would come right away, kinder, more forgiving. *He looks all right. This is hard because I love him so much. This is all a part of living and dying. I'm a good son.* And then there was the third thought-wave, as dark as dark gets. *I'm never going to end up that way, I swear to God I won't. It's why God made guns.*

Bodie turned his head, saw Nate. He pushed against the wall with a bare blue foot to move his chair back. His toenails needed cutting. "Hey, Boy Wonder," he said.

"Hey, Pop."

Then there was silence. Same as it ever was.

Nate never knew where to sit when he came to visit. There were two of the metal chairs, but he never wanted to even touch them. He wasn't about to sit on the bed. That would be somebody else's son. He stayed where he was, standing in the doorway.

"You look like you just woke up," Bodie said.

"I did."

"You're limping. I heard you coming down the hall."

"I got shot in the leg. How's Carl doing?" Nate said.

Bodie had a roommate: another retired cop, dead to the world in a cranked-flat bed, needing a shave, half naked in open pajamas, skinny as King Tut. Carl Karlich was in his late nineties, a grizzled Westerner, a for-real lawman who'd come down to Los Angeles and the LAPD from Bass Lake in the High Sierra when he was forty, in 1967. Nate could smell the old timer's breath and body odor from here. Every part of these visits had become so familiar.

"They're closing in on him," Bodie said. "It's getting funny." He put on a codger voice, closed his eyes, rocked his head back and forth like a man in the middle of a nightmare, *"No, Bart! Oh God, no! They're there! They came back, the whole gang! Behind the bank! Where's my shotgun? Gimme my shotgun!"*

Nate said, "You should have been an actor."

"Yeah," Bodie said. "Me and Bruce Willis, it's like looking in a mirror."

Bodie Cole wasn't that old—in his midsixties, still barrel-chested with a full head of hair. When he was sitting up, he combed it every few minutes, quick, strong, almost angry strokes, a signature habit of his. You wouldn't call it a nervous habit, Bodie wasn't the nervous type. He wore the same outfit all day and every day, like a uniform: a white Fruit of the Loom T-shirt and khaki pants. He had diabetes, which made his legs and feet swell up. (And pancreatic cancer, though none of them knew it yet.) Every few months, a new doctor would rotate in and tell Bodie they should cut off his feet. Bodie always declined. And there was no way that Nate would override his father and sign off on it, though each of the new doctors tried exactly once to get him to do it.

"I saw you out there on the bench," Bodie said. "I thought maybe you weren't coming in today."

Nate didn't have anything to say to that. He knew better than to lie.

"They're talking about taking out those eucalyptus," Bodie said. "They can kiss my ass."

"You need to piss or anything?" Nate said.

"I'll let you know," Bodie said, with a sharpness in his voice that told Nate it was going to be one of the good visits, when his old man was more or less himself.

Carl groaned in his unquiet sleep.

"They issued all of us one of these," Bodie said, and held up a device the size of a ring box with a push-button on it. "A button. I'm supposed to hit this instead of doing anything myself. They said to think of it as 'calling for backup.'"

"Did you tell them they could kiss your ass?" Nate said.

"Yes, I did," Bodie said.

Nate slid some white socks over his father's ugly feet and took him outside, into the sun. Bodie wouldn't use the wheelchair they'd issued him. Walking anywhere with his father took ten times as long as it would have in the normal world. It was like learning how to partner-dance when you were a kid, one-two, one-two-three, everything slowed way down and backward. Nate worked hard not to let his impatience show. Bodie winced every third or fourth step, turned his head to do it. So Bodie was doing a little pretending of his own. It was like learning how to die when you were a sick and busted old man.

And then they were back outside under the gum trees. Bodie sat down, hard, on the same bench where Nate had done his procrastinating. "Is it ever going to rain again?" Bodie said.

"It drizzled a little the other night, about six minutes' worth."

"That only makes it worse, not even enough to wash things off."

"Did you hear about this new county plan?" Nate said. "Tanker rain, once a month."

Bodie adjusted himself on the bench, wincing when he moved. "You know what I hate more than anything?" he said. "Not seeing something coming. I used to make fun of guys who said, *I didn't see it coming*. I always hated that. Well, Goddamn it to hell, I didn't see this coming…"

Nate thought how good a bottle of beer would taste. He didn't drink anymore.

"You seem a little rattled," the father said, "like you're only half here."

Nate didn't say anything.

"Sit down," Bodie said. "I get so tired of everybody looking down at me."

Nate sat on the bench. He let the wind breathe through the trees a minute. "So I roll in on an aftermath deal," he began. "Thirteen-year-old kid, probably a gangbanger, shot elsewhere and brought home to lie in state in the front bedroom so his mother and aunts can wail over him. Actually, the mother was quiet, now that I think about it. We're there, South Central, trying to fill in the blanks, just my gunner and me, and the dead kid's twin brother makes an appearance. Twin. One kid's dead in the bed, the same kid is alive, standing right in front of me. Or so I think at first."

"Goddamn," Bodie said.

"But I don't have time to process anything because now a couple of motorcycles with shooters come down the sidewalk and open up, punching holes in the front wall, including with a fifty cal. I hit the deck. My gunner is killed. The twin brother takes one in the shoulder, and three of the wailing women get killed and two spectators out in the front yard."

"Damn," Bodie said. "Talk about the Wild West…"

"It gets better. I follow up with the wounded twin at KingMem who comes out of surgery okay, and another shooter comes in the recovery room and kills him while I'm standing there."

Bodie laughed, more of a grunt. "Whew!"

"Yeah. But, after that, I had a pretty quiet night. I went home, played some music, fired up a *Romeo y Julieta*."

"Blacks or Browns? The dead."

"It's not that simple anymore, Pop," Nate said.

Bodie just stared at him.

"Blacks," Nate said. "The twin boys, the women. The boys' dad just got out of Lompoc. Coincidence, I guess. The shooters were Browns, at least the two who came to the hospital."

"Anybody throw signs?"

"It doesn't work that way anymore," Nate said.

"It still works that way," Bodie said. "*You* just can't read the signs. Some new alphabet."

"I wouldn't be surprised." He thought about the Inca coin thrown on the bed. As the blood spread.

"An old gangbanger told me once..." Bodie said, winding up. Nate had heard this one twenty times. Fifty times. A hundred times. He wondered what it meant that nowadays his father didn't bother to start his stories with the standard apology about probably repeating himself. *Did I ever tell you about the time...?* Nate could have supplied his father's next lines but he didn't.

So Bodie continued, quoting the old gangbanger, "'We're all in gangs. You cops are gangs, same as us. You have your colors, we have ours. You have your guns, we have ours. You do your business, we do our business. You have your women who you're trying to impress, so do we. You live in your neighborhoods, so do we. You have your OGs—you call them by names like Captain and Lieutenant and Chief—and so do we...'" Then, the punch line. "And then the old gangbanger said, 'You ain't going nowhere, neither are we.'"

Nate nodded. For some reason it sounded more true today than it had every other time.

◆◆◆

NIGHT FELL. NATE LIKED to be up in the air when night came on. Something about being above the surface of the earth—even a few hundred yards above it—made him feel more in control. He was thinking about what his father had said about not seeing it coming. That was what Nate thought about nightfall. If he saw it coming—if he could look east and see a thicker dark moving in or look west and see the last hump of red across the water—then maybe, *maybe* the night had less of a chance of taking him down.

He flew over Montana Avenue in Santa Monica, coming out of Brentwood. He looked over the side. It wasn't even six o'clock yet, and there was a line out on the sidewalk for a new restaurant everyone was talking about, at least the people who talked about restaurants. Il Cielo e Infinito, the new joint was called. The sad thing was it had replaced a red sauce garlicky checkered-tablecloth joint called Vito's that was one of Nate's hangouts, or had been, and his father's hang out before him. Progress. He banked to port over Pacific Palisades and the Pacific Coast Highway. The lit-up Ferris wheel rotated lazily out on the pier. He looked down at the glass and chrome and white walls of The Shinola, a private club. Something was going on tonight. Quad searchlights swept the sky, the beams cutting through the coastal fog that rolled in this time of night almost every night. A pair of air cabs hovered above The Shinola's parking lot as a line of cars trying to get in sniffed each other's butts.

Nate climbed until he was above the marine layer, up into the clear blue-black. "Il Cielo e Infinito" was Italian for "sky and infinity," another way of saying, "the sky's the limit." Not for him. For him, the sky was just the first ten thousand feet of whatever was above and beyond all this all-too-human shit.

His new gunner was waiting for him, standing on the roof of HQ, his hands behind his back, parade rest, like a dope—the same kid from the end of the night last night.

"Why aren't you down in the squad room, cleaning your guns or taking another shower or something?" Nate said as the hatches came up and he got out.

"Sorry, sir," the kid said, snapping to. "I wasn't sure what you were expecting me to do, sir. I asked the captain and she said—"

"You don't ever talk to the captain," Nate said, walking away from the Crow. "You don't talk to anybody. What I'm expecting you to do is to keep me from getting killed and, if you have any extra time, keep yourself from getting killed."

"Yes, sir," the new gunner said, trying to keep up.

"And don't call me 'sir,' call me...don't call me anything."

"Right."

"And don't say, *right*," Nate said. "You don't have any way to know if I'm right or wrong. How could you? I mean, look at you."

"No, sir."

"But I am right, one hundred percent of the time," Nate said, walking on. The young gunner held his tongue, a fast learner. Nate stopped, turned. The kid almost ran into him. "You know that coach you had, the one who yelled at you and called you names and was always in your face but you knew that it was only because he really cared about you and wanted you to grow up to be— you know—a man someday?" The kid was about to nod yes but caught himself. "Yeah, well, that's not me," Nate said. "If you're really lucky, maybe there'll be a day like six months from now when I'll realize, *Hey, that kid is still around...* and I'll give you a big smile and ask you what your name is and if you have a girlfriend and who your favorite band is."

"Understood," the kid said.

Nate left him on the roof lot nodding and doing a nervous dance as if he had to pee.

It was still in early, so the squad room was nearly empty, empty of higher-ups anyway. Nate picked a path through the desks that kept him from having to talk to any other CROs or gunners, got a cup of coffee, pulled a couple of tabs off of the duty board. He went down a floor and stepped into the door-less glass box that was the home of the Gang Unit. The GU wasn't much more than a couple of desks and a sagging couch that looked like it had come from somebody's house. Or from the curb out front. Taped on the glass wall was a poster-size picture of a punk throwing his gang's sign, one so elaborate it took both hands, an elbow, and a stuck-out tongue.

Three GU cops were lounging, including Whitey, the Black, who'd been on the back patio at the house on South St. Andrew Place.

"Business slow?" Nate said.

None of them liked Nate. The one who disliked him least was Korean, named Il Cho, or Cho Il, Nate could never remember which it was. The other cop was some permutation of Latin American, Juan Carlos. Or Carlos Juan? Maybe they'd like Nate more if he got their names straight. Race mattered in the gang business.

"What's happening with the Twenties these days?" Nate said.

"The Incas took most of their good stuff," Il Cho said.

Whitey Barnes didn't look up from the dub-player in his hands when he said, "Well, now the king is back. Long live the king."

"Derrick Wallace," Nate said.

Il Cho unsuccessfully concealed a sideways look at Juan Carlos.

"They say he found Jesus," Juan Carlos said, also not looking at Nate.

"Yeah, right," Whitey said, sour, eyes still on his screen. "Jesus must have a short memory."

Juan Carlos laughed, ugly.

Il Cho said, "You were there at the hospital when the second boy got it, weren't you, Cole?"

"Yeah, whodunit, Cole?" Whitey said. "We're hearing conflicting reports. Not that anybody really gives a shit."

"I didn't see a thing," Nate said. "I was flirting with a nurse."

Whitey looked up from his game, watched Nate leave.

Chapter Ten

There was a busted dinner-hour robbery at a kimchi joint in Koreatown. These days in LA almost every CRO call was a homicide. This was a robbery-homicide. Double homicide. Nate purposefully took the long way there, hoping the coronettes would get impatient and bag the robber and the manager and split. Nate had a short-term goal: to get through the night without seeing another dead body. He landed on the roof of a florist's shop that used to be a bank, left the new gunner with the Crow, and came down an exterior fire escape to the street.

He was right, no bodies. The restaurant was packed, hungry customers stepping over the puddle of blood, fighting over the tables near the windows. The coroner's assistants had come and gone. One of them was named Suzanne. She and Nate had some history, recent history. She'd left him a note, written across the bottom of the body-run form. *You mad at me?* it said. "What, I was supposed to stay over the other night, cuddle? You were dead to the world. I almost put a tag on your toe." Among cops and coronettes, being dead and being sexually spent were more or less the same mockable thing.

Before Nate could finish the wrap-up in the restaurant, there were gunshots. Outside. Loud, meaty, a big-bore rifle. The diners paused—momentarily—decided it probably wasn't *right* out front, whatever it was, and went back to their spicy rolls and dumplings. Then came the sound of a muffled loudspeaker, a voice from the sky, like unintelligible orders from an ordinary, overworked God. A helicopter was somewhere close, a big boy with thudding blades.

When Nate came out of the restaurant, Gunner No-Name had come down from the roof, on full alert, shotgun at the ready. "Bear," No-Name said.

"So I see," Nate said, looking up at the big helo hovering one street over, churning up street dust. It was an old Sikorsky, a repurposed Russian warbird, good for heavy lifting. The side door was open. A rifleman sat there with one leg hanging out while another team member rappelled down to the street.

"Where was it?" Nate said.

"In front of the McDonald's. It came right down the street."

"They'll do that," Nate said. "When I was your age, bears shit in the woods. There was even a saying about it. Let's go."

Before the two were a hundred feet along the sidewalk, there came the big bass drum of another gunshot from the next street over, what sounded like a handgun this time, big-bore. Finishing the job.

Then they were airborne again. "You all right back there, No-Name?" Nate said as they flew out of K-Town and leveled off. Of course, the sky was clear, the city lights below just far enough down to be pretty.

"Yes," the kid said, warily.

"Take the stick a second, will you?"

"Sir? What? I mean…" A Crow wasn't equipped with dual controls.

"That was a joke," Nate said. The kid laughed the world's smallest laugh.

"Nate Cole, code one-eight-seven, two down, MacArthur Park," Radio Carrie said on the heads-up display, three-dimensional, close enough to kiss.

"*I can't take it anymore, Carrie!*" Nate said, like a drama queen, italicized. "*I've seen too much!*"

She smiled. It was a thing of beauty, her smile. Wherever her face came from, it conveyed the improbable idea that there was no place she'd rather be than here, with him, looking into his eyes, crossing Los Angeles, flying backward on a Thursday night.

"Don't you have a stolen bike in Tarzana for me or something?" Nate said. "Or maybe a baby deer looking for a drink of water, down out of Angeles Forest, roaming Old Pasadena?"

"That would be within the purview of Animal Regulation & Control, Nate Cole," Carrie said with another smile.

"The thing is we were going to go grab some dinner," he said, a lie.

"Ten-four. I'll reassign. Out," Carrie said and disappeared. Was that a wink?

Nate banked into the kind of diving turn meant to give a new gunner something to talk about back at the squad room and then they were headed south.

◆ ◆ ◆

TIME WAS, EVERY BLACK-AND-WHITE cop car in Los Angeles carried the motto: *To Protect & To Serve.* Now, officially, it was: *Always There...* But, unofficially, the motto was: *Keep The Lid On (Whatever It Takes.)* CROs answered calls—went where they were told to go, went where the flare-ups were—but they also flew by their own lights, followed their instincts. All CROs were detectives. At least that was the way it was with the ten-thousand-hour pilots like Nate, who knew LA in a way the office-bound, earthbound cops never would. Nate and No-Name walked up a narrow street. All the signs were in Spanish, the colors brighter, different tunes on the soundtrack. On both sides of the street were clothes shops, restaurants, places that still sold bootleg dubs of movies and music on rolling racks that spilled out of the store. This was way downtown, deep in. It wasn't Alvaro Street, wasn't a fake Ensenada. Nobody was waiting for the gringo tourists to arrive in a topless sightseeing bus to experience some local color, *traditional delicacies,* and lackadaisical margaritas. There wasn't a sombrero in sight, no strolling mariachis. And nobody was smiling.

"Hey, look, No-Name," Nate said, walking, "we're the only Whites."

No-Name shifted his shotgun strap from one shoulder to the other.

As they passed the next restaurant, Nate pointed with his thumb and said, "Empanadas."

When they turned right down an alley, the scene changed. It was as if they'd walked into a hip art gallery, fifteen-foot-tall paintings on both sides, both walls, Inca art, gang billboards, the kind painted without fear that anyone was going to come by and make you stop it. Or paint over it. No-Name was wide-eyed. This felt like what it was: a boundary.

"*Algún día estas paredes deberan caer...se desmoronarán, y caeran,*" Nate said.

"Sir?" No-Name said.

"Someday these walls shall tumble, crumble, and fall..."

"Is that from the Bible?"

"Almost. Los Lobos," Nate turned and said.

Pink pastries rolled around on a U-shaped assembly line in a baked goods factory. The air was sweet, too sweet, way too sweet. The shift workers wore white—as if it were a medical facility—and hairnets, which made them all look foolish, tamed. They were almost all young girls, Ecuadorian or Peruvian with a few Cubans. And notably, a few White American girls, too. Of course, no Mexicans. Nate had left No-Name behind in the alley. Nate stood just inside the door. The whole scene made him feel too much like a cop.

Nate spotted the woman he'd come to see. As he started toward her, he snatched a pastry off the assembly line. The floor supervisor—a Latin whip-cracker who didn't look like he'd laughed once since he got the job—hadn't lifted his eyes from the tablet in his hand but he knew Nate was there, knew who he was and what was probably going to happen next. And how he'd be expected to respond.

"They let you wear those sexy boots?" Nate said to the young woman on the assembly line. Her name was Miranda. She was Venezuelan, had been in LA since she was two. She liked what he'd said about her sexy boots, in spite of her "tough grrrl" stance. Her hands never stopped moving, sliding the pastries into plastic sleeves.

"Did you hear about my thing?" Nate said. "The shooters. At the hospital."

"I don't know nothing," she said.

"It was Incas though, right?"

"That's what people said."

"I don't know, I'm not so sure," Nate said. "I think somebody maybe wants us to believe it was Incas. What'd you hear, any specifics?"

"Any name I gave you would be wrong."

Nate liked her. She was smart. He knew her story, or some of it. She had a baby and a husband who had trouble keeping his eyes looking straight ahead. She was carrying a full load at LA City College and paying for it herself. She wanted to be an architect. There was something about that that almost made Nate choke up every time he thought about it. Architect. He wondered if there were any people in her life who thought she was smart. He was fairly certain no one had ever told her.

"That's OK, I don't want to get you in any trouble," he said. He took a bite of the pink *pan dolce*. "How's that kid, your cousin?"

"He's good. We got him in an art magnet."

"Hey," Nate said, looking around, pretending he'd just noticed. "White people work here now. What's up with that?"

"Since all the Mexicans went back," Miranda said.

"So is that progress? I keep forgetting what they want us to think about each other."

She smiled a smart smile.

Nate tossed the pink bun in a recycling bin. "You need anything from me?" he said. "Besides diabetes medicine."

Miranda took a second. Her hands pushed two more pastries into their plastic sleeves. She looked at him. "Somebody said the gunman at the hospital was an old dog named Razor. He's not Inca. He's not anything. He used to be a Twenty, long time ago, or maybe a No Fear."

Nate said, "There were two of them. The old guy was with a young one, a kid with a cross inked on his cheek. That mean anything to you?"

She shook her head but she wasn't looking at him anymore. Her hands had stopped too. Cops were coming in through the same door Nate had come through, a six-pack of uniformed officers. They called them Streets. Right behind them was Whitey Barnes, the sour GU detective, and, behind him, Il Cho. The third gang cop, Juan Carlos, already had some Salvadoran boy pushed up against a wall, squeezing the kid's face between his fingers.

"This has nothing to do with me, I swear," Nate said, before Miranda could even ask.

One worker made a break for it. Two Streets chased him down. When they caught him, they pulled his T-shirt over his head to reveal a back full of Inca art.

Miranda said, "I trust you." It was something Nate would think about later.

Nate went over and got in Whitey's face. Whitey always wore white shoes, like a car salesman or a strip-mall lawyer. Nate accidentally stepped on Whitney's toe.

"Hey!" Whitey said.

"Sorry. What are you guys doing? Tracking me?"

Neither one of them answered the second question. "Just shakin' the bush," Whitey said. "Lettin' 'em know we're here."

"I think they know already, Whitey," Nate said, moving on. "Leave my CI alone."

"Is she chipped?" Whitey said, a petty challenge that stopped Nate in his tracks. Legal immigrant workers had data chips under the skin on the backs of their hands.

"You guys know it's going in the other direction now, right?" Nate said.

Cho felt the need to defend his partner Whitey. "Don't assume, man," Cho said. Whitey smirked. Nate split.

As he was walking away up the alley with No-Name, Il Cho came out of the factory and caught up to him. "Wait," he said.

Nate waited.

"Did you get anything from your CI?" Cho said.

Nate told him about the old gangster with a lobster claw—maybe named Razor—and the second gangster, the kid with the cross on his cheek. "You know either one of them?"

Cho shook his head. Nate believed him.

Chapter Eleven

The sign came on. The name of the mortuary—*Funderburk & Son*—was in blue neon, cursive, what passed for low-key these days. The low brick building was midblock on one of the re-regentrified streets in Compton. It was dinnertime, an hour away from dark, almost quiet. The traffic was light, almost workable. A hulking ganger stood out front, arms folded. He glared at Nate as he approached—a warning shot. "Hey, how're you doing?" Nate said. He was in his CRO flight suit. He'd left No-Name with the helo across the street on the roof of the Fellowship Hall of the Followers of the Messiah First AME church.

Up front in the viewing room, the reconstructed Wallace twins were on display, side by side, shoulder to shoulder in a single pine coffin. It looked handmade, the coffin. Nate wondered if there was some New Age craftsman in the community who made pine caskets in his garage. If so, God bless him. Nate had a thing about funerals—as in, he had been to exactly one—but he had heard that caskets now were made out of recycled pop bottles and beer cans. On an easel next to the coffin, a heart-shaped screen showed silent footage of the boys when they were little. A banner read: *Samuel & Nathan*. It was very still in the viewing room, no music, no street noise.

Derrick Wallace was on his knees beside the pine box, his head bowed as low as it would go; he didn't yet know he wasn't alone. Nate waited just inside the double doors until Wallace's prayer was done—or the prayer gave up and lifted his head—before he spoke.

"Being alone must feel strange. The quiet, after all that noise. Prison."

"Who are you?" Wallace said, getting to his feet.

"How long were you in, five years? Five years of noise."

"Who are you?"

"I was there. At your house, at the hospital." Nate's flight suit said the rest.

"I'd like to ask you to leave."

Wallace's polite, measured tone was a surprise. Maybe it was Jesus talking.

"A changed man," Nate said. "So you found some peace up there. Good for you. Any port in a storm. And it's always a storm, isn't it?"

The edge in Nate's voice didn't surprise Wallace. He knew cops, had always had cops in his life. He knew how they talked, walked and talked, trying to make you fear them, thinking fear was the same as respect. Over the years, he'd come to respect a cop or two. He'd never feared one. He suspected the CRO before him now didn't in any way think that he was a changed man. Both men knew who he had been, knew Derrick "Zap" Wallace had put a good number of boys—other men's sons—into boxes. Or at least his gang the Twenties did, in wilder times. Two men were standing there, a cop and a criminal, both in deep. However secretly conflicted either man was didn't much matter. The past doesn't care what you think about it.

Nate said, "I don't think the first thing I'd do is pray if they killed my sons."

"No?" Wallace said. "What would you do?"

Nate stayed put at the back of the room. "I think I'd charge right back into it," he said. "That's what they're telling you, isn't it? Your people. That it's time to get back into it, time to kill somebody."

Wallace wished he hadn't said anything. He just looked at the other. A flat look he'd learned in Lompoc. It was hard to read anything into his face beyond the long-term generalized anger.

"I had a friend who was a salesman," Nate said. "High-end diagnostic medical gear. He drove a sweet old Jeep. He worked hard but he needed to get into the woods every weekend just to stay halfway uncrazy. One day he shows up with a new BMW. He said his boss, his friend, made him get it. It wasn't a joke. I said why and he said, 'Because he knows I can't afford it.'"

Wallace took a step toward the side door.

"You don't have to go, I'm done," Nate said. "I didn't mean to intrude. I just wanted to tell you about my friend and his BMW. And to say I'm not so sure it was your old enemies who killed your boys."

He walked back up the aisle and left the man with his sons, alone with the Alone.

◆ ◆ ◆

NATE ATE A STEAK at The Original Pantry Cafe, a 24/7 eatery downtown at Ninth and Figueroa in the shadow of the last of the office towers to the south. It was a cash-only place that had been owned by an LA mayor for years, so the crowd had always been políticos and the businessmen and businesswomen who traded with them. And cops. And mid-level drug dealers. Working stiffs. Over the years, it was known especially for steaks and pancakes but, things being the way they were now, you only got a steak if you knew one of the waiters. And you had a hundred bucks. Nate knew Cubby, who had been there forever. And he had a hundred bucks.

Nate sat at the counter, always. When his contraband steak came, it was covered by a thick crusty slice of sourdough almost as big as the plate, Cubby's idea of a joke. Nate left the bread tent over the steak the whole time he ate it, sneaking under it each time he cut off a chunk, his idea of a joke. With the first bite, Nate had to swear out loud, it was that good. Or maybe because it had been that long since he'd had a steak.

At a table in the back corner, beside a row of tall wooden step-in boxes called "phone booths" in another era, two men in business suits sat across from each other, one of them crying. The crying man kept looking at the man across from him and then he would look away and his tears would catch the light. Nate could see both their faces, the way their table was situated. The man who wasn't crying did all of the talking. He seemed resolute, very controlled, but after a minute he was the one who reached across the table, pushing aside a plate with a piece of pie on it, and took the crying man's hand in his. It was ten o'clock at night. Nate tried to figure it out. Had they come here from the office? They dressed alike, standard-issue suits, middle-manager uniforms. Neither man had loosened his tie. Did they work together? How had their day begun? Did the breakup start during the day, over a vid-phone? Were they going back to work after this? Did they have lives apart from each other, lives postponed—or stepped out of—for this, tonight? Was anyone in Los Angeles happy, paired-up and happy? Was *happy* gone with every other gone thing? Had they passed a law against it? Nate thought about the pretend secretary in the story bar the other night, the longing in the air, the lone woman in the deepest shadows. She was there when he came in, alone with a glass of red wine in front of her, her back straight, as if she thought she might be judged for her posture. He was a cop. It was all about the details. He had scanned the story bar when he came in, noted details and drew conclusions, even if there was no official or even practical reason to do so and all without thinking about it. Details. Her posture, her position in the room. The way she had crossed her legs. The way she *didn't* keep time to the music. Red wine, not white. The glass almost full, not empty, not almost empty. The way she had kept her eyes on Jane on the stage, what *didn't* exactly seem like lust in her eyes. She hadn't looked over at them, at Nate and Ava, not once. Who was she? Did she have a place in the world? Wasn't that always the question: *Is there a place for me in the world?* Was there any place where she felt at home, at ease, herself? Why was she there?

Why was Nate here? Then it hit him: it was one of Ava's haunts. She'd talked about the beef shortage. Ava had a hundred dollars too. Ava knew Cubby too. When he'd come in thirty minutes ago he'd been looking for her, he realized now. He wondered what that meant. He decided it didn't mean anything, or nothing worth thinking about. Whenever he found himself thinking about himself and his motives for more than a minute or two, it made him want a drink. He sawed off another piece of steak.

"Seen Ava Monica lately?" he said the next time Cubby came past.

"Not lately," Cubby lied.

Nate got up to pay and split. He thought of ordering a ham and cheese to go for No-Name—standing by on a roof two businesses down—but decided the gesture would be too considerate too soon. He left an extra twenty for Cubby, bought a bag of bootleg nicotine mints from a kid standing just inside the door, and went back out into the night.

No-Name was standing next to the Crow, eating his own sandwich. It was wrapped in wax paper, probably homemade, the bread dark and hearty, wholesome-looking. Nate wondered if the kid's mom had made it, baked the bread. Maybe she was a hippie mom, a back-to-earther, a Five-Ruler. If she was, now her boy was a gunman for the cops. How'd she like them apples? It was something else he didn't need to think about. No-Name snapped to attention when he saw Nate coming across the roof and started to wad up the grub.

"Finish it," Nate said.

"No, I'm ready," No-Name said.

Nate popped the rear deck on the Crow and pretended to care about something under the hood. "Finish it," he said again. "I'm in no hurry. Tonight we're just running out the clock, trying to keep it as boring as possible."

No-Name unwadded the sandwich and ate the rest of it in three bites. The look on his face was dangerously close to happy. Nate Cole had said a dozen words to him. And one of them was "we're." It was a start.

◆ ◆ ◆

A HISSING SOUND. NATE WAS thinking it sounded like a snake about to strike, even if he'd never actually heard a snake hiss in real life.

"What is that?" he said.

A spooked young street cop crouching beside him—eyes wide, a gun in his hand—just shook his head, fast. Either he didn't know what the hissing sound was or he couldn't talk right now.

They were in an alleyway beside a dirty Salvadoran restaurant, La Nacional.

"I guess we'll find out," Nate said.

The kid nodded, fast. He was turning white. And he wasn't even Caucasian.

"You might want to start breathing again," Nate said.

The kid nodded.

"It's all right," Nate said. "I've done this a thousand times."

The kid nodded some more. "Yes, sir. I know who you are."

It was headed toward eleven o'clock. When the call had come in, Nate and No-Name had been fifteen air miles away over East LA circling a silver-roofed house where one of Whitey's informants had said the old dog named Razor lived. This call was a Code 11-99—a cop in deep shit—and Nate had somehow intuited that this particular shit was *his* deep shit. In the chatter on the radio, he'd recognized Il Cho's excited voice. Now Nate was down the alley, where it dead-ended, next to a steel door and a Dumpster and a high window, the restaurant's kitchen. He looked back. Another Crow was landing on a rooftop a half block away. In the middle of the street was the forty-year-old Bell Twin Ranger which had brought in Il Cho and Whitey Barnes. And Juan Carlos.

The GU guys had been first on the scene, "talking" to somebody. Three other Crows were on the ground in the vicinity. All the CRO pilots had the sense to come in quiet, drop right straight down out of the sky on WhisperMode and jog in on foot. Two street cops had been on foot patrol a block over when whatever went down inside the restaurant had gone down and the all-in 11-99 call had come. The streets had cleared out the café's customers. It was small, only four tables. It was close to closing time, so there had only been three people in the place, an old man and a couple, a Salvadoran girl who looked about thirteen and her grown-up boyfriend, flirting over flan. The people in the neighborhood had known when they heard the big helo to shut the doors and windows and turn off the lights and TV, put the kids in the bathtubs, and lie low. It was quiet. Almost.

The hissing. It was coming from the kitchen. Along with Juan Carlos's yowling. Or was he calling out to God? It was a pitiful cry for help and not the metaphorical kind. It was hard to take, about as nakedly human as anything ever gets. Nate was right under the window up high on the alley wall, a window with an exhaust fan stuck in it. It was as if the fan were blowing out the sound of Juan Carlos's torture, amplifying it. Along with whatever the hissing sound was. Water running? Spraying? A broken pipe?

Nate looked back. Where was Il Cho? When Nate had first landed, they'd seen each other, talked for a second. "Juan Carlos went in on his own, through the restaurant to the kitchen, looking for your guy," Cho had told him. "Whitey and I were sixty seconds behind him. Whitey told JC to wait for the knockout team. He wouldn't wait. We pulled back." Then Cho had gone back up to the mouth of the alley. Nate had told No-Name to go with him. The Gang Unit cops rolled without gunners, a macho thing.

The rookie street cop still crouched against the wall, shaking like a 5.0. Nate put a hand on the scared cop's head to steady himself and then put a boot on the kid's right shoulder, used him to step up onto the Dumpster. He was right under the window. He stretched up, trying to see into the kitchen. He came up slowly until the clattering exhaust fan was blowing greasy air right in his face. It smelled like hot oil, tortillas, and pork. And gas.

Nate couldn't see much through the spinning blades, just two men, Juan Carlos on his ass on the floor, the other guy standing over him with a big knife that caught the light every once in a while. In the moment, neither man was saying anything. Juan Carlos had stopped howling. Nate couldn't see much. Before he thought about it, he stuck his fingers into the fan, right at the hub, seized the blades, stopped it cold. Juan Carlos's tormenter shot a look up in the general direction of the high window. It was the kid with the cross on his left cheek. The young gangbanger knew something had changed but he didn't know what and he didn't look directly at the stopped fan. If he had, he and Nate would have been eye-to-eye, just like in the recov room at the hospital. He had a twelve-inch kitchen knife in his hand and blood all over his cook's apron.

Juan Carlos was cut all to hell, little cuts, big cuts. Half of his nose was hanging off. He was plopped down on an overturned white plastic lard tub, his hands behind him, tied or taped, his upper body strapped to one leg of the steel cook table with power cords. There was blood all around on the floor, looking for a drain. Juan Carlos said something or tried to say something but his mouth wasn't working anymore. The cook with the cross on his cheek put down the knife, saying something to Juan Carlos. It didn't seem possible that Juan Carlos's eyes could get any more wide open but they did. This was headed somewhere bad fast. Juan Carlos clinched his eyes shut and dropped his head.

The stalled fan blades kept fighting Nate, cutting into the skin of his fingers and palm. With his other hand he dug into the chest pocket of his flight suit, found a ballpoint pen, and jammed it through the blades. He took his hand away. The blades didn't move. He leaned in again, looked down into the kitchen. He cocked his head. There was the hissing sound again. And now the kid had a cheap lighter in his hand. He jerked Juan Carlos's head up and pushed the lighter into his face so he could get a good look at it, but Juan Carlos's eyes never opened.

The ganger had his thumb on the strike wheel of the lighter.

Nate jumped down off the trash box.

Il Cho and Whitey and two CROs and their gunners were coming his way, up the alleyway. "They said wait," Cho said. "A Spec-Ev team is two minutes out." Or maybe it was Whitey who said it: everything was running together. Spec-Ev meant Special Events. Right.

Nate charged headlong toward the service door into the kitchen. It was a steel door but beat up and loose in the frame. The gunners, including No-Name, were all still ten feet back when Nate kicked open the door. It banged against something inside—metal to metal—and came bouncing right back at him. Nate put his arm up just as the door hit him and all in the same moment saw what was behind it. A tall propane tank. Now the hissing was like a whole sack of snakes.

In a second that expanded almost into timelessness, the kid with the cross on his cheek turned and looked at Nate there in the doorway. On the boy's face now was the same flat look the old dog Razor had in the recovery room when he'd killed the second Wallace twin.

The kid sparked the lighter.

In the fraction of time before it blew, Nate hit the deck and dove toward Juan Carlos, knocking him off the bucket, getting him down onto the slick bloody floor. The explosion had no color, was just clear force, clear heat, most of it coming right back out the open doorway, blowing down No-Name and the other gunners and the rookie street cop.

Nate came crawling out of the kitchen, holding Juan Carlos in his arms.

In time, higher-ups arrived in a double-wide helo with twenty antennae on the roof and took charge of the scene. The aftermath. A commander who had some history with Nate stepped up while the EMTs were cleaning him up beside the Dittbenner. The man looked down at Nate for a melodramatic moment before he said, with an edge, "He was already dead before you charged in."

Nate had gone back to the kitchen, had seen the what the fire did to the kid with the cross on his cheek. He wished he hadn't.

"Thanks," Nate said and called the man by his first name.

Meanwhile, Whitey stood across the way, drinking from a bottle of water, talking to Il Cho but looking at Nate with a look on his face that was hard to read.

Ninety-seven. Ninety-eight. Speaking of aftermath.

Chapter Twelve

A pack of feral dogs trotted down the middle of Mulholland, the leader a Welsh corgi. It was late, after shift. Nate was out walking, away from his place in the hills above Cahuenga Pass, still in his flight suit. He'd unzipped it to the waist, stripped to his white tee, made a knot of the sleeves over his hips. He wore a Dodgers cap. Other than the dogs, there wasn't much traffic, just the occasional speedhead in an electric Porsche with the top off, silently coming out of nowhere, blowing by—wild to be wreckage forever, as the poet said. The air had a spent feel.

"We tend to get the best results, see the most growth, when you have a face to connect with the voice," the voice said and waited. As voices go, it was warm and round, a man's voice. Somebody's uncle? A wise professor? A big brother? Or was that too obvious?

"Enter," Nate said to the midnight air.

And with that, what had been just a voice in Nate's earpiece turned into a disembodied face and torso, a man projected out in front of him at eye level from a lens in the brim of the hat, a man six feet away. Nate kept walking. The projection of the figure retreated apace.

"Hello, Nathaniel," the man smiled and said. He was middle-aged, graying at the temples with sharp blue eyes, handsome though not in a steal-your-wife, intimidating way. "I'm Jeffrey. Or, Dr. Stone, if you need that," he said, still smiling that smile.

"Really, a sweater?" Nate said and smiled a different kind of smile.

"I think I'm going to *like* you," the other said with miscalibrated enthusiasm.

The walk-and-talk thing was weird. "I'm going to sit down," Nate said. "This is making my head hurt. It's disorienting." Ahead was a wide place in the road, an overlook with a bench and a view of the Valley.

"Disorienting? How so?" the other said.

Nate sat on the bench and said nothing.

The view of the man in the sweater automatically widened and pulled back and now he was sitting too, sitting in the middle of Mulholland in an Eames swivel chair with an ottoman in front of him. And now he had legs. He had his shoes off, was in his stocking feet, the shoes on the pavement beside the chair.

"That's *very* interesting," the man said in response to Nate's nonanswer. He wrote something in a paper notebook, that way they do, then looked up. The air behind him was thick with looping bats eating bugs, screeching, blacker than the night. Real bats in the here and now.

"Change," Nate said.

A young Pan-Asian man with rimless glasses now was in the same place in a clear plastic bubble chair, unsmiling, like a villain in one of the Bond movies Bodie Cole had raised Nate on. The bats were still there in the background.

"Change," Nate said again.

A matronly, big-breasted woman.

A younger woman. Somehow, the program knew Nate's type. He didn't drink anymore but when he did—when he stepped into the red dark in one of his favorite dives after a shift on a Wednesday night—this right here was exactly what he would be looking for. And yes, he would end up telling her just about everything about himself.

"Change," he said again, before she could smile and hook him.

Next up was a man who looked more than a little like Bodie but younger and fit. And on his feet. Young Bodie stood there gazing out at the grid of the Valley. He looked back at Nate, about to speak.

"Freud," Nate said, a joke.

Blink. Sigmund Freud was sitting there in another chair, smoking a pipe, looking impatient, some combination of brilliant and bored.

"Stone, come back," Nate said.

And Jeffrey was back in his chair, now wearing a sports coat instead of the sweater.

"Did Freud smoke a pipe?" Nate asked.

"Yes," the other said. "And twenty cigars a day. He died of oral cancer. One of his pipes, a style known as a quarter-bend Canadian billiard, is in the Smithsonian, a gift he made to his longtime secretary."

Nate said, "How much of this do I have to do?"

"It's not mandatory," the good doctor said. "I would hope you don't think of what we're doing here that way. We want you to think of it as…calling for backup. But, having said that, nine hours and twenty minutes of talk-time is the average for most officers."

Empower. Or, rather, Empower™. That was its name, whatever face they put on it, whatever sweater or sports coat or skirt they wrapped it in, whatever pipe or rimless glasses they stuck in or on its face to fool you, to make you open up, relax, confess. Predictably, Empower™ depended upon the subject relinquishing his or her personal power, will, sense of control. It needed to mess with your head, and to do that, it needed you to let your guard down. In San Francisco, the cap was probably a Giants cap.

It wasn't that Nate had disobeyed an order when he didn't wait for the knockout team. Something else had rattled the higher-ups, had gotten Empower™ called down on him. It was that there had been more than a hint of…*crazy* in what he'd done a few hours earlier that night in the alleyway. Charging into that kitchen—a kitchen full of gas and with a dead-ender holding a lighter—looked a little…suicidal. The brass weren't trying to stop their cops from killing themselves—What are you going to do?—but the LADCCR did have an interest in keeping their down-in-the-dumps CROs from taking out other cops and civilians with them when they went.

"Your father was a cop."

"Is that a question?"

"No."

"Yes," Nate said. "He was a motorcycle cop. Then he started taking the tests, rank-running, and ended up a detective, the first motorcycle cop to ever do that, maybe the only one. I saw him Sunday. At church. He lives out in Sherman Oaks, in the house I grew up in. He remarried after my mother died, coaches a Little League team, still runs five miles a day, is active in Liberal politics."

"He must be proud of you."

"I don't have any idea if he is or not."

"Is life good, yes or no?"

Of course the virtual doctor was hoping for a quick, revealing answer, but he didn't get it. Nate got up from the bench, went over to where the Bodie look-alike had been looking out at the greenish grid of lights. A Streamer took off from Hope Airport in Burbank, headed north, rising, and banking. The planes were all but silent with their six props and steam engines. It left six silent white trails over Universal City. It made Nate wish he was up in the air, going anywhere. He'd read something in the liner notes of an LP of old bluesmen. *We didn't know where it was we was goin', but we knew where we was wasn't it.* When Nate glanced over his shoulder, his interlocutor was on his feet again too, with his shoes on again, the chair and footrest gone. The bats were still there behind him too, looping like crazy thoughts.

Nate turned back around to look out at the lights and didn't answer the question about whether or not life was good.

"That is *very* interesting," the doctor said, after nine seconds of silence.

◆ ◆ ◆

DERRICK WALLACE STOOD OUT on his front porch, trying to find some peace, not having much luck. The house on South St. Andrews Place was on the side of the street that was elevated a bit. From the stoop he could see the towers of downtown and a ghost-image of the mountains behind. Between here and there, helos crisscrossed the city with their blinking running lights. Like sparks above a fire.

It was three in the morning. It was never quiet anymore in LA. Horns honked, outlaw dogs barked, and there were occasional bang sounds that were either car wrecks or gunshots. He cocked his head. Someone somewhere out there was playing an old song called "Sleepwalk," an instrumental. Or maybe he was dreaming it up. It was already an old song when he'd first heard it. When he was six or seven? Probably on a car radio, cruising around Inglewood with the older boys on a cooled-off Friday night. It was the first song he'd learned the name of, except maybe for "Jesus Loves Me" or "Happy Birthday." The memory made Wallace feel something, something like a warm hand placed on his chest, but the feeling went away when the song faded out, wherever it was coming from.

Men argued in his living room behind him. He could make out every third or fourth word. It was like nights in prison, meaningless angry bullshit. The cop who had walked in on him at the funeral home was right about one thing: the noise in prison. Always there. Wallace had endured four years and six days of it. Somebody's favorite song became torture when it was played over and over.

The name of a sports team got turned into a taunt, a slur, a curse word, another reason for the men to beat on each other. Always there. Men cried out in their sleep, and other men told them to shut up. Prison was cold surfaces and stale air and aggressive men talking bullshit for hours and hours and hours, repeating the same lines exactly the same way day after day, night after night. There were no editors in prison, nobody cutting out the repetitious parts and certainly not the profanity. No one was cutting for length. That was the point of prison.

He had "accepted Jesus Christ as his personal savior" eighteen months into a seven-year sentence and, as a consequence, from that point on found that he didn't much give a damn about most things on a day-in and day-out basis. Once he had bought into the improbable idea that his numberless wrongdoings were "sins" and that his sins were forgiven—removed from him "as far as the east is from the west," his hulking, murderous cellmate had said—Wallace didn't feel the need to expand his faith-walk much past, "Do unto others as you would have them do unto you." He lived by that. Or tried. There was one Bible verse he'd stumbled across that spoke to him, a line from the Book of Job that went, "Man is born unto trouble, as sparks fly upward." That was where it locked in for him. Faith. Or, to use their word, *Redemption*. It came to him several months after his initial conversion that Wednesday noon in a circle of metal folding chairs in a corner in the chow hall— tears in his eyes, unexpectedly broken down to some basic version of himself— when he had been asked by some other murderer or thief or baby-raper whether he was ready to throw in with Jesus, and he had nodded yes, staring at the glassy linoleum. They had made him stand up to repeat it. That was a part of the deal. Yes. He knew he wasn't born all over again but he did think—from that Wednesday on—that somehow he had gotten a pass for all the bad he'd done. Or at least a reset. Since then, he was just living, trying to walk in the light, upright—even if he was, like everybody else, born unto trouble.

The screen door opened, his wife Jewel. "Derrick, you have to come in," she said. "Or get them all the hell out of here. What are you doing out there?"

So he went inside, following her. Jewel kept going straight on through the living room and went into the kitchen without looking back at him.

There were five of them, led by the one called Nix, a blunt instrument if ever there was one. All of them were Blacks. Three were hip to hip on the overstuffed velvety eighties-style couch, which had belonged to Wallace's mother. The house that Wallace had grown up in, raised by his mother and grandmother, wasn't but six or eight blocks south of 5163 South St. Andrews Place. Whites lived in it now. The men on the couch kept crossing and uncrossing their legs, agreeing or disagreeing with the line Nix was pushing but without much conviction, trying to avoid taking a stand, not wanting to say anything they'd have to follow through on later. The fifth man in the living room was a grossly obese gangster from Long Beach named Madison, the kind of fat person you used to see all the time but didn't see much anymore. He sat in the lounger that was Wallace's chair, not that the fat man knew it was Wallace's. If he had known, he would have moved. If the man named Madison had any real friends in the room, they would have told him.

Nix was on his feet, stomping around, pointing at people, thinking it was leadership. He wore high-waisted rust-colored pants, a cream-colored shirt, and blue shoes. He was the one who'd sent the tricked-out Caddie to pick up Wallace at Lompoc. "You can't ignore this, Zap," he said.

"I can ignore anything I want, Nix," Wallace said evenly.

He gave Nix a look that shut him down, a look that reminded every man in the room of the Zap Wallace they had known before he went to prison. Then he sat down on the bench in front of the upright piano with the pearly inlaid scrolling on the front, sat down with his back to them. The piano had been Wallace's mother's too, like the couch. He tapped three times on a white key. He didn't play piano, but—with all the ways prison can change a man—no one would have been much surprised if he had played "Moonlight Sonata" start to finish.

"I'm just saying we need to move on them or Incas are going to take it all," Nix said.

One of the men on the couch stuck his neck out. "We got to get back in the game. Get in on this Mexico thing."

Madison in the reared-back chair said, "Come on, Zap. For real."

"Don't call me that," Wallace said and tapped the same key three more times.

◆ ◆ ◆

WALLACE WAS AWAKE ON his back on one of the beds in the boys' room, on the backside of the house. Jewel came in, wearing a nightgown, a blinking phone in her hand.

"Nix keeps calling, Derrick."

Wallace just shook his head. Jewel walked out, left him lying there staring at the ceiling.

There was a faint sound, a whoosh-whoosh. He got up, fast.

Wallace came out onto the porch, down the steps, and out onto the little strip of lawn, with a gun in his hand. He raised it and fired eight reckless rounds in the general direction of the hovering Crow. He knew who it was.

Chapter Thirteen

The morning broke eternal, over on that other shore.

Razor was a stack of shoulder and back and legs and arms, the whole mess just lying there on the cement with that lobster claw coming out one side, palm up, as if waiting for a tip. There was no face or even a head—at least not that you could see—because he'd gone headfirst off the Avenue Twenty-Six Bridge over the Pasadena Freeway and the concrete-lined river beside it, the Arroyo Seco. The Arroyo Seco was a seasonal river, the only kind LA had now. *Seco* meant dry.

Ninety-nine.

It was the ninety-ninth body Nate had stood over. The last few days, the numbers were rolling up faster than the digits on the gas pumps of yesteryear. Today felt like the day he might break a hundred. He looked up. The Avenue Twenty-Six Bridge wasn't that high, not more than forty or fifty feet, which meant it wasn't on anybody's Top Ten List of preferred SoCal suicide spots. You'd do better going off any of the hotels downtown or the middle O in the Hollywood Sign, if you were up that way anyway and had a little flair. Who would kill himself going headfirst off a bridge this low? Nobody. Except maybe a USC diver who'd just found out he hadn't made the Olympics.

Whitey was up on the bridge, leaning over the railing like a fisher-person. Nate half expected him to spit.

He looked back down at the nasty pile of flesh and bone. The smell was starting to get to him. "I'm thinking maybe there's a bullet in there somewhere," he said. Il Cho was next to him. They hadn't yet assigned a cop to replace Juan Carlos on the gang squad, so Cho was working back-to-back shifts. He looked it.

The trickle of water that was the mighty Arroyo Seco was twenty feet away from where Nate and Cho were standing. You could just step across it.

Nate had set down his Crow a respectful distance away from the bridge and the body. No-Name stood at parade rest next to the bird, actual parade rest, feet apart, his hands clasped behind his back. A few other cops were on scene, another helo in addition to the one overhead pulling scan-and-record duty. Nate was hoping the coronette he saw from time to time would draw the body haul-off, the one who'd left him the teasing love note at the kimchi joint. Suzanne. He could hope all he wanted, but the ladies from the coroner's office didn't seem to be in much of a hurry to join the party. Or maybe they were elsewhere, working their asses off on a busy morning, bagging up the overnights. The day before yesterday, Nate had made a point of avoiding them, arriving on scene after they'd done their thing and split. Now he was stalling, wishing they'd show.

"His wife said he was depressed," Il Cho said.

It made Nate laugh. "No way," he said. "This guy was in his sixties, maybe seventies. A man that age knows who he is, good or bad. He wasn't suicidal. The suicidal don't know who they are anymore, they just know who they *were* or who they meant to be. I saw this one up close, on the job, with a gun in his good hand. I looked him in the eye. He knew who he was and he was just fine with it."

"I guess," Cho said. "Ostensibly."

"Besides, somebody who works with a gun doesn't jump off a low bridge when he wants to kill himself. What, he was out of bullets? It'd be like a carpenter using his shoe to pound a nail."

"So you think somebody shot him and then threw him off."

"I do. But you know me, I always think the worst of people."

"The Incas, covering their tracks?"

"That wouldn't be the most interesting answer but that's probably it."

Il Cho didn't say anything. He was bone-tired and it was only an hour into his shift. He sighed, loud enough for everybody except Razor to hear him. "But you don't think that's what happened," Cho said next. "So who did it? Zap Wallace, the Twenties? They tracked us tracking Razor?"

"I think that's what we're supposed to think. It makes a lot of sense. But, then again, maybe Derrick Wallace *is* a changed man. You know me, I always think the best of people."

Cho looked up at the blank, dry sky. "Where are the coronettes?"

Nate squatted beside the mass of blood and bone and polyester. He cocked his head sideways, trying to see under the shoulder blades. "Who called it in?" he asked. He looked across the concrete wash. No neighbors, no houses or apartment blocks, no scrub brush, just the graffitied backsides of industrial buildings. This section of the Arroyo Seco was too grim even for the shadow-dwellers.

"Johnny Santo."

Nate stood. "Santo's *my* guy. Why didn't he call me?"

"He talks to everybody," Cho said.

"That hurts," Nate said, though it didn't hurt at all.

◆ ◆ ◆

"Ostensibly," Nate said out loud.

"Sir?" No-Name said.

They were bulldozing their way down the crowded noontime sidewalk on South Spring Street, a couple blocks over from Pershing Square, headed south. Nate didn't know where or what for. Truth be told, he was just walking. He couldn't get the snapshot of the bloody pile of human meat out of his head. Ostensibly, he was looking for Razor's woman. Il Cho had said the wife worked in a downtown rag shop, silk-screening T-shirts. She was the one who said he'd been depressed.

"You wonder where we're going," Nate said over his shoulder.

"No, sir…"

"Of course you do."

"Yes, sir."

"Ostensibly, we're looking for a widow," Nate said. "Ostensibly."

No-Name knew not to say another word.

Like a car crash, a white-haired boy, five or six, ran out of nowhere and banged into Nate, throwing his arms around one of Nate's legs. White-haired. Nate's grandmother—a long, long time ago—sometimes used the word *towhead* when she was telling a story about the old days, in Nebraska. He didn't remember if it was a racial/ethnic slur or what. She was a nice old lady, probably wouldn't think of speaking ill of the flaxen-haired.

Nate looked down at the kid hugging his thigh, the boy's blond head right next to his service pistol in its tactical holster. No-Name was about to fling the boy to the concrete and possibly shoot him.

"Hey, buddy," Nate said to the top of the lad's head. "What's your name?" No-Name backed off.

A young man, twenties—apparently the boy's dad—caught up to the boy, apologizing. Father and son, they were skin and bones.

"It's all right," Nate said. "What's your name, boy?"

Now the boy looked up. But didn't open his mouth.

"He's stopped talking," the skinny father said, and put a period on it. He pulled him off of Nate, muttered another apology, and stepped away, went to another man in the crowd on the sidewalk, a man in his early forties who might have been the boy's grandfather. The menfolk were wearing threadbare bib overalls, as if they'd stepped out of a diorama over at the Natural History Museum. Or *The Wizard of Oz*.

Nate watched the men and the little boy as they flowed south with the crowd. At the next corner, Fifth Street, a woman in a cottony dress came out of a Goodwill Store that once had been a big bank, a backpack over her shoulder. The boy went to her. To his mother.

◆ ◆ ◆

THE DAY HAD BURNED down to nothing. An hour and a half away from dawn when it would start up all over again, Nate stood at the window in his bedroom, watching the traffic slither through the pass below.

"It's four in the morning. Where in the hell are they all going?" he said.

The coronette was in the bed, naked, uncovered. She was tall, even out of her work boots, flat on her back. Tall and tan. She was lying there feeling powerful and safe and wonderfully wide awake.

"Home," she said.

"Home from where?"

"Bars and Twelve-Step meetings."

Nate was naked, too. He turned away from the glass and found his boxer shorts on the floor, pulled them on.

"You want me to go?" the coronette said. Her name was Suzanne.

"No," Nate said.

"I'm done with you," she said.

He came away from the window and got in bed beside her again. "No," he said. "Stay." He leaned back on the pillow.

She rolled over on top of him, straddling him, and stared at his face, comically close. "You actually mean it," she said, looking deep into his eyes. "What's happened to you?"

"Nothing," Nate said and put his hand on her upper leg, where it curved toward her back.

When she was asleep, snoring into the pillow, he got out of bed and went to the radio room. He stood over the table against the wall, his gear. In the half-dark, the transmitter looked like a futuristic city, the uncovered tubes like glass office towers. He flipped up the toggle to ON and the VU meter lit up, warm, literally incandescent. While the vacuum tubes shook themselves awake, he stepped to the tall record rack and sorted through the LPs and found what he was looking for and sat down at the board. The mic was open, but he didn't say anything. The needle on the VU meter quivered anyway, alive, anticipatory, picking up the sound of his breathing. Or maybe it was her snoring in the other bedroom. He'd wanted some comforting human noise in the house; now he had it.

He slid the record out of its sleeve, blew off the dust that wasn't there, put it on the turntable, and gave it a spin it didn't need. He set down the tone arm, side one, track one. He cut the mic and leaned back in his chair.

And thus it was that Leonard Cohen and his Suzanne—leaning out for love, wearing rags and feathers from Salvation Army counters—joined the two of them there in house and whoever else might be tuned in. If anyone was.

Chapter Fourteen

"Señor Passarelli!" the woman said again, much louder than the first time.

A big man walked across the lobby of a rundown downtown hotel, across the brown linoleum that hadn't seen a shine in twenty years. The tall front windows were uncovered but so dirty that there wasn't much light coming through, just a splash of it on the floor. Yellowish light. Not golden. There was a world of difference between dull yellow and golden, the man was thinking, and the light in Los Angeles was yellow. Not golden. No matter what they said.

It was hot and the hotel lobby wasn't air-conditioned, only the rooms upstairs. The big man was wearing a dark brown suit with a matching vest and a tie that probably should have been on display in a museum somewhere. It was knotted in a half Windsor up under his Adam's apple. When he knew he had to head out to Los Angeles, he got his one suit out of the closet and bought three crisp white shirts from the local men's shop to wear with it. He wore the suit on the airplane and had worn it every day since he'd arrived, and he was going to wear it every day for as long as he had to be here. It still smelled like mothballs but less so each day. Hot as it was, he hadn't loosened his tie as he walked around downtown, even when he was on the full sun side of the street. He didn't think it would be right and he didn't change his mind when he saw everyone else on the sidewalks dressed as they were dressed, some wearing next to nothing, looking as if they were headed to a party.

"Señor Passarelli!" She came out from behind the front desk. She was a Latina, a señora.

He kept walking, ignoring her. He was still thinking about yellow versus golden. He had a favorite movie that was about gold, looking for gold, men looking for gold down Mexico way. *The Treasure of the Sierra Madre.* Humphrey Bogart was in it and a "gnawed old bone" of a codger played by Walter Huston. It had been his father's favorite movie, and the two of them watched it so many times it became his favorite movie, too, probably for the same reasons it was his father's favorite, for what it said about the actual nature of things, about what really mattered. What was true and not what a man merely wished were true. Now that he thought about it, the movie was one of the few things his father had passed on to him. Not that his dad didn't love him, not that he wasn't generous. It was just that his father all his life had been dirt-poor and diminished—even in stature—because of it. But the two of them would sit with bowls of home-popped popcorn and watch this movie about gold, about looking for it and against all odds finding it. (Holding onto it was another matter.) In one scene, the men were sitting around a potbellied stove in a beatdown hotel in Mexico—even more beatdown than this one—talking about gold, how come it was worth twenty bucks an ounce, which wasn't a joke amount of money then. Howard, the old man, who knew what the younger men had no way of knowing yet, answered by telling them that only one man in a thousand ever found gold, and so one man's find represented not only his toil but that of the 999 other men who looked for it and never found it. Gold. Though you might as well substitute "peace of mind" or the steadfast love and devotion of a good woman.

Just as he reached the elevator, the insistent señora caught up with him, touching his arm.

"What?" he said, making it sound like a curse.

"Señor Passarelli."

"What?" He pulled a white handkerchief out of his breast pocket and dabbed at his sweaty forehead.

"Do you speak Spanish?" she said.

"No. Why would you ask me that?"

"Because you said you were a Spaniard," she said. "When you checked in."

The elevator doors opened. He stepped in. "I'm Italian," the big man said. "I never said I was a Spaniard."

Just as the doors were closing, she jumped into the box with him. As his hand reached out for the controls, she beat him to it and pushed the button for the tenth floor where his room was. He breathed out through his nose and stared ahead, stared at the framed Certificate of Assurance of Safety & Dependability, which he noticed was dated November 11, 2004.

Up they went. "The Chinese own many of the buildings downtown now," she began. She was a rather small Latina. Until the last few years, most people assumed she was Mexican, though she was Colombian. "Of course they built these new electric cars that are so popular, the Chinese. *El Chino*, we say *en Español*. I have nothing against them. They say that they have the largest factories in the world in China although unfortunately they pay their laborers much less than what is paid in other countries, even countries such as Korea."

The brown-suited man looked up at the numbers. The two blinked on.

"I would estimate that they, the Chinese, now own half of the buildings you see when you go for your walks each day. At least a third. Certainly a good number of the hotels, including the Otani. Possibly half of the hotels."

At six, the big man said, "Why in heaven's name are you telling me this, woman?"

"This hotel has been bought. By the Chinese. Not the government, a Chinese man."

"*Un hombre chino*," the big man said dryly.

"No one likes change," the Latina said. Her name was Valeria.

The elevator stopped and the doors opened immediately, as if the lift couldn't wait to shed its passengers. The big man got out, turned to the right, walked. The carpet was frayed. Green. The hallway was long and dim. The light from outside was minimal—a painted-out double-hung window at each end of the hallway—and the hotel management was too mingy to turn on the overheads in the daytime, even though electricity cost next to nothing now. He walked fast.

She kept up. They passed by twelve doors. "We were owned by wealthy Mexican nationals. I never met them, the owners."

They reached his door, the third room from the end. He turned to face her, standing close enough to poke her in the eye, though he wasn't the kind of man to hit a woman. "What do the Chinese want from me?" he said, one word at a time.

"They require advance payment for weekly guests who have no credit card," she said. "They are lacking in trust, unlike the Mexicans. Or myself."

He unbuckled his belt and undid the top button of his brown suit pants. The woman took a step back. He unzipped his trousers and parted the tail of his white shirt to reveal a canvas wallet attached to a band circling his waist like a girdle, what was known as "The Wary Traveler's Friend." He unzipped it horizontally and removed a sheaf of bills. He took hold of her right arm and pulled her closer and lifted her arm and flattened out her right hand. From the deck he dealt into her palm fourteen bills of various denominations.

"That's for two more weeks, though I can't imagine being here that long," he said and, leaving his pants unfastened. He unlocked his door and went into his room without looking back.

"God bless you," she said as the door closed.

He stood in the middle of the room for a moment, loosened his tie and pulled it off and threw it on the bed as he walked to the window air conditioner. He'd left the AC running three hours ago but now it was turned off. Somebody had been in his room. He looked around to see if anything had been disturbed, if anything was missing. Everything looked all right. Maybe the unit had auto-shutoff. Maybe it knew when there was no one in the room anymore—although it didn't come back on until he turned the knob, cranked it up to HI.

He took off his suit coat and unbuttoned the vest as he hung the coat in the shallow closet. He had a gun tucked into the back of his pants, a little "pimp gun," a .25 chromed semi-auto Colt with pearl grips that had been his grandmother's. He dug it out of his waistband, rubbed the small of his back where it had dented the flesh, and threw it on the bed next to the tie.

He checked under the mattress. His other gun was where he'd left it.

Of course his name wasn't Passarelli. But Passarelli was a real person, alive somewhere, if he was still alive. He had been thinking about ol' Passarelli ever since he had heard his name called out in the lobby. They hadn't been friends, exactly, he and Nico Passarelli, whom the other boys called "Pass." Where he'd grown up, boys played sandlot baseball. It was in northern Georgia, so the scrappy field they'd laid out actually *was* a sandlot, dotted with sandspurs that kept anyone from playing barefoot. The big man was outsized even when he was ten or eleven, always the biggest kid, but Passarelli was the next biggest kid in the group. Neither of them was very good at ball, except when it came to smashing one into the trees every fourth or fifth time at bat. Passarelli always made fun of him because he was poor and his glove had a hole in it.

"Hell, I was lucky to *have* a glove," he now said out loud. "Used to make fun of me because I couldn't swim. Not everybody grew up with a swimming pool."

The room smelled like a clothes hamper. A man's room. He looked around. Newspapers on the floor, the trash can filled with the fliers they handed you every ten feet on the sidewalks in Los Angeles, coffee cups on the dresser, one of the white shirts thrown over the television, which he hadn't even turned on. When he'd checked in, he'd told them no maid service.

Not that the place couldn't use a woman's touch, he thought self-pityingly as he sat on the unmade bed.

Chapter Fifteen

Ava had a dog. For exactly one month, which was all Ava and the dog could take of each other. It had been her stepfather's dog, a Jack Russell terrier, which her mother had wanted nothing to do with upon the death of her second husband. This was in the last year before the Domesticated Mammals Release Law went into effect, emancipating all the dogs and cats, basically anything with a face that looked even remotely like a human face. When Release Day came—July 4, 2022—the weepy law-abiding "pet owners" delivered "their" dogs and cats to centralized locations, the parking lot of Union Station in the case of Center City Angelenos. Goodbyes were said and the uniformly confused animals were loaded aboard Electro-Freightliners for transport to their new homes in the wild in less advanced states, like Idaho. Almost everyone complied. A few holdout citizens hid their pooches and kitties behind drawn shades, feeding them "people food" and double-bagging their shit to avoid detection. The less rebellious just turned their pets loose up in the hills.

But that was three years ago, in 2022. Before that, Ava's stepfather's dog would sit beside her refrigerator for hours, looking up at her with the most annoying and pitiful look. The dog knew there was food in that food box and that Ava controlled the box, could open it whenever she wanted and retrieve that food, which was all that really mattered to the dog, which the dog knew would make everything right.

That was the look on Beck's face.

He was standing down on Sunset Boulevard below Sunset Tower. It was noonish. Ava had just gotten up. She hadn't even brushed her teeth. She'd stirred out of thick slumber when a wayward seabird had slammed into her fourth-floor bedroom window. She had stretched, taken off her sleep mask, gotten out of the sultan-size bed, fluffed her hair, crossed to the living room, and threw open the drapes, then looked down to check the traffic.

And there he was, Beck, looking up at her with that hangdog, pitiful, annoying look.

"Sheesh!" Ava said.

He couldn't see her up there at her window, no way. Still, she could feel his desperate, questioning eyes on her. She hadn't talked to him since the night in her office when she had taken his money. She'd ignored all his calls and messages. She hadn't told him anything. She hadn't told him about finding Cali at The Shinola, looking for all the world like a hooker, a clinically-depressed hooker. She hadn't told him about Cali's "manager," Action Man. She hadn't told him about tailing her to the apartment in the Marina or about the sad little seashell night-lights and the empty dirty white suitcase and finding her dead. And she sure as heck hadn't told him about the cold boot.

She was about to close the drapes and go brush her teeth when she saw that Beck wasn't alone. Except in the cosmic sense. Someone else was watching him watching Ava's building. Parked on the other side of the street, up the strip, was the classic Bentley from the parking lot of The Shinola. Mr. DL. Or rather, his driver. The tall shrugging gun-toter was out from behind the wheel, wiping something nonexistent off the hood as he eyeballed Beck a hundred feet away. Then he pretended to check the rear tires. Then he came around to the back of the car, put his foot up on the bumper, and pretended to tie one of his shoes. Smooth.

Beck never even saw the man spying him, his eyes fixed on Ava's fourth-floor window.

"Go away," Ava said in her scold-the-dog voice. "Both of you."

As if he'd heard her, Beck lowered his head and ran his fingers through his hair, exasperated. He turned his back on the Sunset Tower and went over to sit on a bus bench. He looked over his shoulder again, a perfect three-quarter profile, like an actor's eight-by-ten headshot. He wore the same million-dollar silver suit. Ava had only seen him in the middle of the night before this, yet here he was, handsome as ever. Somehow he got better looking the sadder he was.

Along came a subplot. A half block to the east, a vintage black Volkswagen bug jumped out of the creeping outside lane of traffic and drove up the sidewalk. A girl was driving. Everyone was honking, furious at her for violating protocol, for being impatient, for acting exceptionally. She parked the bug on the sidewalk right across from The Tower and jumped out and waved gaily at the honkers and zigzagged her way through the cars and trucks.

And then she was standing right in front of Beck.

"And who are *you*?" Ava asked, from a great height.

The girl looked familiar. She was Ava's size and build, had the same color hair, cut like Ava's. She wore low high-heeled boots and a tight catsuit with a flip-up hood, though it was un-flipped. The whole outfit was completely inappropriate for the middle of the day on a Thursday.

"Wait! You look like *me*," Ava honked. The girl was ten years younger than Ava, which made the look-alike lass extra nervy.

Beck lifted his head and looked at the girl, who went straight to chewing him out, gesturing theatrically, pointing one way down Sunset and then pointing the other way and then pointing at Ava's building. *Indicating*, they call it in acting. Beck hung his sorry head. Even without seeing his face, it was obvious he didn't want the girl there, ragging on him like this. In spite of herself, Ava felt sorry for him.

The Bentley gunman was watching intently, not even pretending not to be watching.

Beck reached into his pocket and gave the girl some money. Magic, she gave it a rest. The girl said another line or two, tilted her head to one side empathetically, and said something else. Beck nodded. She said something else. He nodded again. She shook his hand that way girls do when they're trying to convince themselves they're grown-ups now and turned around and threaded her way back across the four lanes to her black bug, almost skipping. She got into the VW, turned the key, cranked the wheel, and waved out her window, all friendly-like, until someone—meaning a guy—let her back into the outside lane as if she'd never left. And off she went. At a half mile an hour.

Ava growled.

She took a shower and got into her work clothes and toasted an onion bagel, buttered it, and went back to the window, hoping that…

Nope. Beck was still there, looking up at Ava's fourth floor window again.

"Fine!" she said.

A few minutes later, Ava had him by the arm, walking him down Sunset to Carney's, a hotdog joint retrofitted into an old Coast Starliner train-car planted diagonally on a $5 million lot. The chilidogs were twenty-eight dollars.

"Drink," Ava said. She pushed the cup of joe across the red-top table.

"It's been three days since I—" Beck began.

"Actually, two and a half…"

"I couldn't help but think the worst," he said.

"Well," Ava said, "the starting point with Cali was that she was *dead* so you could say the worst was—"

"She's not dead, I told you that. I would know if she was dead." Then something overtook him, overtook his face, starting in the eyes. After a moment he said, in an altogether different voice, "At least that was true then, when I hired you the other night, in your office," he said. "That's what I thought then, that she was alive. I don't know what I feel now." He looked for the words and then said, pitifully, "Now I'm getting…mixed messages. Mixed emotions."

"Hey," Ava said, "if wasn't for mixed emotions I wouldn't feel anything at all." She looked down at the three feet of Formica between them. Holy cow! One of her hands was reaching across the table to take his hand. She stopped it in time.

Beck hadn't noticed. "You'll tell me, either way," he said, a question, a plea.

"Yes, I will."

"Even if—"

"Yes, even if."

"I just think it would be better to know."

"How could it not?" Ava said, getting up. "Now it's time for me to get crackin'. And it's time for you to suck it up, big fella." She pulled him to his feet, straightened his suit, patted his lapels.

"Do you need more money?" Beck asked, already reaching into his pocket.

"No," Ava said. "No." Today was one surprise after another.

◆ ◆ ◆

"*TROUBLE IS LOOKING FOR someone to drain,*" Vivid sang on the juke. It was a good song.

The dive bar was on Main in Santa Monica, four or five blocks away from anything even close to hip. It had a name, but "Dark & Dank" would have been good. Or "Dante's Abandon-All-Hope Lounge." It was a quarter-full of day-drinkers and fifty-cent criminals. And actors who no longer had representation. Ava had just stepped in off the sunny street and stood waiting for her eyes to adjust. She had tailed the black VW with the ten-dollar help of Edward Chang who had a tap into the traffic surveillance cam circuit and his own bootleg vehicle recognition software. It wasn't that difficult. There weren't but six old Volkswagens in LA proper and only one that was black. The bug was parked on the sidewalk out front. Ava groped her way toward what she hoped was an empty stool at the bar and sat down, all before Vivid finished her cautionary tale.

VW Girl was the bartender. She was working the place alone. She had her back to Ava, putting a new spool of paper into the old-school cash register. She looked even younger than she'd looked seen from on high. Maybe it was her outfit. She'd gone from the knockoff of Ava's catsuit to blue hot pants and a white short-sleeve shirt knotted in front just high enough to expose her belly button. Her high-heeled boots had been replaced by white sneakers. It took Ava a minute, but then she realized where the look came from: Dallas Cowboy Cheerleader, 2001.

"Who *are* you?" Ava said.

When the girl turned around, her face lit up and she said, "You cut your hair!"

"Six months ago," Ava said. "Who *are* you? Do I know you?"

"It's so cute," the girl said. She sounded about sixteen.

"Thanks, I like yours too," Ava said. It came out nowhere nearly as nasty as she meant to sound. "Yours is just like mine from six months ago. I saw you with Beck. Who are you?"

"I can't believe this!"

"I know, me either. Who are you?"

"I'm you," the girl said. The line sounded like she'd rehearsed for use in the unlikely event she ever got to meet Ava Monica. "Or," she said quickly, "I'd *like* to be someday. A detective, a woman detective. Well, I already am, a detective. I'm licensed. You're my inspiration. I studied and took the test and got my license after I saw you on TV the first time. You were talking about the Galton case."

"You're a detective," Ava said. Ava's questions were all becoming statements. And vice versa.

The girl pulled a business card out of her top and put it on the bar. It had a drawing of a cute girl with a big ol' magnifying glass. Her name was Chrisssy. Yes, with three S's. That's all it said, "Chrisssy" and "Investigations" and a number.

"I thought you were a whore," Ava said.

"No," the girl said. "No!"

"Beck," Ava said.

"What?" the girl said.

"I saw you with Beck, out in front of my place."

The girl looked caught, embarrassed. A woman at the end of the bar, who could've been a Ziegfeld Follies girl a hundred years ago, rattled the ice in her rocks glass and held it up. VW Girl, grateful for the interruption, pulled a bottle out of the well and went to her.

When she came back, she said, "Birmingham."

Now it was Ava's turn to say, "What?"

"He said his name was Birmingham. I think it's English. He had an English accent anyway and said he was from Britain. That's the same as England, isn't it? Birmingham isn't his name?"

"Beck," Ava said. "His name is Beck. I guess."

"I am so sorry," the girl said. "I can tell you're angry and that's the last thing I want. I didn't think it would matter. I didn't see how it would hurt. I just thought what a coincidence it was, that he wanted to know about you and of all people he looked *me* up."

"He hired you."

She nodded. "He came here to the lounge. He was sitting where you're sitting. Well, one stool over. I told him I was…undercover, working here. On a case. He told me he had hired you to look for his girlfriend, Cali. Her hat blew off when they were at the beach and she swam in after it and he never saw her again…"

"What else did he tell you?"

"Just that he was a businessman from London and he needed to know if you were legit—*Well, yeah!*—and where you lived. I told him that everyone knew where you lived, The Sunset Tower. But of course he isn't from LA. Are you mad?"

"How did he find you?"

"I'm in the book. With a picture. I don't have an answering service like you do with Penny so when I get a call I pretend *I'm* the service."

"You know about Penny."

"She's so sweet. I call and we just talk. I feel like I know so much about you."

"He gave you more money today," Ava said. "What was that for?"

"To follow you. To tell him where all you went, who you saw. He's desperate and…" She trailed off.

"And what?"

"He thinks you're not telling him everything you know. He thinks…" She looked down at the bar, wiping it idly.

"Stop trailing off like that," Ava said. "He thinks what?"

"That maybe you found Cali and you're…that you're, I don't know, holding her hostage or something. He told me to threaten you, if that's what it took. Are you mad? I'm so sorry." She retrieved her purse from under the bar.

"What are you doing?" Ava said.

"Giving you the money he gave me," she said. "Don't hate me."

Ava glared at her until she put away the money. She turned for the door. "Don't follow me," she said. "I follow people, people don't follow me."

"But…" the girl said.

Chapter Sixteen

Remnants of the future were all over LA. Driving along on surface streets or flying low over the city in a helo-cab, an angle would poke out at you—or a color or a shape—pull you out of *Now* and throw you head first into *Next*. Everywhere you went there were run-down "futuristic" car washes and hamburger joints, mirrored office buildings, flying saucer houses in the hills, glass box houses in the flats. On the face of an otherwise blank apartment building there'd be an aluminum disk with golden arms sun-bursting out from the center. A decoration.

Or was it a declaration? *Come tomorrow!*

When academics and historians catalogued Southern California's iconic architecture, they tended to dwell on the hot dog stands shaped liked hot dogs or the teepee tourist courts on what had been Route 66 coming in through Rancho Cucamonga or the big doughnut on the roof of Randy's. But those were just jokes. They were cartoons. The futuristic designs all over LA weren't cartoons, they were *movies*—sci-fi—that challenged Angelenos to look ahead, to dream, to be unwilling to accept the ordinary. To say *No!* to the here and now. The futuristic designs were advertisements for tomorrow and—like all advertising—were meant to keep you dissatisfied.

Ava was parked in front of a pink apartment building on the street that crawled up Beachwood Canyon toward the Hollywood Sign. The day was ending—dying like an actress in a silent film, histrionically—which meant the pink tone splashed onto the face of the otherwise white apartment building had an exclamation mark after it. Pink! Three aluminum chevrons flew across the front of the two-story building, like spacecraft flying off to a sky battle. The place was called Villa Ventura.

Ava was just killing time, waiting for dark, waiting to go do what she knew she had to go do. She was listening to a pirate radio station, The Beach Boys, "Wouldn't It

Be Nice," which she just now realized was futuristic, too. *Wouldn't it be nice if we could live together in a world where we belong?* The song was wistful and sad and happy and bold and naïve, all at the same time. Very SoCal, she thought. The song made her think of her dad. He had liked The Beach Boys, though he was about as far away from being a surfer or a hot-rodder as it was possible to be, a Pasadena accountant who wore suits to work right up until the last day when he collapsed face-first onto a ledger on his desk, eyes open, getting one last look at that bottom line. Ava was thirteen when he died and it had nearly destroyed her, though she'd been at an age when it seemed best to stuff it down, not let it show, crying in her closet or on the back of a horse going around the ring at the Burbank Equestrian Center. (Her mother had made her take dressage lessons, trolling for a second husband.) *I wish they all could be California girls…* Ava had heard her father singing as he shaved one morning. Was that what her father had against her mother, that she didn't smell like the beach? The song ended and the pirate DJ came on, spoke a line or two. He had a deep and dark voice, the kind of voice that sounds familiar even the first time you hear it. He sounded lonely but used to it, like Los Angeles.

She got out, leaned against the front fender. The air smelled good. Orangey. Blossomy. The light was almost gone. It still wasn't late enough to go do what she had to go do. She looked up toward the hills. Over time the trees along Beechwood had grown toward each other over the street, blocking the view of the hills. All that was visible of the Hollywood Sign was the enormous Y.

"Good question," Ava said.

So Beck was two-timing her. Perfect. She'd tried to tell herself that she had seen it coming, but she hadn't. When it came to Beck, something was clouding her vision, misdirecting her away from her usual wariness. What was it Penny had said? *The slavish devotion of a top-notch guy.* Was that it, just that Beck was good-looking and somebody's slave? (And maybe even a little dumb?) This latest thing with VW Girl didn't make sense. Beck had just found "Chrisssy" in some directory of detectives? Of all the gin joints in all the towns in all the world, Beck walked into hers, Chrisssy's? He found the one girl detective who happened to be obsessed with Ava Monica, the *first* girl detective he'd hired? And… *Birmingham?* An English accent? What was that about? Beck didn't seem that devious or…*capable*, if the truth be told. He didn't seem smart enough be dodgy. But he *was* good-looking and presented himself well. So was that it? Sometimes the explanation for something is the thing that has the least to do with logic. Ava had learned that the hard way.

Two hours later, Ava was back behind the wheel, still at the curb in front of the pink apartment building, when along came the black VW putt-putting up Beachwood with its buggy, perpetually surprised eyes. Ava watched in the side mirror. The VW nose-dived—as if Chrisssy had hit the brakes when she saw the Hudson ahead—but then she came on forward and turned into the driveway that led back to the carports behind the apartment building.

"Hey," Chrisssy said, uncertainly, coming out front to the curb after she'd parked in back. She still wore the blue shorts and the knotted belly-button-revealing blouse. She carried the catsuit and boots she'd had on before. "I thought you were done with me," she said.

"I'm just killing time," Ava said.

"OK…" Chrisssy said, shaky.

Chrisssy's one-bedroom apartment was Deco-ed out just like Ava's digs in The Sunset Tower, white on white on white with pearlescent bowls on crème-colored end tables and black torchiere lamps in the corners of the living room to give some edge to the shadows. It was neat and clean and perfect-on-a-budget and…more than a little disturbing. It made Ava feel old, old and creepy, as in Marlene Dietrich in *Sunset Blvd.* If they weren't careful, somebody was going end up floating facedown in the pool.

"I love what we've done to the place," Ava said.

Chrisssy just stood there, kneading her hands. "I really am sorry," she said. Something had changed in her. Now she sounded halfway like a grown-up.

"Forget it," Ava said. "At one time or other we've all followed someone around, dressed like them, cut our hair like they cut their hair, wore five hundred high-heels like they wore at noon on a Thursday on the strip. Called her office to work up a friendship with her answering service person Penny."

"I go to thrift shops," Chrisssy said, very small.

"By the way," Ava said, "Cute car, kind of like my Hudson before it grew up."

A luxe silver martini shaker, some bottles of go-go, and a silver ice bucket sat on a glass console table that served as the bar.

"I could use a drink," Ava said. "You know how to make a martini? Or are you one of those this-isn't-my-*real*-job bartenders?"

"Gin or vodka?"

"Please…" Ava said, by way of rebuke.

Chrisssy started toward the kitchen for some ice.

"You can change out of your costume first if you want," Ava said and plopped down on the white glazed cotton couch. "I'm in no hurry. I'm just hangin' and doppelgängin'."

Chrisssy disappeared into her bedroom and returned wearing the catsuit and boots.

"No," Ava said simply, waving her away. "Try again."

Chrisssy exited.

A picture on the cover of a tabloid newspaper on the coffee table caught Ava's eye. It was a snapshot of the lithe Black in the swank tux singing "When Sunny Gets Blue" on the stage of The Shinola the other night. The headline asked: "VIVID?"

"Holy crap," Ava said. "Really?"

She snatched it up, thumbed through to the text. There was another surreptitious snapshot from inside The Shinola, the lithe White poetry-reciter, The Duke. The head read: "VIVID TOO?"

"Holy crap, too," Ava said. They were right. Didn't anyone just want to be themselves anymore?

Chrisssy came back in a wispy dress and heels. "What?" she asked. "Holy crap, what?"

Ava tossed away the tabloid. "Nothing," she said.

Chrisssy modeled the change of clothes. "Is *this* acceptable?" she said, sort of snotty.

Ava said, "Whatever makes you feel good about yourself." She had a dress just like it in her closet. This had never happened. No one had ever bit her style. Well, except for underwear. Chrisssy didn't seem to be wearing a brassiere; the dress was unbuttoned enough to show off the lack thereof.

Wait. Maybe Chrisssy *really* liked her, in that late-night cable TV *your-skin-is-so-much-softer-than-mine* way. Ava was a teeny bit flattered in spite of herself.

Chrisssy exited stage right with the ice bucket and came back with it full. She stepped to the bar and went to work. The silver shaker made a sweet, end-of-the-day sound when Chrisssy loaded it and gently swirled it around.

"Do you want an olive?"

"Well, I guess you don't know *everything* about me, do you?" Ava said. It was almost as if Ava were flirting. Flirting with herself? Her younger self? Now *that* was creepy. Chrisssy came away from the bar with what looked like a principled, timeless martini. Ava took it, took a sip. An eyebrow went up, all on its own.

Chrisssy sat on the front edge of a white chair across from the couch, her hands in her lap. She looked down at her crossed legs, pinched a pinch of silk over her knee and then let it fall. Before long she had a tear in her eye. Fortunately, it was the left eye so she could turn her ahead away from Ava to keep her from seeing it.

Ava saw it. People were always crying around her.

"This is too complicated," Chrisssy said. "I don't understand what he's doing...Beck or Birmingham or whatever his name is."

"Where are you from?" Ava said.

"Oklahoma."

"Why is it always Oklahoma?"

"What do you mean?"

"Everybody is always from Oklahoma," Ava said. "The girls, anyway. What's so awful about Oklahoma?"

Chrisssy turned her full face to Ava. The tear was still on her cheek but at least it hadn't been followed by another. "I was born there. It was boring. Flat. I felt like I always knew exactly what was going to happen next. Forever."

Ava liked her.

"Where were *you* from?" Chrisssy said.

"Here," Ava said. "So I've *never* known what was going to happen next."

"He was my first real client," Chrisssy said, sadly.

"Jeez, now *I* feel bad," Ava said. Maybe this was what it was like having a best friend, she thought. Or talking to a therapist. But which of them was the therapist?

"Will I get in trouble?" Chrisssy asked.

"What do you mean? Trouble with who? Whom."

"I don't know, the authorities. For taking on a client who was already your client."

"Yeah," Ava said, "that damn Detectives' Code of Honor. You don't want to run afoul of those boys."

Chrisssy smiled but still didn't relax.

"Do you have a boyfriend?" Ava said.

"Not here," Chrisssy said. "Not anywhere now, I guess."

"Grab a sweater," Ava said and drank up.

Chapter Seventeen

On the other hand, sometimes LA and its architects looked ahead to the past. The Garden of Allah had been a Hollywood haunt on the corner of Crescent Heights and Sunset in the twenties and thirties, the party pad of a Russian silent film star that was turned into a hotel and bungalows when she went bankrupt. Alla Nazimova ended up living in a few rooms in an apartment on the back corner of the property—beyond the pool shaped like the Black Sea—while all around her movie stars and directors and writers and hangers-on drank and diddled each other. Maybe she joined in. Maybe Alla Nazimova liked the present just fine, unlike almost everyone else in Hollywood. Maybe she'd come from someplace that was deadly dull and at least this wasn't deadly dull. There was a private bar where the girls dressed like boys and the boys dressed like girls, a restaurant with a help-yourself kitchen, the pool, the grounds, rented rooms, bungalows. Everyone left their doors open, so as not to impede the flowing party. "A light-hearted, unrealistic place…" gossip columnist Sheilah Graham called it in 1939. Natch, Hollywood changed—just the sinners, not the sins—movie stars fell and the GoA emptied out and went to ruin. In 1959, a bank bought it up. Developers bulldozed it, threw up a branch bank and fast food joints and an acre of hot striped asphalt, prompting Joni Mitchell—who lived up Crescent Heights in Laurel Canyon—to complain about those who paved paradise and put up a parking lot. Or so some said.

But lighthearted unreality proved hard to suppress and in 2018 another group of developers tore up the parking lot and rebuilt paradise, brick for brick, tile for tile, stucco wall for stucco wall, fountain for fountain, palm for palm. It was so compulsively identical to the first Garden of Allah it seemed—even for Hollywood—a little mental, as if some time-ruined rock star or actor were behind it. They didn't even think to call it The *New* Garden of Allah.

By now it was after midnight. Ava was parked on Crescent Heights, in the front row of a hundred-dollar-a-spot parking lot. They were just sitting there, Ava and Chrisssy, lit by the glow of the Hudson's dash lights. The old, quirky music on the radio kept fading in and out. Playing now was a sad song called "A Whiter Shade of Pale" that sounded like it could have been written about LA. Or even about the Garden of Allah, old or new. The DJ had introduced it by asking, as if in no way were it a settled matter, "Life is good, isn't it? All in all?"

"What are we listening to?" Chrisssy said.

Ava hadn't said anything yet, was just staring at The Garden across the street, on the other side of the four lanes of stalled traffic. The new/old hotel was lit up—red and green and yellow—but somehow it didn't look all that inviting. The up-lights made the palms out front look like they were on fire.

"The All-Night Man," Ava said. "We could all use one of those, right?"

Chrisssy tried to see what Ava was seeing across the street. "Thank you for letting me come along," she said. "I just want to learn."

"Watching and waiting, that's the work," Ava said.

A private helo dropped out of the sky and landed on the motor court in front of the hotel. A black limo helo. A dressed-up couple got out, ducking down as they ran toward the entrance. You could hear them laughing, all rich and fun, even from across the street.

"Have you felt an earthquake yet?" Ava said, still not looking away.

"A five-point-one the first week I was here. I had just moved in."

"Talk about not knowing what comes next."

"I told my mom it was LA saying hello, telling me I'd come to the right place. She didn't think it was very funny."

"Did anything break? Besides the space-time continuum."

"A picture of my boyfriend fell off the shelf."

"You need to stick everything down with Silly Putty," Ava said absently. Since they'd parked, every line Ava had said she'd said absently. "I lost a perfectly good glass menagerie in the La Habra quake. The only thing that survived was the unicorn."

"Why are we here?" Chrisssy said. She wasn't being philosophical.

"The Garden of Allah. The top floor of the main building, people go to heal after plastic surgery," Ava said. "You don't leave your room. They bring everything in. You don't have to worry about anybody seeing you with bandages and stitches and bruises. Or if it's not surgery, people seeing you slightly crazy. Sometimes people will check in just to fall apart for a week or so, with someone keeping an eye on them."

"I've heard about the stars, the parties, the drugs."

Ava said, "Friends of ToD."

"Who's Todd?"

"You really are from Oklahoma," Ava said. "ToD stands for Tail of the Dragon. It's a drug. Speedy, trippy. It came out of nowhere a few years ago. A friend of mine calls it the coke cocaine would take if cocaine wanted to get high. It's brown, looks like a ball of wax. You suck on it like a cough drop. So I've been told. It's stupid expensive. It comes from the tip-end of the tail of this lizard that's only found in Venezuela. Or maybe it's Honduras, somewhere where they have lizards. The tails grow back. So it's sustainable."

Chrisssy said, "Did he ever hit on you? Beck or whatever his name is."

Now Ava looked at her. Waited.

"He was all over me when he came to the bar," Chrisssy said, almost sounding embarrassed. "I guess that goes with the territory, huh?"

"Yeah, I guess," Ava said, almost wistfully. "Come on."

Ava opened her door and got out. Chrisssy followed and they crossed the packed street, one in front of the other. People left walking space between the front bumpers and back bumpers for jaywalkers. Of course jaywalking wasn't illegal anymore, just rude, rubbing it in, that you were getting somewhere and they weren't.

The hotel had a wide motor court out front, an entrance paved with Saltillo tile. The limo helo still idled, parked like a car. Ava strode toward the front door of the hotel. The doorman was smoking a jay, which was completely legal but also considered rude. For the same reason.

"What are we doing?" Chrisssy said, trying to keep up with Ava.

◆ ◆ ◆

CALI WAS ASLEEP. SHE was on her side with a sheet over her, her face a whiter shade of pale. She looked deader than she'd looked when she'd been actually dead, but she was breathing, her shoulder rising and falling.

"She looks so lifelike," Ava said. "Cali, Chrisssy. Chrisssy, Cali."

Chrisssy just stared. "So this is her?"

"Yep. When she wakes up, she'll brush her hair out of her eyes. You watch."

"Why is she here?"

"It's complicated," Ava said.

"So Beck was right. You did have her or at least know where she was."

"It's complicated."

"He's really desperate to get her back. There's no telling what he might do. He said things like, *If I can't have her, then—*"

"They always say that," Ava said.

"He asked me if I knew anybody who could 'take it to the next level.'"

"What does that mean?"

"It scared me," Chrisssy said.

Cali hadn't moved a muscle. The two women stood over her, like concerned relatives or best friends bedside in a hospital. Only they weren't really concerned and this wasn't a real hospital and the beds weren't hospital beds. The thread count of the sheets was probably in the thousands. The headboard bore a Garden of Allah™ insignia, for those who awoke in the night or of a morning and couldn't remember where they were. The linens were gold-colored, the pillows probably filled with flamingo feathers. Someone had combed out Cali's hair. Her blonde hair spread out over the golden pillowcase made her look sort of beautiful, like something out of the past, or the future. Or a comic book. Right now, anyway, she looked like someone worth chasing, or at least someone near impossible to get over or forget.

It was a nice little room, a $1,500 room, with a narrow wrought-iron balcony. The double doors were open to the night, the gauzy curtains shifting on the breeze. The floor was covered with white Berber, just as in days of old. The furniture—a pair of easy chairs, a dresser and a desk and chair—was made of heavy, dark wood and didn't seem like reproductions. It looked like furniture out of the Hearst Castle or the Doheny Mansion. On the desk was a Tiffany lamp that matched the octagonal shade covering the overhead light. Soft. Everything was soft. Healing. Illusory. It was stagecraft, as were all overpriced rooms-for-hire.

Ava walked out onto the balcony. The pool below in the courtyard was like a photographer's light table, jade, empty of swimmers. She breathed in a little of the night. She had paid off the desk clerk, a pudgy man/boy in this twenties who spoke in whispers because someone had told him people with money always had hangovers. Or something like that. It had taken $300 to buy their way up. The desk clerk knew the girl upstairs was a nobody, so there wasn't much reason for him to be cautious. He also knew who Ava was and what she did for a living—and that she bribed her way through life. The clerk had eyed Chrisssy with a pitiful hunger. If Ava hadn't been there, he would have let Chrisssy go up for free, maybe even tagged along.

"She looks like Vivid," Chrisssy said, still standing over the bed.

"You think so?" Ava said, coming back in off the balcony.

"Wait. Is that why you were gaping at that story about Vivid?"

"I wasn't gaping. I was working, noticing stuff."

"He didn't say that she looked like Vivid," Chrisssy said. "Birmingham."

"That's because he didn't hire you to look for her. You're following *me*, remember?"

"She looks exactly like her."

"You should see the other ones."

"What other ones?"

"The Vivids. The ones who are actually trying to look like Vivid. I think this one was, or is, just a friend of hers. I don't know, I don't think she looks that much like her."

"She's friends with Vivid?"

"What, you're a fan?"

"A little. I like the way she keeps changing, keeps you guessing."

"Now don't you start copying *her*, Chrisssy!" Ava mocked.

In this light, alive, Cali did look like Vivid, at least more like her than she had looked in the looping picture in Beck's locket. Or out in front of The Shinola with black hair, fighting with Action Man. Or on the lobby directory down in the Marina. Or dead, on that other balcony.

"I thought she'd be older," Chrisssy said.

"People used to say that about me," Ava said.

"She doesn't belong here," Chrisssy said. "In LA."

Ava didn't know what to make of that line, other than that sometimes people say things about others that are really about themselves. Chrisssy had such a sad look on her face, looking down at Cali.

Ava had to get away. "I have to tinkle," she said. "Take over. You're on duty."

"What are we doing?" Chrisssy said. "Just guarding her?"

"We're waiting until she wakes up or we wake her up and then we take her to…" Ava let the ellipsis hang in the air. Oh so many ellipses these days, so many thoughts trailing off inconclusively. "Well, I don't know where we're going to take her. But, as God is my witness, we're going to take her…somewhere!"

"We should call him, Beck. Or Birmingham, whatever his name is."

"No," Ava said firmly. "I'm not turning her over to him until I figure this out or… Well, I don't know what needs to happen before I turn her over to him. So… no. No Beck, no Birmingham." She waited until Chrisssy nodded.

In the bathroom, Ava checked herself out in the mirror above the sink. She ran her tongue over her red lips, fluffed her hair. She was thinking, *Who* are *you?* She almost said it out loud. What was she doing here? How had she ended up doing this for a living? Whatever this was. With this case, she half felt like a pimp, like Action Man. How did that happen? She was about to move on to the next existential query when she heard voices outside, girl voices, alarum.

Cali was up on her knees in the bed with Chrisssy holding her by the wrists. Cali was panicky and angry and unblinking, as if just coming out of a chase dream. She was also all the way naked.

"Cali," Ava said.

When Cali saw Ava she went slack. Chrisssy let go of her wrists. Cali's hands fell into her lap. Chrisssy couldn't take her eyes off of her.

"You remember me, right?" Ava said.

"I recognize you," Cali said, wearily. "I don't know your name."

"Ava. Ava Monica. Beck sent me to find you."

Cali brushed her hair off of her face.

Ava looked at Chrisssy. *See?*

Cali collapsed back against the headboard. She made no effort to cover herself with the sheet or anything else. "Beck. I don't know who that is," she said, with almost no inflection. Her panic was gone, replaced by…surrender?

"Birmingham?" Chrisssy offered.

"What?" Cali said, turning to look at her. It was impossible to say if she was confused or alarmed at hearing the second name. "Who are you?"

"This is Chrisssy," Ava said, before Chrisssy said something that would only confuse things further for the poor girl. "She works with me. We're going to get you out of here. We're not going to do anything to hurt you."

Ava started opening and closing dresser drawers, looking for clothes. The drawers were all empty. The surfer EMT miracle-worker could have at least thrown some of those white panties and tees and jeans from the apartment into a bag before he dumped her here. Then she looked in the closet. A single dress hung on a Lucite hanger, a brand-new dress. And not a cheap one, a cute one with a floral print. Or maybe they were butterflies. Size zero. Ava threw it to Chrisssy. It floated through the air prettily, the only light-hearted thing in the scene.

Chapter Eighteen

Beck was alone in a booth in Barney's Beanery with a lot of money in front of him, two banded stacks of clean hundreds so crisp and new you could smell them, the kind and amount of money that said, *I can fix anything, no matter how far gone.* That lie. The big man who had been sitting across from him until a minute ago had left his fedora behind on the table, next to the cash. Who wears a brown fedora in LA in 2025? Beck put the man's hat over the money and looked around. He thought about just pocketing the cash and walking out of there—forgetting all about this—but he knew he wouldn't/couldn't/shouldn't. For one thing, the man would probably track him down and kill him. He looked over his shoulder. Where was he? The other man had suggested Barney's as the meeting place, even though Beck had called him and not the other way around, Beck who'd decided it was time to go to the next level. Then he'd been made to wait alone for a half hour before the man showed.

It was the middle of the morning and Barney's was a bar-with-food, not a restaurant-with-a-bar, so it was just barely open. Twenty minutes ago, the bartender had punched up a song on the eighties-style jukebox. A guy sitting at the bar with a plate of eggs and a Bloody Mary in front of him had waited a second and then got up and went over and yanked the plug out of the wall. It was early like that.

Beck polished a spoon with a paper napkin. Suspended over one of the pool tables was a gaudy motorcycle. What had they called them back then? Choppers, hogs. Barney's idea of decorative art. Beck made a face. Who hangs a motorcycle from the ceiling in a restaurant?

Barney's Beanery was on Santa Monica in WeHo, West Hollywood. It had been there a hundred years. Literally. The lead singer of an LA band, The Doors—who sang of breaking on through to the other side—had climbed onto the same bar in the nutty sixties and taken a whiz and gotten banned for a week or two. Old-timey blues singer Janis Joplin spent the last night of her life in Barney's, shooting pool, before breaking on through to the other side alone in a motel room up Highland next to the Hollywood Bowl.

Beck didn't know Barney's history or much care about it. This was a different Beck, more focused, less heartsick. Or not heartsick at all? Was that possible? Had his desperation driven him to this version of himself, dry-eyed, resolved to some new sense of reality about Cali? Or maybe this was a new, stuff-it-down Beck. Barney's was the kind of joint with fifty sports screens, the kind of bar where the women only showed up at night, the kind of place where women-broken men put up a good front for the sake of the other men. Maybe this new Beck was just responding to the setting, acting, playing yet another role. He didn't even seem as handsome or as rich-looking today, though he was wearing the same million-dollar suit and had the same million-dollar face.

A girl brought a cup of tea to the table. "He doesn't want anything?" she asked, hooking a thumb in the direction of the empty side of the booth.

Beck said, "Who knows?"

She looked down at the fedora, shook her head, and went away.

Beck picked up the wedge of lemon on the saucer and put it aside, pretending to be offended by it. He thumbed opened the cheap tin of creamer, looked into it, and then poured a splash into his cup. He watched the milk swirl around in the tea, stared at it until it came to rest. It was as if it reminded him of something. Or was it some*where*? Clouds back home? Wherever that was.

Then the big man was back, standing over Beck. He just stood there for a long, pregnant moment, looking down at him. Finally, he slid into the booth again. It was a tight fit. He was a man with the kind of weight that once said *prosperous, notable*. Big like a banker in a black-and-white movie. It was hard to say what his heft meant now, here in LA in 2025. He wasn't going to be a movie star, that was clear, maybe a character actor. He was younger than his clothes would suggest—the fedora and matching brown suit and too-wide tie—but he wasn't all that young, probably in his forties. He looked like somebody's gruff uncle or a travelling salesman, somebody out of another time, possibly trying to get back to it, something everybody knew was flat out impossible. He never smiled, as if smiling was something he'd put away, grown out of, had no time for now. He had black hair that must have been dyed. Nobody but a Kentucky coal miner had hair that black at this man's age. It was greased up and combed back in a Sunday-go-to-meeting almost hick kind of way. He had said on the phone for Beck to call him "Don" but it obviously wasn't his real name.

When he'd walked in off the street and Beck saw him face to face for the first time, Beck had thought he looked like a tough, a brutal man. Who else would be caught up in a thing like this? He'd scanned the room, ID'd Beck, come over, thrown his hat on the table, and squeezed into the booth. The money had been put on the table. Then the big man had looked at Beck with an unblinking, judging look, said he had to "take a slash," and then he'd gotten up and walked away, leaving the cash right out in the open. A hard case, or at least putting on a good act. Still, looking at him now across the table again, Beck saw in the man's eyes at least a hint of humanity. Or was it empathy? Maybe he was as desperate as Beck, in his own way. Maybe more desperate, more heartbroken. But whatever else was there, there was a very intentional look in those eyes, a look that Beck told himself he should remember, that it would be *healthy* for him to remember.

The man lifted his hat off the table and put it on. The money was gone.

"Don" slid out of the booth. "Give me whatever addresses you have for her," he said.

Beck handed him a folded white piece of paper. "The first one's right around the corner, a big white building. There's a...a bench out front. What are you thinking in terms of time?" Beck said, his voice quavering slightly.

The big man just shook his head. "I don't know," he said, annoyed by the question. "Yesterday. Tomorrow. Today. A week from today."

Beck nodded, stung.

"I don't like Los Angeles," the big man said. "I guess that's as plain as the nose on your face." The second line was almost an apology for the first line or how he'd said it, how he'd bit off the words. One got the idea that he didn't apologize much. "Nothing personal," he said.

Beck hesitated, then said, "What do I do now? Are you going to call me or am I supposed to call you?"

"I don't understand why you would ask me that," the man said, standing over him.

"I...I don't know if this is the right thing anymore," Beck said. "I don't want to think about her being hurt unnecessarily."

The man just looked at him.

"I'll call you," Beck said.

Then the man did something that caught Beck off guard. He put a heavy hand on Beck's shoulder and just left it there. He was like a preacher on the front steps of the church after the sermon, or after the funeral. Or like a father with his son. Or the other way around. It was as if he were trying to get something across to Beck, something elemental. He wanted punctuation.

He squeezed Beck's shoulder. That was it. Beck expected him to say something else to seal the deal, but he just left.

◆ ◆ ◆

THE BIG MAN LOOKED up and snugged his hat down tight. The sky was churning overhead. It looked like dirty water circling a drain. To the south, down low, sat fat cumulonimbus clouds a thousand feet high, like clouds in an illustration in an old Bible or on the edge of an ancient map. Or like faces, disapproving gods or pouting babies. The clouds were dark and dense but he knew that didn't mean it was going to rain, really rain. Nowadays, they said, LA rain was almost as rare as LA snow, and it had rained just the other night, a two-minute drizzle and that was that. They said lately that had been the norm, stormy skies that looked like rain but then the rain never came or just a meaningless two-minute drizzle. There it was: LA in a nutshell. All show, no go. Dry. The big man hadn't even noticed the nothing showers the other night. He'd stayed in his hotel room and missed it altogether. The downtown streets weren't even wet the next morning. And certainly not clean. He came from a place with real rain, summer storms so intense you had to pull off the road, driving rain too rainy to drive in.

He looked left and then set out walking to the right, west. If somehow it did rain, he would keep walking. He had someplace to be now and his gait showed it. Somebody driving by would think, *There's a fat man going somewhere.*

The old silver D. L. Bentley was parked down the street. The tall gunsel behind the wheel started it and eased forward. The big man glanced back and saw the car but didn't make anything of it. The driver hiked his shoulders reflexively and sped forward, turned right at the first light.

The big man went straight on Holloway Drive into a canyon of modern high-rise apartment buildings. He didn't know it but he was already lost. He felt the apartment buildings leaning over him, judging him. Every apartment had a wide balcony and a picture window; still there wasn't a soul to be seen anywhere, nobody at a railing or framed in a window looking out at the sky or looking down at him. Not a single soul. Twenty million people lived here, and unless you were downtown about the only place you ever saw them was in their ugly cars stuck in traffic or in weird restaurants and gaudy bars. Nobody strolled.

What did the woman see in this place?

Or anybody else? He'd been almost everywhere, coast to coast, top to bottom. He'd never been out of the country but he sure as hell knew the United States. He had spent a good part of his life on the road, for one thing or another. Most of his life had amounted to the same thing: coming into a city or town, checking into a hotel or motel, meeting a man, cutting a deal, signing on the dotted line or shaking the man's hand, looking him dead in the eye so you could know if he was going to do what he said he'd do, hold up his end of it. You did what you said you'd do; that had been his life, for better or worse, high dollar or low. Oh, he'd done some business with women a time or two, or tried to. It had never seemed to work out to either party's satisfaction. He didn't know how to *close* with a woman. He could never tell if they were being straight with him, if they even halfway meant the words they said. Look them dead in the eye and you might as well be standing on the beach somewhere, looking out at empty blue water.

"I mean, they *paint* their eyes," he said aloud.

He wasn't alone on the sidewalk anymore. A few people were coming at him from whatever was up ahead, probably headed toward their cars parked on the street, fretting about the possibility of rain. Or the *impossibility* of it. They weren't out strolling, that was for sure. None of them paid him any mind. One thing he liked about Los Angeles, maybe the only thing: nobody thought a thing about a man walking down the sidewalk talking to himself. Here they'd probably call the cops on you if you *didn't* talk to yourself, if you kept what you were thinking bottled up inside.

He walked until he was out the ass end of the canyon of apartment buildings. Now he was walking past the backs of restaurants with the busboys outside smoking and shooting the bull beside the trash cans. They looked him over good and he looked them over good too. He might have been guilty of a number of things, but being afraid of action wasn't even on the list. One of the busboys said something in Spanish and the others laughed roughly. If it had been dark, he figured they probably would have jumped him. Or tried to. They weren't that far away. They weren't kids either, probably gang members. He stared at them until they stopped looking at him. They had no idea how close they had come to getting their asses kicked. He was full of aggression and frustration that wanted an outlet.

"*Hasta la vista,*" he said, looking over one last time.

At last he came to the Sunset Strip. The long way. The sidewalks were as jammed with people as the street was jammed with automobiles. On the sidewalks, people divided up into lanes too, keeping to the right, sticking to the rules. It seemed to be working. The people out of cars were moving faster than the people in cars. The big man merged into the human stream on the sidewalk, heading westward. He said, "Excuse me" to a dozen people before anyone stopped and read the address on the paper in his hand, the paper Beck had given him. The fourth person he said "Excuse me..." to gave him a dollar coin without looking at him. Finally a young man in preposterous yellow high-waisted pants stopped, looked at the address on the paper, and pointed in the other direction— pointed east—without saying anything.

The man turned around and started walking eastward. He regifted the buck to an older, legless lady in a motorized wheelchair with a string of pearls around her neck and a scrawled cardboard sign that said...

Mother, Father Raped at Hollywood Bowl
On 2 Separate Occasions

"What are the odds?" the big man said, continuing on.

"That's it, a buck?" she called after him. "After all I've done for you?" He looked back at her. He couldn't tell if she meant what she'd said to be funny. Or the sign, for that matter. That was Los Angeles in a nutshell, too.

Then he found it: a high white old-fashioned apartment building with rounded corners all the way up, white with black trim. Ten stories, with what looked like a single penthouse apartment that took up the whole top floor. The place had a circular drive out front. He had to admit he liked the looks of it. It had character. It had been there awhile. They hadn't painted it orange. He stood across the street from it.

He told himself he was just getting the lay of the land—casing the place, coming up with a plan—but the truth was he wasn't ready for this, wasn't even ready to cross the damn street. He sat down on the bench. He sat there like that for all of the afternoon, until it went dark. Or half dark. Of course, it never did rain.

Chapter Nineteen

It was nine o'clock at night. "You can't sleep anymore," Ava said. "Get up. Brush your teeth. Wash your face. Eat something. Pretend."

Cali stirred just enough to establish that she wasn't dead again. Ava kept poking her until she got out of the bed. Naked. Cali stood there a moment, then sat back on the edge of the bed with her face in her hands.

"Today is the first day of the rest of your life," Ava said. "Or tonight is."

Ava left her sitting there on the bed and went to take a shower. She took her sweet time, too, violated all kinds of city water-conservation diktats, hitting the flow button again every time it shut itself off. She took the kind of shower she used to take when she had been a school girl, tipping her face up into the downpour as if she were outside in the rain. Or in a Clairol shampoo commercial. Or under a waterfall in Hawaii, though she'd never been to Hawaii. When she was a little girl, she had taken long showers because they were a place to hide from her mother. Ava didn't know what this particular twenty-minute shower was about, who or what (or when?) she was hiding from now. But she was enjoying it.

Then Sean the Resuscitator, the surfer EMT, called.

"Yeah, what?" Ava said when she saw his face.

His eyes went wide. "You have a vid-phone in your shower?"

"Most people have the decency not to look," Ava said.

"I just...I..."

"What?"

"I just wanted to make sure everything was cool with the deceased babe," he said.

"She sleeps a lot."

"That's cool, that's what happens. So everything was cool at The Garden of Allah?"

"Frozen," Ava said.

"Excellent," he said.

"Pleasure doing business with you, Everett," Ava said, reaching for the bye-bye button.

"Whoa," he said.

"Whoa what?"

"If you are asked to rate my service, you should know that an eight, nine, or ten means you are—like I think you said—very satisfied."

"What you do is illegal. Completely. Who is going to ask?"

"I value your business."

"Who's going to ask? The cops? The DA? American Medical Association?"

"Pssst."

"What? *Pssst* what?"

"That's who would ask. P-S-S-S-T. That's the rating service for, you know, sketchy transactions."

"I want to go live on another planet," Ava said, reaching again for that exit button.

"Wait," he said.

"What!"

"I was wondering, could I, uh, speak to the babe?"

Ava sent him on his way.

The mirror was all fogged up when Ava got out of the shower. She didn't wipe it off. Lately, seeing herself naked—flat-footed, with no makeup—didn't make her happy. Time was when her naked flat-footed self made her happy. And it wasn't that long ago. She used to *like* mirrors. Now seeing herself in a mirror was like running into somebody she used to know. LA was a hard place to have a birthday. It was filthy with mirrors. And worse, there were all those Calis, newly arrived from wherever, who were their own kind of looking glass. She threw on a fluffy white robe and knotted it at the waist. She brushed her teeth and combed out her wet hair. The fog in the bathroom was starting to clear. Before it got *too* clear, she looked at herself, turned to a three-quarter pose. Her breasts still made her happy.

"Money in the bank," she said.

When she came out of the bathroom and walked past the guest bedroom, she was expecting to see Cali back in bed. Actually, what she half expected to see was the window standing open, the gauzy curtains blowing out into the night like a white flag. She expected sirens, Crows, TV news crews. Was that why she had lingered forever in her shower, to give Cali the time to do the wrong thing?

"But that would mean I'm a bad person," Ava said to herself.

She found Cali sitting at the little round table in the kitchen over by the window, eating as if she hadn't eaten in a week. Or ever. A bagel, a bowl of Cheerios, a bunch of green grapes. A leftover sparerib from a barbecue that operated *sub rosa* in South Pas. A big glass of milk. Breakfast at nine o'clock at night. She was still naked, of course. Ava stood in the doorway watching the girl stuff her face. She couldn't help but stare at Cali's perfect body. She had a surfer's tan, thin stripes of white flesh over her hips from what must have been an itsy-bitsy teeny-weeny bikini. Naked, barefoot, her blonde hair loose and beautiful, Cali had never seemed more like a girl than she did now. A California girl. Now Ava really felt old.

"Who brought you the dress that was in the closet at the hotel? Or, said another way, who brought you the dress and why are you not wearing it now?"

"I never liked wearing clothes," Cali said between bites. "I always pretended I did, went along with it like everybody else. Because I had to. Or I thought I did."

It was only then that Ava remembered the three identical bright pretty dresses in the closet at the apartment in the Marina. Butterflies. Or maybe they were flowers. Was this one of them?

Cali got up, opened cabinets until she found the dishware—Ava's mother's china—then poured herself a cup of coffee from a saucepan sitting on a burner on the stove. Ava had never seen anybody do that—warm up yesterday's coffee on the stove. It felt like something country people would do, but Cali was about as far away from a country girl as a person could be.

"You could have made another pot."

"I don't like to waste," Cali said. The milk bottle was still on the table. Cali poured two splashes into her cup and took a sip. Then she got up, gathered her dishes, and took everything to the sink.

"You don't have to do that," Ava said. "I have a woman who comes in."

"Thank you for your hospitality," Cali said. If she was being sarcastic, she wasn't nearly obvious enough.

Cali started washing the dishes. She seemed lost in thought. Ava remembered CRO Nate Cole's line downtown at the story bar: *"Young Mom Washing the Dishes is next, I think."*

"So who brought you your magic butterfly dress?" Ava said.

"I don't know," Cali said.

"Somebody did. They left it in your closet at the hotel. I guess they figured you didn't need any underwear to go with it. Maybe that narrows it down."

"I didn't see anyone come in. I don't even know how long I was there."

"Two days."

"Who brought me there? You?"

"I...enabled it," Ava said. "The guy who brought you wasn't the kind to think about bringing along a dress for you."

"Once I woke up and there was someone there. I think. A man. A slender man. Very."

Ava thought: very skinny man...the Bentley driver, the gun-toting shoulder-shrugger? The Shinola's manager Silky Valentine was skinny too. And so was Action Man, come to think of it. Almost everyone was skinny now. It was almost against the law not to be.

"So a skinny man you didn't know put a frilly expensive dress from your closet at home into your closet at The Garden of Allah and left? No note, nothing?"

Cali didn't like Ava's tone. "Maybe I dreamed it. I've been having the sickest dreams," she said, arranging the dishes in the dish drainer, drying her hands, and sitting back at the table with her coffee. "You're a detective, right? That he sent after me?"

"Yeah. You broke his heart." Ava poured herself a cup of the warmed-up java. It wasn't half bad. She stayed put in the doorway.

"I broke *his* heart," Cali said. "Mine was broken a long time ago. My spirit, too. It's what men do, break you."

"Tell me about it," Ava said.

Cali just stared at her coffee.

"No, seriously," Ava said, "tell me about it."

Apparently that wasn't going to happen. Not yet, anyway. Instead, Cali asked, "Who was that with you? The girl my age. Where is she?"

"She was working with me, for one night. She went home."

"Home to where?"

"Beachwood Canyon. Down the hill from the Hollywood Sign."

"I thought you meant *home*-home."

"Nobody ever goes home-home."

"What's her name?"

"Chrisssy. With three S's, if you can believe it."

"She's on the run from a man, too," Cali said. "It's so obvious."

"It is?"

"Of course. What was the name you said?"

"Chrisssy."

"No, in front of the club. And then again last night, in the hotel, or whatever that place was. You said a man's name."

"Beck. Don't get cute."

"What does he look like?"

"I guess a lot of guys fall desperately in love with you after you run into the ocean in the middle of the night to drown yourself, huh? Hard to keep track of all of them."

Cali looked at Ava as if she had just spoken a line of complete gibberish. "What did he look like?" she asked again.

"Dreamy."

Cali sank down into herself, as if something had pricked her internally, not a fatal wound but one that hurt just the same. She took a sip of her coffee, held it with two hands, like a little girl with a cup of cocoa her momma gave her, home sick from school. When she put down the cup, she stared at the back of her hand. Her left hand. She wasn't wearing a ring.

"Good Lord, he asked you to marry him?" Ava said. "He ringed you? He didn't tell me that."

Cali got up and walked out of the kitchen.

"You have to talk to him," Ava said after her.

"Talk…" Cali said, walking off. "I think he wants just a little more from me than that."

After a moment, she came back wearing the filmy bright pretty dress. With nothing underneath it. Somehow she was even sexier clothed than when she was naked. She looked like a model, a California girl in a fashion spread, hot as the sun, cool as the breeze.

"You've been so long at the beach you even smell like the sea…" Ava said.

"That kind of creeps me out," Cali said and left for the living room.

Ava called after her, "It kind of creeps me out that you had three of those exact same dresses in your closet."

Nothing. Ava went after her. "So I can call Beck and you guys can talk somewhere?" she said.

Cali was in the living room, looking at the silver-framed pictures that covered one wall. They were all casual shots from more than a few from years ago, Ava with boyfriends and then man-friends. Lush locations, suns dropping, moons rising, white teeth and Chablis, and what cinematographers called the "golden hour." *Life is good* was the subtext. There wasn't a single picture that hadn't been taken in LA—something that Ava had likely never realized—and only one picture of her father, none of her mother.

"There are no women," Cali said. "No other girls, no women. You don't have any women friends." The last wasn't a question.

Ava came in. "You're the one who tried to kill herself."

"I was out of my head," Cali said. "Or all the way into it. The pills were sitting there. I took a handful."

"You tried twice. You swam into the ocean in front of the Rings of Saturn restaurant. On your last date with him."

"You said that before. That never happened," Cali said. "Somebody is pulling your leg."

"That's called denial."

"Yeah, I deny that it ever happened. I took the pills out on my balcony but I didn't swim into the ocean on a date with anybody. I wouldn't do that. Maybe you're thinking about yourself, what *you* feel like doing sometimes."

Ava was getting honked off. She went to the window and yanked open the drapes. It was almost ten o'clock, the nighttime ten o'clock. She looked out over the strip at the Hollywood Hills, the zigzagging climbing streets, the houses theatrically lit. The close sky was battleship gray, that typical blank Los Angeles night sky. Ava wished she were out there. Alone. Riding around. Cali was right: Ava didn't have any women friends. Unless you counted Penny, who may have been virtual.

Cali watched her a minute before she said, "I'm sorry. I didn't mean anything. It's just that everybody's story seems like the same story to me lately."

Ava turned away from the window and said, "Everyone's story is different."

"People should be happy, don't you think?" Cali said.

"That's not the business I'm in," Ava said.

"But what do you think? We have just this one life. People have a right to be happy."

Ava said, "What about Beck? Does he have a right to be happy?"

"There is no Beck."

"You mean metaphorically, right?"

"I don't know what that means."

Ava was about to tell her what *metaphorically* meant when Cali came over to her at the window. She came over and wrapped her arms around Ava, just held her, as if *Ava* was the one who needed consoling, for believing the foolishness she believed.

Ava didn't pull away. Where's the harm in letting a crazy, pretty, semi-naked girl hold you?

But then Cali broke it off.

"What?" Ava said.

Cali had looked out the picture window, looked down, and seen the big man on the sidewalk staring up at the building. He was wearing the hat and she couldn't see his face but she didn't need to.

◆ ◆ ◆

CALI WAS CURLED UP on the bed in the guest room.

"You're not going back to bed," Ava said. "We're going out."

"I'm not going out there. I can't."

Ava left the room and came back a second later with a pair of shoes. And a raincoat. "Just in case," Ava said, handing everything to Cali.

"It's not going to rain," Cali said. "It never rains here."

"Still and all, everybody has a raincoat, honey," Ava said.

"You keep saying things as if they explain everything but they don't."

"Put the shoes on, before I smack you. Baby steps."

Cali sat on the end of the bed and slipped on the shoes. "They're too loose."

"Yeah, I know, I have big feet. Everyone has bigger feet than you do. Except for those poor little girls in China whose mothers bind them."

Cali stood. She brushed her hair off her face.

Ava said, with some finality, "I know Beck doesn't exist in your mind but I just called him anyway. He's staying at a hotel in Beverly Hills. We're going there and you're going to talk to him."

"Please, no," Cali said.

Ava took her by the upper arm, the way cops do.

They rode down to the parking garage in the elevator. Cali looked like a convict being led to the gas chamber.

"You don't have to do anything you don't want to do," Ava said. "Just talk to him. He's a blubbering fool but he loves you."

The elevator doors opened and they stepped out, Ava still holding onto Cali as if she expected her to rabbit any second. "I feel good about this," Ava said. "We're headed toward some closure, for everybody involved. It's going to be all right, sweetie. Have you been to the Beverly Hills Hotel? It's lovely. Pink and green, if you can believe that."

When they got close to the Hudson, the car sensed Ava's presence and came to life, the headlights blinking awake. Behind them, the iron garage gate rattled and began to slide aside. Ava put Cali in the passenger seat up front and got behind the wheel. The door locks clicked.

It was right about then that the big man in the fedora appeared. He stepped out of the bushes just outside the open gate and started down the slope.

Cali saw him before Ava. She stopped breathing.

"Where to, Ava?" the car said.

"Hold on," Ava said. She saw the big man.

He stopped ten feet in front of the car, blocking the way out of the garage. Standing there with his hands on his hips, he was like a wall, a wall wearing a brown suit.

"Hey," he said, hard, looking through the windshield at Cali, ignoring Ava.

"Who are you?" Ava said.

Still with his eyes locked on Cali, not looking at Ava, the man drew a gun from under his coat. It was a blue revolver with a barrel a foot long, almost a joke-gun, like something out of the past or out of a cartoon. He kept the gun lowered, at his side, as if it was the answer to Ava's question.

"Oh," Ava said.

The man took a step closer. "I don't want any trouble from you," he said to Ava. "I would guess you don't know who I am, but I know who you are. I'm going to need for you to let her go, right now."

"Where to?" the Hudson said again.

"The Pink Palace," Ava said. "Go!"

"Go!" Cali said.

The man took a step forward until he was right in front of the bulbous nose of the Hudson. He wasn't going anywhere, his big body was saying. Even a humungous Hudson wasn't going to get past him. The way he stood there said everything depended on the Hudson not getting past him. But he still hadn't raised the gun.

"Come on, go!" Ava said to the car.

"Obstruction," the Hudson said, maddeningly matter-of-factly.

As if enough wasn't going on, it was then that the other bad actors arrived: the Bentley screeching up to the mouth of the garage, the skinny gunsel behind the wheel and Action Man in the passenger seat in a purple suit, leaning forward. The old car's smoking exhaust made it look like it was coming out of a cloud. The big man turned toward the round staring headlights—recognizing the Bentley from in front of Barney's Beanery—and raised the hog-leg pistol. Action Man jumped out of the front seat, leaving the door open. A second later, the gunsel was out from behind the wheel.

Now there were three would-be Cali-snatchers. When the skinny gunsel saw the big man's shooter, he dug into his shoulder holster for his piece, going full gangster, shrugging his shoulders as he drew down on him. Then it was Action Man's turn. He pulled his piece too, but not so smoothly. He was wide-eyed and seemed to realize that the shiny outsized automatic in his hand looked like just another silly accessory to his ridiculous purple outfit.

"This isn't even loaded!" Action Man said, trying stupidly to make it a threat.

"You're an idiot!" Ava said behind the wheel. "Why are you even here?"

Action Man said weakly, "Give her up, Ava! This has gone beyond you!"

"He's here to kill her," the skinny gunsel said, meaning the big man in the hat. "Let us take her."

The big man's shoulders sagged, as if his feelings had been hurt by what the gunsel had said. He just shook his head and lowered his gun.

"Go!" Ava said to the car again.

"Obstruct—"

"Fine!" Ava grabbed the stick herself and shoved it up and mashed the gas. The Hudson lurched backward, ramming into a concrete support.

"Obstruction!" the Hudson said, too late.

"Oh, right…" Ava said, woozy. She'd hit her head on the car door post.

Cali was on the floor on the passenger side, hunkered down.

The big man holstered his gun and took a step forward, peeking over the dash. "Come on, now," he said to Cali with unlikely tenderness.

Action Man started down into the garage toward the Hudson, acting fearless when he was anything but. "You, get back!" he said to the big man. He mistakenly thought he wasn't a threat anymore because he'd holstered his gun.

Cali tried to open her door to make a run for it, but the wreck had jammed it. She rolled down the window to climb out.

Action Man didn't get far. The big man turned away from Cali and the car, rushed him, grabbed a handful of purple, and threw him against the wall. The Bentley driver, who'd decided it was time to wrap this up, came down the ramp and stuck his gun in the big man's face until he backed up a step.

Action Man got his wind back, found his own gun, and waved it at the big man. "That's right, back off! It's loaded! Regardless of what I said before, it is loaded!"

"Point it at him," the gunsel said to Action Man. "Look unpredictable."

Action Man tried. The gunsel went to Cali's side of the Hudson. Cali cowered, scooted across the seat toward Ava.

"T-Bone, no, just leave me alone!" Cali said.

Ava stirred, half out of it. "T-Bone?" she said.

All she saw was a blur, the silk of the butterfly dress being yanked out the passenger-side window.

The gunsel carried Cali toward the Bentley.

"Please, T-Bone, I can't anymore," she said.

"Quiet," the gunsel said. "You'll be safe at the castle." He put her in the backseat of the Bentley and got behind the wheel again.

Action Man waved his gun around a bit more and then jumped into the Bentley.

The big man had dropped to one knee, bent over, as if he'd been hit although no one had fired a shot. The gunsel backed up the driveway fast through a fresh cloud of smoke. The big man drew himself up to his full height and stepped up the drive.

He had a real name: Tom Hadley. He watched the Bentley speed away. He turned to look back down into the garage. Ava was climbing out her window. Hadley looked her in the eye. He seemed as if he were about to say something—or, worse, *do* something—but he didn't. He turned his back on Ava and walked toward the street.

Ava got out of the Hudson—still wobbly—and went after him.

Hadley was already gone, out of sight or blended into the coursing crowds on the sidewalk. A half block up, the old-fashioned Bentley was attempting an old-fashioned getaway, honking and nudging cars, changing lanes, headed west at ten miles an hour. It would have been cinematically fitting if Cali had been looking out the back window imploringly, but she wasn't.

She was on the floor in the back seat, her back against the door, still not herself—in more ways than one—thinking about the concept of the lesser of two evils.

Or was it three?

Chapter Twenty

It was Bodie's gun, a Sig-Sauer P226 9mm. Nate turned it over in his hand. And in his mind. The Sig had been a standard-issue cop gun back in the day. It weighed two and a half pounds loaded. It was no-shine black, black as soot, nothing gun-blue about it. He kicked out a bullet, a jacketed hollow-point. Bodie had hand-loaded his rounds, a cop's idea of a craft project. Nate fingered it, felt the care with which it had been made, made by his father's hand in a whole other time when things mattered that didn't seem to matter anymore. Or maybe it was just a bullet. Maybe Bodie hadn't really given two shits when he'd "crafted" it, had just cranked out a couple dozen of them in the garage in Sherman Oaks some Saturday when the Dodgers on the TV went five runs down in the second inning and he gave up on them.

Nate was sitting on the edge of the roof of his house, legs hanging over the side, facing Cahuenga Pass, the traffic below, the hills on the other side. The sun was almost down, making the vista in front of him all postcardy, a lovely lie.

"He had a rough night," the voice on the phone had said. It was eleven in the morning when the call had come and Nate was dead to the world.

"What does that even mean?" he had said.

The woman on the phone could have come right back at him with attitude of her own—smart-ass, hard, biting, or institutionally cold—but what she'd said was, "He was hurting and scared. He didn't sleep. He didn't eat his dinner. He was yelling at Carl. He ate some of his breakfast and he's asleep now." She wasn't giving him the real details and he knew it. *The mercy of God must be near*, he thought, a line from an old Dylan song. He couldn't remember which one, a song Bodie liked.

As soon as he'd heard the nurse's voice, he pictured her, though he couldn't remember her name. She was the one with the two little boys who played soccer and a husband who might have been their coach. She kept pictures at her station. She was pretty, had brown hair—the kind of woman it was easy to imagine as a girl back in her high school days. But she didn't look like that now. Now she had kids and a husband and probably a banged-up father of her own (or a father-in-law) that she or somebody like her was watching over through long, bad nights.

Nate dropped the magazine out of the gun, pressed the extra round into place, and loaded it again with his palm. He racked the slide and armed it, then set the gun down beside him on the white gravel of the flat roof.

"Can you see me?" he asked the air.

"I try to picture you and respond accordingly," the Empower™ therapist said. "Your words paint pictures." This time the fake doctor was standing—wearing a cream-colored suit and pale blue shirt open at the neck—floating out in front of Nate, suspended over the pass with the red taillights and white headlights of the traffic three hundred feet below him.

"You should be barefoot," Nate said.

"Why's that?" Dr. Stone said, tilting his head.

"The taillights under your feet look like coals, embers."

"Where are we?"

"I'm on the roof of my house. You're over the one-oh-one freeway, midair. You look like you're standing on burning coals. Remember that thing where 'confidence coaches'—or whatever the hell they were called—had people walk across burning coals to learn how to... *self*-empower?"

The virtual shrink wasn't programmed for wordplay so he missed the pun, the sarcasm. "Wait a minute..." he said, *thinking*. He blinked twice. "Yes, fire-walking! In the low two thousands. What do you think made your mind click on that, Nathaniel?"

Nate ignored the question.

"Are you back on active duty?" the therapist said after five seconds.

"Never left."

"I thought, following an on-duty fatality you took some time away to reflect and heal."

"You need an update, Doc. That whole suspended-with-pay thing went out ten years ago. Now we just put on a clean shirt, pull up our socks, reload, and salute. Actually, we reload first."

"I see," Jeffrey Stone said.

"But not literally," Nate said. He picked up the Sig again. "You can't literally see me."

"No. Unfortunately. They're working on it."

Nate lifted the pistol, pointed it casually at the sky, straight up. "Picture this. I have a gun in my hand. I'm sitting out here on my roof with a gun in my hand, bare feet over the side, like I was on a dock in Key West. What do you think about that?"

"Why do you have a gun in your hand?"

"To a cop, a gun's like a socket wrench."

"But you mentioned it."

"I woke up early this morning. I was standing at the sink in my bathroom, looking at my handsome self in the mirror, and the thought came to me: *Tonight you're going to want to take a backup gun.* Just like that. So I got it out of my underwear drawer, cleaned it, loaded it, now here it is in my hand, ready for whatever the night brings. What do call that, a premonition? Or Generalized Anxiety Disorder?"

"Do you find yourself going up onto your roof to sit alone often?"

"You mean more often than before I almost got myself blown up in a Salvadoran restaurant kitchen?"

"Yes."

"No, I've always been a moody bastard. You can ask my ex-wife."

"You said in our third session that you'd never been married."

"Pamela Anderson," Nate said. "It didn't last all that long. Sweet girl. Shy."

Dr. Stone went to the cloud again. After a moment, he smiled.

Nate hated that smile, in all of its permutations. "Why do you exist?" he said, to bring the robo-shrink back to earth.

"I'm sorry?"

"Why am I not sitting in an office with a human being in front of me?"

The program hesitated, almost as if it had feelings and they were hurt.

"Forget it," Nate said. He didn't like hurting anything's feelings. He and Bodie had had an old classic Chevy truck they were restoring and hot-rodding before Bodie got sick. He'd thrown a tool at the engine and called it *a piece of shit!* and felt bad for a week.

"No, I was formatting…formulating an answer."

Nate waited. Some of the pinkish/yellowish light went out of the sky, turning to night. The traffic below went to full stall.

"The counselors were getting burned out," Dr. Stone said, "exposed as they were to so much very specific human pain. As the city became more dangerous—more deadly—the caseload increased exponentially, overwhelming the office and the men and women who worked there."

"The shrinks started offing themselves."

"Yes, some of them. But that's always been true. It's a high-stress occupation. So much human pain."

"Jeffrey, you'll tell me if *you're* feeling a little blue, won't you?" Nate said.

The therapist smiled that smile again and ran a hand through his hair, that way models do in commercials when they want to appear complimented. Or hide their unshakeable self-confidence.

Nate took off the Dodger cap with the projector in the brim and sent it spinning over the Cahuenga Pass, like a Frisbee.

◆ ◆ ◆

GUNMEN ON BOTH SIDES, Incas and Twenties—all told, close to fifty of them—were shooting up the funeral, standing right out in the middle of the street, most of them with a gun in each hand just as they'd seen in the movies they'd grown up on.

"That's for Samuel," one Twenty said, standing over an Inca, shooting him in the face.

"And this is for Nathan," another Twenty said, firing two shots at the wide eyes of another Inca who'd slipped in the blood and fallen.

It was a night service though the whole street scene was lit like noon, lit like an arena. The funeral had only just started. The gangbangers weren't waiting for the solemnities inside to end and paid no mind to the swarming Crows overhead or the CROs and gang cops on their loudspeakers telling them to break it up. The curtain had gone up when the double-wide pine box came out of the back of the black MBZ hearse—on an air-gurney that made it look like it was floating—and sailed all by its lonesome up the steps into the old brick church. The pallbearers—bearing nothing, standing in two lines, heads bowed—flinched with each shot.

The screenplay had been written, at least the first act, and they were all caught up in the enveloping action: just pulling trigger, ducking and diving, shuckin' and jivin', happy to be bit players, extras, stuntmen. The shooters on both sides seemed surprised when their mags went empty and they had to jam in another. (Only the good guys run out of bullets in the movies and they were all bad guys.) Those who caught a round looked as if they knew it wasn't real, just a scene. Even the dead.

The Gang Unit cops watched the clash from their oversized helo, above it all. Whitey looked down out the open hatch, smiling dumbly, as if he were watching one of his games on his dub player. Il Cho was newer to all this and was anxious, gripping a handhold over his head, his heart racing.

"It's hard to tell 'em apart from up here," Whitey shouted over the sound of the whipped wind. "I wish they'd go back to colored bandanas or something. Hoodies. Remember when they all wore hoodies?"

"Take us up higher," Il Cho yelled to the pilot, gesturing with a thumb. A gunship was coming in, crossing underneath, shooting out cans of dispersal gas, what the cops called Vitamin D.

"Shit," Whitey said, "it was just getting good."

Down below, an Inca snatched up one of the canisters spewing out the yellow gas and held it up to his nose and breathed it in, grinning up at the sky like crazy. Whitey dug it.

Nate was inside the church in a black suit and tie, sitting at the outside end of the third row, not hiding but also trying not to shove anything in their faces. There were not a lot of Caucasians there. In fact, not a lot of anybodies. Most of the pews were empty, friends and even family scared off, sending their condolences electronically or with plastic flowers. Nix and Madison were in a row near the back. Standing against the side wall was one of the twitchy men who'd been on the velvet couch at Wallace's house.

Derrick and Jewel Wallace were in the front pew to the right of the aisle, staring straight ahead. So far the purple-robed preacher hadn't said a word. Pastor Lamb had just stood there up front through ten minutes of recorded music, street music, apparently the boys' favorite tunes: brash, assaultive, joyless *unlove* songs that—at least for Nate—went at least a little way toward explaining how this could have happened. Nate didn't exactly know why he was there. Or why he'd made No-Name stay on the roof two whole blocks over where he'd parked the Crow. If there was ever an occasion a CRO needed a gunner at his side, this was it. The walls and doors couldn't keep out the gunfire and the shouts and cries from the street.

And then the pastor spoke. He began the service with a question.

> *What is Man that You are mindful of him*
> *And the Son of Man that you carest for him?*

The text was from the Bible somewhere, but the Black minister looked up at the ceiling and spoke the question as if it were *his* question, as if it had kept him up last night. He said it again, the whole thing, *"What is Man...?"* He spoke the words with a weariness that didn't seem theatrical. Then he lowered his gaze and looked at the assembled, went from face to face. He picked out a young man—a stranger he'd never seen in his church—and spoke directly to him, as if it were just the two of them. It was a common preacher's trick. "Some people believe Man is little more than an animal," he said to the young man. "And there are those others who would lift Man almost to the position of a god. What is Man? What *is* Man?"

The singled-out, apparently unchurched young fellow shifted in his seat, wondering if he was supposed to offer an answer. Mercifully, the pastor looked up from him and spoke again to everyone assembled. "On a good day, family, I see both points of view," he said, "see that *there are depths in Man that go down to the lowest hell, and heights that reach the highest heaven,* as the Holy Writ says. But that is on a good day. A good day. On a day like today, I don't know. Can we all admit that, today, we don't know?" A few amens.

There was a *crack!* Nate flinched, then turned. A shot from the street had punched a hole in the stained glass window up over the empty choir loft in the back of the sanctuary. No one seemed surprised, and only a few others turned to look. In a movie—or a child's poem—the slug would have drilled a fresh hole in one of Jesus's outstretched hands or bagged the dove over his head with the olive branch in its beak. But here it was just a random shot and a random hole, a black dot, night sky where blue glass sky had been.

Wallace turned to look up at the stained glass window, then looked forward again. Pastor Lamb spoke a next line.

"Stop," Wallace said.

The reverend looked at him, nodding for a good ten seconds. He then stepped down to Jewel and Derrick Wallace and put a hand on each of their shoulders and said something between their two faces. Only Jewel cried. Wallace just nodded, almost impatiently, and then led his wife toward a side door with an arm around her waist.

Everyone stood. No one seemed surprised by the way it had ended.

Nate left by the same side door Wallace had used, not that he was going after him.

He took the back way down the alleys over to where he'd parked the bird and managed to see not one body. No-Name seemed surprised to see him walking up, coming out of all that chaos on the street, alive and all, unshot.

Chapter Twenty-One

I t was three in the morning in the Fashion District, or what had been the Fashion District. Nate had landed as close as he could without getting himself and No-Name killed and the Crow stripped for parts. Now the two were wading into the deep dark of a "neighborhood" they called the TMZ (for a reason lost along the way), a half block of hollowed-out buildings east and south of Center City, down where LA's rag trade had been. It was a nasty zone. Down here, cops and even firefighters went in, didn't come out. Nate's pulse was racing: three in the morning on a weekday, everything creepy quiet. A perfectly good night to die. No-Name was walking point, clear-focused all around, and had the shotgun off his shoulder, close at hand.

"I don't think we'll get shot," Nate said to his gunner's back. "I doubt there are many guns down here."

"I'd guess spears and clubs," No-Name said.

Nate was about *that close* to asking the kid what his name was. They were three blocks in and still hadn't seen a soul, which was not as comforting a thing as it might seem. Then, ten feet ahead, what looked like a pile of trash moved. Two human beings, sleeping or… something. No-Name drew down on them. They jumped up and scurried into a bombed-out building through a doorway with no door. A beat-up sign said:

AMERICAN APPAREL

Squatters' rights had made the West. It had made California, sure enough made LA. The history of the West was the history of generations of good people who just wanted to live in peace…on somebody else's land. In this case, the squatters had taken over the bombed-out shell of the Fashion District, dug in, created the TMZ. But those verbs were too strong, wrong. What they'd done was more passive-aggressive than any commonly recognized form of taking over or digging in or creating. The squatters knew squat about intentionality. It had long since been beaten out of them by circumstances. Or drained out of them by their own weaknesses. At first—during some particularly rough patch in the local economy—it had just been a few transients creeping south from Skid Row to the TMZ, looking for *empty* and stopping when they found it. This was five or six years ago, around 2020. Then a few more came. A month later there were too many to count, not that anybody had any inclination to count them. Toward what end? Up on Skid Row the people living on the street had their do-gooders ministering to them, but down here there weren't any do-gooders, official or unofficial.

The whole place stayed dark inside and out, somehow even at noon on the brightest, hottest summer day. At night, there might be cook-fires, but of course there were no streetlights. If there had been streetlights, the squatters would have smashed them out. They wanted it dark. Everything was dirty, everyone was dirty. It was hard to tell the women from the men. There were no children. How could there be? Even feral dogs trotted three blocks south to avoid going through the TMZ, picking up the pace and looking back over their haunches until they were past it. The cops took their cue from the dogs.

A rock or chunk of concrete came at them out of the night, just missing Nate's head. No-Name brought up his shotgun again but maintained his trigger discipline.

"We could come back tomorrow," Nate said.

But they didn't turn back. CROs wore helmets with brilliant lights mounted fore-and-aft, mini-NightSuns to be used as needed. Nate tapped the switch on the side of his helmet for the forward-looking spot. At the flare of light, No-Name jumped. It was like tossing a phosphorus grenade out in front of them.

"Sorry," Nate said.

No-Name lit up his high beams too. His lights were on his shoulders, perched like ravens.

They went another block, then stopped to figure out where they were. A black bear loped across twenty feet in front them. In the moment, it didn't get much of a response from either man. It was just a moving shadow with red eyes.

Ahead was a six-story building with a big N painted on the side, up high, high enough to have been some kind of advertising from the fashionable past.

"There," Nate said.

An hour ago, after the funeral, they'd been sent out on a run to Chinatown: a family of eight arguing in a one-room apartment. Even with the CodeBox translator clipped onto the strap over Nate's shoulder, twenty minutes on site didn't get him any closer to figuring out what was what, who was who. Much less who was right, if that even mattered. When they'd gotten back to the Crow, there was a message waiting, floating in the air in the cockpit.

It was Johnny Santo, the CI.

"*Hola!*" Nate had said, though it was a recorded message.

"I got something for you," Santo had said. He kept looking over his shoulder, as before on the screen in Nate's kitchen, as if he were about to be busted for talking to a cop. "Down in the TMZ, top of the building with the N on it. Tell me when you think you can be there and I'll be there. The N Building, the roof, N like *nada*. Don't fly in. Tonight. Tell me if you can't make it. It's important."

Nate called Santo back. No answer. He left him a message and said he was on the way.

When they were at the base of the N building, at the foot of the stairs, No-Name said, "You want me to go up with you?"

"Well, yeah," Nate said.

A dirty child, three or four, wearing just a pair of shorts but no shoes, stepped into the doorway in front of them. So maybe there *were* kids in the TMZ. A hand jerked the boy (or girl) back into the shadows. The kid had sad, tired, dirty blue-gray eyes Nate would remember later.

"Turn off the spots," Nate said.

They went dark, waited a second for their eyes to adjust, then started up the stair-steps, feeling their way with their hands on the wall, No-Name in front. The shell of the building was brick but the stairs were iron, mounted onto the wall and fairly solid. The staircase had likely been the fire escape in the old days. The elevators would have been in the middle of the building, taking fashion designers and models and executives up and down—never moving fast enough for them—as they prattled on about things that must have seemed very important in the moment.

"Get thee behind me, Satan," Nate said to No-Name.

No-Name let Nate go ahead of him. The gunner looked back down the dark steps behind them, thinking he'd heard something. He had.

Nate had Bodie's Sig in hand. "Just so you know," he said, "for future use, this is the kind of place where a snitch wants to meet when he's going kill you."

"Yes, sir," No-Name said.

They came out onto the roof but found it only marginally lighter. As far as they could tell, Johnny Santo wasn't there. There was sound, a footfall on gravel. No-Name's jitter-meter was redlining.

"It's all right, be cool," Nate said, clicking on a pencil-size red-lens flashlight.

He found them: a family—a mother and a father, two little kids—huddled next to a cardboard tent across the roof, trying to decide whether to run or when. The mother had her hand across the girl's mouth to keep her from coughing and giving them away.

"It's OK," Nate said to them. "We're the police."

The mother took away her hand and the little girl coughed violently, from deep in the chest, sounding like a sick old man who'd smoked Lucky Strikes his whole life.

"Go on, go. You don't want to be here right now." Nate used the sweep of his flashlight to show them the way to go. The family gathered up what few things they had and abandoned their pitiful home. They only went a few feet before they stepped up onto the parapet of the roof. For a second, Nate had the horrible thought that they were all going to jump off, but then he saw that there was a wooden plank bridge over to the next building. The family scurried over, even the boy, four or five, whose father waited for him to cross before bringing up the rear. They were Whites, more pairs of blue eyes shining out of dirty faces. The boy looked back across the black chasm between the buildings, right at Nate, as if he wanted him to acknowledge something that way kids do.

Was it the towhead who'd hugged his leg up from the Goodwill Store?

The world lit up. NightSun, the light from on high, the light of Authority. God when God has gone home, punched out. A Crow was landing. Nate wasn't used to this point of view, being on the ground with a lit-up bird coming down on top of him, and he couldn't help but have the standard reaction: shock and then anger. Something about a Crow made you want to shoot at it. But then the light bouncing up off the roof illuminated the face of the cop/pilot—a CRO named Tucker—a friend, a veteran with twenty years in the air. He wiggled his fingers in greeting, turned off the fireball, and descended blind the last ten feet.

As the helo settled, the hatches came up and it was Il Cho who got out of the gunner's perch. Tucker, who apparently already knew more than he wanted to know about whatever this was, stayed in the bird.

"Hey," Nate said as Cho walked toward him, as the rotors slowed and the wind subsided. He had already holstered Bodie's pistol. "What are you doing here?"

"What's your gunner's name?" Cho said, before anything else.

"I don't know," Nate said. "Why?"

"Could he go sit in the bird with Tucker?"

Nate looked at No-Name and pointed with his thumb at the Crow.

◆◆◆

THE SHORT VERSION FROM Il Cho was: Whitey was up to no good.

"So what else is new?" Nate said.

"He's working something with this Twenties/Incas thing. I don't know what it is but he's right in the middle of it, cheering it on."

Nate said, "I just figured he was breaking windows."

"What do you mean?" Cho said. He wasn't much on metaphors.

"A guy owns a plate glass business. Business is off, so he sends his son out at midnight with a pellet gun."

"It's more than that," Cho said. "Something big, real money."

"Like what?"

"I don't know. Something about Mexico."

Tucker had cut all the Crow's lights except a blue-tone overhead in the cockpit. Cho kept looking around. He couldn't see much of anything. What light there was ended before the edge, the parapet.

Cho was all kinds of anxious. "I won't go to Internal Affairs," was the next thing he said.

"Did they make you do that Empower™ thing?" Nate asked.

"This is serious," Cho said, looking Nate in the eye. "It got Juan Carlos killed, almost got you killed. I had to tell somebody."

"Who sent you to the Salvadoran restaurant?"

"Nobody."

"I thought you said you got a ten-twenty on the Inca kid with the cross on his cheek from one of your CIs."

"I didn't say that."

"Maybe it was Whitey who said it."

"I came into work and Whitey was already suited up and getting Juan Carlos all jacked about it," Cho said. "Then we were in the air. Whitey and JC went into the restaurant to check it out. JC apparently right away saw the Inca kid in the kitchen, through the little window, just went for it. I wasn't there. Whitey said he told Juan Carlos to wait for backup."

"You understand that Whitey knows everything you're thinking, right? He's been at this a long time. I guarantee he's ten steps ahead of you."

"I don't think so," Cho said.

"Watch your ass is all I'm saying."

Nate looked over at the Crow. Tucker was reading a paperback in the blue light. "Why'd you want to meet down here, in the kill zone? We could have met out at the beach or something, had a fish taco."

"Johnny Santo said you picked the place."

"What?"

"When I met up with him to pay him off for the bridge tip, I told him I wanted to see you about something, private, away from everybody, and would he set it up. Whitey was ten feet away. Johnny called back a half hour later, said you said meet here."

"You think Johnny didn't turn right around and call Whitey?"

Cho got a look his face. He hadn't been at this all that long.

"Forget it," Nate said. "I'm like you, so trusting of people."

"Shit, look out," Cho said, and jumped back a step and went for his gun.

Nate spun, the Sig leaping into his hand. In the same moment, the hatch came up on the Crow and No-Name jumped down, landing with his feet apart, the stubby shotgun already in hand.

Squatters. Ten or twelve of them, ragged and dirty, coming across the roof, coming up from below. Tucker reacted, flipped on the Crow's side-floods, lit up the rooftop, *over*-lit the scene, as if the rooftop were a stage in a no-budget little theater somewhere, a shabby local production of *Les Misérables*. The raggedy squatters were slow-moving. They were bunched up, all looked alike. Some of them had clubs, two-by-fours, or baseball bats. And they weren't all men. They were all White, except for one young Black and what looked to be his son. Another half dozen of them followed the first wave, spilling up out of the staircase.

"Is it now?" they started saying, first one of the ones in front, then the others. "Is it now?" They were like the creepy chorus in the same bad play.

Now more of them were coming from the other side of the roof, crawling on all fours over the plank bridge from the adjacent building, including the blue-eyed family that had fled just minutes ago.

"Check your six!" Nate yelled.

No-Name turned and saw the second flank.

Nate raised the Sig over his head. "Get back!" he said.

"Tell us. Is it now?" They kept coming on both flanks. No-Name fired a shotgun round into the air. They kept coming forward.

Tucker cranked up the Crow, started the blades turning, panic preflight.

"Come on, get in!" No-Name ordered Nate and Cho.

The cops dashed to the two-man helo, intending to make a four-man helo. Il Cho, who wasn't a small man, climbed up into the raised gunner's seat while Nate jumped in beside Tucker up front, practically sat in his lap. The Crow was already rising.

No-Name jumped onto the skid. The starboard-side back hatch was still up.

"Get in," Nate said.

No-Name shook his head, disobeyed the order, stayed on the skid as the squatters swarmed forward. The Crow was six feet off the deck when one squatter jumped and seized hold of the skid under No-Name's feet. No-Name kicked the man away with a boot to the face. The man fell away but another squatter jumped and grabbed hold of the skid where the other man had been.

"Let go!" No-Name hollered at the hitcher.

Another man jumped and wrapped his arms around the first squatter's waist, piggybacking. The engines strained. The helo wasn't rising any higher.

The Crow wasn't made for this—three men in the cockpit and a gunner on the skid—and it certainly wasn't made to lift two hangers-on. The bird drooped to one side, seconds away from crashing. No-Name tilted down and shoved the shotgun against the shoulder of the closest man and fired. The squatter fell away, his face frozen into a nightmare look, leaving his hand and arm behind. It took a second for the squatter's fingers to let go of the skid. With the weight off, the Crow rose, fast. The piggybacking second squatter landed hard on his back on the roof, his arms still around the waist of the now one-armed man.

Tucker clicked on his NightSun. The other squatters threw up their hands to shield their eyes and fell back, and the helo rose, up and out of there.

Chapter Twenty-Two

Less *Les Mis*, more *Grapes of Wrath*.

The day was done, gone, down to ash. Nate was laid out in a chair in his living room, a bottle of water in his hand, staring at the wall, a projected image there. It was a black-and-white still, floor to ceiling and as wide as the room. It captured a moment in time, out of the far past, an unstriped two-lane highway, a barbed-wire fence alongside it, a black car cresting a low hill. A 1934 Dodge Deluxe Sedan, if Nate had it right. Time was, Nate knew the shapes and names of cars, the way some other kid knew his dinosaurs or his ballplayers and stats. New cars, old cars, bold cars of the future flying off the pages of *Popular Mechanics*. This was when he was eleven or twelve, dreaming of the day he could get behind the wheel and break free. The Dodge looked to be running wide open—blurry—as if just barely escaping the inescapable thing behind it, a roiling black wave, blacker than either the car or the road, a dust storm a thousand feet high.

The picture had a name: *Doomsday, Texas Panhandle, 1936*.

Suitable hard-times music—gut-bucket blues and Depression-era jazz and folk tunes—played in the background, from the other room, tonight transmitted out onto the airwaves without comment from The All-Night Man. If he had any listeners, they'd be wondering what had gotten into him.

"Go," Nate said.

A second and third and fourth picture came up, shots of brown powdery dirt piled against fences, drifts as high as the top row of barbed wire. The stills gave way to newsreel footage accompanied by the sound of ninety-year-old wind.

"Go," Nate said.

The fifth picture: a late-twenties Hudson Super-Six sedan loaded to just shy of cracking an axle, strapped on top with a mattress and iron headboard and a pair of straight-back wooden chairs and along the sides with a white suitcase and a washtub and a sack of flour—all they had, whoever they were and wherever they'd come from. The Hudson was somewhere out in the desert, crawling past a highway sign, a black badge: Route 66. A canvas water bag hung off the stanchion for the missing mirror on the driver's side. A stunned boy and girl—there was no clearer way to describe them—looked out the back window. *California Or Bust* had been painted down the side by one of the adults.

"Go," Nate said. When nothing happened, he said it again, impatient in that way only a modern man can be.

And there she was. There *they* were. It was as famous as any American photograph, a tired-eyed migrant mother sitting on a box in a lean-to tent with her two girls clinging to her, the girls' faces turned away. It was taken at an ag camp off US 101 in the Central Valley at Nipomo, 165 miles north of LA, March, 1936. *Migrant Mother.* Eyes trying to see tomorrow. That the woman and probably her daughters were long since dead didn't make it any less sad and unsettling to look on.

"Go."

Nate was restless, stressed. He was lonely, though he wouldn't call it that. He'd come back from downtown, from the rooftop in the TMZ, thinking about all the blue-gray eyes. He wanted a drink, badly, but he'd settled for water. And old pictures of blowing dirt and desperate White people. Maybe it was the heat. Or the dry. It had been close to a hundred in Los Angeles every afternoon for a week and it hadn't really rained for two months, unless you counted the ten-minute shower the night he met Ava Monica downtown at the story bar. That didn't count for rain, even if she had come into the joint in a raincoat, as if it had been pouring out on there on the street. He had thought about ragging her, making a joke about it, but he hadn't. Everybody pretends in different ways, pretends they're somewhere else or some*one* else or that it's some whole other time instead of: now, here, *you.* He was as guilty of it as anyone.

And his old man was worse. The LP playing in the background was Bodie's record, Woody Guthrie…

> *I just blowed in and I got them Dust Bowl blues*
> *I just blowed in and I'll blow back out again…*

What's a young LAPD motorcycle cop living a block off Ivar in Hollywood in the sixties—at least until he could find a woman to marry who'd make him have a kid and move to a house in the Valley with a pool—doing listening to Woody Guthrie sing about the Dust Bowl?

> *I seen the wind so high it blowed my fences down*
> *Buried my tractor six feet underground...*

Nate took another slug of his water. It wasn't Bombay Sapphire gin but it was good, bottled in the mountains. Bottled in glass, ten bucks a bottle. It came from snow melt and High Sierra springs, not like the soulless pipe water from the big de-sal plants that nowadays kept LA hydrated and sort of almost halfway kind of green.

The living room wall was blank. The projector had come to the end of the queue.

"Current," Nate said. "Zone seven. New Dust Bowl."

The News. *Here, now, you.*

First came the sound of a very-present wind—ten-channel now—howling, moaning, whistling, sounding like a beast dying. Then came the visuals, vivid, enormous churning clouds of dust, blowing across the living room wall, rattling Nate's windows. In the pictures, it came in under the doors, dusting everything—section after section of farmland in 2023 Oklahoma and Colorado and Texas and Missouri, blown away by the brown wind—people holding onto their hats, leaning into it, tumbleweeds crossing the interstate. The images were so crisp and clean and high-defined that they seemed unreal, the clearest things in the room.

"Stop," Nate said. The wall went blank again.

He didn't need to see any more. It had been all over the news: two years of drought, Sirocco winds blowing without a break for weeks at a time, "Dusters" and "Okies" fleeing dead farms and dead farm towns, a repeat of the Dirty Thirties but collapsed into twenty-four months. The backstory was as predictable as all history is: topsoil gone, over-farmed/over-machined land, the wrong crops planted, boom and bust. That very American mix of greed and optimism. Before he stopped it, the last footage had shown lines of beat-up RVs now turned to desperate purposes as they plowed into the curtains of dust drawn across the highways, headed west. Again. The New Migrants.

Nate didn't need to see the faces looking out the windows of the RVs. They'd come where history told them to come, come west to work the fields and vineyards and the almond and apricot orchards in the Central Valley—and the factories in LA—where the Mexican migrants had worked before the massive Oaxaca Find two years ago that had brought oil wealth to Mexico and called *los nacionals* home. Mexico was the new Saudi Arabia. The New Okies had come and—as before, in the thirties—there were too many of them and not enough work. And, as before, not all of them were from Oklahoma. "Okies" was a slur. They came from several states, some all the way from Arkansas. Some of them had gone north to Oregon, some had landed in the East Bay—Oakland and Fremont—and some south to LA. None had gone home to Tulsa or Stillwater or Muskogee or Colorado Springs or Topeka or Springfield. For now, there was nothing much to go back to. Some of them—Nate now knew—were there that very night in the TMZ, still coughing up the dirt in their lungs.

He went into the radio room in his second bedroom and sat at the control board. He still had nothing to say to his vast audience of a dozen or so night owls. Tonight, he was just listening to the music. Scratches and all. The album he was broadcasting was a Library of Congress recording, and it sounded a thousand years old, as if it had been found in a cave somewhere.

> *I had good gal, long, tall, and stout*
> *I had to get a steam shovel just to dig my darlin' out...*

He looked over at a gap under the window shade. Light on the sill, dawn. The All-Night Man had run out of it once again: night.

◆ ◆ ◆

WHITEY BARNES HAD A nice place down in Baldwin Hills. Two-story, columns out front, like a little White House. Or a plantation house. It was nice enough to make Internal Affairs take notice, if they'd known about it. They didn't. The current governor was a real man-of-the-people—rode a bike, ate nothing but raw vegetables, fruits, and nuts, lived in a Craftsman cottage on a modest street in Santa Monica. Except his boyfriend was a pop star with a $50 million house a half mile away in Brentwood. Everybody downtown joked that there was a tunnel and the governor could walk in the front door of his humble un-air-conditioned bungalow, take the elevator down, and the electro-roller would jet him over ten blocks so he could come up into his real house and eat a rib eye. So maybe Whitey had himself a tunnel running back to Inglewood and his legal residence.

Nate was hovering at two thousand feet above Whitey's place, too high to be noticed by anyone on the ground. Besides, day and night there were so many Crows and EMT wagons and fire rigs crisscrossing Los Angeles they didn't even catch the eye anymore unless they had a siren whooping. Nate curled around to where he could see the backside of the house. Whitey had a swimming pool. Nate smiled. Nobody could get a variance for a swimming pool anymore. It was kidney-shaped and had a cover stretched over it, painted the same green as the artificial lawn around it so that it looked like a putting green. Whitey had a tennis court, too, though the net was down.

Nate was alone, lone-wolfing it. No-Name was probably at home, curled up in his jammies, wondering if it was too late to enroll at Long Beach State, train for a job where no one was trying to kill you or hang off your skid. Nate looked west. Sparkles, dark blue water. The way the light bounced off the Pacific made him feel something. What was that sensation? Oh yeah…pleasure. It was almost enough to make him think about making some changes in his life, maybe not sleeping past noon every day. It wasn't even nine o'clock in the morning. He hadn't gone to bed, had just put on another Dust Bowl record while he watched the sun break over the hill on the other bank of the Cahuenga Pass, the 101 already clogged with commuters who'd be lucky if they made it to work by noon. He'd brushed his teeth, stepped into the shower and out again, then into his body armor and a fresh flight suit.

He hadn't shaved. He thought maybe he'd grow a beard, even knowing he'd be mocked for it by friends and enemies alike.

"It *is* you," said Carrie, appearing before him in the cockpit.

Nate said, "I thought I had you turned off."

"It's not possible to turn me off," she said.

"I could lose my job, just by listening to you say that line. 'Acquiescing to harassment,' I think it's called in the handbook."

"Los Angeles would be the poorer if you weren't protecting and serving us, Nate Cole," she said. "Are you growing a beard?"

"It's growing itself," Nate said. "So this is you in the morning."

"This is me. Where are you?"

Of course she/it knew exactly where he was, down to the half foot. Her question helped remind him that Carrie was part of The Grid, that she *was* The Grid. But where's the harm in pretending she was real? She knew Nate about as well as anyone else in his life. They'd spent more time together than almost anyone else who came to mind. They'd laughed, they'd cried. They'd worried about each other. They'd told each other, "Take care..." They even sang "Happy Birthday" to each other. Nate had made up a birth-date for her—11/06/91, the number on his Crow's tail—and she didn't correct him. She was flattered. Or some twenty-two-year-old Sri Lankan guy who'd programmed "her" was.

"I couldn't sleep so I'm pretending to work," Nate answered. "I'm south, running down something for one of my CIs. But I was just thinking about going out to the beach, maybe even go over to Catalina. Land on the sand, blow their minds, eat some calamari."

"I've never seen it," she said. "Catalina. If you go, leave your down-lens on for me."

"Did you bring your bikini?"

"Where's your gunner?" she said.

"Home in bed, I hope," Nate said. "Let me ask you something."

"Go."

"Do other CROs learn their gunners' names?"

"I keep telling you, Nate, I only have eyes for you."

"Good song. The Flamingos."

"Do you want me to sing it for you?" she said.

Below, a private transport was hovering over Whitey's house, getting ready to land on the tennis court, a tennis court without a net.

"Next time," Nate said, and clicked her away. Then he reached under the dash for the comm-line switch he'd installed, bootleg, and cut the link to HQ. Nobody needed to know where he was.

He went up another five hundred feet—almost omniscient—whipped into a one-eighty, and fell in behind the hired transport bird that had lifted off from Whitey's. He looked west at all that sparkling water and the little range of smooth mountains beyond that was Catalina Island. Next time.

◆ ◆ ◆

AUTOMOBILE AND TRUCK ASSEMBLY plants had folded left and right in the years since the last of the Swarzenegger nukes went online, the electric Feds came along, and "Detroit" moved to 中国. No industry took a knockout blow like the one the RV business took, a sucker punch in the first round when filling the tank in a Winnebago went to $1,000 about the same time the government went to shaming—and then fining—RVers for spending their money inappropriately, "without sufficient regard for others." Everywhere all at once no one wanted to be seen stepping up into or down out of a motor home, even if they were using it to go see Grandma in Sun City.

So why then was Nate looking down at a parking lot full of brand-new RVs?

It was up north in the high desert—Antelope Valley—fifty miles by air from Baldwin Hills, a parking lot behind an old dead Ford factory. Or it *had been* dead. Ford had built the plant ten miles outside of Palmdale in 2017 to turn out a hybrid with a forgettable name that some unforgettable-name-creation company in San Francisco had come up with. Ford had bought robots, hired a few union humans for the sake of appearances, and cranked out a thousand automobiles a day for two years, parking them door to door, head to tail, in a five-acre fenced lot. They were all painted beige. Then it ended, at midnight on a Thursday. The plant was shut down, locked up, the last of the cars loaded onto railcars on the spur out back, and that was that.

But now this was this. An RV factory in 2025? Nate was hovering at ten thousand feet. The Crow's undercarriage target & track camera threw the scene below onto his monitor. The unit had a long lens, gave him a view that was like standing on a hill fifty feet away. He watched as a tall and wide door on the smallest of the Ford plant's four buildings rolled up and a fresh RV was birthed. The model wasn't much changed from the old days: a boxy behemoth, shiny two-tone brown. Gas-powered. He could tell it was gas-powered but the motor wasn't warmed up, coughing white smoke out the tailpipe. It sped out of the plant and was driven at a good clip to its place in the front row in the lot, next to a sibling. On the far end of the lot were a dozen bare-bones truck chassis waiting to be built upon. The big garage door was already descending. The RV driver stepped down out of the motor home, trotted across the asphalt, and slipped under the door, barely making it before it closed. Somebody was messing with him, workplace humor. It was 115 degrees down there.

Whitey's transport had been on the ground ten minutes, parked inside the fence close to the side of the building. The long blades still rotated slowly—probably something to do with keeping the bird's AC going—but Whitey hadn't gotten out. Then a second transport blew in. A man with a shaved head—Nate guessed Central or South American—got out of the back of the second helo, as if it were a limo. Getting out was a struggle for the shaved-head man because he was crippled up, dead legs. A second man came out with him who could have helped, but the helper never helped, just stood by. The first man was strapped into a MotoWalker in a sitting position. He rolled out of the back of the helo—roughly, in fits and starts—and then the robotic device took him upright, brace-bars straightening and locking into place. They were like stainless steel crutches and came up under his armpits to hold him straight, with small retractable wheels on the ends so he could roll. The man squared his shoulders and ran his hand over his shaved head. He was only disabled from the hips down. He was wearing a flashy grape-colored suit wholly inappropriate for the location and the time of day and the season of the year. Or the decade. He was short, when you subtracted the extra three or four inches the MotoWalker had just added. He wore reflector sunglasses.

Whitey still hadn't come out of the first helicopter.

Nate centered the camera sight on the machine-assisted man. "Capture," he said. A recorder started recording. "Close on the face. Track and ID." The lens came in tighter, tight enough to see the blue cloudless sky reflected in the hombre's shitty-looking sunglasses. Nate reached under the dash and relinked to the home office.

"Ignacio 'Nacho' Iberriz," a man's voice said almost immediately over the radio. "DOB: Eight–twenty–eighty-nine. Place of Birth: South America. Principality: Unknown, possibly Peru. Current Address: Multiple Addresses, District: East Los Angeles, Boyle Heights. Citizenship: Unknown, possibly Peruvian."

Nate was missing his radio girl Carrie. Radio Ron didn't have much personality. "Occupation…" the radio voice began.

Nate interjected a guess, "Uh…orthodontist, Pasadena."

"Laborer," the robo interrupted, "Unemployed since two thousand fourteen. Incarcerated: two thousand six to two thousand ten—Men's Correctional,

San Luis Obispo. Two thousand eleven to two thousand fourteen—Lompoc. Two
thousand nineteen to two thousand twenty—High Desert Prison / Susanville."

"There you go," Nate said.

"Physicality: Differently-Abled since two thousand twenty-one."

"And the gang affiliation I'm guessing would be—"

"Inca."

Ignacio "Nacho" Iberriz was still standing out there in the high desert sun.
Whitey was still making him wait. More workplace humor? Iberriz apparently
had enough waiting and pivoted and started to locomote toward Whitey's helo.
The MotoWalker was designed to roll on its wheels until it came to a change in
whatever surface was underneath that necessitated a step. Then a wheeled foot
would rise—the brace-bar unlocking and breaking at the knee—and set down.
And then it was the other leg's turn. The device had an unexpected grace to its
movement, as if it had been designed by an injured runner or dancer.

The hatch opened and Whitey got out. The automatic eye of Nate's camera
detected the new action at the other helo and quickly shifted, finding Whitey.
It closed in until his face filled the screen.

"Scanning for ID…" the voice said, the program back home at Parker Center
going to work.

"Yeah, I know who he is," Nate said and reached under the console in a
hurry and killed the link, lest there be a record of who was where when. Coming
out behind Whitey was another man, another Brown man. "But I don't know
who *you* are," Nate said.

The third man was tall, barrel-chested, wore a white, crisp *quayabera* shirt
and shiny black skinny-toe Western boots. And a black cowboy hat. He wasn't a
cowboy. He looked like a businessman, but a businessman from somewhere else,
somewhere harder and tougher than LA, somewhere where the sun beat down
even hotter. Import / export would have been a good guess. The drug trade. Nate
considered switching on the identifier again but thought better of it. The tall
man was standing too close to Whitey to risk Whitey getting ID'd too and all
of it going into the system. Besides, something told Nate this third man wasn't
going to be in anybody's book, at least not in the US.

The Black cop introduced the two Browns and they shook on it, whatever
it was.

Chapter Twenty-Three

"I'm gonna miss you, Johnny," Nate said, watching Johnny Santo come out of a Mexican restaurant with a woman-not-his-wife on his arm. He was sucking on a mint, probably the free kind from the bowl next to the cash register. He was wearing that polyester Jesus Malverde shirt again and had a spring in his step, practically merengue-dancing down the sidewalk, looking about as satisfied with life as a man ever looks. In LA, anyway. Two CROs with their gunners, who just happened to be walking by at the right moment, closed in on him from different directions. The gunners already had guns in hand, so Santo lost his *it's-all-good* look in a hurry. He raised his hands so as not to get shot outright. Nate's friend Tucker was one of the CROs. Tucker engaged Santo in conversation while the other CRO patted him on the belly. Big surprise: Johnny Santo had a gun in his waistband. And he was still on parole, too.

Nate was across the street in the shadows. He watched as they took his gun and turned him around to cuff him. Santo was nonstop running his mouth, plea-bargaining. Nate knew what he was saying, could almost read his lips, "I work for Il Cho, call him. I work for Whitey Barnes, call him. He'll tell you." Johnny had sense enough not to use Nate's name in vain. He knew he'd betrayed Nate when he'd sent him to that roof in the TMZ, probably at Whitey's behest.

Nate wasn't enjoying this nearly as much as he thought he would. He stepped out into the light to let Santo get a look at him. He didn't want to rub it in, but he it was always good to let a man know who'd dropped a dime on him. Good advertising: let a CI see what happens to a snitch who gets too big for his britches and starts playing one cop against another. Get it out there on the whatchamacallit, grapevine. But what Santo had done was worse than just playing both sides of the fence, working with Nate and with Whitey, and being used by both. He'd sent Nate to the top of the N Building knowing Nate could die up there. If the squatters had clubbed Nate dead or thrown him off the roof, Santo could have been an accessory to cop murder. But that didn't happen, no thanks to whoever had come up with the idea of a 3:00 a.m. trip to the Fashion District. So, in terms of the actual justice that often precedes the official kind, Johnny Santo was getting off easy. He'd just have his parole violated and go back to prison for a year or two where'd he get a swinging new orange wardrobe and lots of time to think. And see old friends and plan some heists.

The woman who was Johnny's date picked now to walk away. Tucker looked across at Nate. Nate shook his head no. He didn't care, let her go.

The restaurant that was the backdrop for this sad, predictable melodrama was the Casa Vega. It was out in the San Fernando Valley—on Ventura Boulevard, Sherman Oaks—where Nate grew up. Nate watched as a couple of high schoolers came out, laughing too loud, looking like they were on a date. It was already an old, impossible, *survivor* restaurant when Nate was in high school. *Menudo rojo* on Thursdays, beer-soaked carpet, *sombreros* tacked on the walls, catching dust and hiding spiders. Lots of dark corners. The Mexican ladies who were the waitresses—they seemed old to Nate back then but probably wouldn't now—didn't check IDs. As long as you ordered the big combo plate and tipped like an adult you could drink all night, margaritas and shots and brown-bottle Bohemia beer. One weeknight, High School Nate had been there with his crew and—though the red air was as dim as a Crow cockpit on a midnight run—he'd seen his father in the shadows with a woman. A woman-not-his wife. In a booth, a little alcove. Bodie was leaning close, laughing at something she'd said that probably wasn't all that funny. What made it a doubled-down surprise for Boy Nate was that the woman was older than his mother by a good ten years. And not as pretty. It was about then that young Nate started drawing some conclusions about human beings, conclusions that grew harsher as time went by. He didn't know if Bodie ever saw him that night. He left the other boys behind and got up to take a leak, went out a fire door to the parking lot, and walked home. Or somewhere.

Across the boulevard, they had Santo cuffed. Another Crow had shown up, was hovering, lighting up the scene. Nate decided to split. But then he looked down. Apparently, his feet had other ideas. His feet were taking him across the street. It was a weeknight but early evening, so the street was fully clogged.

His feet had to climb up and over the bumpers of the jammed-up, nose-to-tail Feds, four lanes of them. He really hated Feds.

"What the hell were you thinking?" he said to Johnny when he was two feet away. He didn't say it in a mad way. Nate actually sounded like his feelings had been hurt. A cop with feelings?

"Shit, I don't know," Santo said, sadder than sad. Then—meaning Tucker and the other CRO—he said, "Tell them, Cole. Tell them I'm your guy."

"Well, that's the problem, Johnny. It looks like you weren't my guy."

"No way, man."

"Whose idea was it?"

"Nobody. What?"

"Who did you talk to after Il Cho told you to set up a meeting with me?"

"Nobody."

Nate waited.

"Nobody," Santo said again. But this time it sounded almost like, *White-y.*

"I'll check in on your wife and kids every once in a while," Nate said, turning to leave. He meant it and Johnny Santo knew it.

Santo tried to stop him. "I maybe got something for you, Cole, something big, coming from the Incas and maybe the Twenties, too," he said.

Nate wasn't lured. But he only made it a few feet before he stopped and came back. "Whatever it is, don't tell it to Whitey," he said. "I'm serious. He'll kill you."

◆ ◆ ◆

It felt almost like a date, not that there were flickering candlelight and wine and long lingering looks. No-Name was itchy, bouncing around in his chair, not sure what this was about, wondering if he was getting fired, not having a clue how the adult world worked. He'd ordered spaghetti—the cheapest thing on the menu—after Nate had said he was picking up the check. Actually, what Nate had said was that the restaurant didn't let cops pay, but No-Name knew that wasn't the truth.

"You were good. On that roof in the TMZ," Nate said.

"It was intense," the kid said.

"What's your name?" Nate said.

"Blake. Blake Rockett," the other said. "Two Ts."

"Your name is *Rockett?* For real?"

"Yes, sir."

"Sweet."

The kid looked down at his untouched spaghetti. Nate could tell he—*Blake Rockett*—was taking a second to appreciate what had just happened with his pilot, his CRO. Maybe he was already thinking ahead to telling someone about it—a girlfriend, or even his mother.

"Do you ever watch war movies, Rockett?" Nate said.

"Yes, sir."

"Anytime in a war movie they have a guy, a soldier or a sailor or an airman, take out a picture of his girl back home, the guy dies in the next scene. It's like a given. Did you ever notice that?"

"No, sir."

"Don't be that guy," Nate said.

Rockett nodded, taking it to heart but not understanding what he meant.

"What's your favorite band?" Nate asked.

Chapter Twenty-Four

Wild Oak Drive rose and curved, and curved and rose until it ran out of houses, and it was just dusty pavement and scrub brush, stunted oaks and dried-out undergrass, what the firefighters nowadays called "fuel." Wild Oak Drive felt like a road to nowhere. It was in the middle of the city but didn't look like it. It wasn't all that late, but there was no one around, except for Ava behind the wheel. She was not herself. Or maybe this was who she really was. She was hurting, bruised, and not just from the crash in the garage. Over the last few days, things had gone from confusing to outright bad. Funny, but she was missing Cali. They'd snatched Cali, whoever *they* were. Ava was alone, *noticeably* alone, feeling more alone than she'd felt in a while. Loneliness usually wasn't a problem with her, but tonight it was. It had overtaken her, like a big rogue wave.

She had Edward Chang on the line. "You're sure about this?" she said. For now he was all she had in the way of company, which was just plain pathetic.

"Darris Laines. *DL*. One Thousand One Wild Oak Drive," Chang said, never sounding more Chinese, laying it on thick tonight for some reason. Maybe he thought it made him sound more authoritative. Maybe he was getting ready to raise his price. "Can't miss it. Twelve dollars. Keep on going." Yep. It used to be ten.

Tonight Chang was just a disembodied voice, no picture on the dash talk-screen. "How come I can't see your handsome, probably Asian face tonight?" Ava said. "I'm just getting a blankie on my screen."

"Technical glitch," Chang said. A second later, a blurry screenshot appeared on the dashboard screen, Chang frozen at his console with a puzzled look on his face, a pic out of the memory bank. It buzzed, pixilated, disappeared, returned.

"Is that your mom in the background?" Ava said. "I always wondered."

"Keep going. Almost there."

A canine something-or-other—a dog or a coyote or a mix of the two—ran across the road right in front of the Hudson. Ava hit the brakes, skidded to one side on the sandy pavement. The canine hit the brakes too, looked her right in the eye across the hood, then trotted on. Peaceful coexistence.

"Keep going," Chang said. "Go more."

Ava didn't go more. She stopped the car. "There's nothing out here, Changster," Ava said. "Tumbling tumbleweeds."

"Around the next curve it straightens out."

"How do you know exactly where I am? Are you tracking me?"

"You can't miss it. It's all lit up. Darris Laines." Actually, what he said was *It's all rit up.*

Ava set out again, steered around a blind curve. Wild Oak Drive straightened out, leveled off, and ended at a cul-de-sac, just as he had said.

And there it was.

"What the hell?" she said.

Uplighted, as if ready for its close-up, Mr. DeMille, was a one-tenth-scale copy of Griffith Observatory. It was a house, a big house, a mini-mansion if not a full mansion. And behind it and above it—a half mile away, on the downside of Mount Hollywood—was the real Griffith Observatory. It was like some kind of depth-of-field demonstration. Or an acid trip.

What sort of person wants to live in an optical illusion?

"DL. Darris Laines. Twelve dollars," Edward Chang said.

"How did I not know about this?" Ava said.

"You don't know everything. Twelve dollars."

"Check's in the mail, Chang," Ava said and punched his lights out.

The motor courtyard out in front of the house was empty, no sign of the Bentley with the DL plates. Off to one side, separate, was a four-bay two-story garage. The garage doors were down. Lights were on upstairs over the garages. Was it the gunsel driver's apartment? The mansion itself looked dead, deserted, even with all the dramatic lighting. It was perfect, if a fake, copycat thing can be perfect. It had the big dome in the middle with wings jutting out on either side of it, each with a smaller dome atop the end. All the domes were clad with copper. The structure itself was of poured concrete, painted white. On either side of the twelve-foot-tall front doors were five skinny windows, blacked out. It looked like a fortress, a castle. A museum. A mausoleum. A gift shop for the real deal?

Ava got out, closing the door of the Hud with her hip. Right about then—as if welcoming her—a micro-dust storm blew through, literally adding some atmosphere to the scene. She turned her head as if she'd been slapped and flipped up the hood of her catsuit and set off for the house. No neighbors, no human sounds in the night. The setting wasn't helping her mood.

"*Down at the end of Lonely Street...*" she sang softly.

But maybe Cali was in there. What had the skinny gunsel said? *You'll be safe at the castle.* She stopped short of the first circle of floodlight in front of the house. The closer she got, the bigger the scale of the crazy. She slipped along the front of the four-car garage. The windows in the garage door were six feet up. She could jump up and try to see if the Bentley was home but she decided it might seem undignified, if anyone was looking.

"You only have one opportunity to make a first impression," she said, using her mother's voice.

She thought of doing some recon, get the lay of the land—go off into the brush, circle the place to see if she could spot Cali inside—but then she looked down at her inappropriate-for-reconnaissance footwear and walked straight toward the tall, tarnished, copper one-tenth-scale front doors. Sometimes you just ring the bell. She rang the bell.

A pair of surveillance cams positioned high to the right and left opened their eyes and the entryway lights brightened. Unless it was all on autopilot, someone was home. She pictured the wily gunsel/driver looking out the video peephole and shrugging his skinny shoulders, cracking his neck, and adjusting the gat tucked under his armpit.

"This is not exactly my best angle," she said to the cameras.

"You're beautiful," a disembodied voice said, immediately. "If you were any hotter, you'd set fire to my sagebrush." It wasn't the gunsel, that was for sure. This disembodied voice was professional-strength, a trained voice, a voice of authority. A SAG voice, or at least IATSE.

Ava was already thinking, *Is that...?* when the two doors opened inward and there was Dallas Raines. "Darris Laines" was Dallas Raines. He was wearing a suit and tie. And cowboy boots. At midnight.

"That's right, it's me," he said. And for punctuation, right there in the doorway, he showed off his golf swing, minus a club, the most famous of his various signature moves. His younger fans, which probably included Ava, had no way of knowing he'd swiped the move from another television star who'd gone off the air forty years ago.

He was a TV weatherman. Through week after week and year after year of mostly utterly predictable SoCal weather, there he was, first on Channel 7, then on Channel 9, and then on Channel 2. When the television news converted to targeted zone broadcasting, he became his own channel, *Dallas Raines and The Weather System*. Somehow, he was on the air—live?—every time you looked for him. Days and night, seven days a week, year-round, Christmas Day, Yom Kippur. Most people had assumed he'd long ago been digitized and automated. "Look up!" was his signature sign-off; that and one of the best smiles in Hollywood, which was saying something. His gimmick was he meant it.

Ava said, before she thought to stop herself, "How *old* are you?"

"Sixty-nine," he said, without apology. "I was twenty-three when I came to this market." He smiled that smile. This close, it was powerful.

"Do you have a Bentley with DL plates?" Ava said.

"No, I don't," he said. "But would you like to come in for a cocktail?"

"It's kinda late," Ava said. It was nine o'clock.

"There you go!" he said, as if she'd answered *Yes!* He slipped his arm around her waist and—like the trophied ballroom dancer he also was—perfectly turned her toward the interior of the house. But before they made it inside, another robust gust of dry wind blew in. Dr. Raines—he was fully credentialed in his field—let go of Ava and strode out onto the motor courtyard. Fists on his hips, he glared up at the night, as if the dust devil had been a personal affront.

◆ ◆ ◆

SO THEN AVA WASN'T as lonely, or at least wasn't thinking it about anymore.

She waited at Chrisssy's door. It opened. Chrisssy had been asleep. It was just after midnight.

"Oh, hey," Chrisssy said.

"Those are endearing," Ava said, meaning Chrisssy's flannel pajamas, sky blue with puffy white clouds. But where were the bunny slippers?

Ava came on in. She turned on a table lamp on one of the crème-colored end tables.

"What's up?" Chrisssy said.

"You can do computer stuff, right?"

Chrisssy nodded. "I guess," she said.

"I need you to find an address for a guy, the guy I usually use to find an address."

"OK?" Chrisssy said.

"Ten dollar," Ava said, imitating Edward Chang's sketchy accent.

"What?"

"Come on, wake up, honey," Ava said. "If you want to be a PI, don't go to bed so much. To *sleep*, anyway. Edward Chang. Local. He might be Chinese, but I've always had my doubts. There's a good chance he lives over a Chinese restaurant. In Chinatown. With his mother."

Chrisssy sat at the mirrored desk and fired up her computer. A large screen on the wall in front of her came to life. Chrisssy yawned and started tapping on the keys as the keyboard lit up under her fingertips.

Ava started, "He sent me to a house up in the hills where 'Darris Lanes' was supposed to live. In short, he sent me—on purpose?—to the wrong guy's house. What I asked for was fairly simple: the address of a 'DL' with an old Bentley. And he sends me to Dallas Raines's house. Do you know who Dallas Raines is?"

"It's a *who?*" Chrisssy said, still typing. "It sounds like it would be a *what*. It rains a lot in Dallas, in Texas generally."

Ava was feeling around on the face of a small TV on a credenza in the dining room area. "How do you turn this on? It's like a hundred years old, right?"

"The remote," Chrisssy said. "Buttons. It's not *that* old."

Ava found the control stick on the divan. She pointed it at the TV and clicked it on and started scrolling through the channel index. Chrisssy was already writing on a pad of paper with a pen, a pen that had a plastic daisy on the end where the eraser should have been.

"There!" Ava said. On the little TV, Dallas Raines stood in front of map of SoCal. "Do you think he broadcasts from his house? All night? He'd have to. He's always on."

"There isn't ever any weather here," Chrisssy said. "Haven't you noticed?"

"He said it could rain tomorrow. Told me that personally."

"*Could.* Like a one-percent chance."

"Still and all…"

Chrisssy handed Ava the paper. "It's not Chinatown," she said.

"Forget it," Ava said. She still had her eyes on Dr. Raines. "Watch this," Ava said. "This is how he always ends it."

"Look up!" Dallas Raines said and smiled that smile.

"How *old* is he?" Chrisssy said.

Ava turned away from the TV on the credenza, dug into her pocket, and pulled out her stack of mad money. She fanned off two hundred-dollar bills, which she put on the glass console table. Chrissy looked as if she was going to cry.

She walked toward the door. "I got another job for you," Ava said. "For in the morning. Find Beck or Birmingham or whatever his name is. Follow him around. You have to do this right because he knows you. Do you know how to do that, tail somebody without them spotting you?"

"With a partner, right?"

"You don't *have* a partner," Ava said. "Just be cautious, tricky, stealthy." She made a diving motion with her hand. "*Under*cover." She made the opposite motion. "Not *over*cover."

Chrisssy nodded.

"Five hundy a day plus expenses. Tail him. Keep your distance. Call me if he goes anywhere or does anything that makes you say, 'You know what? I should probably call Ava.'"

Chrisssy nodded bigger. She waited until Ava'd closed the door before she pumped her fist.

Chapter Twenty-Five

Edward Chang lived in a modest Costco tract home out in the IE, The Inland Empire, Riverside. By the time Ava got out there, it was almost 3:00 a.m. and all the fun had leaked out of the idea that she was going to kick his ass for sending her off after the wrong DL. She parked across the street and turned off her lights. The drapes were drawn but there were lights on in the house, including the front bedroom on one end. Shadows moved across the drapes now and then. From what she could make out, Chang was sitting in front of a computer and a bunch of monitors—big surprise—and someone else was coming in and out of the room. His mom? Worse, a wife? Ava seriously thought about just driving away and letting it go. But she didn't. She never just let things go. She called him up on the comm.

When he came on screen, he looked worried.

"I'm out front," Ava said.

He looked more worried.

"It's all right," she said. "Come on out."

Nobody had grass anymore, not real grass, at least nobody in the middle-class Inland Empire. Gravel, baby. All the front yards in the ten-mile-square housing tract were white gravel. Edward Chang's "lawn" also sported a peeling white birdbath—dry as a bone—with a chubby angel baby sitting cross-legged on the rim. Edward Chang came out the front door, saw the Hudson, and crunched across the gravel to it. He was wearing Converse All-Stars and cargo shorts and a black T-shirt that said in white letters, *What's Your Story?*

Ava was out of the car, getting another look at her creased back bumper.

"I know what you are going to say," Chang said. Now he had *no* accent. He sounded like a reporter on TV, a Nobody from Nowhere.

"I *knew* you didn't live in Chinatown," Ava said.

"I never said I did." He came right out to the last foot of his yard. He had his hands in his pockets. He had a round face with the expected straight black hair. Ava was thinking he looked more Korean than Chinese, but she was a White; Whites made the same mistakes about non-Whites, over and over.

"Yes, I believe you did," Ava said. "But you were drunk."

"I don't drink. I don't drink and I don't get high. Except gaming."

Ava leaned against the rear fender. "OK, so who is DL?" she said.

"Who or… what?" The pause was most melodramatic.

"Don't get cute. It's too late, in more ways than one."

Edward Chang looked up and down the row of houses, as if someone might be watching. None of the other houses even had lights on.

"David Lynch."

"David Lynch?"

"The director," Ava said.

"Yes. And so much more," Chang said. "A remarkable man, even to those of us who might be seen by some as his declarated enemies."

"You mean *declared*."

"If you prefer."

That was the most words Chang had ever said to her. For now, Ava put a pin in the "enemies" thing and said, "He has a silver Bentley? Right?"

"Silver, unconverted, gas-burning, twelve-cylinder. Nineteen sixty four-door S-two Saloon. He bought it when *Twin Peaks* was a hit."

"And then he bought—"

Chang cut her off, nodding. "That's right," he said. "Ding ding ding, ladies and gentlemen, we have a winner. In twenty eighteen. He bought it from the State of California when *Be.Here.Now.* crossed the five-hundred-million-dollar mark in remunerated downloads." This new Edward Chang was so proud of everything he knew that the average person didn't know, or at least hadn't looked up online. He was cocky, a whole other person. Ava wanted to smack him.

"I heard of it," Ava said. "A video game."

"Think what you will, but *Be.Here.Now* wasn't a video game."

"So what does DL stand for? Besides 'David Lynch'? What's the *what?*"

A solitary car, a Fed, was coming toward them from the far end of the street. At twenty miles an hour, with one headlight burned out. Somebody on the night shift, or the Dawn Patrol. Chang waited until it was past them and then waited until it reached the next corner in the development before he gave her the answer.

"Dark Lighthouse," he said.

◆ ◆ ◆

AVA WAS BACK TO feeling lonely. That wore off fast.

She stopped at the all-night Charge-'Em-Up on La Brea, then headed north. It only took an hour to break free of LA traffic. For most of the hour, she had the pirate radio guy for company. She'd decided she was his only listener. He was talking about the Dust Bowl and then the New Dust Bowl. He'd played a song she'd never heard, a nasally folk singer–type who sang, *"You don't need a weatherman to know which way the wind blows..."*

How did he know?

The Hudson was running smooth, in spite of its dinged bumper and jammed door and hurt pride. It was as if it were glad to get out of town, open up, burn up some atmospheres. About Encino, the hot-stripped roadway began. The Hud slipped to the inside lane, dropped its skid-drag, got a good connection, and said, *"Mmmm...thank you."* The electrified highway was one of the few new things in the new world that worked as promised. For now. It was another rushed government project. A couple of years after the twenty-two baby nukes up and down the coastline went online, the overwhelmed governor decided to try to revive the motor-tourist business. The open highways connecting cities and towns were *too* open, empty. No one was going to hit the road in a dinky Federal. Feds had a top speed of thirty-five before they started shaking like a palsied old person and their open road range was measured in minutes. A few holdout land cruisers were still out there rocking and rolling—the usual suspects, Cadillacs and Lincolns and Hyundai Big-9s—but who could pay for the gas now that it was coming from Mexico? The open-road gas stations all became *Nuevo Mundo* stations and—before long—most of them were closed *Nuevo Mundo* stations.

The answer—in California at least—was to power up the highways. A machine that moved at two miles an hour dug a flat groove into the middle of each lane and laid down a six-inch-wide copper strip. Older autos were converted and sleek new electric models called OpenRoaders were engineered. Essentially, open-highway cars were slot-cars, just like the kids' toy from the last century. A skid dropped down from the undercarriage and touched the hot-strip and away they went. They could go nonstop until you got to wherever you were going or you needed a pit-stop. When that time came, you disengaged, the onboard batteries took over, and you steered or were steered over to the outside lane, where the slow locals were. The juice was free. The State made its money from the reprieved motels and roadside restaurants and tourist attractions. Not that California wasn't still bankrupt.

Ava stopped in Summerland just south of Santa Barbara for an egg-and-chorizo burrito. She ate it in a beach park, sitting in the dark on a picnic table next to the kids' playground, looking out at the water and the stars that curved down to touch it. A string of exhausted offshore oil rigs were in the foreground, close in, still fully lit to keep the sailors from running into them, looking like the lowest stars.

She remembered a night with her parents in the car, in Pasadena, coming back from something or other at the Flintridge Country Club, which her mother had made her father join. They were arguing, back and forth, taking all the easy shots at each other. Her mother had said something like, "You're such a grump. You always act like you'd rather be anywhere than with me and my friends."

And her father had said, "You know where I'd like to be about half the time? I'd like to be working on a goddamn oil platform out there off Summerland! Where there are no women!"

Ava had been in the backseat, looking out the window, wearing white gloves. She'd thought it was funny. Now, sitting at the picnic table, it was a story that seemed to be trying to make some other point; she wasn't sure just what. Whatever it was, it wasn't funny. *"I wish they all could be California girls..."* her father's song, came into her head again as the high-tide black waves collapsed in front of her with a sound like hesitant applause. She hauled back and threw the last third of the burrito into the surf—hoping there was still something out there to eat it—and a minute later she and the Hudson were back in the groove, headed north.

When the day broke, Ava was a hundred miles above Santa Barbara, rolling north along the coast on the mostly empty California 1, the primer-gray Pacific off to her left, the brown hills on her right. The car windows were down. The air was funky in that seashore way. The new light angled in through the open passenger-side window. There were no trees on the hills to break the beam of the sun so it didn't flash. The steadiness of it appealed to her. She literally warmed up to it. The whole side of her face felt as if it were glowing. Or as if she was blushing, something she hadn't done in who knew how long. She looked over. The brown hills all wore tiaras now.

"Up and at 'em," she said and went faster.

She came through the little tourist town of Cambria at ten in the morning, only slowing down enough to keep from getting a ticket from the cop who was always lying in wait down the side street by the bank. (It had once been a bank, now it was another gallery selling *Plein Air* landscapes and polished redwood burls.) A new wine shop sat next to an old wine shop next to the gallery. She could have stayed on the highway and bypassed the town altogether, but she wanted to see if all of her favorite places were still there. She had spent more than a few weekends and weeks in Cambria, with friends and alone, when she just had to get out of LA—something everyone who lived in Los Angeles understood.

Business was good, the town full of electro-travelers. The cop had pulled over a white El Dorado convertible, the driver and the officer laughing as he wrote the ticket. They both waved at Ava as she came around them. She almost stopped for a fancy coffee but instead kept on all the way through the town; she then crossed over the main highway to the two-laner that went along Moonstone Beach, with its motels lined up shoulder to shoulder facing the sparkling water. Her favorite spot to hole up, The Little Sur Inn, was still there and apparently prospering: the lot was full and a no-tech No Vacancy placard hung on hooks off the bottom of the wooden signboard.

Moonstone Drive gently returned her to Highway One, the way north.

"Auto-drive?" the Hudson Man said.

"No, I got it," Ava said, her mood darkening a bit now.

Chapter Twenty-Six

Below Hearst Castle out on a point on the ocean was a dramatic stand of three-hundred-foot-tall eucalyptuses, as big as they get. The trees leaned toward the mansion above—toward *America*, if you thought about it—pushed that way by a hundred years of prevailing wind that came all the way from…somewhere. Below the trees was a curving sandy beach and a surf line that broke right, toward a long wooden pier. An offshore breeze stood the waves up, easy six- and seven-footers, green and clear.

Cali had one all to herself. She had the beach all to herself. She was on a longboard, a red-striped Dewey Weber, wearing a white bikini that tied on the sides. She was tan in a way she hadn't been just a few days ago, the kind of tan a person has to *relax* into. She wasn't smiling, but she looked gentled, in the moment, in the here and now. Happy? Possibly. Why not? Was happiness really just a choice? She certainly looked far away from her troubles with Beck. Or whomever. She eased down the face of the wave and gracefully turned—these classic old boards didn't pivot—into a section that threatened to collapse but never did. She kicked out, then paddled out to catch another. When she reached the landscape of gentle swells beyond the shorebreak, she glided to a stop and sat up, still facing out to sea. A leopard shark circled her, close enough for her to see the spots. She looked over the side of the board. She could see her toes, her pink-painted toenails. She wiggled them and giggled. It seemed to her that she could see all the way to the bottom, what looked like a mile down. A pelican floated over. She looked up at it, tracked it, slowing it down and changing its color from gray to turquoise. To better match the water and sky. There was so much gray in the world. She made it pink and let it fly on.

"This is perfect," Cali said. She turned her head. She could hear the wind breathing in the trees on the point. "This is perfect. I'm perfect." She said it again, *"I'm* perfect."

A swell lifted her and she saw the woman on the beach in a purple dress.

"Margo!" Cali said, delighted. "Margo Channing..." The woman in the purple dress was looking out to sea, with a hand over her eyes for a visor, but Cali didn't know if she could see her.

Cali waved. The woman took a step closer.

◆ ◆ ◆

AVA HAD STEERED OFF the highway to an oceanfront observation point shy of the mansion. She was guessing there'd be a gatehouse ahead, so she'd stopped well before the road that led down to the point. She had the observation pull-off all to herself. The highway coming up from Cambria had been empty, too. Maybe the tourists were all still asleep in their borrowed beds back down the way on Moonstone Beach. No hurry. It was only a two-hour drive to Big Sur, the next wonderful place on the way north. Ava parked the car, started down to the beach, then realized she could lose the shoes, went back, steadied herself against the doorframe, unbuckled the buckles, and threw her red pumps into the front seat.

"Back so soon?" the Hudson said.

"Go to sleep," Ava said.

She walked along the beach toward the pier and the point beyond. She was coming in on the down low. Ahead, the point with the landmark stand of eucalyptuses. It was a good half mile beyond the long wooden pier. Everything up here was outsized, a landscape for giants. There wasn't a soul in sight yet but no signage, nothing that marked the beach as out-of-bounds to outsiders. And so far, no electrified fences or robo-dogs. Or even cameras, unless they were implanted in the eyeball of the screeching gull overhead, holding in the same spot, riding the wind.

Ava stopped cold. Ahead were dark bulbous shapes on the sand. Blobs, furry blobs. It looked as if someone had cleaned out the closet of an old society maven and thrown around the mink coats in a fit. Then one of the fur coats flippered some sand onto its back to warm up. Its neighbor lifted its head and barked a rebuke. At least it sounded like a rebuke to Ava. She wasn't much of a Nature Girl, though she sometimes liked to pretend otherwise with a Nature Boy. She gave the sea lions a wide berth and walked on. The warm sand felt good to her, too, the sun and the sand. The sky was cloudless. It was a beautiful day. Unassailable. She could see why someone would want to escape to this, or at least give it a try.

William Randolph Hearst had officially named the estate "Le Cuesta Encantada"—The Enchanted Hill—but he himself just called it The Ranch. Everyone else called it San Simeon. David Lynch, when he bought it from the State in 2020, named it—or renamed it—Xanadu. The grand house with its fifty-six bedrooms and nineteen sitting rooms had proved too grand—not even Lynch's ego could fill it—so after six months he let the tours and tourists back in and moved himself and his friends down to more modest quarters in a renovated building below on the point, what once had been Hearst's private train station, at the end of a spur line that came up from LA.

A few hundred yards more and Lynch's train station house was visible through a broad grove of orange trees. The trees had uniform dark green leaves and were thick with fruit. The grove looked so perfect Ava wondered if it was all fake, a good bet. The drought that had tried to kill off the Central Valley was still lingering hereabouts. It had all but wiped out the vineyards below Cambria. The train station house was a hundred yards up from the beach. No one was around it, though it didn't looked deserted. It was big. It would have been called a mansion, too, if it wasn't just down the hill from Xanadu. It had a pleasing, old-timey shape to it. No wonder, it was a copy of Union Station: arched entryway, high round windows, red Saltillo tile everywhere, and a central clock tower—though the hands were missing, which no doubt was intentional.

"Margo! It's been forever! How are you?" Cali said to Ava, coming in, dragging the surfboard by its nose through the shallows.

"I'm good," Ava said, with only a little bit of questioning in her voice, standing a few feet up from the reach of the sliding suds. "Are you OK?"

Cali gave her a curious look. "Of course," she said. "This is where I belong. Remember when we used to talk all night about finding the place where you belong? Your proper place in the world? You're so pretty. I had forgotten how pretty you were."

All right, Ava thought, she's high. Though she was still in the shallows, Cali turned loose of the board, let it drop, and walked away from it. It started to drift out.

"You'd better get that," Ava said.

Cali turned and looked at the drifting surfboard. "No, it's all right," she said. "It's part of the program." She threw out her arms and came at Ava and hugged her tightly, just as she had hugged her in Ava's living room, out of the blue. "Margo, Margo, Margo..." she said.

"We have to talk," Ava said, still in the embrace.

"Of course we do," Cali said, releasing Ava, smiling a radiant smile. "Catch up." She threaded her arm through Ava's and walked her toward the house. "Come meet my friends," she said. "You're barefoot. That is so perfect."

And so they walked arm in arm through the perfect orange grove. It *was* bogus. Not a single piece of fruit was on the ground, not even any fallen leaves. Ahead, the house waited for them. Under the tallest of the archways, the dark wooden front doors stood open. The same doors had been closed a minute ago, when Ava had first seen the house.

Cali leaned over and kissed Ava on the cheek as they went in.

"Is...DL here?" Ava said.

"Do you know about DL?" Cali said. "That is so cool."

The cavernous great room was appointed with Deco furniture and accessories, stained glass lampshades on Mission end tables next to club chairs and rolled-arm sofas, rugs over the red tile. Warm light, softened by proximity to the ocean, angled in from one of the high round windows. It still felt like a waiting room in a train station on Sunday morning. And everyone had already boarded. Perhaps that was the intention.

Around the room on the Navajo white walls were outsize posters: *Eraserhead. The Elephant Man. Blue Velvet. Wild at Heart. Twin Peaks. Mulholland Drive.* And hung up over the mantle and the mouth of the fireplace was the artwork for *Be.Here.Now.* Behind the three-word imperative was an image of David Lynch, staring right at you, more than a little Big Brotherish.

"So what's he like? David," Ava said. "Is he here?"

Cali wasn't hearing anything Ava said. She too was looking around at the high-ceilinged room and all it held, as if she had never seen it before either.

At the other end of the great room was a large painting, the centerpiece of the room, even more than the *Be.Here.Now.* art. Ava gave up on getting anything out of Cali right now that made any sense and walked toward it.

It was the lighthouse from the print in Cali's apartment in the Marina, the red lighthouse on the rocky point in daylight with the ragged California coastline behind it—the spikes of Big Sur in the distance—all of it under a cloudless blue sky. And with the cones of black light—antilight?—shining from the lens.

The brass plaque on the bottom rail of the frame read: *Dark Lighthouse.*

Then Cali was standing at Ava's side again, looking up at the painting, too. "That's David's company. Do you ever see Esther or Doreen?" Cali said. Before Ava could respond—or even process the question—Cali looked around and said, "Where *is* everybody? Sleepyheads. You have to meet all the girls. We're all in this together. We're the California Girls!"

Ava wished she had some duct tape so she could wrap up Cali, throw her over her shoulder and get her the hell out of there. But then a girl in another white bikini walked in from somewhere, yawning and stretching fetchingly and rubbing her eyes.

"Hey," the new girl said, from across the huge room.

"Syndy, this is my friend Margo," Cali said, turning, indicating Ava. "Margo was the first person I met when I went to New York for a year when I was seventeen and trying to be a model. We had this apartment, oh my gosh, that was so small you had to go outside to change your mind."

The new girl held out her hand to shake.

"Ava," Ava said.

"Hi, Ava," Syndy said. "I love that name. How do you spell it?"

"A—V—A?"

"I love names that have the same letter at the beginning and the end. Names like…" But she couldn't think of another one in the moment.

"Palindromes."

"What?"

"Like…*wow*," Ava said.

"Really…" Syndy said, nodding, agreeing.

"Mom. Dad. Eve. Eye. Gag. Bob. Pop. Boob."

"Huh?"

Cali watched Ava and Syndy talking. What they were saying didn't matter. Not really. *This is a subplot,* Cali was thinking. *No, an aside.* She wondered how it could be that Margo hadn't changed at all since New York. Then she remembered the thing that was crucial always to remember: *I am in control of this.* She thought, *I created Margo. I picked the purple dress because that was what I remembered.* Cali looked in the direction of the arched hallway at one end of the great room, the hallway that led to the bedrooms. *Where was everyone?* When she looked— was it *because* she looked?—two more California girls came out, rubbing the sleep out of their eyes. All of the girls were younger than Cali. Cali smiled at the sight of her friends. But where was David?

"There are my girls," David Lynch said, coming in from another room.

Cali ran toward him. All the girls encircled him, pushing in to give him some sugar.

Except, of course, Ava.

Lynch had noticed her but didn't seem suspicious at seeing her there, a stranger, an outsider. He looked at her, then looked away. He acted like what he was: the master of the house. The way the multiple Calis were acting, dancing around him, Ava wondered how long he'd been away. Then she remembered that they were all just girls and were easily excited.

David Lynch. Here was another Dallas Raines, a man of a somewhat advanced age who didn't look it. *Eraserhead*—Lynch's first film—had come out in…what? The late 1970s? When the director was just out of film school? Ava was never much on math—her father's profession aside—so she gave up halfway through trying to figure out how old Lynch was. Eighty? He looked fifty, with the same angular face he'd always had, a face topped off by a shock of tall hair you couldn't stop looking at. The hair was white now, which made the whole effect even more striking.

"Who wants some dessert?" Lynch said loudly, though it wasn't noon yet and no one had eaten. He was speaking figuratively…

Because then Vivid walked in. There was a good deal of squealing. Vivid had waited in the wings in the dining room to make her entrance. She was a blonde again. Her lipstick was properly smeared. A tribute to herself? She wore a little black dress and—could it be?—the gold open-toed heels the Shoemaker had made. Behind Vivid was a moderately handsome and very well-groomed man in a sports coat and khakis who looked familiar to Ava. John Tern! The politician on the poster in Cali's apartment. Mr. Empathy! Behind Tern was the gunsel who drove the Bentley. The gunsel was carrying a bunch of luggage, struggling with it so much he apparently didn't notice Ava standing across the room.

Vivid went directly to Cali and kissed her on the mouth; then Vivid waved at Ava as if they were best friends, too. Cali watched Vivid as if she were wondering which part of this was real.

"Same here," Ava said, reading Cali's mind.

◆ ◆ ◆

THE CALIFORNIA GIRLS—THERE WERE five of them, including Cali—changed into identical butterfly dresses. They were all still barefoot and as cute as five buttons. Ava wondered whose idea the costume change was. Theirs? A cue from Lynch? An order from T-Bone, the gunsel? Mental telepathy? They were all sitting on the floor with their tanned legs drawn up underneath them, in a circle around Tern, who seemed to be delighting them with a story that appeared to have a lot of moving parts, requiring gestures and changes of voice.

Vivid had slipped away for a nap. Followed by Lynch.

Ava was still standing apart from the others, under the painting of the weird lighthouse. The gunsel brought her another margarita, as nice as could be. She now knew from the snatch in her parking garage that his name was T-Bone, not that Cali was the best authority on people's names.

"Why, thank you…T-Bone," she said, handing him her empty glass.

"No salt," he said. He shrugged his trademark shrug.

"So are you like…his butler?"

"No!" he said. But then he got over his indignation. "The cook went back to Mexico. Retired. Rich. We're short-handed."

"Did you drive the Bentley up here?"

"It's out back, on a flatcar. On the train."

"He has a train? I didn't hear a train."

"Electric," T-Bone said.

"So who was the big guy in my garage with the big gun?"

He looked surprised that she was asking. "Ask your what-you-call-it…client."

"Beck? I don't buy it. Why would Beck hire him? For what?"

"To back you up, I guess," T-Bone said. "Or do what you couldn't do. Or wouldn't do. Direct action. Muscle. He's from out of town. Way out of town. We've been watching him. Or maybe he was watching us."

"He was pretty scary, all right," Ava said. "I guess that was the idea. By the way, Action-Man is an idiot."

"Yeah," the other said.

They both looked over as Lynch came down the hallway from the living quarters into the great room again. He'd apparently changed into a fresh outfit. It was hard to tell because he always wore the same thing: a black suit with a white shirt open at the neck, no tie. Black-and-white, like an old movie. He stood over the circle of girls and Tern, appearing to enjoy Tern's charisma.

"So, was he helping Vivid with her *nap*?" Ava said.

"He's not going to let you take her," the gunsel said. "I know him."

"I just want to talk to her. Once the drugs wear off."

"She's not high. DL is against drugs. He won't allow them." With that he walked off toward the kitchen with her empty glass. "I'm making tacos," he said. Or at least that's what Ava thought she heard him say.

She dove into her fresh drink. She remembered that she'd read somewhere that David Lynch had his own brand of tequila. In Lynch's case, that didn't mean that he'd bought a south-of-the-border distillery. It meant he cooked off his own split agave hearts, extracted the juice, fermented it, distilled it, aged it for seven years, and then bottled the end product. And he'd designed the label. He did, however, let Texas field hands tend to the spiky agave plants, which took seven years to grow to maturity. Which meant, Ava guessed—taking another sip—that the master of the house had unnatural patience. When Lynch looked over at her, Ava raised her glass. In recognition of his patience, if nothing else.

Cali saw the two of them looking at each other. She blinked, as if trying to change things.

◆ ◆ ◆

"Unfulfilled desire is life's bedrock experience," David Lynch said, now standing behind Ava. She almost jumped out of her skin. She was at a window with a third drink, looking up the brown hill at Xanadu. Casa Oxymoron.

She turned. Lynch was shoeless, wearing white socks. "You snuck up on me," she said.

"That's what the Buddists say," he said.

"*You snuck up on me?*"

"They call it *dukkha*. Unfulfilled desire, also translated: *unsatisfactoriness.*"

"I hear *that*," Ava said. She started to take another sip of her margarita, thought better of it, put it down on a table. Two or three days from now she'd have to drive again. Or at least find her car.

"Wouldn't you like to join us?" Lynch said.

"How do you mean that? Amble over there with the other gals or...drink the Kool-Aid?"

It was clear that Lynch didn't feel like arguing with Ava. Or proselytizing. And it was easy to see that he hardly ever did anything he didn't feel like doing. "She wants to be here," he said. "She needs to be here."

"You mean Cali?"

"Do you know that she chose that name herself? Cali SoBrite."

"You're kidding."

"Be on your way," he said, without anger, turning. He turned back and pointed at her. "Be on *your* way."

The last thing Ava saw on her way out—on *her* way out—was the gang, now including Vivid again in a black wig on the floor in a circle in the great room, kneeling around Lynch who seemed to be explaining something intently. The way Lynch talked to them—pointing at each of them in turn as he recited his lines—made the scene seem ceremonial. And when he bent over and touched each of them on the ear and they closed their eyes, nodding, it made Ava's skin crawl.

Chapter Twenty-Seven

"Earwig," Edward Chang said.

"Eww…" Ava said. She was driving back down from Xanadu toward Cambria, had the Hudson on auto-drive because she was so flummoxed. And still half drunk, though the DL tequila was dissipating. "You mean that thing that crawls in your ear while you're sleeping and burrows in and eats your brain?"

"*They* don't call it that, they just call it… I don't even remember. The Daisy or The Dongle or The Dreambug. They like words that start with D or L. Everybody else calls it an earwig. You stick it in your ear and it digs in and goes into your bloodstream."

"Literally?"

"Yes."

"Whatever happened to *Myst?* Or *SimCity?*"

"What?"

"Never mind."

"It loads and you're off and running. Only most people just sit in a chair and *think* they're running."

"What did you call it?"

"Isolational Imaginable Immersion. *I I I.* The basic node-hub has been around ten years but for *Be.Here.Now.*, the techs at Dark Lighthouse and the master himself kicked its ass and dunked the user all the way. DL personally came up with the robo-earwig to administer it. There's the genius."

"Maybe. How long does it last?"

"That's where the Stackers come in—outside hackers. We found a way to modify it. The stock earwig parks at the base of the brain and goes to work.

But then, at the appointed hour—Game Over—it kills itself, breaks apart, flushes out of your system. It's gone in three hours and thirty-three minutes."

"The Mark of the Beast divided by two," Ava said. "Coincidence?"

"What?"

"Got it, Changster. It's gone in three thirty-three. Now I believe you were about to toot your own horn."

"Some people—we Stackers are scattered across the globe in six different countries, including the Dominican Republic—are dedicated to freeing up globally any and all factory-encrypted code that—"

"I'm almost to where I'm going, Chang. Leave out the agitprop."

"We hacked into the earwig, modified the base design. We give it away free. Or for a small donation." He paused. Then he looked so so smug as he said, "Ours lasts up to ten days."

"You sit in a chair for ten days?"

"You can still do your business, if you know what I mean, but mostly, yeah, you sit there for ten days and when you come back you're really hungry."

"So it's like reading a really good, really long book."

"I wouldn't know," Chang said.

"What does it feel like?"

"Whatever you want to feel, wherever you want to go, *whenever*, with whoever you want along for the ride. Or whomever you want as your enemy. But that was yesterday's game. It's not a first-person shooter. It can be as complicated as you want to make it. You're in control. Sorta."

"So it's exactly the *opposite* of being here now."

"I guess, yeah," Edward Chang said. "That's sorta genius too, when you think about it."

Ava said goodbye just as Chang began to say something. Maybe, "Be careful."

She cruised along for a minute then said out loud, "I think it's fair to say I tried." She'd done everything she could, right? What now? She'd head for home, find out what Chrisssy had learned tailing Beck, find him, tell Beck the truth— "*She's gone, Babycakes, she doesn't want you, she has her earwig…*"—and then she would get on about her business.

"That's exactly what I'm going to do," Ava said. She hit the phone button.

Penny appeared on the screen. "Hey, stranger," she said.

"Hey."

"Where have you been?" Penny said.

"On The Magical Mystery Tour. How many times has Beck called?" She was remembering what the gunsel had said about Beck hiring the big man in the big brown suit.

"Zero. Goose egg. *Cero. Nada. Null.*"

"You're kidding."

"*Nein.*"

"He called nine times?"

"No, he didn't call once. *Nein* is German for no."

Ava thought a minute. Now Beck *not* calling annoyed her for some reason.

"I think he's moved on, Ava," Penny said. "I'm wondering if you should, too."

Ava rang off, wondering if she should get a new answering service.

After another mile or two, she put on her blinker and the Hudson took the turnoff for Moonstone Beach. The traffic was lighter than when she had blown through that morning. Now it was midafternoon. She looked over as they rolled past the first of the inns and motels on the strip.

"Slow down," she said to the car. "Where's the fire?"

The Hudson obeyed and slowed to a crawl, even let a car in. *The Fog-Catcher, Cambria Pines Lodge, The Fireside Inn, The Sea Otter.* Ava smiled at the names. She looked over at the water, how it broke over the rocks, swallowed them up. The tide was high. The surfers were out, surfing as if the rocks weren't there. An open, beach-facing parking spot presented itself. Ava took it as a sign.

"Park it," she said.

The Hudson pulled in and shut itself down, and Ava got out. She took in the scenery for a second, then crawled up onto the hood and sat with her back against the windshield, like she used to do with her dad when they would sneak out and go to the last drive-in movie in Los Angeles, in Burbank, to spite her mother. Maybe the sun would burn out the last of the tequila. Beck could wait.

It was like a beach party movie. What caught Ava's eye was a teenage boy, young—not more than twelve or thirteen—young enough that he still liked to surf with his dad. They were wearing wetsuits though real winter was a month or more away. Matching red wetsuits. The father sat on his board out beyond the break, rising and falling, watching his son, protective but in a way the boy wouldn't notice. The father was on a longboard. The son was on a shortboard, a board shorter than he was tall. The kid danced all over his wave before coming off the top upside down and still spinning. The father just shook his head, laughing. It was possible that the father understood that the chances were his life would never be better than it was right then, but probably not. Ava watched the father and son, wishing she was either one of them. Or at least to be them right now, here and now. She'd even take being the mom, who sat on the beach with her knees drawn up to her, her arms around them, watching the show, apparently happy. Ava tried to remember if she'd ever seen her mother with a look like that on her face.

She felt a little lost, Ava. Not geographically. Being lost geographically was almost impossible now. If you were *lost* lost these days you could call up a live satellite shot and there you were, Charlie. All you had to do was zoom out until you saw something you recognized and off you went. (It cost the lost person a hundred bucks, to keep people from doing it for kicks or mooning the sat-cam.) Ava wasn't *lost* lost. She knew exactly where she was on a map. Not to put too fine a point on it, but she was lost in her own narrative, in the road trip of her life. Something about the case—something about Beck and Cali—had bumped her gyro. She'd gotten lonelier day by day since the night she'd walked down the hallway in her office and seen Beck sitting there in the half dark.

She thought of the last time she'd been here—Cambria—the last time she'd stayed at the Little Sur Inn. It was on the fifth anniversary of the week her brother died. She'd come up alone. The two of them were six years apart. He was the baby. Jacob. Jacob Weiss. He used the family's real name. He and Ava fought a lot, but mostly as a way to bond against the tyranny of their parents, though they didn't know it then. (They also didn't know their parents weren't all that tyrannical, compared to what was out there in the world.) Jacob wasn't like anyone else in the family. When there's a boy and a girl, a son and a daughter, it's common to say one takes after the father and the other takes after the mother, but Jacob had always seemed as if he'd come from some whole other family, Ava thought. Or was it that that he was just himself, a mystery that might someday be solved? It turned out not to be so.

She looked across the street at the inn, thought about checking in. The *No Vacancy* sign wasn't hanging off the hooks anymore. She could spend the night, eat a lobster, drink a bottle of wine all by herself, get up in the morning, and maybe make another stab at getting Cali out of Little Xanadu. About now she was wishing she'd stepped over to the circle of girls and taken Cali by the arm and led her away. But she hadn't done that. She'd bailed. She'd seen enough. Cali wasn't her problem. Beck was.

And, besides, everyone kept saying Vivid was getting ready to sing. There wasn't any reason to think that would cheer her up.

Ava didn't check into The Little Sur Inn, didn't eat a lobster all by herself in the restaurant or drink a bottle of wine staring into a video fireplace in the Mopey Single Lady Suite. She didn't make a plan to go liberate Cali in the morning. She just climbed off the hood and got behind the wheel of the Hudson, backed out of there, crossed over the main highway again, and drove into Cambria—not intending to stop—hoping she could get south to San Luis Obispo before dark. That was the target she was aiming for: to get to SLO at sundown and home before midnight. Nonstop. That was the plan. It was always good to have a plan.

But then, surprising herself, Ava pulled into a charger station in the middle of Cambria to top off. She could have paid outside, but she went in. Truth be told, she stopped at the station because was hoping for some last bit of human contact before she headed back to LA, even if it was just the Cambria High School sophomore running the register. She bought a bottle of water and a premade sandwich. Egg salad. The kid said she'd made a good choice. No one had said anything even remotely like that to her lately.

Actually, she wasn't hungry. She threw the sandwich onto the seat as she got in, cracked the seal on the water, and took a slug.

"Ready?" the car said.

"Ask me something easy," she said. She tapped the shifter to put it in Go.

"Excuse me," a voice said. A man's voice. A gentle voice, already apologetic.

And there was the face to match. A man with a sunburned face looked in the passenger-side window, careful not to lean in too far, not wanting to seem aggressive or dangerous. He was wearing a sun-bleached denim shirt, bleached almost white.

He extended his hand to shake. The apologetic tone continued as he said his name. "Gene Lindgren."

"I can't help you," Ava said, by rote. "I don't have any change. I'm sorry."

He withdrew his hand. "I wasn't asking for change. Well, not that kind." He came within fifty miles or so of a grin. "Over there, that's my family, my wife and daughter, Betts and Bridget," he said, pointing toward the outside of the station's restroom where a woman kneeled, cleaning a little girl's face with a wet paper towel. The wife didn't look up.

They were Whites. In the moment, that seemed to matter. Ava opened the glove compartment for her purse.

The man held up his hand to stop her. "I told you. We're not asking for money," he said. "We were just hoping for a ride. Out of here. Anywhere south, as far as you are going. I hate to ask but we're stuck here."

The daughter rode up front, the husband and wife in the back. The Hudson was a two-door; Ava had to get out and let them in because of the jammed passenger-side door. The wife told Ava their names again and said they were from Missouri.

"Originally," the little girl added. She wasn't more than eight or nine and wore a cotton dress that looked like her grandmother could have made it.

"Bridget is a pretty name," Ava said.

"Thank you," the little girl said, straightening her dress.

"She's named after my best friend in college," the mother, Betts, said.

Gene Lindgren turned to look out the back window, as if he was glad to be seeing Cambria shrinking away behind him. He turned forward again. "My great-grandfather had a Hudson," he said. "Hornet."

Ava steered onto Highway One south. The road was empty. The hills were treeless through this section, covered in just dry grass. There wasn't any wind. A barbed-wire fence ran alongside them. The sun was dropping. The light was the color bad painters can never get right. The Hudson found its groove and Ava took her hands off the wheel.

The little girl had her hands folded in her lap. "How old are you, Sweetie?" Ava asked.

"Eight," the girl said. "I'll be in third grade, when I can go back to school."

"We came out to work in the vineyards," the man said from the backseat. "Or tried. They're all dried up. Someone lied to us, took most of our money."

"So what are you going to do in LA?" Ava said. "Do you have family there?"

"We hope to get to Mexico," the man said. "Work."

"My grandma died," the daughter said, as if it was just another fact to report. The little girl couldn't take her eyes off Ava. "You're so beautiful," she said. "Like a movie star."

Ava reached over and tucked the girl's blonde hair behind her ear. "You're adorable!" she said. "I think you should come live with me in Hollywood. We'll be best friends."

"All right," the girl said, seriously. "I'd like that."

Ava wasn't used to talking to kids. Actually, she wasn't used to thinking before she spoke, wasn't used to being anything other than a smart-ass. She wasn't used to *poor* desperate people, only rich ones. She looked up at the mirror, caught the mother's eye. "I'm so sorry," Ava said.

"It's all right," the woman said. "This hasn't gone the way we meant."

The man looked out the window, tired inside and out. But at least they were moving again.

Another half mile of road passed underneath. "I have a sandwich," Ava said.

Chapter Twenty-Eight

She was just a little girl, seven or eight, White. Nate didn't know much about children, how to tell how old they were. How could he? She was lying on her back in the sand with nothing around her, stripped naked except for a turquoise tee with a sparkly Princess Pam design across it. She was sunburned, as red as if she'd been cooked in a pot. She was more or less whole. None of the real predators of the deep had bit her, but she'd been chewed on by smaller fish or crabs or birds. The wounds opened up the skin to show the seawater-bleached meat underneath. Her brown hair was in ropes, sandy, like any other girl-child on the beach. Fortunately for all of the cops, her eyes were long since closed.

"You have kids?" Nate said to Il Cho.

"No," Cho said. "I just bought a house I can't afford. Maybe next year. I have a niece, my brother's daughter."

"What grade do you think she'd be in?" Nate said, still looking down.

"I don't know. Third or fourth?"

"Do they even still have grades in school anymore?"

"I guess," Cho said.

Nate turned away. He needed something else to look at. Up the way was the Hotel Del Coronado, wooden, white-painted, red-roofed, with bay windows and spires with old-timey lightning rods. It had been built a million years ago yet somehow was still here and still in business, the pride of Coronado. Coronado Island technically wasn't an island—a narrow strand went all the way down to Imperial Beach and Chula Vista—but everyone treated it like an island, the tourists anyway, a place to get away from it all. Ferry boats and water taxis and twenty-passenger helos came across the bay from San Diego. For those who wanted a bridge, down south there was a high span that curved over from the mainland, a suicide bridge second only to the Golden Gate when it came to vertical traffic. Speaking of getting away from it all.

"That place is bizarre," Nate said, eyes on the old hotel. "Did you ever stay there?"

"It's supposed to be haunted," Cho said, turning away from the dead girl, too.

"What isn't?" Nate said.

Hotel guests—including whole families—stood a hundred yards away watching the commotion on the beach, all the helicopters in the air and on the ground. It had all begun at daybreak when the first runner came down the sand and found the scene and the call went in. The San Diego Police had immediately brought in the LA Gang Unit and LA's famous coroner to assist and advise. Nate had a friend who was a San Diego CRO, a woman. In SD, things were ever so slightly more civilized, and so there were several female CROs. LA had one. Nate's CRO friend had called him and two minutes later he was lifting off the roof of his house.

"You have to see this," she'd said.

TV news helos hovered a thousand feet above the traffic from the working cops. Whitey was down the way, talking to a woman reporter who would occasionally look up at the sky, at the camera.

"This is going to be a big story," Cho said. "Whites." He didn't say it with any rancor.

"I guess," Nate said.

He looked back down at the little girl. Her face was puffy from the hours in the water. He wondered if her kin would even recognize her when they were brought in for ID, if any of them were still alive.

One hundred.

Here it was, the hundredth body Nate had stood over. Not that his coworkers were going to stop everything and have some kind of ceremony, give him a commemorative coin like they do in AA. Today there wasn't even going to be a pause in Nate's personal body count. He looked down the beach. Another twelve bodies had washed up overnight. Twelve. And the girl made thirteen. All White. Screeching terns circled in full riot mode, anticipating the feed. He decided he was done with the counting thing.

"Is it now?" Cho said, mostly to himself.

"I was thinking the same thing," Nate said.

They were seeing the faces of the Okies on the roof in the TMZ from the other night. They started walking down the beach toward the beached bodies. Cho pointed ahead. "Mexico. What is it, ten miles? Somebody said the current flows north, they probably went into the water in Mexico if they ended up here. At least they made it back home."

"I guess," Nate said.

He'd set down the Crow on the hotel parking lot. No-Name Rockett stood by it, hands behind his back. Nate waved him over. This was a teachable moment, if Nate could only figure out what the lesson was.

◆ ◆ ◆

THEY ALREADY HAD SOME answers so they called a press conference. The live news coverage started with a panning shot of six dead men and one dead woman dressed like a man. All Latin. Browns. Wherever they had been shot and killed, the six had been dragged onto a dock in Long Beach. The image was meant to convey that the story had started here—Long Beach, the LA harbor—and that it was ending here, too. Or the authorities wanted it to. The close-up of the dead gave way to stock footage of a rusty freighter stacked with containers, most of them with Chinese writing on the side. HÆRVÆRK was written across the ship's stern. The camera held on the word a long moment, as if with time it would start to mean something.

Then came a wide shot of cop brass, a White cop standing at a microphone with a grove of multiracial cop-trees behind him.

"Why aren't *you* up there, Whitey?" Nate said.

Twenty CROs and the gang cops and a couple of higher-ups sat on desks and stood around in the squad room downtown, watching the show. The CROs had allowed their gunners in. They were at the back of the room, Rockett among them. It was a day to remember.

"I'm like Batman," Whitey said. "Nobody knows who I am."

That got a laugh. Nate didn't join in.

"How come they never had a Black Batman?" some wag said. "They had everything else."

Il Cho was trying to watch the press conference. He had a sad, unsettled look on his face.

"They never had a Chinese Batman," another Asian cop said.

"Keanu Reeves," a CRO named Baker said. He was a Genesis CRO, on the job/in the air less than a year.

"He was Hawaiian," the Asian cop said. "Half."

"And he never played Batman," Nate said.

The joke had played itself out so there was a silence. Then a sergeant said, "Can't we all just get along?" The man wasn't known as a comedian, so most of the men and women weren't sure if they were meant to laugh. So they didn't.

"Touché," Whitey said.

The *Thirteen Dead on Coronado!* press conference got boring fast, nobody asking or answering the real questions. The TV director, wherever he was, sensed his audience's boredom and cut away from the cops to the feed from a drone gliding over the still-uncovered bodies, like any other bird of prey. For narration there was only the sound of the wind. The director would probably win an Emmy.

The cops in the squad room had already begun to wander off.

Whitey was alone in the Gang Unit office when Nate came in.

"What are you hearing?" Nate asked, just for fun.

"Nothing," Whitey said. "They'd been loaded into a container somewhere and the container was on deck on the cargo ship and it got loose and went over."

"So when did it crack open?"

"I wasn't there."

"Who worked this end? Who loaded them in Long Beach?"

"I guess those dead gangsters on the dock. I wasn't there. They could have loaded them anywhere, then trucked them in. I wasn't wherever that was either."

One the dead gang members on the dock wore a white *guayabera* shirt and black pointy-toed boots, like the tall cowboy businessman Nate had seen with Whitey at the RV factory in the High Desert, only this one had three or four bullet holes in him around his heart so the shirt wasn't so white anymore. And he wasn't tall.

"Who was the cowboy?" Nate said, his vagueness fully intentional.

"You were watching the TV, Cole. They IDed him. *Something Something Juan Something.* I never heard of the man. May he rest in peace. I'm sure his mama's upset."

"He wasn't in your gang book?"

Whitey tapped his forehead. "This is my book. You trying to get jumped into the unit with us, now that JC is gone?" Whitey said. "We'd love to have you. You could do all the flying. I know Il Cho thinks the world of you."

"Were they Inca?" Nate said. "The people on the dock."

"The Incas don't smuggle people. And they aren't in TJ. I think you're going to find out these gangsters were from Tijuana."

"Where were they headed?"

"Who?"

"The people in the cargo container."

"China?"

"That's a long trip."

"There was Chinese writing all over everything. Supposedly there are jobs waiting there, in China, if you can get there and get in. I sure wouldn't want to do it. Does all this have something to do with you, Cole?"

"I don't see how it could," Nate said, on his way out.

◆ ◆ ◆

NATE HAD BEEN HALF afraid Rockett would turn chatty now that Nate had learned his name, but the kid had been real quiet all shift, since the morning in San Diego. Maybe he had a sister the age of the girl on the beach.

It was ten o'clock, moonless, dark. Or at least as dark as the West Side ever got. Money meant light. (And more water.) Nate looked over the side. They were low-flying over the flatlands of Beverly Hills, businesses and halfway-normal houses and apartment buildings on tree-lined streets with sidewalks and bright streetlights: 90210. It looked peaceful, which meant all the crime was indoors. Or riding around in Bentleys. He flew over Beverly Hills High. Century City was ahead, the Westside business towers, most of them still lit up, all forty floors. The protocol for routine patrol-flying in a 'scraper zone was to elevate and go over the top of the buildings, but Nate stayed at the same altitude, flying between the towers at five hundred feet, spooking the white-shirt guys and gals still at their desks at ten o'clock. Served them right.

"What's your dad do, Rockett?"

No response came from the second seat for a couple of seconds, as if Rockett was coming out of sleep mode. Not that he'd been asleep. "I don't know," he said. "I don't know him."

"What about your mother?"

"Teacher."

"Do they still have grades, like third grade, fourth grade, fifth grade?"

"Yes, sir. But she teaches college English." A few more seconds went by before Rockett added, "Restoration Drama."

"My favorite," Nate said.

Carrie popped up on the display, all business. A *Crime in Progress, Violent* call.

◆ ◆ ◆

CROWS WERE COMING IN hot from three directions. The action was out in the yard in front of a single-family house in Mar Vista, a middle-class community between the 405 and the beach towns. Nate had to slalom in, dodging a tree or two and a too-low news rig before he landed on the top deck of a parking structure up the street from the scene.

Nate and Rockett ran down the middle of the street. The house was four houses in from the corner. Across the street was an elementary school. Schools nowadays all looked like prisons to Nate, high-fenced with light stanchions on the corners. An early-in Crow hovered, lighting up the scene: a bloodied man and woman fighting in their front yard, screaming at each other. A real grass front yard. Real grass usually meant a homeowner who still cared about personal property. It wasn't easy to keep a lawn green with a five-gallon-a-day pipe water ration. The front door to the house stood open. The white downlight from the Crow flashed off the blade in the man's hand as the man and woman flailed away at each other, pushing and shoving. They were husband and wife—Vietnamese or Cambodian or maybe Thai—screaming at each other in a language nobody on scene understood, the husband with the butcher knife over his head as if ready to strike again, his cut-up wife screaming *"No!"* at him. They weren't shutting up, not for a second, not even to take a breath. It looked for all the world as if he meant to kill her and right now.

Nate was still carrying Bodie's Sig. It felt heavy and…perfect in his hand. There was no other word for it. Rockett kept his weapon holstered for now but he was right beside Nate—a gunner's job was to protect his CRO, not take out citizens who were only threatening each other. Four other CROs were on scene, taking up positions behind whatever they could get behind, all with their guns drawn and their gunners guard-dogging them.

CROs were yelling, "Drop it! Drop the knife!" Some fool said it in Spanish.

Nate scrambled up for a closer look and dug in beside Baker, the rookie Genesis CRO from back in the ready room who might have been first-on-scene. When Baker saw Nate, he started talking, answering questions before Nate asked them. "She's cut all to hell," Baker said. "It started in the house, broke out here. He's got her blood all over him. We've got to take him down, but they're standing too close together."

"Go slow," Nate said. "You never know."

Baker nodded but had no idea how to slow anything down.

Overhead and across the street, a news bird was dropping in for a better angle, its own spotlight already fired up. The regs said they were supposed to stay a thousand feet above the Crows, but this was too good a show to go by the rules.

Nate looked over his shoulder, saw it coming. "Look out," he said, cool.

Baker turned just as the news helo clipped a light stanchion in front of the school. There was a metallic scream and the news-bird dropped like a rock and went sideways all in the same moment, nearly taking out the legit Crow lighting the scene. The Crow pulled up and went right fast as the news-copter plowed into the asphalt playground, beating itself apart on the way down. Somehow, there was no fire. And least not yet. They weren't close enough to see if the pilot/reporter had bought it.

Nate turned back to the business at hand. New cops were running in, higher-ups. "Gunners, if you get a shot, take him down!" a senior CRO called out. "Anybody!"

Rockett looked at Nate. Nate shook his head.

The man with the knife over his head hadn't even noticed the crash, though something had shut him up. Now *she* was the only one screaming, saying the same thing over and over. Now the man seemed ready to cry, not that he wasn't still murderously angry. He spoke in a defeated, fatalistic voice and took a step toward her, the knife still in hand. Every gun on the yard came up. The wife kept saying her line over and over.

The husband was a second away from getting ten bullets in him.

Then came a new voice. "No! It's her! It's not him, it's her!" It was the Asian cop from the squad room, the Keanu Reeves guy. The husband and wife were still shouting at each other. "She's telling him to kill her. He took the knife away from her. Something happened in the house. He took the knife away from her. She cut herself."

Then he listened to the woman and said, evenly, "She killed their children."

The lead CRO stood and took a cautious step toward the husband. The Asian cop was right behind him, shouting something to couple the in Vietnamese. The woman kept crying out angrily but now dropped her knees. The grass around her was already covered with blood. The husband just stared at her and threw the knife off to the side.

Cops ran for the house, including Baker, less of a rookie than before. He'd gone from Genesis to at least Exodus.

"SoCal is coming apart at the seams," Nate said, as they walked back to the Crow.

◆ ◆ ◆

NATE CLOSED OUT THE night circling the TMZ, cruising, lighting it up, looking for any sign of the New Okies. He hadn't told Rockett where they were headed as they flew away from the craziness in Mar Vista and felt him tense when the downtown towers passed under the belly of the Crow. He had no intention of setting the bird down in the TMZ again, but Rockett didn't know that.

Nate was stiff and sore from all the hours flying. He still had beach sand in his boots and was sunburned on his face and neck. The sights on Coronado Beach had followed after him all day, like a panhandler with his hand out. The sound of the wind still whistled in his ears. The smell of the bodies was in his nostrils. What he'd seen that morning had *The End* written all over it, yet still it felt like the beginning of something. To Nate, anyway.

There was nobody to be seen in the TMZ until the ninth or tenth orbit. Whether it was the sweep of the NightSun or the soft whirr of his rotors, they woke. When Nate was starting to think they'd *all* gone south—all died—they emerged. They looked the same as before, but now there was a hundred or more of them—on the ground between the dilapidated buildings, coming out onto the roofs—all with their heads tilted back, dangerously expectant.

Chapter Twenty-Nine

The next day the rest of the story came out. The *HÆRVÆRK* was pursued down the coast, overtaken and boarded by Mexican authorities a hundred miles offshore of the State of Oaxaca. The ship was well out into international waters, but Mexico had a reputation for hard-ass enforcement when it came to immigration. The captain and crew were completely unaware of the men, women, and children they'd misplaced on their uneventful voyage south. Or so they said. It only took another day for it to come out that the freighter was known for human cargo. Every trip, the ship carried one or two boxcars of living breathing humans in among the containers of scrap metal and shredded plastic and refurbed Priuses. The ship's *modus operandi* was to run south to just offshore of Mazatlán below the end of the Baja Peninsula and offload the North Americans into smaller boats for the run to the coast. From Mazatlán, trucks would haul them overnight to the corporate farms in southern Sinaloa. Apparently the smuggle had been going on for six months or more, since the oil boom had turned things upside down and reversed the direction of the illegal border-crossings. Mexico further tightened legal immigration restrictions and erected their own electrified fence—a fence that killed—five miles in from the border with the US, but that only drove up the smugglers' prices. The labor shortage was a constant. Will met way.

Before it had even passed Ensenada, the *HÆRVÆRK* had hit heavy seas and at least two of the containers carrying the would-be farmworkers went over the side. The boxcars were sealed shut. They would have floated. There was no way to know when they cracked open; possibly on the rocks of one of the dozens of unnamed islands off the Mexican coastline below Rosarito Beach, some just barely over the border. All told, twenty-eight North Americans had drowned. Thirteen bodies rode a current north to Coronado, six washed up on Mexican beaches, and nine were unaccounted for, their names put forth by relatives left behind. Because the dead were White, the investigation—at least in the US— was manned to the maximum. And expedited. The wrap-up was tidy: the perpetrators on the LA end—the dead on their backs on the docks—were from a Tijuana gang come north to collect the money and load the passengers. The TJ gangsters had been shot and killed in a gunfight aboard an old Chris-Craft yacht trying to escape south from Long Beach. There was no local connection. Or so it was said.

Otherwise, Nate's gut told him. He had a judge friend who hated cops. All it took was a phone call and a matchbox of the hipper-than-thou drug Tail of the Dragon—which technically was legal but extremely hard to find—and Nate got satellite and drone surveillance of Whitey's house in Baldwin Park. The judge threw in access to pickup / destination info from Whitey's favorite air cab company. So, just like that, Nate knew where Whitey was at any given time, probably knew more than Whitey's wife or girlfriend did.

This morning, Whitey was in church, the same church where Derrick Wallace worshipped his infinitely forgiving (or forgetful) savior. Coincidence? Whitey had brought his wife along. They'd arrived early in an air cab for the eleven o'clock service, the service the devout favored, the one that went three hours with a two-hour sermon. Nate was on a roof down the block with a pair of recorder-binocs. He'd given Rockett the day off on the chance the kid had a spiritual life of his own. Or liked football. Or just needed a day to delete the head-pictures of the dead on the beach down in Coronado.

It was a hot and windless Sunday. Nate had found some shade beside a rooftop water tank but was still sweating. He wondered if church ladies still fanned themselves with cardboard fans with the wooden handles, the kind supplied by the funeral homes for advertising. The first hour of the surveillance of the church had been entertaining: rocking, thumping music escaping out the open windows. Nate could even hear the right-on-the-beat clapping of the congregants. Like they say, Sunday morning is the most segregated hour in American life.

When he was in middle school, Nate's mother found a bag of pot in his jacket pocket. It wasn't good weed and there wasn't much of it, but it got him sentenced to Sunday School for six months. His mother—her name was Cher— supposedly didn't tell Bodie, so the old man must have wondered what was up with his son and wife's sudden turn to religion. She picked a Presbyterian church in Encino with a "contemporary worship service." From the first punitive Sunday on, she let Nate drive there and back, although he'd just turned fifteen and couldn't even get a learner's permit yet. He never got the link between the Bible-ing and the mostly lame Christian rock and getting to take the wheel of the family Camaro, but he didn't question it. One Sunday morning his mother said, "You are probably wondering why I am letting you drive. It's because I want you to learn to the rules of the road from me and not Bodie." After six weeks, she told him he didn't have to go anymore. She was a nurse and had started working Saturday-night-into-Sunday-morning shifts. Though his sentence had been commuted, Nate went to the church on his own for another three months, on his skateboard. He'd even played drums in the "praise band" until his friends found out about it. It was then that he learned that Whites—most White Christians anyway—couldn't keep time. Whenever the long-haired worship leader shamed the flock into clapping along, half of them would lose the beat immediately. It was embarrassing. Tribally.

The service was ending. The doors of the church opened, letting out—like a held breath—a swell of organ music. Two sharp-dressed deacons emerged, secured the doors, tying them back with red cords. One of them brushed something off the other's shoulder, which made the second deacon flash a radiant smile before he pushed the first man away, pretending to be angry. The deacons were just teenagers. They made Nate think of the murdered Wallace boys. The pastor in his purple robes—he who'd officiated at the truncated funeral—was next out. He stood there on the top step, tapping his toe, looking like he wanted a cigarette. The music still hadn't ended; then it did. The first of the brethren emerged. They were a fancied-up crowd—dressed competitively, Nate thought—bright colors, matching shoes, and hats on the women and men. Old School. These days, almost nothing felt more retro than religion.

Whitey and wifey came out, Whitey steering her with a hand on the small of her back. She was a handsome, full-figured woman in her fifties. She wore a pale blue dress with shoes and a lid to match, a hat that looked, from Nate's vantage point, like an upside-down shoe. But what did he know about fashion? The reverend, Pastor Lamb, tilted toward her and took her hand and pulled her closer with the sort of attention first-time church attendees always got, at least the ones who hadn't come in off the streets. Then he reached around her to shake Whitey's hand. Whitey looked like a man who thought he'd just wasted three hours. He all but pushed his wife away from the preacher and down the steps. He walked her across the car-clogged street and pointed her toward the Yellow AirCab idling in the front half of the parking lot with two other air taxis, then he turned to watch the front doors of the church.

Nate had a good view of the whole street. Most of the church-goers were on foot, from the neighborhood, and they began to stroll away, as if it were another century. Some women—and one man—even had parasols. Whitey was hard-scanning the crowd, eyeing everyone who came out. As the deacons were untying the doors to close up, Il Cho emerged into the sunlight, apparently the last one to come out. Cho wore a Sunday-go-to-meeting suit, too. And wingtips. He looked one way and then another until he found Whitey across the street. Cho looked at him and shook his head. No go. Whitey stayed put, waited as Cho crossed the street. The two cops talked on the sidewalk. After a minute of it, Whitey shook his head—frustrated or annoyed or both—and walked away from Cho toward the idling air cab and his wife.

Cho watched and waited until Whitey's cab lifted off.

A block north of the church, the Gang Unit helicopter hovered fifty feet above the street, whipping up the dust. A sky-ladder hung from the underside of the bird. When Nate approached, Cho was a second away from putting his foot into one of the loops to be hoisted up. It was how they embarked and disembarked when there was no landing spot. Routine but hairy. If you slipped or lost your grip, the loop auto-tightened around your ankle and hauled you up upside down. It worked for dead bears, too.

"So was he there?," Nate said loudly to Cho to be heard over the helo.

When Cho turned toward Nate, he had a surprised look on his face, a look that could be read a couple of ways. Cho looked up at his pilot, spun his finger in a circle, and the helo lifted and roared away, the carbon-cord ladder retracting.

Cho said, "Until he saw Whitey. Then he disappeared."

"Derrick Wallace is a smart guy," Nate said. "Whitey doesn't think so, but of course Whitey thinks *he's* smart. What were you going to do, arrest him for something? Try to drive him in deeper into whatever he's in?"

Cho hesitated, then said, "Whitey believes Wallace is out of the game, not wanting to get back into any of this, that his wife doesn't want him to have anything to do with it now. Whitey said he just wanted to make sure."

"So Whitey thinks a guy going to church means he's out of the game?"

Cho didn't say anything.

Nate said, "Did you find out any more about the Tijuana guys dead on the dock in Long Beach?"

"One of them was a woman."

"Remember the good old days, when smuggling was just drugs and guns? The Yellow Submarine?"

"Why'd they call it that?"

"You don't like The Beatles? I thought Koreans liked The Beatles."

"I like *new* music," Cho said.

The GU helo came around the corner again, ladder already lowered. It held back a bit, hovering over the next intersection. It was like a big dog with its leash in its mouth, wanting to go for a walk. The pilot was watching the two of them intently. He was Whitey's guy.

Nate got right in Cho's face. "Get the hell out of here!" he said.

"What?" Cho said.

Nate wasn't a half-bad actor. He even managed to draw some blood up into his face and bug out his eyes, get in the moment. Cho was only confused for a second. Then he spit an angry line of his own back at Nate. He tipped his head to one side, cracking his neck, a move he'd seen in more than one Hong Kong action flick. Il Cho *was* a half-bad actor.

Cho pointed at the pilot and gestured with two fingers and the pilot flew forward to pick him up. Cho and Nate shared a smile that couldn't be seen from the cheap seats; then Cho hooked the toe of a Florsheim Imperial in the lowest loop on the sky-ladder and rose.

Nate did a one-eighty and strode off, his back projecting mad as hell.

◆ ◆ ◆

A BIG WHITE COP IN a CRO suit walking up a sidewalk in Boyle Heights with a bright video screen in hand and no gunner. It was a good way to get killed. It was only nine o'clock, but it was full dark. Most of the streetlights long ago had been shot out and the night's moon had already risen and didn't amount to much. Nate was on Whittier Boulevard, way upriver in Inca territory. The gang's hook-beaked eagle was splashed over everything: the buildings and bus benches and sidewalks, even a school. He was walking four or five blocks east of the house that was Razor's last known address, the silver-roofed house that he had been circling when the call came in about the havoc across town at La Nacional, the Salvadoran restaurant. He remembered what his CI Miranda had said, that Razor wasn't Inca, that "maybe once he was even a Twenty or a No Fear" but wasn't in any gang anymore. Maybe not, but Razor had lived right in the middle of Inca turf. Neutrality didn't seem very likely, not tonight, not here.

Nate had made a couple of passes at a thousand feet, then set the Crow down on a patch of plastic grass in a park, a piece of turf that had been a soccer field for the locals until the Controllers realized they had lost control. The local *futbolers*—Browns mostly—weren't signing up on the official schedule, much less filling out the liability release forms. They were just playing, whenever the hell they wanted. With their own ball. Unsupervised. So the city had yanked out the lights by their roots, packed up the goals, and—just to be safe—dropped three or four boulders in the middle of the field, making it unusable for anything except picnics. And rapes.

Whittier Boulevard had traffic, slow but moving. Every head in every Fed pivoted toward Nate. Occasionally a sho-nuff low-rider would creep past, stuck in traffic like everyone else but not minding it as much as the others. A reminder of better days, all dressed up with everywhere to go. Nate kept walking, reading his screen. All he had for now were dots on a map, one red dot that was supposed to be Whitey and five or six other yellow dots around him, unknowns. They were on an open lot on a corner, only the lot wasn't exactly open. When he'd flown over, he had seen that it was covered by a tin roof, blocking his view.

Nate had "dotted" Whitey, sending a command drone to individually target and move with him. The command drone then coordinated secondary drones and worked up map-views and sat-views: *The Whitey Barnes Show.* The system was all computerized, which meant it didn't involve a human being once a nameless unionized clerk somewhere checked the electronic "paperwork" and touched the *GO* button. When Nate woke up that morning and checked his screen, the surveillance system had asked him, as the sole data reader, if he wanted the subject dotted. Nate had said, *Why, yes, thank you, I believe I do.* The program should have asked for Nate's authorization for full track-and-trace surveillance, but it didn't. So the dotting wasn't exactly legal. It was what they called *illegal.*

Nate felt a little... *illiberal* about it. At least for a couple minutes, while he was brushing his teeth.

Nate closed the screen. He knew where he was going. Ahead.

He went two more blocks. He was feeling too many eyes on him so he ducked down an alleyway, stepped over a couple of cardboard condos, went up an old iron fire-escape ladder on the first building he came to, and climbed over the low wall onto yet one more flat roof. He'd lived half his life on flat roofs. He trotted across the gritted tar paper, parallel to the street, and went up and over the parapets until he got to the corner. He dropped into a crouch and crept up to the front wall, staying low, though it was his experience that people almost never looked up at the tops of the walls around them, not even criminals—especially criminals.

He straightened up, came up like a periscope. He had a clear view of the open lot cater-corner across the broad intersection. The tin roof made the scene look almost cozy, like a patio, a hangout. No grass, but there were two picnic tables and some white plastic Walmart chairs. During the day, old men probably played chess there. Whitey Barnes stood next to one table, drinking a bottle of Mexican beer, six men standing around him in postures that said respect. Or at least fear. Whitey's posture said everything was *cooool*.

Nate dropped back down. He leaned his shoulder against the front wall, dug out his screen, snapped it open, set it to night-read red. The map was gone, replaced by a live feed in thin color, a view from on high that angled in under the tin roof. He looked up at the gray night sky overhead, trying to spot the drone. Nowadays the little bastards had chameleon skin, fitted with a camera that read whatever was above and painted everything down-facing to match. One of them could be ten feet overhead with you feeling the breeze from the rotors on your upturned face and you couldn't see it. Nate touched the zoom control and went in for a closer view. Four of the men stood with their backs to the street, facing Whitey. A fifth person was in shadow in a chair, but not one of the white plastic chairs. Nate could see the face of the sixth man but he didn't know him. He could tell he wasn't anybody important.

One of the standing men wore a black cowboy hat. And was tall.

Then the food truck came. With a building roar that meant big engines and twin-rotors, a freight-hauler came down the boulevard at two hundred feet, lights blazing, a roach coach clamped to its belly. It was good that Nate was

more or less the color of shadows around him because the big rig flew right
over his roof, slowing, turning. Nate peeked over the wall for a look. The huge
rig orbited the intersection three times, waiting for the traffic to clear, then set
down. People had heard the racket and were already coming out of the bars and
cars up and down the street. The helo uncoupled from its cargo—gave everyone
another moment to admire its brute self—then revved up and rose, leaving the
food truck right in the middle of the X. Before the street-dust settled, a young
man in a white apron jumped out of the back as "La Cucaracha" played on the
truck's horn. A side awning came up. Greasy smoke was already rising out of a
blowhole on top, another form of advertising.

It was a repurposed RV, a Winnebago. It looked new.

Whitey and the men strolled out from under the tin roof. Apparently what
Nate was seeing was a meeting of the Inca board of directors. The six came
out, led by Ignacio "Nacho" Iberriz in the upright MotoWalker. Iberriz wore
his cheap reflector sunglasses at night, too. The other men, including Whitey,
moved aside and led him ambulate forward onto the street, then closed in behind
him. Iberriz turned to the underling Inca and tipped his head toward the food
wagon and then toward Whitey. Whitey put up a palm to say, *No gracias,* but the
runner was already running off to score some chow for him. The Incas were
showing off for Whitey.

Nate didn't get to watch any more of it because there was a sound behind
him. Footsteps but…softened somehow. He turned, quickly, but not in time to
do much about what came next. Two men were coming at him across the roof,
almost at a run, one with a gun in his hand. They never took their eyes off him as
they stepped over a couple of junk pipes. They were barefoot. *Incas.* In the space
between one quickening heartbeat and the next, Nate pictured them running
through a jungle. Nate was already trying to get to his feet and at the same time
going for the Sig Sauer in the holster strapped to his leg, but they were moving
too fast. Not much more than a second had gone by and it was already clear that
this wasn't going to play out in any way that was in Nate's favor.

O O D A… The OODA Loop. It sounded like the latest dance craze but it was a
mindset training mnemonic for soldiers and cops. *Observe. Orient. Decide. Act.* Nate
blew right through O and O and D and was trying for A—going for the Sig—when
the men reached him. One gangster stepped on Nate's gun hand and the other
man punched him in the face three times. At least they weren't going to shoot him.

Then they shot him.

Or the one Inca did. No warning, no sense to it. It didn't seem like part of the plan. Sometimes a man will use a gun just because it's already in his hand. The shot was so close and so loud and came so immediately—like a door slamming—that it made Nate think maybe he was already dead, that he had been blown away into Whatever Comes Next. But then the onrush of pain in his face told him otherwise. *Do the dead feel pain?* Another second passed. His face and whole head hurt so much he couldn't feel anything else. He couldn't begin to pinpoint where he'd been shot. Maybe he wasn't shot. Maybe the shooter somehow had missed him, but how could that be? From three feet away? Nate realized his eyes were shut. When he opened them again, there was the smoking gape of the pistol. *It's a shitty little thirty-two cal,* he thought, hopefully.

O O D A. He exhaled roughly, let his head flop to one side, played dead. It was the only thing that came to him to do. He waited for the kill shot. Instead, they picked him up, each man grabbing a handful of flight-suit shoulder and a pant cuff. Nate figured they were going to throw him off the front of the roof and that would be the end of it, but they didn't; instead, headed with him toward the back edge of the roof and the fire escape. They were taking him somewhere. To show him off or to kill him in front of the boss? Or in front of Whitey?

He was still playing dead. The Incas had their hands full carrying him and they'd forgotten about the gun still in his holster. Or maybe they had bought his act. OODA. Nate came back to life and went for his Sig again. The man on the right side was young and had a young man's reflexes. He reacted fast, letting go of Nate, dropping him. The other Inca grunted and was about to bitch at his coworker for dropping the cop when he saw what was happening. The first man was already taking care of it, stomping on Nate's right wrist, breaking it with a crack that could have been heard down on the street. The first man snatched the Sig out of Nate's crippled hand, looked at the piece admiringly for a half second and tucked it into his waistband.

Where were they taking him? They threw him off the back of the roof, like a sack of potatoes. *Uno...dos...tres...* Throw. It was only twenty feet to the street. Newton would know how many seconds, from release to landing. One? *The same for a feather as for a stone...* Actually, time didn't matter because somehow, just his luck, they'd tossed Nate right into a wormhole—a portal between realities—and he had all the time in the world to fall. Anybody who flew anything had this selfsame recurring dream: somehow the hatch comes open and you're falling, falling, falling, looking up at the aircraft getting smaller, smaller, smaller, going on without you, the wind whistling past you or you whistling past the wind, in the company of birds, clouds seen from the inside, eyes wide open, your legs and arms flailing as if you were a swimmer backstroking it, in the most horrible kind of danger but never hitting ground.

Not yet, anyway.

Nate landed on his back on a cardboard box, a box with an unfortunate man sleeping in it, maybe a man having a dream of another man falling out of the sky onto him.

Chapter Thirty

The doors were golden and twenty feet high, the kind of doors a poor person might expect to see upon arrival in heaven. But this was Beverly Hills. At three in the morning. Nate knocked again. With his left hand. He had already rung the bell but there was enough party noise coming out from inside to make him think he should probably just go on in.

Then the door opened, letting out an explosion of laughter.

It was a naked woman with a Ping-Pong paddle in her hand.

"Love-Thirty," Nate said.

"That's tennis," the naked woman said. "This is table tennis. It's scored differently. You think I'm thirty?"

"I'm a friend of Bruce's," Nate said. He could see past her into the living room, which was grand and glassy and cold as ice, marble-floored and filled with white couches and chairs and titanium coffee tables and people who looked like models in an ad for some overpriced thing guaranteed to make you happy. A video-fire roared in the fireplace. Nate could see all the way through the house to the lit backyard where the Ping-Pong table was. And the pool. And the tennis court. And another pool. More happy rich people were out back, eight or ten of them. She wasn't the only nude woman. Nate's air taxi lifted off from the motor court behind him. He couldn't fly the Crow in his condition.

"Wait here," the girl said. "I'll inform Dr. Lark he has a gentleman caller." She turned around and walked in. She had a remarkable backside, Nate thought, even in his banged-up broken gunshot state. He did as he'd been told, stayed put. The Ping-Pong girl stopped and turned back toward him. "I was kidding, you idiot," she said.

Nate apologized for being an idiot. She waited until he walked past her and slapped him on the ass with the Ping-Pong paddle. He winced. He hurt all over.

He thought about shooting her, then remembered his holster was empty. He was still in his flight suit.

"You're a mess," she said. "Are you a cop? Is that blood?"

"Fake," Nate said. "I'm an actor."

"No, you're not," the girl said, authoritatively.

Bruce Lark was a friendly-looking gray-haired man in his forties, dressed all in loose white and barefoot. Nate found him out by the pool, sitting by himself on the end of a chaise lounge, drinking some kind of green drink you couldn't see through. Dogs were everywhere, running in and out of the house, little puffball Beverly Hills dogs, illegal dogs. A white cockatiel flew across the yard from one perch to another, for dramatic effect. Nate stood there a second, kicked away a Pomeranian that looked like it was thinking about some ankle-nipping. When the dog yelped, Dr. Lark came back from wherever his thoughts had drifted to and saw Nate.

"I got shot," Nate said.

"That's never good," Lark said.

Then they were in the examining room, out in the guest house. Lark came in and flipped on the lights. The swinging door whooshed closed behind Nate. It looked like any other doctor's office. Lark went straight to a sink, rolling up his sleeves, scrubbing in. A standard stainless-steel table was center stage in the middle of the room with the standard lights over it and the standard wheelie tray beside it. The steel table didn't look too inviting, so Nate stood just inside the door until Lark looked at him. Nate stepped over to at least stand next to the table. Lark activated some kind of sterilization tank and went into a cabinet for a package of wrapped surgical tools. He opened two of the packages and threw the metal gear into the sterilizer. On the walls were bone charts and nervous system schematics. For dogs and cats.

"My wrist is broken, too," Nate said.

"You start skateboarding again?"

"I never quit."

"Strip. Where's your gun?"

Nate just shook his head, didn't want to talk about it. He unzipped his flight suit and let it drop. He'd bled more than a little. The bullet-wound was in his left shoulder, just above his "bulletproof" vest.

"That, too," Lark said, meaning the vest.

Nate cringed as he unfastened the blood-soaked body armor and pulled it off. It was stuck to him. Lark patted the steel table as if it were a bed and Nate sat upon it.

Lark was gently examining Nate's right arm—a nasty-looking compound fracture that wasn't going to fix itself—when the Ping-Pong player stuck her head in.

"You need me?" she asked. She was still naked, only now she wore a nurse's cap, apparently not a joke. Now Nate was naked, too. Or almost. Just his boxers. She covered her eyes, pretending to blush.

"No, I got it," Lark said to the nurse. "But put some clothes on. Buddy is fully erect out there."

She winked at Nate and left.

"Buddy's a dog," Lark said. "The Yorkie. Lie back." The table was full-length. And cold. Lark started poking at the bullet wound in the soft part of Nate's left shoulder. The wound was only an inch or two above the heart, though neither man was going to talk about that.

"Are all these dogs yours?" Nate said, to have something to say instead of howling. Lark had moved his gloved fingers to the pain trigger.

"People bring them back for dinner parties. I hate dogs," Lark said. "Well, I don't hate 'em. I hate *these* shitty little ass-kissers. I got a cat around here somewhere."

Lark unwrapped a syringe and took a vial of something blue out of a med-cabinet. He drew out a dose and poked the spike into the meat right next to the gunshot wound. He went back to the tool tray for a refill and then numbed up the wrist, too.

Nate tried to think of something offhanded to say, a crack, but he wasn't really feeling it. "You been all right?" he said, after a second. It was something the sober said to each other. Nate and the doctor had met in a West Side twelve-step meeting, court-mandated for Lark.

"I'm so happy I can't stop crying," Lark said. He'd started to clean both of the wounds, painting them up with orange disinfectant. Nate just stared at his friend's hands, the way they moved, the deliberateness of them, the control, the efficiency, the *gentleness* which—Nate was thinking—seemed feminine in the best kind of way, though of course he'd never say that aloud. "Straight through," Dr. Lark said of the gunshot.

"That's always good," Nate said.

Bruce Lark had been a doctor to rich people for ten years when he became addicted to morphine and a mix of the most perfect prescription drugs known to those in the know. Things went surprisingly well for him for three or four years. He was working long hours, booked solid, bright-eyed and bushy-tailed, lots of energy. Then the curtain started to close and the house lights came up. Well before anyone suspected anything, Lark had thrown in with some celebrity patients on a $10 million Mexican brown heroin deal. It blew up, and in the end he lost a lot more than did his famous partners. The celebrities went into rehab, talked about it on every TV show there was, and saw their careers expand, while Lark lost his license to practice medicine. For all time. On people. Actually, he wasn't licensed to be a vet either, but that was how he lived and kept the homestead: the outlaw vet for outlaw pets.

"Where were you when you got shot?"

"On a roof, Boyle Heights."

"Heroin is dirt cheap all of a sudden, starting about two weeks ago." To Lark it wasn't a non sequitur. "The market's flooded, coming in from Mexico, some new way I guess. It's crazy strong, too, laced with Fentanyl. I know of three people who died. Since Tuesday."

Lark let the syringe take another long pull on the bottle and then again stuck the needle into Nate's wrist. Nate watched Lark's face as he thumbed in the dope, wondering what wellspring of faith or fear or discipline kept him out of the medicine cabinet. It was ten feet away, day and night, right across the room, right here at home.

"You'll remember this next part for the rest of your life," Lark said, taking hold of Nate's arm with both hands to set the bone.

◆ ◆ ◆

NATE FOUND HIMSELF ON the chaise next to the pool. Apparently the others had either gone home or gone quiet. The night was crystal clear, stars and everything. Even a shooting star. Two! Or maybe it was the drugs. Nate never took anything anymore, not even an aspirin. He was afraid to. Like most men, he was the leading authority on his own weaknesses.

"You want some sushi?" Dr. Lark said, materializing, standing over him.

"No." Nate's forehead itched. He reached up to scratch it, clunked himself with his brand-new cast. It was dyed black.

"Don't go anywhere for a hour," Lark said. "Just sit there. You want a smoothie?"

Nate shook his head. He was watching a beautiful cougar walk across the lawn like it owned the place. Dr. Lark stepped toward the big kitty with his hand held out, which slightly increased the possibility that it was real.

Chapter Thirty-One

A steady stream of people moved past the front window of The Original Pantry though the sun wasn't down yet and the show at The ObamArena didn't start until ten. The concertgoers were mostly kids—and wannabe kids. They were singing the hits as they flowed past on the sidewalk and in the street. They would finish one song and someone would choose the next and then they'd all be singing that one too, as happy as could be, that kind of happy that has anticipation right at its core, like children on their way to Disneyland. They were packed so tightly they kept tripping over each other, their laughing apologies added to the lyrics they sang.

Nate surprised himself: he knew a couple of the songs, not that he was going to sing along. He was sitting at the counter using a steak knife to scratch the itch down inside his black cast. He wasn't eating a hundred-dollar steak, though he probably should have been; could have used some red meat to help replenish the blood he'd lost. Cubby looked over at him with the standard waiter question on his face. Nate gave him the *That's right, I am* still *not drinking* look. In the old days, Nate drank enough red wine at The Original Pantry to supply a wedding in an Italian village. Good times. And then they weren't. But getting shot and beat up and thrown off a roof was a real test of his will. Or his ability to surrender to the one kind of painkiller the doc had used to numb him to set his arm and yet not the other, the kind that came in a bottle.

Cubby came over with a fresh cup of coffee as hot as a volcano. The Original Pantry's cups were the same squat heavy cups they'd had for a hundred years. After a nuke attack, all that would be left of downtown LA would be cockroaches and Pantry china. And maybe Cubby.

Il Cho came in off the sidewalk, harried. "Did you know it was going to be like this down here?" he said. He took the stool next to Nate.

"This is where I need to *be*, man," Nate said, like a beatnik on *Dragnet*, his favorite show when he was four.

"Why did you want to meet down here?" Cho said.

"I was going to be here anyway. I thought it would be convenient for you. Did you drive? Where'd you have to park?"

"I took the Red Line. You OK?" He was looking at the cast and the bruises on Nate's face, pretending not to.

"A lightning bolt couldn't stop me," Nate said.

"Everybody was talking about it. You know how it is: if the cop doesn't die, it's like a joke."

"It's good to know I'm in their thoughts and prayers."

"Can you fly like that?" Cho said, pointing at Nate's cast. The cuff of the flight suit wouldn't snap over it.

"I'm letting my gunner take the stick." Rockett was sitting near the door, alone, his Streetsweeper on the white paper tablecloth. Nate said, "He's got the worst table manners, but he's only eleven."

"They said you wouldn't let them take you to the hospital."

"It wasn't me who called the EMTs." Nate was well past wanting to talk about what had happened to him in Boyle Heights. He pivoted on the stool to face Cho. "Did Whitey say anything about it? About me?"

"No. And I was with him all morning."

Nate still didn't know if he could trust Il Cho. He couldn't read him, or couldn't read him all the way through to The End. Cho had come to Nate with his suspicions about Whitey, shared in the craziness on the rooftop in the TMZ, told him about Johnny Santo's double-cross. So there was that. All in all, Cho had talked a good game, but Nate still didn't know exactly where he stood. After all, he was a Gang Unit cop. With Whitey. He wasn't a CRO.

"So you're the one who wanted to meet," Nate said. "What?"

"I went up to Palmdale," Cho said.

"You found the place."

"I counted twenty RVs in the lot. You said there were ten or twelve."

"They're making food trucks out of them."

"All of them?" Cho said.

"Maybe they're going to export them," Nate said. "To someplace where gas is cheap."

"Incas are doing this?

"It's all very confusing." Nate's coffee had cooled off enough to drink it, after he'd put an ice cube in it. He took a sip.

Cho said, "What were you doing on a roof in Boyle Heights?"

"Getting more confused by the hour. Until they tried to kill me."

The crowd outside seemed to surge and suddenly the door flew open and there before them was a teenage girl, as if coughed up by the beast out front. She had pink hair and carefully smeared makeup that was part of her look. Behind her, the chorus on the sidewalk kept moving. The Original Pantry patrons stared at the girl as if she were famous or an alien. Or a famous alien.

"Sorry, guys," the girl said and turned and went out the door.

"You'd better go," Cho said to Nate.

◆◆◆

Les Belles du Nuit.

THERE WAS VIVID, A hundred feet high, in costume and full makeup and black, chopped-off, serrated hair, a Parisian waif with pleading eyes. It was a huge moving image billboard on the front wall of the arena, a "live" loop of the waif's face. Every once in a while, she'd blink, in case anyone thought it was a still. *Beauties of the Night* was Vivid's new road show. It wasn't nearly enough anymore for the biggest of the stars to simply come onstage with a band and sing and dance, perform the hits, maybe change costume once or twice, touch hands along the front of the stage and then come out for a *Who, me?* encore or two. These days, fans could sit home with their twenty-speaker sound systems and realer-than-real holographic projections and have the *basic* concert experience for free, alone or with friends and with their drugs and alcohol closer at hand and not overpriced. As with drugs, what once had been enough wasn't enough now, not for the shows with thousand-dollar cheap seats.

Judging by the image on the billboard, Vivid had immersed herself in the role, let go of a good deal of her vividness. Vividity? The mop of pink or silver hair was gone. The trademark smeared lipstick was gone, the sunken black eyes, even the dot over her lip. She looked sad, and getting sadder, as if the weight of the world was on her now. Or at least the weight of Paris. For tonight, anyway.

Without warning, three enormous helicopters—one in front, two behind side by side—flew down Figueroa, coming in from the north at five hundred feet. They were the new-model firefighter birds with doal rotors and 1,100-horsepower unmuffled engines—converted Navy bomber helos. They looked like red silos coming down the canyon between buildings. As one, the crowd pressing on toward the concert arena looked up and cheered. Maybe most of them were already high and anything big and loud and unexpected made them happy, even repurposed warships.

Nate watched the big helos thunder over. He was standing atop a box truck on the edge of the arena's jammed front parking lot. Rockett was up there with him. The truck bore the logo of a theatrical lightning company, part of Vivid's crew. As the fire wagons continued on south, Il Cho jumped up onto the truck's front bumper. Apparently he'd been down on the pavement in the crush of citizens. Nate waved him on up. Cho stepped onto the hood and then onto the roof of the cab. He climbed as if he were afraid of denting personal property, a concern that hadn't occurred to Nate, who saw almost everything in life as an emergency situation.

"They picked the wrong night for that," Cho said, meaning the fire wagon flyover.

"The fans think it's part of the show," Nate said.

Now that the big 'copters were gone, the crowd was singing again. It was almost touching in the human unanimity it showed. Or terrifying.

Nate thought it odd that Cho was still there, hanging around. Nate and Rockett had left him inside The Original Pantry. He'd said he was going to eat and then go back to work, clock in for a shift. Now here he was. If Nate let his paranoia hold sway, he'd wonder if Cho was somehow doing Whitey's bidding, keeping an eye on Nate, trying to find out what he knew and what he didn't. But that would be paranoid. Paranoia was one of the things that had taken the fun out of smoking weed and drinking for Nate.

"Is there any way we can get inside?" Cho said, looking out to the crowd.

Nate smiled. "Are you a Vivid now, Cho?"

"A what?"

"Maybe you're just a belle of the night," Nate said. "Come on." He jumped straight down to the hood of the truck, denting it good with his Doc Martens completely on purpose.

Rockett followed, denting it worse, having learned from the master.
Cho came down Cho-style: carefully, respectfully.

◆ ◆ ◆

Ava Monica wasn't paranoid enough, Nate thought. An odd duck was tailing
her and she hadn't noticed him. She was down on the main floor, sipping a Coke,
munching on a tub of popcorn, her eyes on the skyboxes on the left side. The man
tailing her, watching her, looked country, from down south, maybe—a big man
in an out-of-fashion three-piece suit. Brown? The colored lights and the dimness
of the arena made the suit look gray or even red. He wore a fedora.

"Nice hat," Nate said. He tended never to say things ironically.

Nate was at the railing in the loge, one level up from the floor. It was half past
ten and the crowd around him was happily impatient, already standing on their
seats, clapping. At least they weren't singing anymore. Ava hadn't seen Nate.
He was behind her and above her and she was looking in the other direction. The
hat man who was still watching her hadn't moved a muscle. He was down on
the first floor with her, but he was almost all the way across the arena and under
the overhang of the loge. He looked like someone who was used to waiting and
watching. Maybe he was a PI. Or a deer hunter.

Then another man—a younger man wearing a Vivid T-shirt as a "disguise"—
came up to the man in the suit. He said something in big man's ear—three or
four sentences—and pointed up at the skyboxes. He seemed like a Junior G-Man,
an intern PI, a mook. Everybody has to start somewhere. The big man nodded
and dismissed the younger man, and then his eyes went back to Ava. A booming
announcement told people to take their seats. People obeyed. The crowded aisles
and jammed stairs didn't make it any easier for the younger snoop closing in on
Ava. The place was so packed and she was so preoccupied with the skyboxes that
she never spotted the second man. Or the big man. Or Nate. Unless she was doing
a great job of pretending. She definitely wasn't paranoid enough.

Ava put her drink cup and popcorn tub in a trash receptacle like a good
person and started walking through the crush of fans, not looking back. A tunnel
between the stands was marked Exit. She took it, going upstream against the fans

rushing in. The youngish man tailing her went after her, but the crowd did its part and pushed him back.

Nate thought about going after Ava, but then remembered why he was here. He looked around for Il Cho, but he wasn't back yet. Cho had said he was going to get a beer but that was half an hour ago. Cho wasn't a very good liar. Nate had left Rockett out on the street. The kid didn't seem disappointed at missing a Vivid show, especially one with a French name. Plus, they wouldn't have let him in with the shotgun and Rockett had gotten attached to it. It was his favorite fashion accessory. It went with everything.

Nate looked up at the skyboxes Ava had been eyeing. What was she doing here? Clearly, she was working. Twelve glassed-in boxes all the way up on the west side of the arena. There were twelve more across the arena from the first, but she wasn't looking in that direction. He couldn't tell which of the twelve skyboxes had Ava's attention. The one dead-center was full of people, beautiful people. Nate took out his binoculars and scanned the partiers. They were dressed as if it were New Year's Eve. Some were in the three rows of seats with a steep rake, while others up in the front rows danced around each other, cocktails in hand, touching each other, complimenting each other. The floor-to-ceiling glass across the front had been moved aside, the better for the perfect people to take in everything without having to rub shoulders with The Imperfect down there below the clouds.

Nate panned across their faces. They had to be somebodies. He could only see three men, including a tall drink of water with white hair wearing a black suit. Nate thought he should know who the man was—an actor?—but he couldn't come up with a name to match the face. And the shock of white hair. The man next to him looked familiar, too. The mayor? A politician? Either that or a used-car salesman on late night TV. A door opened at the back of the skybox and Ava entered. The box was crowded enough that no one paid her any mind. Nate may have been the only one who noted her arrival. He watched as she walked down some steps in a way that made her look like she belonged there. She was wearing her tarnished silver catsuit. In this context, it seemed chic—not that Nate had a clue about such things.

Every light in the arena went out. Even the exit signs, undoubtedly a code violation. Pitch black. The crowd gasped as one. Angelenos were accustomed to sudden disasters—earthquakes and explosions and mudslides (back when it still rained)—but they were still human beings. Instinct made them duck and cover before they realized that this particular sudden thing was part of the show, and they recovered and applauded the darkness. Some dolt whistled and whooped with that kind of piercing concert whistle-and-whoop nobody likes.

Then, it began: a single, pure, phosphorous-white spotlight found a wingless angel in a wisp of a dress hovering high above the crowd. Vivid! Or so it would seem for the next few seconds. The crowd cheered as one, a unified sound that seemed like a release, a sound like the sight of a flock of birds set free at a wedding or an antiwar march. Every eye was on her. She moved her arms slowly, gracefully, treading air, and the strains of a theme began, a sweet, thin, faltering melody. Or notes on their way to becoming a melody.

Nate was thinking that it'd been years since he'd been to a big concert. The audience around him was mostly young but they weren't all young. He wondered if he'd ever had that look on his face at a show with some band or some singer, the look that was on their faces: satisfied already by the first notes of the first song, one song and one image. One Vivid. But not for long, because now the hovering Vivid was joined by another a hundred yards across the arena. And then there was another, this third Vivid swooping down almost low enough for the main floor crowd to touch. They tried, reaching for her, screaming. Before long, there were a half-dozen Vivids, spread out, swooping and soaring. You couldn't see the wires. Nate was thinking there must have been some real advances in theatrical trickery since he'd stopped going to concerts. They really looked as if they were flying, a flock of Vivids.

Which was the real Vivid? The last to appear. Almost imperceptibly, the black void at one end of the arena began to turn blue and very slowly the stage was revealed. A set, a scene, a lamppost, a street. In Paris? Paris in unhappier times? As the blue intensified, the lamppost somehow increased in size until it was as tall as a tree—like an effect in a trippy cartoon—and Vivid herself walked forward from the deeper darkness at the back of the stage, singing the first words...

> There was a boy, a very strange enchanted boy
> They say he wandered very far, very far, over land and sea
> A little shy and sad of eye but very wise was he...

Nate raised his binoculars again and looked up at the middle skybox on the left, turning on the night vision. The tall white-haired man whose name he couldn't remember and the others were all up front at the rail, fully caught up in the spectacle—or pretending to be. Ava was watching the stage, too, but off to one side from Whitehead and the others and with a look on her face that was hard to read. She seemed lost or...*sad of eye?* Maybe that was it, though Nate would be the first to admit that he could almost never tell what a woman was thinking. And whenever he was certain, he was almost always 180 degrees wrong.

He panned across to the next skybox, the next-door neighbors to Ava and her beautiful people. More beautiful people. The next one? More beautiful people. He went from skybox to skybox, all the way around the arena.

And there they were. Directly across from the beautiful people's perch was a skybox on the east side with a different sort of Vivid fans. Il Cho was up front with his back to the railing with a beer in his hand, not a beautiful somebody at all. Behind him were Whitey and Ignacio "Nacho" Iberriz, the crippled *El Jefe* of the Incas, cranked upright in his MotoWalker. And there was the South American cowboy businessman, all of them just hanging out like the best of friends, only the women paying any attention to the show on stage.

By then, Vivid had gotten to the punch line...

> *The greatest thing you'll ever learn*
> *Is just to love and be loved in return...*

Just?

Chapter Thirty-Two

The problem with helping people, especially strangers, is: *How do you stop?*

The day before, Ava had given the New Okie family a ride down from Cambria. When they got about to Westwood, the traffic on the 405 went to full stall. Predictably. It was eight o'clock. The four of them had been riding along, talking easily, taking turns telling stories or even jokes, when the traffic stalled and the conversation with it. After ten minutes of creeping along in silence, the father asked Ava if she knew how to get to downtown LA.

She did. Of course she did. So Ava exited the freeway and took them downtown on surface streets to Union Station, thinking—because she hadn't really thought this through at all—that was where they'd want to go, Union Station. And what, catch an ElectroLiner for home? Home was gone, home had blown away. Gone with the wind. They'd made that clear with the stories they told on the drive south, not that they were asking her to feel sorry for them or even feeling sorry for themselves. They had a kind of pride—all three of them, even the little girl, Bridget—that was almost certainly going to make things harder for them, whatever happened next.

Ava stood next to the Hudson in front of the train station as they gathered their belongings. Now what? What's the last thing you give to the unfortunate before you walk off or drive away, before you leave them in their lives so that you can get back to yours? A smile? Another buck? A big thumbs-up? A piece of advice? A stick of gum? A gun? How do you stop? Ava left the car with the $100 valet and walked the Lindgrens across Alameda to Philippe's. Philippe's claimed to have invented the "French-Dipped Sandwich" in 1918, although another sawdust-floored red-boothed place downtown—Cole's—claimed their chef had come up with it ten years earlier. So Ava fed them, ate with them, French-dipped with them, listened to another story or two, even insisted on three pieces of pie. *À la mode,* too.

"Well, good luck..." Ava said and offered her hand to the father, standing again next to the idling Hudson in front of Union Station. The little girl smiled up at her, clutching the pink Philippe's T-shirt Ava had bought her at the cashier's stand, while her mother stepped onto the old-timey penny scale next to the door.

"Thank you. Good luck to you, too," the man said.

The mother prompted the little girl with a look and a nod. "Thank you," the girl said.

Ava asked them where they were going now, and regretted it almost immediately.

"They said the 'TMZ'?" the man said. "It's supposed to be down here someplace. I don't know if it's an old hotel or a park or what."

Or what.

So Ava took them to the corner of Grand Avenue and Fifth Street—as close to the TMZ as common sense would allow—and this time stayed behind the wheel while they got out. She managed not to say "good luck" again and then managed not to break out sobbing as she drove away. She also didn't look in the rearview mirror.

"A block over from Hope Street..." Ava said to herself. Maybe irony would save her.

"That is your current location," the car's voice said.

"Oh, shut up," Ava said.

◆ ◆ ◆

AVA WAS DONE, OR SO she told herself. She was going to find Beck and tell him face-to-face that Cali wasn't dead. She wasn't exactly *alive,* either, but apparently she was just exactly where she wanted to be. Trippin'. Cali wasn't Cinderella— leaving a shoe behind for the prince to find—she was a Lost Girl, she was in Never-Never Land, playing a childish game, off with Peter Pan. *Be There Then.* Or off with somebody. Not Beck. Sure, she was high all the time. High, low, or sideways, Cali was gone, living in a Beck-less world, and he needed to get on with his life. That was exactly what she was going to tell him. Of course, the *déjà vu* alarm was clanging in Ava's head. She ignored it.

"Penny!"

Penny appeared on the dash-screen. "You're back!" she said. "You have to tell me all about it," she said. "I'm all ears."

"No, you're not," Ava said. "And no, I won't. Who called?"

"No one."

"No one?"

"Well, Dallas Raines, but he said it was personal. He's that weatherman, right?"

"Chrisssy didn't check in?"

"Nope. Well, once, right after you left. She said she was on the Beck case, working it. Here it is…"

Chrisssy's face replaced Penny's on the screen. "Hi, Ava, I'm on the case, working it," Chrisssy said. "The subject is staying at the Motel Sixty on Little Santa Monica. Laying low, looks like. I'm going to surveil said location, avoid direct contact, like you said. Right now I'm getting my hair done." A beautician appeared behind Chrisssy, fluffed up her hair, then pulled it back to show off Chrisssy's cheekbones. "Let's do it," Chrisssy said, apparently to the beautician.

"Call her," Ava said to Penny.

Two seconds later, Penny reappeared saying, "Nope. No answer."

"Call the numbers you have for Beck."

Five seconds later, "Nope. No answer."

"Call the Motel Sixty on Little Santa Monica."

"Just did, while you were watching Chrisssy," Penny said. "He's a guest at the motel, but hasn't occupied his room since Wednesday. No use of bed, bed linens, or towels."

"What about the little strip of paper across the toilet?"

"You're not happy, but you're funny," Penny said.

"What?"

"It's a line from a song."

"I like that lipstick," Ava said, a sincere non sequitur. "It brings out the blue in your eyes."

"Gosh, thanks," Penny said.

◆ ◆ ◆

ABOUT LUST AND LONGING, she was (almost) never wrong, Ava Monica.

It was after 11:00 p.m. when she pulled over to the curb on Beachwood Drive, parked, and got out. She looked up at the Hollywood Sign as she walked across the front yard of the apartment building. They had the sign's lights on—they only turned them on two nights a month now. It drew too many people up into the hills, they said. Too many tourists taking a leak in the bushes, too many suicides.

Ava went around the back of Villa Ventura. Chrisssy's black VW bug was under the unlighted carport. It was covered in dust, powdery dust, as if it hadn't moved in two or three days. Ava wrote *WASSSH ME!* with her finger on the back window.

"I knew it!" Ava said, when after her tenth knock on Chrisssy's door it opened and there stood Beck, wearing nothing but pajama bottoms. His silver hair was mussed and he had a stupid cat-that-ate-the-bird grin on his unshaven face. Shirtless like this, he was a bit fleshy. But still kind of perfect.

"It's Ava, babe," he said, looking away toward the bedroom. "Busted."

At least Chrisssy had the decency to look slightly embarrassed when she came up behind him in the barely buttoned top to Beck's jammies and put her arms around his waist. She had shorter hair now.

"Hey, Ava," Chrisssy said, trying to sound down. "Sorry about this."

Ava heard their confessions at the Formica table in the dining room, after she made Beck throw on a shirt and a pair of real pants. Chrisssy mixed a shaker of martinis without being told. Ava hadn't touched hers, trying to make a point about the utter wrongness of this.

"I'm an actor," Beck said.

"No!" Ava pretended.

"Did you see *The Fire Next Time?*" he asked. "I was Craig T. Nelson's middle son."

"Didn't see it," Ava said. "Or if I did, I don't remember it." Beck looked hurt, which she enjoyed. "What's your real name?" She gave in and took a sip of her martini.

"Beck. Beck is my real name. Roland Beck. Actually, my birth name was…"

"I guess you knew you didn't have to worry about anyone recognizing you: 'Wait, aren't you the actor who played Craig T. Nelson's middle son in *The Fire Next Time?*'"

Beck laced his fingers together on the table top.

"Ava, I'm so sorry," Chrisssy said. "Honestly."

"Hey, what's a girl to do?" Ava said. "The heart is a lonely hunter."

"Wow," Chrisssy said. "That's beautiful. And so true."

"It's the name of a movie, honey," Beck corrected.

"Who hired you?" Ava said.

"Initially, on the phone, when he cast me, he just said his name was 'Don,'" Beck began, heavily, as if this were an audition for an episode of a police procedural. "He said he was from Chicago. He called himself an 'intermediary.' Subsequently, he mailed me my character's profile and backstory and a goodly sum in hundred-dollar bills as well as a cashier's check for a larger sum. All in one package. Along with your name and the address of your office in Westwood. And the name of a tailor. *Mailed* it. He didn't even insure it. He's something of a throwback, out of the past."

"That's the name of another movie," Ava explained to Chrisssy.

"It was remade as *Against All Odds*," Beck added.

"Who was he an intermediary for?"

"He wouldn't say. He called him 'The Mister.' Something tells me she is married, Cali. Or whatever her real name is. To someone from somewhere other than Chicago or Los Angeles. He said as much."

"Florida?" Ava was remembering the souvenir seashell night-lights in the high-rise apartment down in Marina del Rey.

"Nothing I heard said Florida."

"Why did he pick you?"

"The Mister supposedly found me on the Screen Actors Guild Virtual Headbook."

"What else do you know about 'Don'?"

"He described himself as a repairman. But there is clearly some money behind this."

"You mean a fixer?"

"I guess. What he said was *repairman*. In time, I learned that his name is Nico Passarelli. After our third in-person meeting—after you lost Cali for the second time—I pressed him for his actual name and he told me. Nico Passarelli."

"You lost Cali?" Chrisssy said to Ava. "When?"

It made Ava feel like a bad person. "I'll tell you later," she said.

"I think he may harm her," Beck continued, sounding almost like a regular person. "That may not be The Mister's will, but I believe he intends to deliver her back home to him by force."

"Maybe it's her daddy who hired him," Chrisssy said. They both looked at her. "Maybe he just wants his little girl home."

Ava drained her drink. "Here's what you're going to do," she said. Chrisssy took Beck's hand. "Both of you."

They waited.

"Nothing," Ava said.

Only Chrisssy looked disappointed.

Ava's conscience—or something—made her turn off the autopilot and take the wheel, and before she knew it she was idling in front of Vivid's place up on Lookout Mountain. Everyone knew where Vivid lived: on Appian Way, off Lookout Mountain Avenue, off Laurel Canyon. Tonight it felt more like Lookout! Mountain. It was party night, lights blazing, music and squealing. A party before the next big show downtown. The classic silver Bentley was parked against the wall that surrounded the modern low-and-wide house. Ava parked across the street, got out of the Hudson. She walked on by Vivid's house to the end of the street to check out the view. And stall for time. That tiny voice telling her what she should do had gotten so tiny she couldn't hear it anymore over the ambient noise of LA.

What a sight! The night was very clear, if noisy. At Ava's feet was the curve of Sunset Boulevard, clogged with traffic and looking lovely, like a necklace. Costume jewelry? Paste? Directly below was The Sunset Tower, Ava's Sunset Tower. It was as if Vivid wanted a place that overlooked it and all that it represented. At least, Ava told herself that. She counted down from the penthouse and found her apartment. She had left all the lights on. She'd been doing that a lot lately. She wondered if she should talk to someone about it, if she could find someone who wouldn't roll their eyes.

Beyond Sunset was the spread of lights, a twenty-mile view—half of LA—east, south, and west. The grid of streets and streetlights made it all seem thought-out. From up here, it looked like a complicated board game, one played solo and only at night, you against the grid. Above the streets and freeways, crisscrossing helicopters. Any given night there were hundreds of Crows, all headed somewhere fast. Somewhere and back, if the cops were lucky. Tonight there was a ton of air traffic, EMT rigs and fire trucks and other law enforcement aircraft flying on the same level as the Crows. Sky cabs, commercial haulers, and the occasional private helo were restricted to the lower altitudes. Ten miles south, two queues of descending jetliners and the new prop steam planes stretched from LAX halfway to Palm Springs. Two other lines of ascending planes escaped out over the black water. It looked almost as if they were doing touch-and-gos. Out of necessity, every flying thing was outfitted with automatic separation and isolation gadgetry— fore and aft, side to side, over and under—to keep them apart. Sometimes Ava wondered if everybody in LA secretly had been fitted with it, too.

She looked back at Vivid's house. The living room was all glass. The party looked hilarious. Or was it hysterical?

Seeing the planes coming and going made Ava realize she hadn't been out of the state in a couple of years. When this business with Cali was wrapped up, she was going to get on a plane and go to…Paris. No, Barcelona. She was going to go to Barcelona where she'd never been, and she was going sit in bars and eat tapas and drink sangria and make small talk with a handsome unmarried man whose English wasn't good enough to get in the way of the two of them falling for each other. That was it, that was the plan. After she nabbed Cali and got her away from Lynch and Vivid and SoCal and back to her daddy or husband or parole officer or whoever he was. The Mister. Someone who cared enough to send a man—and a woman and a half—after her. She was going to grab Cali by the hand and take her to the airport. Or somewhere.

But it wasn't going to be tonight and it wouldn't be here.

Chapter Thirty-Three

Ava was walking! When she was still a block from the arena, Ava saw a very large electric sign that hung over the middle of the street. It was fully lit up, even though it was still daytime, the sun still well above the surrounding buildings. In letters ten feet high, it said…

L'essentiel est invisible pour les yeux

Figueroa was packed with people, even ten blocks south where she'd left the Hudson. Being among the crowd on the sidewalk and in the street was like being caught in a riptide. She was going where they were going, but even if that wasn't her intention, she still would have been taken along with them. That they were all smiling, laughing, and singing Vivid songs made it a bit less frightening. At least until the energy level cranked up as they neared their destination.

Ava had had a plan—get there early and ambush Cali as she arrived with her friends and enablers—but she hadn't anticipated the level of the chaos. It wasn't the first time. She also wished she'd worn different shoes.

That which is essential is invisible to the eye

The hanging electric sign was self-translating. Give it another minute and it would go to Spanish or Japanese or German.

"It's been a while since I've been to a big show," Ava said to a perfect stranger pressed against her, a girl in her twenties wearing a wig made of foil. They were so close together it was almost as if the two of them were slow-dancing cheek to cheek to the song the crowd was singing.

"I've been to every show since the *Straitjacket* tour," the girl in the silver wig said. She managed to free her right hand from the tangle of bodies and offered it to Ava to shake.

"Vivid," the girl said.

Ava shook the hand and said, "Ava," as they all surged under...

필수 는눈에 보이지

◆ ◆ ◆

EVERYONE IN LYNCH'S SKYBOX was down at the rail watching the show—everyone except Ava, who instead was watching the Cali show. Cali was re-blonded, blonder than the first time Ava had seen her, blonded to within an inch of her life. Of course, Cali had seen Ava, but she was acting as if she hadn't or as if she thought Ava wasn't really there. Maybe it wasn't an act. They hadn't had a chance to talk yet. Ava hadn't dragged her off to a service elevator yet either, but that was the plan. Cali was looking down at the arena floor. She didn't look happy, didn't look sad, though a tear was slow-rolling down her cheek. Maybe it was the song. Vivid had found a pretext for wedging one of her hits into the thin storyline of *Beauties of the Night*, a confusing love song of hers called "I Love You Too (Much)." Vivid was alone on the front edge of the stage in a puddle of pink light, selling the lyric. And especially the parentheses. The show was almost an hour in and the crowd was still wholly engulfed in Vivid-Love, especially those down on the floor in front hungrily reaching out to her.

"She isn't a woman, but isn't she pretty?" a voice behind Ava said.

She turned. "Nate Cole," she said. "Music lover."

"How'd you get in?" Nate said.

"The usual. Stuck a gun in a guy's face, showed him my badge," Ava said, tough, playing a game. "How about you?"

"A hand-job in the stairwell," Nate said.

He was in his flight suit, on the job, though as far as Ava knew he was always on the job. She doubted he had any regular clothes. But he did look good in a flight suit. The left side of his face was bruised from the eye socket to the chin and he had a black cast on his right wrist. She was about to ask him what had happened to him but thought better of it. She knew a joke was the only answer she'd get out of him. Cops.

"Check this out," Nate said, nodding toward the stage. "Watch what happens."

Ava watched as Vivid—not missing a word of the song—knelt to take a wrapped gift from a front-row fan. A second later, a stagehand ran out and took the package from the star and disappeared back into the shadows.

"They call it 'the present' because it's a gift…" Ava said.

"I bet they do the same thing with flowers," Nate said. "She probably has her own private bomb squad." Ava was still watching Vivid. Behind her, Nate was taking a second to refresh his memory about Ava's body while she was looking down at the stage. As if she didn't notice.

"But everybody *loves* her…" Ava said.

"In my experience, that's when they try to kill you," Nate said.

"I'm so glad I don't have to worry about obsessive love," Ava said.

Nate was eyeballing the group down at the railing in the box. "Who is he? White hair."

"David Lynch. And John Tern is a state senator."

"His name is *Turn?*"

"Tern. With an *e*. Don't you ever read a paper?"

"A paper what?"

"Lynch all but created Tern. They have mutual interests. Intellectual property, but not too intellectual."

"Who's the blonde who keeps brushing her hair out of her eyes?"

"You noticed."

"She doesn't look too steady."

Cali turned and looked right at them. She was too far away to have heard what they were saying. She'd just heard Nate's voice. He had the kind of voice that people turned toward, just the timbre of it. In the military world it was called a *Command* voice. In the cop world it was called a *Sit Down & Shut Up* voice.

Cali went back to staring unblinking at the arena floor again. Another tear had followed the first.

Ava said, "She's thinking about going over the rail."

"So you're on lifeguard duty," Nate said.

"Maybe," Ava said. "Why are you here?"

"The usual. Trying to end all the suffering in the world," Nate said. "Or at least in LA. How about you?"

"I don't know," Ava said after a moment, seriously.

Nate said, "How come all of these women are wearing the same dress?" Cali and the others were in their matching butterfly dresses, just like up at Xanadu.

"To please a man," Ava said. "Or to please themselves by pleasing a man. It's something we do in our weaker moments."

"You make it sound dirty," Nate said.

"I guess men do it, too—try to please women," Ava said, though she didn't believe it.

"You got a guy tailing you," Nate said, trying not to sound superior. "Actually, a guy and another guy working for the first guy. Big guy in a crackerjack brown suit. Blondie's daddy, unless I miss my guess."

"I saw them," Ava said, though she hadn't seen them. She knew who the man in the brown suit would be: the big lug with the foot-long gun who'd stood in her path in the parking garage. Nico Passarelli? Don? But she didn't know he was here. Or that he had an assistant.

Nate lifted his binoculars. He wasn't looking at the stage anymore. He'd seen something across the way. Ava tried to see what he was looking at. There was a crowd in the box directly across from them, a multiracial group, unlike Lynch's gang. Cali left the group at the railing and walked up the aisle on the far side of the skybox, pulling Ava's attention back where it belonged. Cali was either headed toward the exit or the little lost girl's room. At least she hadn't dived over the railing. Ava went after her.

"Bye," Nate said, the binocs still to his eyes.

From this vantage point, Nate could see into the depths of Whitey's box. Whitey had just said something that got a laugh out of Ignacio "Nacho" Iberriz and his gunsel, who was never far away. Il Cho was standing off to one side, close to the wall. Cho looked like he didn't belong there, or didn't know how he was supposed to act among all these criminals. Or maybe Nate was just giving him the benefit of the doubt.

Someone else had shown up. Derrick Wallace. Along with his wife Jewel, who was wearing the same basic black dress she'd worn to the funeral of her boys. Wallace looked as if he didn't exactly know what he was doing there either, like Cho. And even here—with love all around—Zap Wallace looked angry, a long way past *Do unto others as you would have them do unto you.* Whitey patted him on the back and handed him a drink.

Ava never returned, at least for as long as Nate stayed in the skybox.

◆ ◆ ◆

Fin. Vivid's *Les Belles du Nuit* was over.

Or rather, the show had moved out of the arena and onto the streets, the twenty thousand fans inside pouring out to merge with the ticketless thousands who had partied outside throughout the concert. The crowd—insiders and outsiders—had arrived singing six hours ago and they were singing still, dancing and jumping up and down. It was almost midnight but not a single *belle* or *beau* showed any inclination to leave. Anyway, how would they get to their Feds and trains through this throng?

Nate had climbed on top of a party bus. The driver was half asleep behind the wheel without one passenger inside. He knew he wasn't going anywhere soon. The crowd extended north to The Original Pantry, thick as they could be. It was the same view south down Figueroa Street. People were jumping as high as they could jump, trying to touch the letters of an electric sign suspended over the jammed street. Nate had no idea what the sign said or even what language it was. What it should have said was *I Can't Get No (Satisfaction)* because they wanted more, all of them. Vivid had come back for four encores and the cheering only got louder with each one until it drowned out the songs. Halfway through the encores, Nate had guessed what was coming next and headed for the exit, ahead of almost everyone.

The crowd outside would surge in one direction and then surge back. From on high the mass of people would have looked like an organism, a living thing trying to perambulate in the most basic, mindless way. Mindless, but happy. Nate spotted the big man in the brown suit and hat with his boy PI. They'd just come out on the far end of the arena. The young man was pushing fans aside as best he could to clear a path for the big guy, but they weren't having much luck getting away from the arena. People kept snatching the man's fedora and putting it on their own heads and then he'd snatch it back. Nate didn't look for Whitey and

Il Cho or Derrick Wallace and the other gang leaders. They'd likely already lifted off of the roof from the city officials' pad. Vivid and the band and backup singers had probably flown away, too. Nate wondered about Ava. Worried? He hoped she had stuck close with the VIPs.

Rockett was back atop the lighting truck, a hundred yards across the way. The party people kept threatening to climb up to the top of the truck. Each time they tried, Rockett lowered his shotgun until they backed off, raising their hands in mock surrender and laughing at him. They were like kids playing fort or King of the Mountain, except one of the kids had a shotgun. Rockett didn't look rattled.

"Good man," Nate said to himself. He said into the radio, "Stay where you are. I'll come your way when I can." Nate had landed the Crow on the roof of an office building behind The Original Pantry, so Rockett was closer to it than Nate. "Don't shoot anybody. This'll break up in a while."

But as it turned out, that wasn't going to happen, because now the rain came. The "rain." The fat red tanker helos returned, came down Figueroa again—one in front, two behind, as before—loud as hell, louder than before. Their arrival was sudden, more sudden than seemed possible with such big things. Earlier in the evening when they'd passed overhead, it had just been for recon. Now they were getting down to business. The twenty-foot spray-arms were cranked out from the sides of each helicopter and the valves were open as they roared in.

Rain. The county had been promising/threatening for two months to launch the program: fake rain from tanker-helos filled with water from the desal plants. (Or was it reclaimed sewage water?) *The Freshening!* it was called, complete with the exclamation mark. The bold/desperate plan was for squadrons of tankers to shower the whole city, neighborhood by neighborhood—one night of rain for each—for forty nights (which meant someone somewhere had an Old Testament sense of humor). The basic idea behind it was to clean the streets and the parked cars and the rooftops, to water the trees and the cemeteries and the lawns that were left, and to buck up the citizenry. No one wanted to see a repeat of the water riots of 2020. So they'd had weeks of debate in City Hall and public information sessions in satellite outreach meetings, a process that was supposed to be ongoing, although tonight apparently someone had decided to just pull the chain and see what happened.

The helos slowed as they came over, causing the raindrops to fatten. With the down-blow of the rotors, it was like being in a typhoon, a friendly typhoon. Nate thought this whole thing was a joke, but, before he could stop himself, he put his head back with his mouth open, looking like an animal howling at the moon. He missed the rain, more than most people. Rain just felt *right*, he was thinking. Rain reinforced the idea that the cosmos wanted you to flourish, he thought. Or at least survive. It was hard to believe, but a heavy rain like this used to come over Los Angeles on a regular basis. Even over a desert town like LA, which is what it was. He remembered something his old man said on a camping trip out beyond Twentynine Palms when Nate was twelve or thirteen. Bodie had said, bouncing along on a rutted road in his truck, looking straight ahead, "It never rains harder than it rains in the desert, when it finally gets around to it. Watch the hell out. And don't pitch your tent in a ditch."

Of course, the Vivid crowd loved the homemade rain. When the tanker helos had made their first pass, everyone had thought it was part of the show. Half of them were wearing T-shirts. Now the shirts came off, now they got waved around overhead like flags, as if they were disaster-at-sea survivors on an island waving at a rescue boat, only in this case they didn't want to be rescued. The three tankers banked slightly. It looked as if they were going to come around for a second slow pass just for the delight of the crowd, something that surely wasn't part of the night's official flight plan. Now some of the women started pulling off their shirts, too.

Below Nate's island, a woman with a child was panicking. Her daughter was getting swallowed up. The people around the mother were too caught up in the wet wildness to read the alarm on her face. The little girl was wearing a glittery Vivid T-shirt. In the next moment, her feet were knocked out from under her and she went down, disappeared beneath the surface. Even over the cheering and singing of the crowd, Nate heard the girl's scream and jumped down off the bus. He clicked on his ShockTouch and waded in.

For the last few years, street cops—and CROs, who occasionally moved (impatiently) on crowded sidewalks—had been equipped with gizmo technology that sent a low-voltage kick to their fingertips. Wires ran down from a unit strapped on the upper arm, connecting to mesh gloves that transmitted the juice. It delivered—with just a touch—a tenth of the jolt of a taser. The cops called it the "Excuse Me." It didn't usually rile the person touched but was an effective people-mover nonetheless.

Twenty feet of fans stood between Nate and the girl and her mother. He parted the Red Sea and then—after he'd de-weaponized his mitts—pulled the girl up to safety. He handed her off to her mother, looked back at the way he'd come in. The crowd had closed behind him. He put the mother and daughter behind him and switched on his gloves again and started back toward the bus.

He spotted Ava off to his left. She was searching the sea of bobbing heads, looking for someone, probably her own blonde Little Girl Lost from the skybox. Nate got the mother and daughter to the bus and then went back out into the crowd for Ava.

"Want me to save you?" he said when he reached her. She was soaked. Her hair was a wet mess.

"I lost the girl," Ava said.

"Come on," Nate said, touching her shoulder.

She jumped back. He'd forgotten he was hot. "Watch it!" she said.

"Sorry," he said.

"Boys and their toys," Ava said.

"So what do you want to do, Ava?" Nate said.

Ava took a last scan of the crowd around her. "Get me out of here," she said.

This time Nate headed in the direction of the box truck, where Rockett was. Ava fell in behind him. Overhead, the three red helos curved around, apparently for a second drop.

"Where'd you park?" Nate said over his shoulder.

Ava's instincts about chaos were as good as his. "Forget the car. We need to get out of this," she said. "Now."

How quickly everything changed and had gone from joy to riot. Ten feet away from Nate and Ava, four or five people exchanged a look, then started in trying to pull down one of the light stanchions, rocking it back and forth until it snapped off and fell, sparking. It wasn't prompted by anything, at least nothing that could be seen. Its bulbous head crash-landed on a kid looking the other way and electrocuted him, his body bouncing around on the pavement. It made no sense at all, but the people close enough to see what happened cheered with the ugliest kind of sound. Light stanchions were spaced every fifty feet across the parking lot. Spontaneously, knots of men and women who didn't know one another started rocking the other light posts back and forth until they snapped off too, sparking and flashing. It was like a light-forest being felled. Then, without warning, everywhere, men and women started beating on each other, pushing and hitting each other, strangers acting as if they weren't strangers at all, were full of hatred, with bad history. And as if on cue, the second wave of bogus rain fell. The churned-up crowd responded like a beast, one beast shaking its thousand fists at the sky. Blood was flowing by now, too much for the fake rain to wash away.

Ten Crows arrived, out of nowhere. The scene outside the arena had been monitored from the start and now some human or robotic scanner had determined that it was time to act, or at least to come in closer to investigate. The NightSuns on their underbellies were blazing, ten brilliant orbs, ten unblinking eyes looking down on the crowd, judging them en masse. Nate looked up at the closest Crow. He could see the eyes of the CRO at the stick, nobody he knew. He waved him off and at the same time keyed his mic. "Pull back! Lift!" Three of the Crows obeyed immediately, ascending rapidly and cutting their spotlights. The other CROs had either seen Nate or heard his voice and recognized him. The Crows all lifted.

Rockett watched as Nate and Ava came toward him through the throng. He jumped off the side of the box truck, landing on his feet on the tarmac with a grunt. It had knocked the wind out of him, but he recovered and crossed to Nate and Ava. Rockett walked point and the three of them made their way through the crush of people, headed south. They stepped over a dead woman, young, blonde, face-down. Ava stopped cold. The dead blonde wore a print dress but it wasn't Cali. Nate gripped Ava's hand to get her past the mess.

Rockett was ten years older.

◆ ◆ ◆

IT WAS AFTER ONE in the morning when Ava made it back down to where she'd parked the Hudson, going the long way, with Nate and his gunner clearing a path on the still-packed side street. The fans had eyed her hopefully, as if she might be someone famous, then went straight to being annoyed that some unfamous someone got a police escort, and an electrified one at that. The riot's bad vibes diminished the farther they got from the arena. There was at least a little shame on the faces around them, mixed in with a lot of confusion. And blood. Ava waved goodbye to Nate and his too-cute gunner and pulled out of the parking lot.

The drive across town took too long and somehow not long enough. She had smooth sailing for a short block or two, then Wilshire was bumper-to-bumper, and Beverly Boulevard was worse. Sitting there, stuck, with the big wheel in her hands, she had the idea that maybe she'd be better off walking, not that she acted on it. Going home, going to bed, alone, wasn't something she thought to do, so she was headed to Westwood to the office. At least there would be a guard at the desk downstairs to say hello to or maybe the accountant across the hall would be working late. He worked all night some nights, too, apparently also had no one at home who would notice.

Westwood. Two thirty. The streets dead quiet. A miraculous parking spot waited for her on Gayley, right below her office window. She shut the Hudson down and got out. After the programmed "rain" downtown, everything in Westwood looked so dirty, so parched and dusty. *Dry as a bone.* She thought of the phrase, standing there beside the car. A city in a drought was like a big boneyard. Maybe the fake rain would be a good thing for the Angelenos—make them think, as they fell asleep hearing it drip off the trees and eaves, that they weren't going to dry up and blow away after all—and get them to start acting accordingly. Then she remembered that the "rain" had seemed to make tonight's crowd want to stomp each other to death.

"Tomorrow," she said out loud. "Tomorrow and tomorrow and tomorrow."

She was ten feet from the front door to her office building when she heard a squeaking noise. It had rhythm to it: *beat, beat, squeak, beat, beat.* She looked south toward Wilshire. It was a man on a bicycle, coming this way, still two long blocks away. A big man, too big for the bike, maybe too big for any bike.

A big man in a fedora. Nico Passarelli!

Ava grabbed the office door handle. It was locked. She looked in. The guard wasn't at his post though the screen on his desk was pulsing and she could hear the chatter and soundtrack laughter of an old sitcom. He was in there somewhere. She pounded on the door. The people on TV kept laughing. She dug in her purse for her keys. They weren't where they were supposed to be.

He closed in. She kept looking for those keys.

"Wait," he said, dismounting awkwardly, almost falling over onto the street. His tone wasn't threatening. It was meant to not just stop Ava but to put her at ease, something all men learn how to do with women they encounter alone after dark somewhere. Then he said something that further disarmed her: "They say you never forget how to ride a bike but…I don't know."

"Leave me alone, scram, I have a gun," Ava said, and widened her stance, the way men do when they are standing their ground.

He leaned the bike against a parking meter post and straightened up and pushed his hat down. "No, you don't," he said. "You don't like guns. That was one of the reasons I wanted to use you."

Ava found her keys, aimed one toward the lock in her office door.

"Wait!" he said. "You don't know who I am, do you?"

Ava got the door unlocked. The guard was just coming back to his desk with a cup of coffee. He saw Ava outside, saw the look on her face, put the coffee down, and came on toward her.

"I'm her husband," the big guy said.

The line did what it was meant to do: it stopped Ava from going in. He was close enough now to put out his hand. "Tom Hadley," he said. "Belleville, Illinois. Some call me Happy."

Chapter Thirty-Four

Sunday morning coming down. The doctor caught Nate in the hallway when he was about ten feet away from Bodie's room. She touched him on the back to make him turn. Doctors don't usually touch people—at least not in the way regular people touch each other—so it spooked Nate, but when he turned, she didn't have a particularly worried look on her face. He'd learned how to read the faces of doctors in places like the Police Sunset Home. Or he thought he had. The doctors had a whole different manner when he was on the job and the dead and dying were someone else's old man. Or son. Cops and doctors on the job talked to one another as if they were letting the other man in on the joke. Here it was different, what might be called *normal*.

She backed into an unoccupied room. He followed her. The door stayed open. She didn't turn on the light. "Old Carl died," she said.

She was in her fifties, had the kind of good looks that lasted, Nate was thinking, even at a time like this.

"I hate to hear that," Nate said. "He was a for-real gunslinger."

"He died in his sleep," the doctor said. "Though with Carl that didn't mean he died peacefully."

Nate smiled. "The bastards behind the bank finally got him."

She smiled back. She didn't seemed rushed, the way doctors always seem rushed. She noticed the cast on his arm. He had his sleeves rolled down. She knocked on it, like knocking on a door. Nate was thinking maybe she was flirting with him, though she wasn't smiling anymore. Then he realized she just needed to put a pause in the scene. That was when she said, "There's something going on with your father. We have to run some tests." So much for being able to read doctors.

Nate came back out of the world of his own vanity and self-absorption. "What is it now?" he said. "What's wrong with him? Do I want to know?"

"We're running some tests. Blood work today and a CAT scan Monday."
She ran her hand across her stomach and abdomen. Nate tried not to think
about what exactly hid in the dark in that section of the human body.

He cursed. One word. She had heard the word before.

"He doesn't know," she said. "There aren't any new symptoms."

Nate nodded. Maybe she knew what he meant by it, the nod, because he
didn't know what he meant.

Bodie was in bed, but he'd propped himself up with an extra pillow behind
his head. He had his comb in his right hand, down beside his hip. He'd been
combing his hair. If he was sicker than he'd been the last time Nate had come,
he didn't look it. Nate stayed in the doorway for a second.

"You've got more hair than I do," Nate said, instead of hello. "Mine is
starting to thin out."

"You've got your grandfather's hair. He was bald by fifty. Maybe it skips
a generation."

"That would suck," Nate said.

"Carl's gone," Bodie said. Both mens' eyes went to the empty bed. Nate
nodded. Bodie said, "I thought maybe you'd think they were just giving him a
bath or something."

"When?"

"What difference does it make?" Bodie said.

"Good point."

"Last night," Bodie said. "He went all quiet, right after he got real loud."
They both looked away from the empty bed. "When I got put here, he was still
pretty much in the here and now," Bodie said. "Goddamn, he was tough. He had
seen some things, *done* some things too, probably. Tough."

Nate took his father outside. Today, Bodie let him push the wheelchair.
Neither man commented on it. They went out under the eucalyptuses. Nate
thought of the trees as belonging to the two of them, their eucalyptuses. Since
it was a Sunday, there were a lot of visitors, on the benches, under the trees. Did
they think the trees were theirs? A windstorm had come through two nights ago
and no one had come in to clean up yet; there was shredded bark everywhere.
No birds were in the branches, as if they'd been scared off, as if they'd all flown
off to wherever birds go when waiting for bad weather to pass. The question was
why hadn't they come back?

A volunteer rolled a cart by, ice cream bars, free. Neither man wanted one.

"Are you going to tell me how you broke your arm?" Bodie said.

Nate thought of a joke answer but, instead, said, "I think I'm onto a dirty cop, a senior guy in the Gang U. Something involving smuggling, maybe smuggling people. Two different gangs, maybe working together. I got thrown off a roof in Boyle Heights."

"We used to kill crooked cops," Bodie said, just like that. "It wasn't about Internal Affairs. Hell, most of us didn't care much one way or another with most IA cases. It would have to be a bad case that we'd find out about or personally witness. Not just a guy who got in money trouble. And not a first offense. It would have to be habitual or particularly egregious. In our faces. We'd kill 'em. It happened twice in my years on the force. And one other time, the guy killed himself, with some of us standing right there."

Nate was used to Bodie charging off down some road in his head. It seemed that the sicker he got—the closer to an end that only he could see, perhaps—the more Bodie had to say, the faster he talked, as if he was needing to get things on the record. Nate would say something that triggered a memory and away Bodie would go, usually starting with a line that was designed to grab Nate's attention, hook him, draw him close. No doubt the gerontologists had a name for the phenomenon, a designation meant to tame it, make it seem less crazy, less...*end stage*. As before, Nate just listened, let him go.

"A robbery detective had a thing at Santa Anita," Bodie said, in the next breath. "When they still let horses race and let people put money on them, right out in the open. Imagine that. It wasn't that he had some kind of skim going on, the usual thing. This guy was working with somebody inside, doping horses and probably jockeys, too. A couple of them died. Horses, not jockeys. We thought he'd let it go then, but he started right back up and when he did, he laid off the previous deal on another cop, a rookie who didn't have a clue and ended up in prison over it."

"So what happened?" Nate said. Bodie had stopped cold.

"Somebody—not me—shot him in the head, out under an old oil well in Alhambra, end of his shift. Cops can't let things like that go on. Not when it's in your face, not when innocent cops are taking the fall or worse. You have to do what you have to do."

You. Nate wondered if his old man meant him specifically. He was still watching the high branches of the stinky, papery trees. It was such a dry, dead day that nothing was moving, not the smallest branch, not one leaf. It was as if the world were holding its breath, this little corner of the world anyway.

"The other day I was remembering when we got our pool," Nate said.

"Nineteen ninety-six," Bodie said. "It cost eight thousand dollars."

"I was seven or eight. You were sitting there with a bottle of beer in an aluminum folding chair. I had these goggles I got for my birthday. You took the bottle cap and threw it out in the middle of the pool. You said you'd give me a dollar if I dove down and got that bottle cap."

"I don't remember any of this," Bodie said.

"I dove down," Nate said. "It was deep. On the second or third try, I got it. I climbed back out, handed it to you. You dug in the pocket of your shorts—you weren't wearing a shirt, just shorts—and you came out with four quarters."

Bodie started to nod.

"You threw them in the pool, the deep end," Nate said.

"*There's your dollar!*" his father said, laughing. Nate laughed, too.

A motorcycle came past, and not one of the new electrics. This one had that throaty my-wife-doesn't-approve sound. Nate looked over as it turned into the facility. It was fire-engine red, a thirty-year-old Harley Roadster. It made a loop around the lot, then stopped next to Nate's Crow at the far end of the lot. The rider got off, dropped the stand, and pulled off his red helmet. It was Il Cho. He looked across at Nate, stayed right where he was.

"I gotta go," Nate said.

"Leave me out here. Sun feels good. I can get myself back in."

Nate bent over the wheelchair and kissed Bodie on the forehead, something he'd never done before, not once. He could tell his dad appreciated it, even if he didn't see it coming or understand why it had come today.

"Thanks for dropping by."

"I'll talk to you later," Nate said, starting across toward the parking lot and Il Cho.

"Sorry about the hair," Bodie said, instead of goodbye.

Chapter Thirty-Five

The CI switchboard was on fire, every snitch in Snitchville calling in. Nate had even gotten a message from Johnny Santo sitting in County, waiting to be transferred up to Soledad. They were like third-graders squirming in their seats, waving their hands, hoping to be called on, get that gold star. And they were all saying the same thing: something about RVs, a line of them supposedly aimed toward LA from some place in the high desert, purportedly headed on to Mexico, apparently to pick up weed. A new big-scale smuggle. Incas.

The first informant of the day was Blind Billy, a legally blind (former) barber in Compton. "I'm not looking to get anything out of this, not a thing," he had said right off that morning there on the screen on the counter in Nate's kitchen, before Nate's KitchenMaid had even made coffee. "You turned my life around. I'm forever in your debt." Blind Billy said the same lines—run together like that—every time he talked to Nate. Six years ago Nate had put together the trafficking case that sent the blind man to prison along with three of his men. Improbably, right there in the courtroom, Billy had thanked Nate for arresting him and—in prison and once he was out again—had continued to thank him with the occasional tip.

But this time something was off. There was subtext in the blind man's video tip. So Nate flew down to Compton to look him in the eyes, such as they were. Billy wasn't at his usual spot on the sidewalk in the green lawn chair out in front of the shop he still owned. The barbers inside said they didn't have the slightest idea where he could possibly be, but then Billy stepped out from the back room. Maybe Billy smelled the turkey. Nate had brought him a smoked whole turkey.

They went into the office to talk. From the start—when he pointed toward the red plastic couch and closed the door behind them—Billy was uneasy, hesitant, acting like a man who had something to say but wasn't sure he was going to say it, who wasn't sure what trouble it would bring down on him if he did say it. Blind Billy was a White man in his sixties. His hair once had been sandy blond, but now what was left of it was dyed red-out-of-a-bottle. "Legally blind" in Billy's case meant that he could make out shapes and shades of light. He had lived his whole life in the Black community. Nate didn't know his personal story, had never thought to ask. There were a lot of Blind Billys in Nate's life, men and women who weren't what they looked like from across the street, men and women with backstories that went a way toward explaining—but not all the way—how they got to be the way they were. Billy wore sunglasses day and night, apparently because he thought they made him look more Black and made people think he couldn't see a thing, which was useful. People spoke to him as if he were fully blind and senseless in all the other ways. They'd say, "There's a coffee there in front of you on the table, Billy." Behind his back, the same wise-asses might say, "Has anyone ever told him he's not a Negro?" though everyone knew he'd lost his sight in high school.

He settled behind his desk and said, "What brings you down here, sir? Did I say something in my message that gave you pause?"

"Everybody's calling me about the RV thing, using the same words," Nate said.

"Like the man says, they're just words unless they're true," Blind Billy said. He looked up at the ceiling, squinting, as if attempting to read something there. Maybe he was trying to remember the words *he'd* used when he'd called Nate that morning.

"Who did *you* hear it from? If you don't mind telling me."

Billy shifted in his chair, made it squeak. He hesitated, then said a name. Then he said another name. "It could have been either one of them," he said. "I honestly don't remember. People come to me with all manner of things. Trying to get a free fade, I guess. Shave and a haircut, six bits. Like you said, everybody's talking about this."

"When?"

"It's happening now, probably already happened. They on the road, brother."

"I meant when did you hear?"

"I imagine I heard about it sometime Sunday. I guess it's an entertaining idea, captures people's attention, RVs."

"And everybody likes more Mexican weed," Nate said.

"Indeed," Blind Billy said. "And there's a drought."

"What about heroin?" Nate asked.

"A ton of it all at once," Billy said, turning toward Nate again. "First there wasn't none, now there's a ton. One if by land, two if by sea."

"Any thoughts about who's behind the RVs?"

"Incas. And a Gang Unit cop is in on it. What I hear."

"A fleet of RV haulers. That would be a whole lot of pot."

"Indeed. But people want a lot of it. They use it as an escape goat."

Nate smiled, stood. He had the turkey in a paper sack. He set it on the desk.

Billy got up to see him out. "It probably was Little Devin who told me, now that I think about it. That'd make sense," he said. It was one of the names he had offered up a minute ago, the second of the two names he'd said. "He's dead," he said. "Found this morning."

"Hope you like the turkey," Nate said. "A guy in South Pasadena smokes 'em. Real wood, real smoke, real meat."

"Real illegal," Blind Billy said, and licked his lips.

Nate had left the Crow a block away atop the building across from the funeral home where he'd walked in on Derrick Wallace. Rockett had given up standing at parade rest beside the bird but he was still alert, head on a swivel. He had his side-arm in hand. Nate wondered if he'd holstered it since the other night's riot. He also wondered if the kid was keeping his own body count. A hundred people had been stomped dead in front of the arena. It was Monday. At least the kid had gotten Sunday off.

Yesterday morning in the cop home parking lot when Il Cho had ridden up on his motorcycle, he hadn't said anything about the RVs in the High Desert but he had told Nate about the goings-on in Whitey's skybox at the Vivid show. Nacho Ibierrez and Derrick Wallace. According to Cho, the get-together had been about making peace between the Incas and the Twenties, clearing the way to do some business together. Or at least not trip over each other. It had stayed tense between the leaders of the two gangs, Cho said. And Cho said Whitey had said, when it was over, that he'd brought together Derrick Wallace and Nacho Ibierrez to play the two gangs against each other. "To neutralize them," Cho said Whitey had said. "To keep the whole thing from happening." Maybe. Or maybe Cho was feeding Nate a line Whitey wanted Nate to hear, to throw him off.

Nate and Rockett flew north.

And there they *weren't*. The RVs. The fenced lot behind the factory in Palmdale was empty. It had held twenty or more new coaches but no more. Gone. The plant looked dead, abandoned. Nate hovered for a few seconds and then circled for another angle, another view. He knew Rockett in the seat behind him was looking down on the utterly empty scene, too. Maybe he was getting used to this. He'd been Nate's gunner long enough now to figure out that the job was a lot of watching and waiting in places where nothing seemed to be happening. Down below, a literal tumbleweed rolled across the lot.

"You like Westerns, Rockett?"

"Not really. My mom made me watch *Unforgiven* once. It's her favorite movie."

"That makes sense. Your dad splitting and all."

"I guess. I never thought of it that way."

"They're morality plays, Westerns," Nate said. "The best ones are black and white."

"Actually, I think she was the one who split," Rockett said.

"Oh," Nate said. Of course.

He pivoted, pointed them south, dropped the hammer. When accelerating, haulin' ass, Crows tilted down radically. At speed, Rockett had the same view as Nate. They were above the 5 freeway, five hundred feet off the deck. It wasn't but a minute before they were over the weird slanted red slabs of Vasquez Rocks. Nothing looked more Western than Vasquez Rocks. Or was it Martian?

"We're looking for RVs," Nate called back to Rockett. "A bunch of them. Rollin'."

As they flew over Mission Hills into the San Fernando Valley, Nate reached under the dash and revived the radio. Carrie appeared instantly. "Where have you been?" she said, almost like a wife. "We have a Yellow Code call."

◆ ◆ ◆

IT WAS A FULL-ON coordinated move on the TMZ; twenty-five helos in formation, a murder of Crows, half of them coming in from the south, the rest in a fan-tail, approaching from the west, north, and east, spread out like fingers. It was the sort of operation that needed a good deal of planning, which meant it was political.

Nate was still ten miles out, watching the show on the heads-up display, listening to the noisy cross-talk on the radio. He recognized most of the voices, comrades in arms. No Whitey, no Il Cho, no GU cops, none of the voices he was tired of hearing.

"Three-six-five," Nate said to the air in front of him.

His CRO buddy Tucker appeared. He was airborne, over downtown, behind the controls, moving into position with his gunner behind him. "Yo. Today your day off?"

"There are no holidays in hell. So what's in the TMZ? Godzilla?"

"Okies. We're doing a 'humane extraction.' Round 'em up, head 'em out. I guess there got to be too many of them down in there."

"Where are they taking them?"

"We're just handling the rounding up part," Tucker said. "We're supposed to make a show in the air to center them, then drop and land and come in walkulating. They want to get it all done by dark, before the suppertime news shows."

"Makes sense."

"You want us to wait for you?" Tucker said.

"Could you? I love a good show of… concern," Nate said.

They didn't wait for him. It looked like war. Nate made a first pass at mid-altitude and then climbed to a thousand feet and hovered, above it all. Below, the helos tightened up the formation for their friendly assault. Nate opened the hatches so Rockett could see. They watched, waiting for the Okies to come out onto the rooftops or run out of the buildings. It didn't happen. After a few minutes, a handful of the TMZ's regular homeless inhabitants emerged between the buildings, looking up. Crows were mostly silent, but not when there were twenty-five of them directly overhead. They started landing, picking roofs on the perimeter of the zone. The long-term squatters disappeared back inside.

Tucker and the other CROs started coming down fire escapes, moving in on foot.

"What do you see?" Nate said.

Tucker clicked on the body cam on his shoulder. He was inside the N Building, where they'd all been that night when things went sideways. "Does that answer your question?" Tucker said.

Not a soul.

♦♦♦

NATE WENT BACK TO looking for the RVs, this time flying south. The empty would-be weed-haulers could've slipped into Mexico already if they'd left Palmdale over the weekend as Blind Billy and everyone else had testified. It was a four- or five-hour trip to Mexico. Two middle-of-nowhere roads went south and southeast through the mountains and desert. Even with the tightening of the border after the oil boom, the crossings at Tecate and La Rumorosa remained. They were old-style, low-tech, and undermanned, with local officials more open to bribery than the *federales* at the big gate at Otay Mesa/Tijuana.

But something told Nate the RVs were still in LA. He flew over a few big used-car and truck lots east of downtown. Boyle Heights. He flew right over the rooftop where his two Inca pals had tried to teach him how to fly. The memory made his wrist hurt. He went farther south, crossed over two freeways and the dry LA River, and scoped out the massive car graveyards and salvage lots in South Gate, dusty rusted acres of The Way We Were. A battered old Winnebago leaned against another dinosaur RV in the back row of one junkyard, but that was it.

"We're still looking for RVs," he said to Rockett.

He headed back toward downtown. Storing the coaches out in the open—even for a day or two—would be a mistake Whitey and the Incas wouldn't make. The rigs were too tall to fit through the entryways for most of the covered parking lots, but Nate circled a couple of those anyway.

Tucker's visage popped up on the heads-up display. He looked beat. "The Okies were gone"The Okies were gone, all of them, when we came in on foot," he said.

"Gone how?" Nate said.

"The regulars down in the TMZ said the Okies all went into one building down in there and never came out. Herded by some gangbangers—Latin. It all happened before we came on the scene, early this morning."

♦♦♦

IT WAS BUMPING ON sunset when Nate decided to look for RVs another way, on screens. He landed on the roof of the glass block that was the CRO headquarters.

He stood there by the Crow a second and looked west. When it got really dry like this, the sky at sundown could look almost like blood. Or that sherbet that was orange and raspberry swirled together. That kind of sky always made him think of The Eagles' *Hotel California* album, the picture on the cover, back when records still had covers.

You can check out anytime you like, but you can never leave...

The song was still stuck in his head as he rode the elevator down, leaving Rockett on the roof supervising the fueling of the bird.

Nate started with the last forty-eight hours' worth of high-sat/low-sat surveillance recordings, elapsed-time coverage of Southern California from Ventura south to Mexico, from Palos Verdes Peninsula east to Palm Desert. The big, high clear brown pictures weren't of much use except to give Nate his bearings and to confirm the drought and near certainty of a dry tomorrow. It wasn't entirely cloudless. In the Angeles Forest above Azusa, out to the east a few miles, a trio of perfectly round cotton balls had gotten snagged in the derelict broadcast towers on Mount Wilson. The high view had another use for Nate: it gave him, against all odds, a sweet feeling, a feeling of home. Los Angeles was inhospitable in all kinds of ways, but it was his home territory. He clicked down to the closer view and zeroed in on downtown, watched that morning's commute. The feed was sped up, which meant the cars looked as if they were actually moving, actually commuting. A running analog clock in the corner of the frame ran through two hours while Nate watched. What was funny was how little forward motion there was, even sped up, how dumb and utterly impractical driving a car in LA seemed.

The video gear had hand-gesture controls. It was like flying with the stick in his hand but without the stick. Nate pointed to the right with his thumb to roll back the time and the footage went in a blur to noon the day before, only stopping when Nate's thumb came upright again. He lifted his right hand and changed the location with a pushing motion that told the View-Master to speed north. Thus he went from the towers of downtown back to Sun Valley and the mountain pass where the I-5 came south past Vasquez Rocks. It was as good a spot as any to sit and watch and wait. Daylight faded and night came on. The spy system used the best military night-vision cameras. The hills stayed black but the freeway turned orange, bright as day.

No sign of the RVs. Nate watched all through the night, which meant five minutes.

Most Angelenos would be surprised to learn of the level of surveillance they now lived under, how close and unblinking the eyes watching them were. Whether they would be angry about it was another question. What did privacy even mean anymore? Tonight Nate had the HQ screen room to himself, but other nights cops would scan LA for scenes to crack jokes about. Nude sunbathers in their fenced backyards. Volleyball girls at Zuma Beach. Falling-down drunks falling down drunk. Unattractive mismatched people getting married at the arboretum. Beautiful guys doing yoga on rooftops in West Hollywood. Dopes stealing cars only to get stuck in traffic a half block away. Hookers hooking. An action movie shooting on a studio backlot, take after take, explosion after explosion. Some Islander taking a leak in his backyard at midnight, drinking a beer with his free hand.

Nate remembered something. The 24/7 surveillance of Whitey Barnes that his judge friend had secretly court-ordered could still be up and running. He logged in. It was still there, still hot. He was presented with a list of options. Between past and present, he chose past, the last thirty-six hours of drone surveillance. Next he chose a View, chose to be looking over Whitey's shoulder anytime he'd been airborne in the last day and a half. And there they were. It took a few minutes of scanning, but there they were. At 3:10 a.m. Sunday morning, Whitey was aloft in the fat and ugly GU helo watching as the RVs came not down the I-5 but instead down the dry concrete wash of the Arroyo Seco, headed toward downtown in a line, lights out, under a sliver of moon. Whitey—and Nate—watched as the convoy passed under the Avenue Twenty-Sixth Bridge, the selfsame arc from which Razor had been thrown, alive or dead.

Whitey's helo stayed high but fell in behind the RVs on the dry riverbed, following them another five miles until the line of them drove into the mouth of a thirty-foot-tall culvert.

Chapter Thirty-Six

Nate and Rockett had their lights on as they walked on powdery dirt. Nate had decided not to fly into the culvert, though a part of him was tempted to try. The suicidal part? There was room, just barely. The apex of the curve overhead was twenty-five feet off the deck. The road in front of them wasn't hard to make out, double-grooves on both sides. It looked like a road—a trail out in the desert—but it wasn't a road at all, just tracks in silt in the bottom of the big pipe. It had been months since any real rainwater had flowed through this underground section of the Arroyo Seco. Dust hung in the air, as if the convoy of RVs had permanently stirred things up. It had been more than twenty-four hours since they'd come through. The tracks were double-grooved because they were duelies, four tires on the back. To carry the extra weight. The rigs were long gone, but, based on the tracks, nothing had come after them either. Until now.

"What do you do when you get a song stuck in your head, Rockett?" Nate said, his voice booming in the cave of the culvert.

Rockett said, "I sing it as loud as I can. It flushes the song out of your head somehow. I used to work at In-N-Out Burger. My manager told me about it. He was studying psychology at Pierce College."

Nate took it from the top, at the top of his lungs.

On a dark desert highway, cool wind in my hair
Warm smell of colitas, rising up through the air...

"I sound good," Nate said. "Natural reverb."

Both men wore helmets and body armor. With the lamps on the helmets and the throw-lights on both shoulders, they looked like deep-sea divers, explorers on the bottom of the ocean, which was about the last thing they were. Rockett had a shotgun strapped to his back, for one thing, and nobody knew they were down there for another.

Nate tapped the side of his helmet. "Is your radio working?"

"It comes and goes," Rockett said. "Somebody is trying to get in, sounds like. My GPS is messed up, too. Where does this come out?"

"Runs about a mile and a half, straight south, comes out again below Olympic. But we don't know if they're using this for a road or a storage facility."

Nate went back to singing "Hotel California." Rockett looked back. They were already a quarter of a mile in from the mouth of the culvert—behind them, nothing but black. He felt movement in the air, like a ball whizzing past his head. Bats.

A hundred yards on, a set of tire tracks went off to the right. Nate stopped singing. The dust had gotten so thick it was hard to see anything more than what was right in front of them or right at their feet. The track was misshapen on the left front, wide. A flat? Nate looked up from the dirt. His headlamp lit it up: a single RV, ten yards ahead, parked against the curved side of the culvert. All the Winnebagos were brown just like the dust and the back window on this one was painted over so as not to reflect light. If Nate hadn't seen the tracks, they would have trudged on past it.

Closing in on the disabled RV was like making an old-school traffic stop, something Nate hadn't done since the Academy. He was all but sure the rig was empty, abandoned, so he was cool. Rockett swung the shotgun off of his back and brought it up to the ready, a crisp, showy motion like a drum major in a high school band with his baton.

"Don't get too into this," Nate said.

His side-arm still in the holster, Nate went forward. He'd guessed right: a blowout. He came around the rig, tried the main door. It wasn't locked. Nate opened the door, letting Rockett and the Streetsweeper go in first. Since the other night when he'd been thrown off the roof, Nate had been a little less cocky than normal, especially when there wasn't much of an audience. The coach was empty, nobody home. Nate stepped in behind Rockett, hit the light switch. An overhead light came on, as did a couple of sconces on either side of the picture window, cheap brass fixtures meant to look like Western lanterns. Nate took off his helmet and went forward. On the floor next to the driver's captain's chair there was McDonald's trash and three crushed red Tecate beer cans. And a stubby joint was in the ashtray. The other captain's chair up front was bagged in plastic, fresh off the assembly line.

The RV was as standard as standard gets: main room with kitchen, bedroom across the back. The king-size bed was covered with an ugly comforter with a saguaro cactus design stitched onto it. Off the three-foot-long hallway was the bathroom, a drain in the floor so you could take a shower standing over the plastic toilet-and-sink combo. The whole thing reminded Nate of a prison cell, albeit a really nice beige and brown Southwestern-themed one.

Looking up, Nate said, "Does it feel a little low in here to you?"

"I've never been in one of these," Rockett said.

The ceiling in the hallway was just a foot over their heads. Fiberglass. Nate pushed up on it. No give. There was a light fixture in the middle of things. He used his helmet to punch a hole in the molded plastic over it and ripped it away. A metal drawer pull had been screwed in next to the bulb, an add-on.

If it weren't for following hunches, Nate would never go anywhere. "Give that a yank."

Rockett grabbed the handle and pulled, and the fixture dropped down, hinged on the backside. They shined their lights up. Crawlspace, another two feet of height over the cabin.

"Feel around up in there," Nate said. "I'd do it but I'm scared of spiders."

Rockett reached up and patted around until he found something. He pulled down an aluminum ladder on rollers. Nate still had his helmet in his hand. He switched on the headlamp to use it as a flashlight and ascended. Up the ladder, he shined the helmet around, slowly, like a lighthouse. Running the length of the coach was a steel box, light-gauge but steel, not aluminum. Handcrafted. It was like an attic, ten feet wide and thirty feet long and just tall enough for a bale of cannabis.

Something caught Nate's eye aft, in the upper corner, like a fuel cap seen from the inside. He came back down the ladder. They stepped down out of the rig and went to the back to the standard-issue ladder. Nate climbed onto the roof, but the top deck had no give. The cargo compartment was steel all around. He pointed the light and found a scoop molded onto the top of the coach at the rear. An air scoop.

Another vent was mounted on the front of the coach next to a rack of fog lights. He was walking forward to check it out when the radio speaker in the helmet in his hand cracked and sputtered, a voice coming in midsentence.

"Say again," Nate said, putting on the helmet.

Il Cho. The signal was loud and clear, at least for a second. Maybe it was because Nate was standing atop a steel box. Cho said, "Whitey knows where you are."

"Generally or specifically?" Nate said. "What does he know?"

"Where you left the Crow." Then the connection broke.

Nate jumped down off the roof of the RV. Rockett was looking back toward the mouth of the culvert, like he wanted to go there. "Let's find the rest of them and get the hell out of here," Nate said, firing up all of his lights and moving back toward the main line of tracks.

Then it came.

It didn't sound like a flood or they would have heard it coming and gotten out of the way. It didn't sound like anything. Nate and Rockett were another hundred yards deeper into the culvert, still following the tire tracks. The dirt underfoot was dry. And then it wasn't. Nate looked down. When he lifted his boot, the footprint filled. Mud. Moving mud.

"Rockett," Nate said.

Rockett was out in front but turned as the mud went over his boots, then up to his ankles. It was like pudding, butterscotch, six inches of moving butterscotch pudding. They both knew it wasn't rain, not real rain. It smelled of reclaimed sewage water, tanker water. The sludge was up their shins now and still rising. Bottles and cans and cardboard boxes floated past, and then a red stop sign, and then a dried-out dead dog. So this was Hell.

"Get to the side," Nate yelled, pointing to dry ground still visible along the sides of the culvert. They set out but didn't get very far very fast. Everything was in slow motion. The flow kept rising. At least the dust was gone.

The mud was up to their knees when the broken-down RV came at them, straight down the middle of the culvert. It was still driverless but seemed full of murderous intent. They tried to mud-wade out of its path, Nate going one direction and Rockett the other. As if in response, the RV began to rotate. It came right at Rockett, turning lazily, and was sideways when it plowed into him. It knocked him down and almost under. Rockett grabbed onto the side mirror and pulled himself up. All of it took three seconds, about as long as it took Rockett to think about what it would be like to drown in mud. He grabbed the top bar of the mirror and chinned up until he could throw his leg over the lower brace.

Nate went after him, in slow motion. The motor home was twenty feet past him now. It was like running in a bad dream. He made it to the back deck of the RV, reached up for the ladder, missed, slipped, then caught hold of it on the second try and pulled himself aboard. He hooked his good arm in the ladder, went up a step or two, and leaned out to see where Rockett was. Rockett was struggling, weighed down by his muddy suit. He looked like a three-hundred-pound man. Nate watched as Rockett threw his leg around the front of the coach, across the windshield, holding onto the rack of the fog lights on the roof. Just then, one of the RV's wheels caught hold of solid ground under the mud and the rig shifted course abruptly, almost throwing Rockett off. Then it shifted again and aimed itself toward the side of the culvert. It crashed against it, crushing Rockett's right leg, pinning him. Nate climbed onto the roof of the RV and came forward. Free of the mud, he moved like Superman. He came out to the front edge. Rockett looked up at him. He was stuck bad. Nate held onto the light rack and leaned down. Rockett seized Nate's broken arm just above the cast, more desperate than he wanted to let on.

Nate howled in pain. "Try again," he said.

Rockett hooked both of his arms through Nate's good arm. It was no use. Rockett was pinned. Nate put both boots on the side of the culvert and his back against the top of the frame of the RV and pushed. It was like some perverse workout in the kind of gym where there's no music. It worked. The front of the rig pivoted an inch or two and Rockett's legs were freed up. Nate pulled him onto the roof just as the coach snagged on the bottom again and turned back toward the center of the culvert.

Rockett was on his back, rubbing his right leg. He tried to get to his feet and fell over. "It's not broken," he said, without being asked. He was wrong, but neither of them would know that until the night was over.

Nate looked ahead, into the continuing darkness, but there was nothing to see. "We gotta get off of this thing," Nate said. "I'm getting seasick."

"Look," Rockett said. Twenty yards ahead off to the right, rungs of an iron ladder climbed the side of culvert. Nate aimed his lights at it and followed the rungs up. At the top was another, smaller tunnel, intersecting. Just then, the RV stopped dead, as if obeying a command. The mud had gone solid, like cooling lava. Rockett hopped down the RV ladder on one leg before Nate could help him. Then they were both on the mud again. They got to the base of the ladder and climbed.

Once they were up top, Rockett said, "Is this another storm drain? It's big."

"A subway line they never finished," Nate said. "Long Beach to Pasadena. Right under downtown."

Nate was already walking in that direction. Downtown. Rockett followed. The second tunnel was darker than the culvert, cut off from the light at the end. Before they had gone a hundred feet, Nate had found something: a stuffed dinosaur. The toy was ragged, as if some kid had had it awhile, but it was clean, hadn't been down there long. Nate looked up.

Another iron ladder climbed the side of the tunnel to an open hatch.

"How close are we to the TMZ?" Rockett said.

"We're right underneath it," Nate said.

◆ ◆ ◆

NATE AND ROCKETT EMERGED out of the mouth of the culvert, right back where they'd gone in. They'd retraced their steps to get back to the bird. The dirt underfoot was dry again but it was obvious the flood had passed through. The pitiful sliver of a moon had gone down. Nate had left the Crow on high ground on the bank of the wash. A premonition? As he moved toward it, he slapped the start switch on the upper left arm of his flight suit and the servo motors whirred and the doors scissored up. Rockett hobbled after him with his bum leg and pulled himself up into the second seat. Twenty seconds later, they were airborne.

Carrie came on. "Goodness. What happened to you?" she said, when she saw Nate.

"Singin' in the rain," Nate said.

He pivoted to fly toward downtown. Off to his port were the red tanker helos, a flying wedge of six of them, crossing and recrossing above the zone between the Arroyo Seco and Boyle Heights, even though the Zone Three news said tonight they'd be all the way out in Brentwood.

Chapter Thirty-Seven

The Crows were at full-throttle, nose-down, leaving Center City on a south-by-southeast course. Off to Nate's starboard was Tucker, who'd ditched his gunner and picked up Il Cho. Nate and Rockett had come in and refueled but hadn't even taken the time to wash off the mud. There was still plenty of night left. Nate had the idea that they had to overtake the convoy by daybreak. After that, it'd be a different game involving too many others, outside authorities. Depending on how long the RVs had to wait in the culvert before loading the New Okies coming from the TMZ, they could've already made the run by now. Of the two roads that crossed over the border east of the big crossing in Tijuana, Nate was guessing they'd be on 94, the Tecate road. He thought that because of the Tecate beer cans thrown on the floor of the abandoned RV. Highly scientific.

He'd radioed Tucker and then Il Cho as he was flying away from the Arroyo Seco and the culvert. He'd also reached out to two San Diego CROs, friends he'd seen again that bad day on the beach at Coronado. After witnessing a thing like that, his thinking went, a man might be looking for a chance to do some good, something to try to get the world halfway back in balance again. In this case, one of the men who might be looking for a chance to do some good was a woman named Carlisle. She had a first name but considered it an insult when anyone used it. She'd been the one who'd called him when the bodies washed up, the one who'd said there was something down her way he needed to see. She was in her midtwenties and flew that way.

But the San Diego Crows hadn't shown up yet.

"I like your bumper sticker," Tucker said, over the radio. At three hundred mph. On Nate's fuselage was a sticker that said, "You're In My Blind Spot." Nate had bought it at a truck stop out in the desert.

"I should get it tattooed on my forehead," Nate said back to Tucker. The Crows were flying as close as two cars going down the freeway. "Are you all right back there, Cho?" Nate said. Cho looked spooked, from what Nate could see of him in the second seat behind Tucker. Nobody liked flying with CROs. Cho didn't like flying, period.

"You guys are crazy," Cho said.

"Where's Whitey tonight, Il Cho?" Nate said. He had tried to tap into *The Whitey Barnes Show* a few minutes ago but it was gone, the feed shut down. Either the time had run out on Nate's judge friend's authorized drone surveillance or Whitey had gotten wise, been tipped off. He probably had judge friends, too.

"He's twenty minutes behind us," Cho said. "I didn't call him. He said suddenly all our CIs were telling him Inca RVs were on the road to Tecate."

"That's good to hear," Nate said, with an edge. "I was half afraid we were on the wrong road."

"He thinks the RVs are empty, just weed-haulers going down to pick up the first load."

"Did he ask why you didn't wait for him?"

"We're all working different things different times," Cho said, defensively.

"If he's in the GU helo, by the time that bus makes the scene it'll all be over."

"Could be that's his plan," Cho said.

"Maybe." Nate still wasn't sure which side Cho was on. Or even what the sides were now or what side *he* was on. The one that wasn't Whitey's.

Cho said, "He wanted to know why you weren't on the comm-link all night."

"Say again?" Nate said, making a fake radio-breaking-up noise with his mouth.

Rockett leaned forward and pointed over Nate's shoulder. "There," he said. Lights. A mile in front of them. A line of lights. "Hot damn," Nate said.

In this section of Highway 94—the last miles before Mexico—the two-lane road was under a canopy of trees, oaks as black as everything else around them. At this speed, the CROs were on top of the convoy in seconds. The RVs were running nose-to-tail. The headlights and taillights flashed through gaps in the trees—white and red—blinking like a quarter-mile-long string of party lights.

"Lift, ease off," Nate said to Tucker. They were flying at a thousand feet.

The two birds slowed to keep from overrunning the RVs and climbed another thousand feet. Nate and Tucker had killed their running lights fifteen minutes ago, over Orange County, and had been dangerously invisible since then.

They'd cut off their comm-links to headquarters at the same time. No Carrie, no access to home base tools and personnel. Whitey and Cho were communicating on their own frequency, possibly in more ways than one.

"Nate," a voice said on the radio, a woman's voice. Carlisle.

"Hey, girl," Nate said. He'd pay for that later.

She appeared on the heads-up. "So we're chasing RVs?"

"Where are you?"

"In front of them a hundred yards. We're at a thousand feet, flying backward."

"Cool," Nate said.

"I'm here, too, mate," another voice said, this one male and Aussie, pretending hurt feelings.

"Tim Tam," Nate said. "Did you guys bring gunners?"

"Gunners and guns," the other San Diego CRO said.

"Go to two thousand feet. We don't want 'em to panic. The drivers are amateurs and probably high."

"I don't think they're looking up," Carlisle said. "Third wagon in, the driver has a woman with her face in his lap, riding along. A blonde. He has the dome light on."

"Jeez," Nate said, not wanting to think much about it, who she might be.

"What are they hauling?" Carlisle said.

"People," Nate said.

"People," she repeated.

"New Okies. Dust Bowlers."

"How many?"

"Maybe twenty in each rig. They're taking them to work in the fields in Mexico. Or to dump in the dark in the middle of nowhere. I'm sure they already got all the money out of them."

"People suck," Carlisle said.

"Yes, they do," Nate said.

"They're slowing down, way down," the Aussie pilot said. "Are you seeing this?"

"Hold," Nate said.

"How far from the border are we?" Il Cho came on and said.

Tucker answered, "We're twenty miles from Tecate."

"Are they stopping?" Cho said.

"Maybe taking a whiz," Tucker said.

Nate was studying the same onboard map Tucker had, the lay of the land ahead. The road in this section was uphill, but there had been twists and turns and hills and valleys before and the convoy hadn't slowed. They'd been running hot ever since Nate and Tucker had picked them up, apparently unaware of the cops above them. Nate looked over the side but couldn't see much. He needed a better view.

"High and live," he said, to the air, to the onboard computer. The Crow had its own link-up for navigation apart from HQ. After a hesitation, the heads-up read: LIVE SATELLITE VIEW UNAVAILABLE. "What else you got?" Nate said. "Dead and low?"

"You talking to me?" Tucker said.

The computer put up an archived daylight sat-view of the area. This part of Highway 94 ran through a mostly unpopulated area, a ranch house or two along the way, well off the road. It was the same story the rest of the way to Tecate, at least according to the archived daylight view.

"We got a mesa up here, top of the hill," Carlisle said. "A gap in the trees, level."

Nate found it on the daylight sat-view four miles ahead. "Got it," he said. He dropped the hammer again and flew forward until he was over the mesa. In real time, looking down, it was just a black hole, blacker and emptier than everything around it.

Tucker stayed right with him. "Hey, look what we found," he said.

Nate looked down and back over his right shoulder. He could make out in the dimness the blind curve of the highway before it opened out onto the mesa. It looked like a good place to stop the convoy. Or it looked like a trap of some kind, a big round bear trap just waiting for something or someone to set down on it and trip it. But who would have set a trap for them? The rigs hadn't shown any sign of knowing the four CRO helos were up there.

After the mesa, the trees closed in again. It wasn't now or never…but it was now.

"We'll take 'em down here," Nate said.

"Affirmative," the other three pilots said.

Nate could feel Rockett tightening up in the gunner seat, getting ready, the adrenaline starting to pump, the blood thumping in his young ears. Nate remembered how it used to feel, heading into something like this. His own pulse was probably lower than it had been eight hours ago when he'd stood on the roof at HQ looking at that bloody Eagles sunset. Was it a good thing that his heart didn't race anymore when a lot was at stake, when with a wrong turn he could wind up dead?

"Carlisle, Tim, come forward," he said. "Tucker and I will be on the flanks, east and west, five hundred feet off the deck, dark," Nate said. "You guys will be at the front door, same altitude, backward, everybody dark, everybody pointed in. Then all at the same time we'll hit 'em with a ton of light and drop in."

"That'd scare the shit out of me," Tucker said. "If I was flying along, stoned, out here in the middle of nowhere." He gave it a beat. "Wait, I already am."

They all moved into position, the San Diego birds north of the mesa, Nate to the west, Tucker to the east, like points on a compass or nine, twelve, and three on a clock.

"Hold up," Cho said.

"What?" Nate said.

"Whitey's coming in," Cho said. "Four klicks out."

Nate looked to port, back toward the far dome of incandescence that was Orange County and LA. A ball of light was coming toward them, growing in size.

"I see him," Nate said. "Tell them to get on our frequency. Let's hope the drivers don't look up. Or have their windows down."

The sound of the GU helicopter would reach them any second, the thudding of the blades and the low-register rough roar of its engine. A Bell Twin Ranger was like a moving van compared to a Crow. It was coming in fast, unmuffled and fully lit up, the way you fly into a poor neighborhood when you want the people on the ground to know the cops are on scene and don't much care what you think about it.

"Stand off, Whitey," Nate said, into the radio. "And kill the light."

A moment slid by before Whitey spoke. "You're the boss," he said.

Whitey wasn't alone. Two more heavy helos were behind the GU bus—flying in a straight line—Bell Twin Rangers, too. One slid out to the right of the GU rig, one to the left, revealing themselves. They were immigration enforcement cops, ICE. It was written on the foreheads of the helicopters, the first thing you saw when they came at you. All three birds killed their lights, obeyed orders, pulled up, and backed off.

"Why'd you bring ICE, Whitey?" Nate said. "I heard you thought the RVs were empty."

"I try to keep an open mind," Whitey said.

"Stay back."

"Yeah, you already said that," Whitey said.

"Here we go," Tucker said. "They're going into the big blind curve."

The motor homes had slowed to a crawl as they climbed the highway toward the mesa. They were bumper-to-bumper when they broke out of the trees. Then they came to a dead stop, the whole line of them. One by one, they turned off their headlights. It looked almost like surrender, except no one was getting out with their hands up. A minute passed with the RVs just sitting there.

"What are they doing?" Cho said.

"Thirteen of them," Rockett said.

"Quiet," Nate said. Then to everyone else, "Somebody dot 'em."

Everybody responded, aiming and firing their light-guns, painting phosphorescent tracking dots on the top deck of each RV.

A full minute passed. Then another. "Are they just going to sit there?"

"OK, on the downbeat," Nate said.

"I don't know what that means," Tucker said.

"Hit the NightSuns. Now," Nate said.

"Wait, wait," Carlisle said. "They're heading out again."

It was as if the lead driver had just been waiting for the convoy to bunch up before he pulled out again. And he pulled out fast. One by one, the rigs sped away, drag-racing across the mesa, lights out, headed for the trees on the other side, a hundred yards distant.

"Oops," Whitey said.

"Hit it," Nate said to his team.

All four NightSuns exploded at once, making it high noon on the mesa. The Crows were so low the light seemed universal, lit up every bit of the scene, threw intersecting shadows across everything. It looked like a rock show. The escaping drivers looked up, squinting, as they sped away. It was impossible to say if they were surprised or not by the arrival of the police. More than a few were grinning big.

"Stay in front of them, Carlisle," Nate said. "Close the gate."

Carlisle and the Aussie pilot were already dropping, positioning themselves between the convoy and the trees and the highway that went on to Tecate. They all but set down on roadway, hovering ten feet above the blacktop, their forward lights aimed at the first RV, like the rudest, highest high beams ever. The idea was to make the lead RV stop.

Nate was hot after the rigs crossing the mesa. The RVs were as close together as boxcars on a rolling freight train. Nate was flying a foot off the road, flying like a twenty-year-old, right on the tail of the last coach, tailgating it.

Tucker was right behind him, coming up on the left flank of the convoy, low to the ground, too, but not suicidally low.

The lead RV showed no signs of stopping. "Carlisle, I guess you'd better lift," Nate said.

Carlisle and Tim-Tam floated up a foot, just enough for the convoy to pass underneath. The driver in the first coach looked up and smiled a satisfied smile. "We got us a cowboy in the front vehicle, a black hat," Carlisle said.

At the rear of the train, Nate and Tucker stayed in position, but the trees were coming up fast. At the last second, Tucker bailed, went high and left, all but trimming the top of the first oak. Nate stayed low and centered. And then all the rigs were back under the trees with Nate right behind them on the tail of the last motor home, close enough to read the expiration date on the license plate. The coaches were still running with no lights. The tunnel of trees was as black as a cannon barrel.

Nate floated up a foot or two and looked up the length of the convoy, all the way to the front. There was a line of phosphorescent targeting dots. He wished he could fire a rocket, or two, or three—until he remembered the cargo. Anyway, Crows weren't fitted with rockets. Yet. He jumped the Crow out to the left side for a different view. Coming up was an open section, not another mesa but at least a short break in the trees.

For a second, he went eye to eye with the driver of the last rig in his left side mirror. He was just a kid, scared, in over his head.

Nate dropped back, waited until it broke clear above—black, starry sky— then jumped up and over the last rig in the line. He skidded across the roof, cutting it closer than he meant. There was no more than a quarter mile of open air. He sped ahead, trying to get to the front of the convoy so he could look the black-hat cowboy in the eye. Thirteen, twelve, eleven, ten RVs… The trees on the other side of the gap were coming up fast. Nate had a chance to pull up and go over the trees but he didn't take it, flew right back into the tunnel with the rigs. There was but ten feet of open space between the tops of the rigs and the overarching oak branches. Nate flew over four more rigs. Nine, eight, seven, six… His NightSun was still fired up, as was his forward-looking light. The drivers had to be seeing him coming in their mirrors, but maybe they couldn't believe that a Crow was in there with them. When Nate came over the fourth wagon from the front, the driver freaked and backed off the gas and the rig behind plowed into him, knocking the RV in front forward again and half out of control.

"We're going to get these people killed," Nate said, to no one. Ahead was a hundred-foot gap between two huge trees. Nate took the exit, turning the bird onto its side to thread the needle. He made it out, shot high.

"Holy shit," Tucker said when Nate popped out right in front of him.

The sky was crowded over the convoy, everybody still moving with it, all with their lights on. A hundred yards ahead, Carlisle was just above the trees, forward of the lead truck, flying backward again. "The road's straightening out," she came on to say.

"Five miles to the border," the Aussie CRO said.

"I can't see you, Timbo," Nate said.

"I'm ahead of Carlisle a klick,"

Nate climbed for a long-range view, oriented himself and pinpointed all the players on the game board, though this was less like chess than a rodeo. Ahead, the terrain was the same—trees after trees after trees, not another open area— no way to get in front of the convoy again.

"Mexico knows you're coming," Whitey said over the radio, just when Nate had forgotten about him. The GU and ICE helicopters were still standing off. "I predict they're going to close the gate in that big new fence of theirs. I almost feel sorry for these guys."

The border was a mile away. Nate couldn't see it. At least, not until a second later the Mexicans fired up the high-wattage tungsten floodlights atop the twenty-foot-tall steel fence that stretched off west and east. So Tecate wasn't the dinky, friendly crossing that Nate remembered as a seventeen-year-old kid with his friends, headed down to surf and drink and buy firecrackers. He should have known. He should have seen it coming. More Mexican lights came on. There was the checkpoint building itself. The gate was closing, all right...but not before a six-pack of armored troop carriers rolled out. Nothing like a country with a lot of oil.

"Now what?" Carlisle said. "I hate to say it but—"

"Pull up," Nate said. "The Mexicans are going to stop them. On our side of the border. They're rolling out APCs. We'll wait a few minutes and go in on foot... Or not."

His voice betrayed him. He'd already figured it out: the rigs were empty. He spun the Crow to see the panorama. The ICE helos were there, waiting, standing off a hundred yards, but the Gang Unit bird with Whitey in it was already gone.

Chapter Thirty-Eight

The .38 round that Nate turned end over end when he had the jimmies got a little more worn down as he flew flat-out toward Long Beach on autopilot. It was coming up on five o'clock. Dawn was already brewing behind him out over the Salton Sea. As fast as the Crow would go, it wasn't nearly fast enough. What he really needed was a time machine. He'd been wrong. He'd been tricked, played. He'd been Whitey'd.

A song was looping in his head, a Velvet Underground ditty about "the big decisions that cause endless revisions in my mind." The question in Nate's mind, causing endless revisions, was what had happened to the people down in the TMZ because of his decision to head toward Tecate. He'd let Whitey play him. Magicians called it misdirection. Pay no attention to the box with the woman in it waiting to be sawed in half. Look over there. Keep your eyes on these thirteen shiny Winnebagos speeding toward Mexico.

So where were they? Where were the people in the magician's box? Where had the New Okies gone this evening, where had they gone? Where was the kid who'd lost the dinosaur in the tunnel under LA? Where had they gone? Home? Home didn't exist anymore for them. Where, then? It was clear they weren't downtown, at least nowhere in plain sight. Who knew where they were? Cho had been on the ground at the border when Nate and the others—including the ICE agents—checked the hollow motor homes while the Inca drivers stood there smirking. (The black-hat cowboy businessman was in the gatehouse smoking a cigarette, making the Mexican agents laugh.) From the way he'd acted, Cho had been tricked, too. Of course in the case of Cho's misdirection, Nate had unknowingly been one of Whitey's shapely assistants helping pull off the trick. Keep your eyes on the thirteen shiny Winnebagos, Cho, it's all about the Incas and RVs.

But what about Derrick Wallace?

Nate had heard a voice in his head when he'd been lifting off from Tecate, that of Blind Billy—the barber in Compton—talking about all the heroin coming into LA now. *One if by land, two if by sea...* Billy had thrown in the line when he was talking about how there had been a shortage of heroin but now there wasn't. Zap Wallace used to run heroin out of Long Beach. He went to Lompoc for it. Derrick Wallace. His Bible was probably still in the backseat of the car, where he'd thrown it when he walked out of Lompoc.

Nate was still a hundred miles out from the LBC, twenty minutes. Rockett was asleep behind him, snoring like a kid in his car seat, one more thing tonight that made Nate feel old. He ran his finger down a directory on the heads-up display. The helo's brainbox sent out the call. Nate still hadn't reconnected to home base and Carrie. He knew she'd ask how things went down south. Or maybe she was in on the trickery, too. It had been one of those nights.

"You there, Baker?" Nate keyed the mic and said.

Baker was the rookie who had been the first CRO on the ground at the front-lawn domestic drama in Mar Vista the other night.

"Yessir," Baker said, quick, at the same time his young face came up on Nate's heads-up. He was at the stick of his Crow.

"You're working," Nate said.

"I've been on the dogwatch all month."

"So lunch is breakfast," Nate said. Rockett stirred behind him—probably at the mention of food—but then went back to snoring.

"My wife's having a baby. I'm taking every shift I can get."

"You know who Derrick Wallace is?"

"Just from TV. His boys' funeral, the shoot-riot."

"He lives in South Central, little house, five-one-six-three South St. Andrews Place," Nate said. "I need you to go by there. You don't have to land, just see what you can see."

"You got it," Baker said. "I heard about the drive-by, then the other son killed at the hospital. You lost your gunner, right?"

"It was a long time ago."

"It was last week," Baker said.

"Call me. Don't talk it up to anybody. Thanks. I'll buy you a crib or something."

"They cost like a grand."

"Then I'll buy you a steak at The Pantry." Nate rang off before the young cop could tell him he was a vegan.

The sky had gone almost yellow while they'd been talking. Nate could see all the way to the coast—a good twenty miles—or at least all the way to where the coastal fog sat, a big white feather bed. Some other day, he might have enjoyed the view, say if he had just gotten up and had his hands wrapped around a cup of coffee, sitting on a roof. Or if he'd been up all night, maybe with somebody instead of being alone and full of regret. But wasn't that what the wee little hours of the night were for? As he sped over Orange County with nothing to do but beat up on himself, he leafed back through the calendar in his head. Baker had been wrong about it being a week, but it was only nine days ago when he and Isaako hit the deck in the front room of Derrick Wallace's house while the machine guns rattled and roared, drilling holes in the wall.

Nate switched off the autopilot. "Wake up, Rockett," he said.

"I'm not asleep, sir," Rockett said, too fast.

"Wake up anyway. Talk to me. So I don't crash."

"Yes, sir."

"Do you care where we're going?"

"No, sir."

"Good man. We're going to Long Beach."

"Good, sir."

"You ever heard of The Velvet Underground?"

"No, sir. It sounds like a strip club."

"It's a band. Check 'em out. It'll warp your mind, in a good way."

Nate had sent Carlisle home to San Diego, then flown off, leaving Tucker and Cho on the ground to close the show at Tecate. Now Tucker came on the radio, out of nowhere. "You're flying like my grandmother," he said.

Tucker was back on his wing, ten feet aft. Cho in the second seat raised his hand in greeting. Both men looked whipped, especially Cho, who had a look on his face that said he was wondering what he was going to do for a living now.

"What's in Long Beach?" Tucker said. "I'm about to run out of gas."

"Plan B," Nate said. "One if by land, two if by sea."

"You think they're just going to put 'em on a boat, sail 'em out of there?"

"I guess we'll see," Nate said.

Long Beach. In full, clean new light, dozens of gulls and the occasional bully pelican screeched and reeled and fought over fish scraps above the marina. Not much else stirred. Across Shoreline Drive were the office towers and the terminus of the cross-city Metro line that had never opened. Downtown was barely alive. On the waterfront were the usual seafood restaurants and a marina. Up and down the bight were hundreds of sailboats, their masts uniformly still and straight. The day's wind hadn't yet come. On the far side of the marina were the sportfishing boats. Beyond that, two wide channels over, it was all business, commercial vessels, Terminal Island, cargo ships, and cruise-line docks: the Port of Long Beach.

Nate looked over at Cho behind Tucker. "You come up with anything from the sat-scans? What about my covered berths?"

Cho answered, "Three big enough and out of the way enough. One is just over from downtown, the end of your tunnel. Remember, we never could find it."

Tucker said, "I don't get it."

"What about traffic overnight?" Nate said to Cho.

"Since the cargo container thing, there have been drones up, wall-to-wall," Cho said. "They're checking every cargo container ten ways from Sunday. Anyway, nothing big going out all night—four or five fishing boats in the last hours, open decks, lit up. Maybe they could be down in the hold, but they all went straight out, then north," Cho said. Images came onto Nate's second screen, sped-up/slowed-down coverage of the commercial boats heading to work, nets out, floodlights hung from their masts. "The last red-and-white Catalina ferry came in at midnight, been at the dock all night."

Then they were above a nondescript tin building on the end of a dock, a covered berth. "It's big enough," Nate said. "And a straight sail-in."

"The other two possibles are on Terminal Island," Cho said.

"Terminal Island is too out in the open and too far from downtown."

"I am seriously running out of gas," Tucker said.

Nate dropped down over the tin building. There was a line of open berths next to it. Nate circled, Tucker hovered. At the opposite far end of the dock, a deckhand looked up as he washed off a small gray sea urchin diver's boat in an uncovered slip. Something about the man said, *I am not a deckhand.* He was a Black but a lot of Blacks worked on the water. Maybe it was the velveteen jumpsuit.

"Capture," Nate said to his target & track gear. The deckhand looked right at the camera, like a fifty-dollars-a-day extra. "Close in on the face. ID." The lens came in tighter.

"Shayne 'Cinder' Block," a radio voice said. "DOB: Eight–fourteen–ninety-nine. Compton, Los Angeles. Gang Affiliation: Twenties. Incarcerated: Two thousand sixteen to two thousand eighteen—Men's Correctional—Yucca Valley…"

Nate cut him off before he had to listen to the rest of the rap sheet. He lifted, shifted to port a hundred feet until he was over a tree-covered parking lot. There was a candy apple red 2020 Cadillac, in case anybody needed something else by way of ID.

Young CRO Baker came on the radio. "You there, Cole?"

"What have you got?" Nate said.

"He's walking. Alone," Baker said. "I was over his house when he came out. He's been walking since before the sun came up, going nowhere as far as I can tell."

"I know the feeling," Nate said.

Tucker said over the radio, "If I don't get some fuel I'm going to drop right into the sea."

Chapter Thirty-Nine

Wallace never went to bed Saturday night, instead staying up in the red velvet chair in his living room, staring at a cloth satchel on the coffee table. It was like a purse. Men carried them now—some men—carried their computers and their mobile phones in them, slung over their shoulders. Wallace had spent the hours of the night staring at it, never touching it, never opening it. The phone had rung a half-dozen times, but he'd ignored it. He drank a beer.

The same group of men as before, minus Nix, had come back to the living room that afternoon, a meeting that lasted into the early evening, until Wallace told them to leave. Wallace didn't sit in front of the piano for this one. He didn't sit anywhere, just stood there until the last man, Madison, was out the door.

By about four-thirty or five o'clock, he'd taken a shower, staying under the downpour for twenty minutes, leaning forward with his hands on the wall, the pose of a man about to be arrested. In prison the showers were short, on a timer, the water rationed, and you only got a shower every other day. Two minutes, five gallons. The prisoners had figured out a routine that got the washing done, but it grated on them, day after day after day. They knew it wasn't about the water shortage. The drought hadn't really kicked in until 2016, and the shower-rationing had begun years before. There was plenty of water, snowmelt from the Sierras. What it was was another way for the Controllers—the men with the keys—to control them. It gave the convicts one more reason to hate them, as if they needed one. And if a man stopped taking showers in protest, they put him in Segregation.

Jewel was awake in the bed behind him as he dressed, standing in front of the chest of drawers and the mirror, though she was pretending to be sound asleep. He knew she was awake and was glad she was pretending otherwise.

If she was awake, what would he say to her? Were they going to sit at the table in the kitchen at 3:00 a.m. with a cup of coffee and *talk* about it? Talk about the distance between them now? Men in prison became well-acquainted with solitude. Every silence was an awkward silence. Were Wallace and his wife going to talk about *that*? Were they going to talk about the fact that, tonight, anyway, he felt utterly alone? She'd made him go out and buy some new suits. Standing in a men's shop, he'd realized that she too wanted him to go back into it: the criminal life, his old life. She wanted Zap back. He'd even seen her huddled with Nix once, talking close and very seriously. He lifted a suit off the rod in the closet. It was black, like his old suits. He took things out of the drawers, dressed, put on a white shirt and tied a tie, put on the suit coat. He looked at himself in the mirror. Together. His exterior was at odds with what was going on inside him.

He kissed Jewel in her "sleep," a kiss that held as much anger as love but was sincere. She didn't stir. He looked back at her from the doorway, wondering if he'd ever see her again. It was just like the old days, though today he didn't have the weight of a gun under his armpit or snugged in his belt. That man would have been Zap.

It was still full-on dark when he came out of the house on South St. Andrews Place. He didn't pause on the stoop. He started up the sidewalk, the satchel gripped in one hand. The neighborhood wasn't quiet: more than a few parties were still going. He'd pass by a house or apartment with a crowd spilling out and music going and come face-to-face with a pack of partiers, leaving—but not going home to bed or to breakfast—heading off to look for another bash with a little life left in it. Some of them recognized him. A cop helicopter was overhead, nothing new about that.

He walked past the church twice before the doors were open. The earliest service was at eight. It was still dark. He kept going and walked over to Leimert Park. In a few hours, it'd be full up with kids and families, picnics. The day broke. The short, sleek helicopter came by again. "You think I can't see you?" Wallace said, to the sky. He set out walking again. When he made the third pass by the church, the service was in full swing, mid-sermon. He went in. It was crowded inside. He slipped into the last pew next to a fresh-faced couple with three dressed-up kids who smiled that *everyone-is-welcome-here* church smile. When the sermon was over, there was another song for what they called "the invitation" or "the call," and Wallace slipped out, leaving the satchel on the pew with a hymnal to cover it.

He was blocks away when a deacon brought the satchel to Pastor Lamb in his office. Lamb was out of his purple robes, daubing at his sweating face with a towel. He waited until the deacon had left before he looked into the satchel. He spilled its contents out onto his desk: a great deal of cash, thousands—*used* money, not crisp hundreds stacked and banded—a half-dozen wedding rings, four heirloom watches, and a small gold cross, such as might be worn by a girl child.

◆ ◆ ◆

BRIDGET LINDGREN LOOKED UP at her father, overheated, her faced flushed. She clutched his leg, as close to him as she could get. "I don't like this," she said, almost without making a sound, almost mouthing the words.

"I know," Gene Lindgren said. "I don't either. It won't be forever."

It was hard to see her face in the windowless metal box. They were all jammed together—standing—and there was only a single, caged light bulb mounted onto the wall at either end of the burnished aluminum box. The ceiling was just inches above the heads of the tallest of them. The floor was metal, too. There wasn't anything like enough air.

Somebody draped a denim jacket over one of the light bulbs to try to cool things off. Several of them nodded their approval.

"It'll probably catch on fire," a woman said.

"There's not enough air left in here for a fire," the man across from her said.

"We're like biscuits in an oven," another woman said.

"We're going to die down here," a man said, red-faced.

"Don't say that," another man said. "The children."

"It's true," a woman said. "This thing's running out of air, now that we're down. You saw the tanks when they led us in. They aren't big enough. There aren't enough of them. These people don't know what they're doing."

Bridget's mother, Betts Lindgren—like most of the others—had a fixed look, staring straight ahead, just trying to get through it. A ten-year-old boy was across from them, his back against the opposite bulkhead, staring at the Lindgrens, but not in a harsh way.

"I have to pee, Daddy," Bridget leaned up and said.

"You just have to go where you are," he said. "It's what they're doing. This will be over soon."

The girl seemed not to question this queer unprecedented thing, or just let it be added to all the other unprecedented things that had come into her life in California. She watched the urine run down the inside of her bare legs. She was wearing a sweet little homemade cotton dress and slip-on shoes with white socks. Nobody in California dressed like her, that she knew. She looked up at her father again, pulling herself tighter against him. Lindgren lifted her up to one of the ventilation ducts. Unseen motors large and small hummed and buzzed and whirred. The whole place never stopped shaking. Some other kid was crying; some other parent tried to calm him.

Chapter Forty

Both Crows were on the dock, side by side. The lookout in the jumpsuit was gone and the red Caddy with him. Rockett got a screwdriver out of the box on the Crow and came back to where Nate, Cho, and Tucker stood in front of the high corrugated tin door on the enclosed berth. The structure didn't look like much, but it was tall enough and wide enough to house a good-sized cabin cruiser. Rockett stuck the screwdriver through the shiny new padlock on the door and gave it a yank. The new lock held together but the clasp fell off. Nate threw open the door. Inside, exposed rafters and corrugated walls were held together with rusting nails. There was the walk-in level and a step-down level around three sides of the slip.

"I don't know what we would have done if it was sitting here," Cho said. He was on the radio to someone and working his screen at the same time.

"Plan C," Nate said.

"So what are we not looking at?" Tucker said.

"The Yellow Submarine," Cho said. "Like The Beatles song, only I don't think it's yellow anymore."

"It never was," Nate said. "They aren't stupid." He jumped down to the lower section of the dock, walking the length of the slip, pacing it off. "Derrick Wallace had it built six or seven years ago," he said. "He was in the Navy, knew something about subs. It ran to Mexico—heroin, cocaine, and pot, like tons—diesel-powered with backup electrical. We never could find it; then Wallace got sent up and it was over." He got to the end of the slip. "It's fifty, fifty-five feet long."

Nate was already out the door with Rockett behind him.

As the two Crows lifted off again, banking to head south, Baker came on Nate's radio. "He went to church," Baker said.

"Of course he did," Nate said.

◆ ◆ ◆

THE OPEN OCEAN WATER was clearer and cleaner than Nate had expected, and a color there wasn't a name for, at least not a name he knew. Below him and forward, a school of flying fish surfaced and dove, surfaced and dove, fifty or more of them. There was something about the way they swam that seemed carefree, even happy. Are fish ever happy? At least they looked as if they knew there were no fishermen close by. The two Crows were cruising side by side again, rotor to rotor a hundred feet off the water. They were out of sight of land, flying due south, headed for Ensenada. Tucker had made a stop for fuel at his base in San Diego, then jetted back out. Ensenada was just a guess on Nate's part but a reasonable one. It was a crowded, chaotic port with several entry points, a lot of liquid real estate filled with sardine and lobster boats, sportfishing rigs, and cruise ships, although now most of the cruise ships bypassed Baja because of new tariffs, now that Mexico wasn't desperate for the tourist dollar.

But Ensenada was still just a guess, and Nate had less confidence in his guesses than he'd had twenty-four hours ago. The sub—with a top speed of twelve knots—would be approaching Mexico in daylight, probably midafternoon. The traffickers could come in submerged and head to some remote part of the port or into another covered berth, if there was one. There was a high likelihood that the Mexican authorities had been paid off, so maybe they'd just come in on the surface, big as hell. If the plan was to stay offshore until dark, it would add another three or four hours to the run, which Nate didn't think would be all that appealing to the smugglers. So there was another guess or two on top of the last guess and the one before that. Nate tried to not to think about it, unsuccessfully.

Nate knew Tucker didn't like flying blind. "We're headed to Ensenada," Nate said. "Highway Three comes out of Ensenada, truck route, goes the back way up to Tecate and the farmlands. Any farther than Ensenada in the sub is a rough haul." Even to his own ear, Nate sounded like a man trying to talk himself into something.

"What if the guy on the dock tips them off?" Tucker said.

Behind Tucker, Cho said, "I had a friend pick him up, hold him out of the system. He didn't call anybody. Besides, radios wouldn't work underwater. We didn't notify the Coast Guard. Maybe we should."

Nate sorted through his words before he spoke. "These guys could panic if they saw a show of force. They could freak and screw up and put the sub on the bottom in a heartbeat."

"The Coast Guard can't go into Mexico, and neither can ICE," Tucker said. "Neither can we, come to think of it."

They all stopped talking while they covered another ten miles, all three— four counting Rockett—trying to picture what lay ahead and get their heads wrapped around it. Nate wasn't going to say it out loud, but he was thinking the sub could also head for Puerto Nuevo, "Lobster Town," south of Rosarito Beach, up the Baja coast from Ensenada. There was a long dock there with closed berths and not a lot of people nosing around on a sleepy Sunday afternoon. Nate knew that stretch of coastline well. For a year or so—years ago—he'd been down in Baja more than he'd been in LA: surfing, sleeping on the beach or with college girls in their motels, drinking dollar beers, eating lobster tacos and chuck steaks cooked over mesquite fires, riding K-38 and Scorpion Bay and Shipwrecks and Alisitos, drinking mezcal, smoking weed, learning the Spanish names of constellations. Bodie had called it "The Year of Not Giving a Shit," but it was the opposite of that, for as long as it lasted.

"Stay on this course," Nate radioed Tucker. "I'm going to head to Rosarito and slide down the coast, just in case. We'll meet up at Todos Santos."

◆ ◆ ◆

MOVING THROUGH THE GENTLE seas, the submarine surfaced just enough to expose the six-foot-tall conning tower, which came to a point fore and aft, shaped to cut through the water and leave almost no wake. On top of the conn was a wide air scoop and a short antenna. It was fitted with four video cameras, which served as a periscope. They were far from land, all but invisible from the side or above. The whole craft—a clunky, crude-looking thing, the engineering and build half homemade and half professional—was painted a color somewhere between the hue of the deep water around it and the blue of the unclouded sky above. It was running full speed ahead, head-down determined, single-purposed, going where it was going like a big dumb animal.

The sub had a crew of three. A scrawny, mixed-race, terminally-tattooed jitterbug, Perry, twenty-six, who referred to himself as "The Captain." An older Mexican man they called "Víbora," whatever his real name was. Víbora meant "viper." Víbora was Inca. The third man was Nix, the Black who'd stomped around pointing at people in Derrick Wallace's living room, he who'd run the Twenties while Wallace was in prison. Perry and Víbora wore navy-blue jumpsuits that looked as if they'd come from Wardrobe. In Perry's case, the cuffs were tucked into unlaced Converse All-Stars. Nix wore what he considered business attire, a beige leisure suit with a chromed .45 stuck in the belt. All three men were armed with handguns. They'd all taken a mix of tranquilizers and speed to make the trip tolerable and had glassy eyes and unpredictable responses. Clamped onto the bulkhead were a pair of shotguns and four full-auto rifles. And a signal-flare pistol, not that they'd want to draw attention to themselves if anything went wrong. It would be an enormous surprise if none of the guns had been fired when the day was done.

Inside, the conn was the size of a shower stall, with inch-thick Plexiglas windows on three sides, facing forward. The helmsman drove the sub in a standing position—standing on the floor of the boat—with a truck steering wheel at crotch level and four pedals underfoot. The bulkheads were fitted with twelve tanks—six on each side—air supply for when the sub was completely submerged and unable to suck in outside air. There was a bucket to piss in. Perry and Víbora spelled each other at the helm. Nix never touched the wheel himself but occasionally pushed aside whoever was on the helm to look out the windows or glance at a rack of screens showing the flickering feed from the vid-cams. The conning tower opened onto the "cabin," an eight-by-twelve cell, just barely tall enough for the men to stand, though Nix mostly stayed put in his white plastic Target lawn chair. Of course, Nix thought *he* was the captain.

This was their first run with human cargo. Aft of the cabin was the cargo hold, an aluminum box. A pattern of holes—in the shape of a peace symbol—had been neatly drilled into the door, no doubt in the pot-running days. Sometimes, from the back, moaning or an angry shout could be heard, but the human noise had subsided once they'd partially surfaced and the outside air had begun to circulate.

"We'll stay up ten minutes, then take it down again," Nix said, not even getting up.

"That sounds about right," Perry said, instead of *aye aye*.

"Put on some music," Nix ordered Víbora. "Something soulful, none of that Mexican shit."

Víbora went over to a shelf wedged into the ribs of the curved hull and flipped through a shoebox of discs left from the old days. He steadied himself with a hand against the low ceiling. His eyes wouldn't focus. The whole ship never stopped vibrating. It was like one of those electric massage chairs in the airport, only there was nothing relaxing about it. It made Víbora wish he'd taken a double hit on the cocaine back in Long Beach when the Twenties ganger had offered it.

"How far out are we?" Nix asked Perry.

"I'd guess two, two and a half hours."

"Send up the ball antenna," Nix told Perry. "We have to link up, tell 'em we're coming in, give them an ETA: estimated time of arrival."

"I know what it means," Perry said, instead of kicking a hole in something. "Release the balloon."

◆ ◆ ◆

US FEDS FLEW FORTY-YEAR-OLD Twin Rangers, but their Mexican counterparts rolled in full-on gunships, brand-new two-rotor helos built by the Israelis, who knew a thing or two about borders. And there was one of them, dead ahead above the Baja coastline, blocking Nate's way south, just waiting for him. It was like a bull pawing at the ground in the *corrida de toros*.

Nate cursed. He was still fifty klicks above Ensenada. He'd come in at Rosarito Beach as planned, then flown down the snaking coastline, just offshore, waiting to sight a conning tower, an unexplained wake, something, anything. He'd already flown over a dozen famous surf spots, famous to surfers anyway. The beaches were uncrowded, the water empty. Nate had wondered why until he started seeing the sharks offshore. He was just below La Fonda, a restaurant and hotel, when he started getting pinged—somebody forward of him. Now he was close enough to see the black-clad soldier-cops inside. Rockett cursed, too. The kid was learning.

Nate banked into a kick-out turn to starboard, heading out to sea again. "Yeah, it's your country, but these are *our* gangsters."

The bull just watched him go.

Nate called a number. Carlisle. "Thanks for last night," he said. She was out by the pool in a bathing suit, the screen propped against her knees.

"You make it sound like a date."

"A cop date. Sad as that is."

"What do you need?" she said.

"A margarita. Or a good-sized boat and you to ride shotgun. I'm off Ensenada."

"Did you find them?"

"Yes and no."

She said she'd see what she could do.

"Something fast," he said.

◆◆◆

RED-STRIPED LIGHTHOUSES MARKED THE ends of the Islas de Todos Santos as unmanned lights that came on at dusk or when a black storm rolled in. Isla Norte, the smaller of the two islands, was a quarter-mile long, flat-topped, with a rocky strand extending out from one end. From above it looked like a stingray, the strand its stinger. Out off the strand was where Todos Santos's monstrously big waves erupted four or five times a year, a deepwater break that since the sixties had been called "killers." At least by the North Americans. *Los Asesinos?* The islands were twelve miles out from Ensenada Bay. Today the surf was ordinary. And empty. Nate came in hot and orbited the lighthouse on Isla Norte. Tucker's Crow was on the ground near the beacon, the hatches scissored up, Tucker prone beside it, apparently doing pushups.

"Come on up when you're done with that," Nate said.

Tucker keyed his mic, "You see anything up the coast?"

"La Guardia Civil."

Cho was sitting on a rock, working a screen. He looked up in Nate's direction.

Nate sped off to the west. Tucker climbed into his Crow. Cho got back in the gunner's seat just as the hatches came down.

◆ ◆ ◆

THEY GOT LUCKY. THEY were ten air miles out from Todos Santos—the two Crows flying nose down at a thousand feet, fanned out, a half mile apart—when Rockett spotted something way below.

"There," Rockett said. "What's that?"

It was a balloon, three feet in diameter, blue-gray, just a dot ten or twelve feet off the surface, bobbing along.

"You got young eyes," Nate said to Rockett.

"What is it? A balloon?" Tucker said.

"Camouflage blue. With a line hooked to something that's moving."

"It's a ball antenna," Cho said. "It's snagged, not fully deployed. It's got to be them."

"I see it and then I don't," Tucker said. "Let's drop in, get a real look."

"Wait," Nate said. He'd seen something below. Or guessed at something.

◆ ◆ ◆

NIX SAID, "TRY AGAIN." Víbora was at the helm. Perry was messing with a radio. "Use the other channel."

An Okie pounded twice on the door with a flat palm and shouted something. The sub had been fully submerged for an hour and the air was stale and thin.

"Shut up!" Nix turned and said to the door.

There were more shouts from the compartment, more pounding. Nix snatched up off the floor what looked like a fire extinguisher but wasn't. It was a tank of gas with a hose attached to the valve and nipple, a red funnel stuck on the end of the hose. Nix stepped over to the door to the hold and opened the valve on the tank. It started hissing. He pressed the mouth of the funnel against the peace sign holes. Immediately, a different kind of shouting came from the compartment, more hands slapping the aluminum door.

"I'm not shutting it off until you all shut up!" Nix said to the door.

They quieted but it wasn't clear if they were responding to Nix's demand or whether the gas—whatever it was—had stilled them. A child coughed violently. Nix kept the funnel pressed against the door. Perry and Víbora looked at each other.

"I tried all three channels," Perry said. "The signal's not getting out."

"Then what the hell, surface," Nix said. "See what's wrong. We're still twenty miles offshore."

Víbora had his hands on the wheel but was big-eyeing Nix. Perry had gone back to fiddling with the radio, now with a new kind of desperation.

"Surface!" Nix ordered.

◆ ◆ ◆

"Climb!" Nate said.

The sub was surfacing. Tucker went right and Nate went left and the Crows both shot higher, climbing like bottle rockets once they were out of each other's way. They climbed to a thousand feet and steered into cloverleaf turns in opposite directions until they came back around, side by side again, hovering. Cho came close to blacking out.

"Stay high, but get over in front of it," Nate said to Tucker.

They watched on their screens through the long-range lenses. The sub—still powering forward—was fully surfaced now. The top of the conning tower opened and a skinny tattooed young man—his whole head was inked—climbed out onto the rolling deck. The sub had a four-foot shark fin welded onto its spine, some stoner's idea of a joke. The skinny man stumbled toward it and grabbed hold, steadied himself, looking aft. The blue balloon was just ten feet off the water, the antenna line caught in a patch of seaweed draped over the sub's tail. The man made his way unsteadily forward again to the conning tower and shouted down into the open hatch. After a second, the sub cut its speed to a crawl. The man hesitated, then went aft again, slipping and sliding on the deck.

"Ten bucks says he goes over the side," Tucker said.

Another man—a Black in a beige leisure suit—appeared in the conning tower, shouting in the direction of the skinny man. The first man shouted back and went on trying to disentangle the drape of seaweed. When the kelp came free, the skinny man lost his footing, went half over the side, saving himself only by seizing another handful of the seaweed. He shouted for help, on his belly against the hull. The man in the conning tower thought the whole thing was funny and didn't move an inch. The skinny man managed to pull himself onto the deck. He didn't look at the man in the tower, just went at the tangle of kelp again, finding the antenna line. He gave the wire a yank to break it loose. The line snapped off. The balloon rose, free! The skinny man made a futile jump to catch it—like a daddy at Disneyland—but it was long gone. It came straight up, caught a wicked fast thermal, and went sideways toward the horizon, out to sea.

Tucker was laughing.

"This isn't good for us," Nate said.

The second man in the conning tower now had an oversize phone to his ear, a sat-phone. The man finished his call and dropped down into the sub, and a second later it started moving forward again at full speed. The skinny man had to trot to make it forward and all but dove down into the conn. The boat was submerging, and this time all the way.

Nate pivoted the bird. From this height, the coastline was clearly visible, with Todos Santos ten miles distant and Ensenada another twelve miles beyond. Nate drew a line on the ocean and headed in, flying the speed of the sub, in the same direction.

Chapter Forty-One

A long hour had passed. They were still five miles west of Todos Santos, still flying above the sub, flying low and slow along that straight line drawn toward Ensenada. No La Guardia Civil helicopters had come out to meet them, so that was good, but second and third and fourth thoughts were nagging Nate. At this speed, it would take another hour to get into the harbor. The sun was dropping, getting close to dusk. That was good for the sub. When dusk came on, the world got sleepy, and people started letting things slide until they stopped paying attention to everything. Especially in Mexico. They'd probably invented Happy Hour.

It was torture for Nate and Tucker to fly at sixteen miles per hour. Like any fighter pilots, they weren't built for slow pursuit. They were all about *Now*, always impatient for the end. CROs always wanted things to get real and get done. Nothing quite made sense to them until it did, in the air or on the ground.

"I got an idea, Tucker," Nate said, dry. "Why don't you go on to Todos Santos?"

"Thank you, Father," Tucker said, and sped forward before Nate could change his mind.

Nate said, after another long mile, "See anything, Rockett?"

"Nossir."

"Water, water everywhere and not a drop to drink," Nate said. "That's what my dad used to say, every time we sailed our Hobie Cat." Memories were dogging him.

◆ ◆ ◆

THERE WAS NO AIR. "Maybe they're all dead up front," one man said.

More than a few of them started considering that possibility, as unlikely as it was. They started grumbling again and the ones up front went back to pounding on the door.

"God damn it!" a despairing woman said. "Surface!"

"Shut up, they'll gas us again," a man said.

The panic ramped up fast. Suddenly they were all gasping, fists clinched, pounding on the low ceiling and the walls. "Let us out of here!"

A white-haired man stood against the back wall of the cargo box, still on his feet although he was likely the oldest among them. His back was ramrod straight and his eyes were clear and bright, the color of the sky on a better day than this.

Without an introduction, he began…

> *I shant forget the night when I dropped behind the fight*
> *With a bullet where my belt plate shoulda been.*
> *I was chokin' mad with thirst and the man that spied me first*
> *Was our good old grinnin', gruntin' Gunga Din.*

It quieted the panicked. Someone even smiled. The children turned to stare at the man, whom none of them had paid any mind before.

> *He lifted up my head and he plugged me where I bled,*
> *And he gave me half a pint of water green.*
> *Though I've belted you and flayed you,*
> > *by the living God that made you,*
> *You're a better man than I am, Gunga Din.*

Up front, the crewmembers were as drained as the people in back but at least now Nix, Perry, and Víbora weren't feuding or casting blame. It used up too much oxygen. Perry was at the helm, on the floor with a plastic jug of water between his legs, his shoulders slumped forward, breathing as if he'd just run a footrace. Nix sat in his vibrating lawn chair, his eyes on the deck. The shouting from the cargo hold had stopped. Through the holes they could hear a man speaking, calmly.

"What is that?" Perry said.

Nix, who was closest to the door, said, "Somebody saying a poem or something."

"Poem," Perry said.

"Tap the next tank," Nix said to Víbora. Víbora didn't get up, just rolled over on his hip, reached up, and started screwing closed one valve, moving a rubber hose to the next tank in line and opening the new valve.

There was no hiss.

"Empty," Víbora said.

◆ ◆ ◆

TUCKER LAPPED TODOS SANTOS and once more started up Nate's line drawn on the blank ocean. He'd already twice flown all the way over into Ensenada, looking for anything, seeing nothing. "They're gone," Cho said behind him. "Or at least they're not here. It's going to be dark soon. No way they'd go in blind."

"Who's going to tell him, you or me?" When Cho didn't answer, Tucker went to the radio, "Hey, Nate."

Silence. Tucker rotated his Crow, a slow spin, came around until his nose was pointed toward the long brown line of the coast. Baja looked a thousand miles long.

"Nate."

Nate returned to the airwaves. "I'm here," he said. Tucker didn't have him on the heads-up screen but he remembered the look on Nate's face when they were on the ground at Tecate. "You go north, check Puerto Nuevo again, then watch Ensenada," Nate said. "At least until the *federales* come out. We'll go south."

"What's south?" Cho said.

"A memory," Nate said.

◆ ◆ ◆

"I GOT 'EM," NATE radioed. "Big as hell."

He was riding high. The sub was a hundred feet in front of him, running due south, submerged except for the conning tower. The sun would be gone in a half hour. The scene below—the golden expanse of sea, the shoulders of the tan mountains, the curving hyperblack coastal highway, the pastels of the sky— looked like a commercial for the Baja Department of Tourism.

"Where are you?" Tucker came on to say.

"Five klicks south of La Bufadora, just offshore of Punta Banda," Nate said. "Come on down. Bring your longboard."

Five minutes later, Tucker was on Nate's port side.

"I can't believe it," Cho said, looking down at the conning tower.

"What do you need me to do, sir?" Rockett said, not over the radio. "When we go in."

"Remind me I'm never wrong," Nate said.

◆ ◆ ◆

THERE IT WAS, CONQUEROO. Until the thirteen bodies on Coronado had overwhelmed him, Nate had kept count of the dead he'd seen. He'd also kept track of something else: the times he had come close to dying himself. What did *close* mean to him? Close enough to see it, feel it, taste it, look into its eyes, shake its hand, learn its real name. By his count, he'd almost died four times. (Being shot and stepped on and thrown off the roof in Boyle Heights wasn't one of them, nor the episode in the exploding restaurant kitchen.) Nate's most recent real brush with Mr. D—number four—had come two years ago, when a shoulder-fired rocket had blown him out of the sky over Van Nuys. But first on the list was Conqueroo, a left-hand reef break in Mexico, when Nate was nineteen.

The Crows hovered at five hundred feet a half-mile offshore of the hideaway cove, like rich people in box seats. Ten minutes ago, they'd watched as the submarine—still half-submerged, only the conn showing—powered in toward shore just past a rocky point. And then it had stopped cold, well out beyond the waves. It hadn't moved again, was just sitting there offshore.

It was an unusual place, a cove with a small river—just a stream, really—coming down from between the low brown hills before crossing under the highway beneath a simple arch of a bridge. The beach was half rock/half sand with the river splitting it. There was nothing around, not even a fishing shack. The whole scene was empty, empty and beautiful in the dusk. There were two lines of surf. The set farthest out from the beach was a roller that never broke, just flexed its muscular shoulders then shoved its mass of water on toward the beach, onto an up-slope on the bottom and then a reef. The reef created the second line of waves, the shore-break. The waves were long and straight, tubular and translucent. From offshore, from the helos' high angle, in the last light of the day, they looked like pastel glass tunnels, too good to be true.

"Does it have a name?" Tucker said.

"Conqueroo. That's what we called it."

"Where are all the surfers?"

"Somebody or something ran 'em off."

"Is that a river?" Cho asked.

"A big creek. Twenty feet across. Freshwater."

"What's up in the hills?"

"I don't know," Nate said, in a voice none of them had heard before. "Never went up there."

"They're surfacing," Rockett said.

Cho was watching the shore through binoculars. "I see boats, coming down the creek. Four Zodiacs with outboards, two men in each boat."

Tucker fired up his track & target gear. "They're coming out through that surf?"

"It's better than having them swim in," Cho said.

"Stay here," Nate said, peeling off from Tucker. He shot out sideways, northward. "I'm going up in the hills."

"The hatch is opening," Tucker said. "The same guy—the guy with the satphone before—is sticking his head up."

Nate cranked into a hard right. A beat later, he was over the coastal highway and then across it. He climbed even higher as the brown hills came up under him. He took up a position above the narrow river, high above it. A dirt road came off the coast and wound up into the hills, came out into a half-open wooded area next to the river, piñon pines with the underbrush cleared away, a campground or picnic area. It was rustic, not much to it—no buildings, not even portable toilets—but it looked sanctioned, government-issued. There were no campers or picnickers— not that it was empty. Two stake trucks with canvas roofs were next to the water, under the trees. A driver sat on the bumper of one, smoking a cigarette, kicking at the dirt. Nate drifted sideways and found another angle. A second man was stretched out on a picnic table.

Nate radioed the others, "I got two trucks up here in a picnic area, two drivers."

"There's a third man, in the back of the truck," Rockett said, over Nate's shoulder.

"Two drivers and middle management," Nate told everyone.

Tucker came back with, "Tat Man is out on deck and a new cat has come out too, Latin-looking. It's happening."

"Here they come," Cho said. "They're bringing the first people up on deck."

"They look half dead," Tucker said. "There are six of them, holding onto each other. Shit, there are kids."

Nate let the Crow slow-drift southward and looked down. The Zodiacs were just coming down the last stretch, transitioning from the river, powering into the ocean, toward the shore-break.

"Stay up," Nate said to Tucker. "Tail at the sun, nose down. So you don't catch the light."

"I don't think they're looking up right now. God damn, are you seeing this?"

Nate pivoted, switched to the long lens. The first of the Zodiacs were punching into the shore-break, an eight-foot wall of water. Each boat had a man in the bow holding onto a rope and a motorman with both hands on the tiller and throttle. There didn't seem to be much wave-timing involved, just bravado and brute force. The first boat made it up and over the wave, cutting through the top two feet of curling water, the Zodiac almost standing on its tail as it powered over. The second boat was twenty feet behind the first on the same line. It had an easier go of it, though the same wave was still alive and kicking.

"They're bringing more people on deck," Cho said. "How much sun is left?" Cho said. "They can't do this in the dark, can they?"

Tucker said, "This makes the RV deal look like a real good plan."

Into all the charged radio talk—Nate and Tucker and Cho talking over each other, running their words together—came a calm voice, Carlisle. "Where are you, Nate?" she said.

"Here. We got 'em," Nate said, fast. "South of Ensenada. Where are you?"

"Waiting off Todos Santos," she said.

"You got a boat for us?"

"A hydrofoil, a whale-watching boat. It'll hold forty. Where is here, how far south?"

"Five kilometers below La Bufadora, the point. They're right now taking them off the sub for the run to the beach. In Zodiacs."

"The *sub*?"

"Guess I didn't mention that. They have a submarine."

Then, company. La Guardia Civil was back, one fat black bird, hugging the coastline and coming south at five hundred feet. It passed on over the cove, continued on without changing speed or altering course. It was not possible that they hadn't seen the action, but they kept on going.

"And there they go," Nate said. "Nothing to see here."

◆ ◆ ◆

BRIDGET LINDGREN WAS IN the first Zodiac going in to shore, pressed tight against her father, under his arm. She was so cold. How could it be so cold, if this was Mexico? The sun was still up and everything was pretty and warm-colored, so how could it be so cold? Then she thought that maybe it wasn't the seawater making her shiver. She remembered how she'd shivered after they'd told her nanna was dead. (What they had said was that they had *lost* Nanna, but she knew what they meant.) They had told her they were staying in that camp with the trailers and tents—and they had hugged her, tighter than ever before, but then they had gone off with their arms around each other and left her in the dark tent, shivering so hard she wondered if a person her age could die just from shivering. Now her father and another father were shouting for everyone to hold on, as if any of them weren't holding on already in every way they could. Though she knew it might make her more afraid and even colder, she pushed herself up until her head was above her daddy's shoulder, until she could see ahead. She'd never seen the ocean until that last day in that town on the coast when they got a ride over from the dried-up vineyards and then another ride down to Los Angeles with the woman. And she'd certainly never seen the ocean *from* the ocean, looking toward the land. So she didn't know what she was seeing in front of them, a smooth hump of water getting humpier and humpier until the rubber boat tipped up with it. She was seeing so many things she had never seen before, and not all good. The open boat kept rising, going up the backside of the wave, the outboard motor racing, sounding desperate, overwhelmed.

Bridget's mother squatted in the bottom looking with both eyes at the six inches of water splashing over her feet. Only the children would have been surprised if she'd jumped over the side. She buried her head under both of her arms. Her husband reached out with his free arm and pulled her close to him and their daughter, just as the bottom fell out from under the Zodiac and it nosed over the shoulder of the wave.

The little girl was surprised by how soft the landing was. The boat dipped, then righted itself, came up again, and then they were surrounded by foam, the wave behind them. The foam was just foam, like a bubble bath. She looked back. The man at the motor twisted the stick more and the engine growled even louder and the boat jumped forward. They had won a fight with Nature. It was something else that was new, and this time, it felt good. Her father squeezed her tighter, but now it was more like a hug *hello* instead of *goodbye*. The motorman smiled at her. He pointed. Ahead was something strange and wonderful. Just as the ocean was ending, a new pathway of water opened up before them, water that was coming *toward* them, toward the ocean. A creek, like the ones at home? It was as if the beach was opened up, split down the middle. The Mexican man standing in the bow turned and shouted something to the motorman and he steered left and rode the new water across the beach and then under a high bridge, into a place of trees, strange as that was. She patted her mother's foot.

◆ ◆ ◆

"WHAT DO WE DO now, Chief?" Tucker said. "The *federales* with their stinkin' badges are gone. It's back to just us."

"Did you say *justice?*" Nate said.

The sun was almost gone. The second Zodiac, headed for shore with the second load, was just pushing through the back of the wave, making it look easy. The third and fourth boats were out in the rollers, on their way to the sub, where the rest of the human cargo stood on deck in a line, like passengers waiting for the train.

Rockett said to Nate, "There's something in the back of that second truck."

Chapter Forty-Two

Nate and Rockett were still high above the picnic area. The drivers below weren't loafing anymore. The first Zodiac was just arriving, driving right up onto a sandy bank under the trees. The Okies jumped out. Whether it was a joke or not, one of the men among them knelt and kissed the ground. One of the truck drivers grabbed the bowline, pulled the boat up higher, and wrapped the line around a tree. The boss man was dropping the tailgate on the second truck, and the other driver was standing beside him. The Okies started toward the back of the nearest truck to climb aboard—just trying to be helpful—but the boss man shooed them away to wait beside the picnic table. He gestured for the two men from the Zodiac to come forward. They disappeared under the covering of the half roof of the truck and pulled out a loaded pallet.

The gray-green picture on Nate's screen showed a stack of packages the size and shape of loaves of bread. A tall stack.

"Is that cocaine?" Rockett said.

"Or heroin," Nate said. "I was hoping it'd be pot, so I could not give a shit."

Nate and Rockett watched as the two drivers and two boatmen formed a human chain to load the drugs onto the now empty first Zodiac. The boss man supervised, the drugs clearly more important than the people. The second of the Zodiacs arrived, pulled onto the bank next to the first. They'd put a white-haired man in the second boat but he wasn't among the first ones off, instead waiting for others to go before him.

"Did they make it?" Tucker said. "What's happening up Shit Creek?"

"First and second boats off-loaded, all good," Nate said. "Where are the other boats?"

"They just started upriver toward you with the rest of the people," Tucker said. "Have we got a plan here? I'm feeling like a spectator."

"Are they loading them in the trucks?" Cho said.

"Whoa! Things just changed," Tucker said, excited. "Heavy firepower." He threw his track & target image over to Nate. The skinny man and the beefy Mexican were coming up out of the conn with machine guns.

"They're loading a boat up here with heroin or maybe coke," Nate said.

"Make money coming and going," Cho said. "That's Zap Wallace."

Nate left the picnic grounds in the hills, dove toward the beach, then cranked left and flew along the surf line. There was no need to stay invisible anymore. If the crew on the sub saw them and panicked—now that the Okies were on dry land—so much the better. Let them panic. Panic had its uses as long as it was the criminals panicking.

Nate dropped and slowed, flying over the wave, the shore-break.

"What are you doing, Nate, reliving your youth?" Tucker said.

"Drop down on the sub, right on top of them," Nate said. "Get big on them. Let's let them get a good look at us."

"That's the plan?" Tucker said. "Scare them?"

"I thought you said Carlisle was coming in with a hydrofoil," Cho said. "Where is it?"

Carlisle's voice came on the radio. "We're ten minutes away. Keep your pants on."

"Stand off with the boat," Nate said. "But you come on in, Carlisle. We could use another Crow."

In the last minutes the sky had gotten lighter somehow, a last exhaled breath of daylight. Nate looked out at the horizon. The sun was touching the water. He dropped down even closer to the top of the tube of the wave and turned left, running the length of it. It was a quarter-mile long. Flying slowly along it like this, it seemed even longer, impossibly long, a wave in a dream, a wave that never breaks. It was what the place was known for. The other thing was the Keyhole—or just the 'Hole. The reef was relatively close to the beach, no more that twenty-five yards out. You'd get in position, watching and waiting, and then you'd see the build and start digging. If you'd timed it right—or if it had timed *you* right—you'd feel it lift, rise under you with such force they joked about being thrown into the sky. If there were other surfers and they saw you dig in and catch it—if they thought you'd earned it—they'd back off, let you have it to yourself, for safety's sake if nothing else. Because three-quarters of the way along the glass tunnel—with no warning, other than legend—the bottom dropped out of the wave. It was like being thrown off a roof. Free fall. If you had anticipated it and gone high, you'd power on across. Otherwise, you met the Keyhole. Nate never thought to call it anything other than that because that's what he'd seen through the jade water, coming up at him. A keyhole. A shape cut into the reef the length and width of a coffin, four feet deep, sand on the bottom. The reef around it would surely kill you—crush you, shred you—but the Keyhole was worse, the Pacific holding you down until your lungs burst, or the wave broke.

Nate didn't remember what he'd thought then—on his back in the Keyhole, the one time he rode Conqueroo—but now, skimming alongside the wave, looking ahead to where it fell apart, he flashed on the other times he'd almost died, for real. Would those scenes have happened—or happened to someone else, some other cop or cop's boy—if he'd been held down a minute longer? A minute. Can a single minute make all the difference?

If the key goes in the lock.

Nate came to the end of the wave, kicked out, flew out over the sub, and came in low, as if daring them to shoot at him. The tattooed man and the Latino man raised their full-auto rifles, but the one in the beige suit shook his head no.

Now Tucker and Carlisle came on scene in their Crows, a real show-of-force moment, even if the cops—a hundred miles into a country not their own—didn't have much to back it up. The timing was perfect. The first boat loaded with drugs was approaching the sub. The throttleman in the Zodiac idled, unsure for now what to do. He grabbed up a walkie.

"I'm opening the hatch," Nate said to Rockett. The hatch scissored up. "Do that thing you did with the shotgun on the roof in the TMZ. Only don't shoot."

Rockett climbed out of his seat and stepped down onto the right-hand skid, holding onto the fuselage with his left hand and single-handing the shotgun with his right.

Carlisle saw what Nate was doing. "I want to do that," she said.

"Go ahead," Nate said.

Then Carlisle's gunner was hanging out the hatch too. Her gunner may have been a woman. Tucker just had Cho in the second seat.

The three helos circled the sub. The Zodiac's throttleman looked to the sub for guidance. It took another rotation of the jacked-up Crows before the shoulders of the Black in the beige suit slumped in resignation. He waved off the Zodiac, then said something to the skinny man and the other crew member, and the two crawled back down into the sub. The boss man looked up at Nate in the Crow and flipped him off, just for the sake of pride and professional discourtesy. Then he climbed into the conn and pulled down the hatch behind him. The submarine submerged a second later.

The boat of drugs pivoted and powered back toward the mouth of the river.

◆ ◆ ◆

THE THREE CROWS CROSSED the highway into the hills, Nate bringing up the rear. The sun was gone, as if the submarine had taken it down with it. All three pilots snapped on their night-vision gear. There was a commotion at the campground. The drug-run Zodiac had come back fast with the bad news and now a clumsier version of the human chain was off-loading its cargo into the back of one of the trucks.

"Let's see if these guys spook as easy," Tucker said. "Lights on or off?"

"Off," Nate said. "For now."

"Where do you want us?" Carlisle said. "Blocking them down on the highway or up here?" All three birds were staying high for now.

"If they get on the highway, they're gone," Cho said.

Rockett had stayed out on the skid with the shotgun. "Get back in," Nate said. Rockett climbed up into the second seat. The hatch came down. Nate was directly above the campground. Tucker and Carlisle were circling, standing off. The night-vision light-booster made everything below gray and green, made the Okies look even skinnier. They were like ghosts floating around under the trees.

All sixty seconds of a minute crept past. The hills beneath them had gone from brown to black in a heartbeat. There was no moon but a lot of stars, as if someone had flipped a switch. Up and down the coast road, no traffic, not a single pair of headlights.

"I'm going back down to the highway," Carlisle said. "Where do you want the boat?"

"Stand by," Nate said.

"Me or the boat?" Carlisle said.

"Both."

Nate looked down at the scene. He'd changed his position to where he was above the dirt road coming down from the staging area in the woods. He dropped down another two hundred feet, until he was not much higher than the hills around him.

"They're starting to load them," Rockett said.

"Tucker. Do what I do."

Nate counted to a hundred...and turned on his NightSun.

The ghosts became real. The Okies were all looking up, doused white as phosphorus, as if this were some kind of mass religious experience. Before they all threw up their hands, covering their eyes from the brilliance, Nate recognized two or three of them from the roof in the TMZ. Some were already in the back of the stake truck. They looked up through the slats in the braces and one hung off back of the truck, all looking up.

The drivers and the boss man scrambled to get in the front seats in the trucks.

Tucker said, "They're not giving up. At least not yet."

Nate waited another long minute and said, "Let them go."

"What are you doing?" Cho said.

"Nothing," Tucker said. "Let them go."

"We came a long way," Cho said.

"So did they," Nate said. "Lift. Keep your light on. Show them the way down the hill."

Tucker rose and flew down the hill, lighting up the dirt road, the escape path.

The trucks came to the coast road and turned north without stopping, a storm of dust coming down the hill after them. The drivers kept looking in their mirrors, waiting for the trap to be tripped.

Nate killed his floodlight.

"Where are they taking them?" Tucker said.

"There's a turnoff, Mexico Three, a couple of miles up," Nate said. "A work road. It turns north toward the big new ag operations."

Carlisle had been listening in. "I'm going home," she said. "Thanks for asking me out, Nate."

"Thanks for coming," Nate said.

"I need a beer," Tucker said. "I'll buy."

"Rockett has to take a leak," Nate said. "Go on without us. We'll catch up."

As the other two Crows blew northward, Nate landed on the beach. The hatches lifted. The rotors stopped spinning. Nate climbed out. He unkinked his legs. He patted the fuselage, the way a rider might pat his horse after a long ride. He'd been in the air behind the controls twenty-two out of the last twenty-four hours.

Major quiet. The kind that almost makes a man want to shout to break it, before it breaks him—that kind of silence. Nate walked away from the helo and took a piss on a bleached-white driftwood log that looked—at least tonight—like a dinosaur bone. With the Crow's engines and radios off, there was nothing to remind the ear of the twenty-first century. Nate thought of those blue eyes again, looking up at him from the bed of the truck. White people, he thought— *his people*, he thought—when some buried tribal thing in him stirred. So he'd let them go. Let my people go. They were let go, left to go on to…something different. Whether it was better or not, it was left to them to find out. Nate buttoned up his flight suit and turned and looked out to sea. His eyes had adjusted to the moonless night. Now he could make out the white tops of the waves.

He looked up at the spread of stars. Ursa Major was on its back on the horizon. He tried to remember its name in Spanish. Ursa was *bear*. It would be *Oso*-something, he guessed. *The Year of Not Giving a Shit* was a long time ago. Osa Mayor! He looked back at the Crow. Rockett leaned against the tail section, rubbing his leg, drinking from a bottle of water. He lifted it in salute.

Chapter Forty-Three

There was that Shinola moon again, tonight just a comma at the end of the only slightly silvery path across the dark blue Pacific. The windows were open, the steady breeze stirring the chrome palms. Perfect. Everything come back 'round again. It was early yet. The club was all but empty. A man played the glass piano, that was it. Ava was alone at a table for three, the same table in the shadows where the black-haired Cali had sat and cried that first night, the first time Ava had seen her in the flesh. She was here tonight, Cali; she'd just gone to the powder room.

She came back. She stood over the table a moment, then smiled at Ava, sat down.

"Your lemonade didn't come yet," Ava said. "My lemon drop cocktail came and somehow it evaporated, so another is on its way."

Cali smiled again. It seemed sincere, if limited. Tonight her hair was a color that was likely her natural color—taffy—which was *near*-blonde but not so obvious. Not so pushy, not so...*Cali*. She wasn't wearing much makeup tonight, just a little color for the lips. She'd already lost her tan. She was wearing a loose, filmy dress. It appeared expensive but it didn't look new. Maybe Vivid had given it to her, a hand-me-down, or maybe Cali had brought it with her to California, the best dress she owned. She wore white shoes more practical than stylish.

She looked beautiful. "Did you really go to New York when you were seventeen to try to be a model?" Ava said.

Cali gave her a look. "No," she said. "What are you talking about?"

Ava realized the poor thing didn't remember what she'd said at Lynch's train station house up at San Simeon, when she's been under the influence. She was about to tell her all about it—it was a funny bit—but then thought better of it. "Never mind."

"I won a pageant, Rotary Club," Cali said, with some combination of embarrassment and pride. "Somebody told me then that I should try modeling. I never looked into it. I wasn't pretty enough."

"Being a model isn't about being pretty," Ava said. "It's about looking younger than you are and older than you are at the same time, for as long as you can pull it off."

"Did I tell you I went to New York?" Cali said.

"I must be thinking of someone else," Ava said. Cali knew Ava was concealing something from her. And Ava knew she knew.

Cali had cut her hair, too, or had a friend do it. Whether it was the new length or something else, Cali didn't brush it off her face anymore, not once since she'd walked in the door and sat down. Had that little Veronica Lake twitch been a feature of *Be.Here.Now*? Or a bug in the program? It didn't really matter anymore. It was gone.

"Like you said, never mind," Cali said.

"That would be a good name for a program, *NeverMind*," Ava said. "But don't tell DL."

"No, I won't," Cali said, rather dully. "I'm sure I'll never see him again."

"Were you using the Lynch thingie right from the start? *Be.Here.Now.*" Cali nodded. "You know, you're smart," Ava said. "*You*. You're smarter like this than you were like…that."

"You mean like Cali."

"Like Cali," Ava said.

Of course, Cali had a real name and now Ava knew what it was, but she wasn't about to use it. She'd seen the slight tremble in Cali's lip from the start when she'd walked in the door of The Shinola. There was no guarantee that this was going to work.

"All you have to do is talk to him," Ava said.

Silky Valentine himself brought Cali's lemonade. He placed it on the table. "It's on the house," he said. He was acting oddly. "Handmade," he said. "From… lemons." He clicked his trademark click twice, but slower than normal, more seriously, not ready to walk away.

"What?" Ava said. "What's wrong, Silk?"

He looked at Cali and then at Ava. "I don't want any trouble," Silky said.

"Then keep those lemonades coming, pardner," Ava said.

He walked off, shaking his head.

"That was strange," Cali said. She really was coming to her senses.

Ava had tracked her down to Vivid's place in the hills, on Lookout Mountain. She had prepared for a full assault, a by-the-book strong-arm snatch-and-run. She'd put on her stealthiest catsuit, got her running shoes out of the closet, even called in backup, Chrisssy, who'd been positioned at the end of the cul-de-sac in case the subject climbed out the bathroom window. Ava and Chrisssy had gone over The Plan twice, studied the aerial of the house, synchronized their watches, had a *here-we-go* hug, and then they were ready.

Ava had been tying her sneakers when she'd said to Chrisssy, "I'm going to call her."

"OK…" Chrisssy had said.

Ava had called Cali. Cali had listened to a sensible sentence or two, said yes.

"Did Vivid drop you off here?" Ava said now.

Cali nodded. "She might come by later. To see me off."

"I'm not sure that's a good idea," Ava said.

Cali said, "She's on *your* side. She thinks I should go home, go back to Tom, go back to Belleville. What she said was, 'California's not for everyone.' She also said she envied me."

Ava waved at Tommy Cairo behind the bar. Where was that second lemon drop?

"Where is he?" Cali said, looking at the front door.

"Don't worry," Ava said. "He's probably riding his bike."

"He has a bike?"

"He had one the other night. He rode it from Downtown to Westwood to my office."

"You don't understand who he is, what he can be like."

"Girl, just give it a chance. He said—"

"What not one of you ever understood was that I love him," Cali said, stopping Ava cold. "I love him and I miss him. I never stopped missing him."

"Oh," Ava said.

"We're not as far apart in age as you probably think," Cali said. "People in California have messed up ideas about age anyway. I'm older than I look and he's younger than he looks. I always wore clothes that were younger and he wears clothes that make him look like a man instead of a boy. Looks aren't everything."

"Maybe I should live in Belleville, Illinois," Ava said.

"That would be hilarious," Cali said, flat.

Ava was going to miss her. How could that be?

"He's probably walking here," Cali said.

"He said he was going to take a helicopter," Ava said.

"No way. He hates to fly. He won't even go up in tall buildings."

"He flew out here."

Cali looked at her. "Really?"

"He told his hired actor Beck to talk about taking the train out, but he *flew* out," Ava said.

"That's so sweet," Cali said.

Ava was still trying to process the wild idea that Vivid might be envious of Cali. Could it really be true that all women wanted the slavish devotion of a top-notch g—of a guy?

Ava said, "Speaking of which…"

Tom "Happy" Hadley was walking up to the table, literally hat in hand. A white Panama. He looked as if he'd lost ten pounds since the night in front of her office. He was wearing a new suit, light-colored—corn-silk blue?—possibly seersucker, almost fashionable. Ava pictured him standing before a mirror in a froufrou men's store in Beverly Hills thinking that the color would remind his wife of the sky back home.

It was an awkward first thirty seconds. Hadley stood over his wayward wife, bowed as if to kiss her, but thought better of it and ended up just bowing. Ava sat back in her chair, mum, letting the two of them talk. Her second lemony vodka treat had come so she had something with which to occupy her hands and lips.

Hadley probably had his case for why Cali should come back with him laid out on three-by-five cards, but he never took them out. Instead, he just talked about home, about people from home, animals, flowers, other animals, weather. It'd been raining a lot back in Belleville. Of course it had. It was normal, a normal place with normal people. Ava could see that just being around his wife turned Tom Hadley into a different man, a man he almost certainly would rather be than the angry, red-faced, gun-totin' man who'd stood in front of the Hudson in the garage. Cali wasn't saying anything but she didn't move her hand when his hand brushed against it on the table. Hadley was being careful, so self-consciously careful. He'd start to tell her about something or someone and then stop himself just before he said something that he realized she might find corny now, too Belleville, Illinois. He was talking about a church function—or was it the Boy Scouts or 4-H or Little League?—and just as he reached what was probably the best part, he stopped and said, "I didn't go."

When he'd first sat down and started talking, he had locked eyes with his wife—as if it were just the two of them in the place and it was do-or-die—but now he started looking at Ava, too, including her in what he was saying, though Ava only nodded and smiled and smiled and nodded.

The whole thing felt as if it could collapse in on itself at any moment.

"How's Mom?" Cali said. It was clear she meant his mother, not hers.

"She's good," Hadley said. "I got a ramp built for the front of her house. I drew up the plans and Lamar nailed it together for me. I made it gradual but she still goes down it too fast. Speed demon."

Cali turned to Ava. "My mother died when I was seventeen."

"Oh," Ava said. "Sorry." She stole a look at her watch.

Cali pushed back from the table and stood. "I need to go to the ladies' room," she said. "Excuse me."

"I should go, too," Hadley said. "I mean, the men's room." He laughed awkwardly.

Cali put a hand on his shoulder and leaned over and kissed him on the lips.

It was like he'd won the lottery.

There was so much familiarity in the gesture, Ava thought, such ease, so many years behind it. Togetherness. A marriage. What a concept! It was as if Hadley's happiness (and Cali's?) only existed in proportion to Ava's…what? Unhappiness? Dissatisfaction? Loneliness? Singleness?

"We should think about dinner," Cali said. "I'm hungry and I know you are, Tom."

Speaking his name doubled his joy, fool that he was. He watched her walk away across the club toward the door marked *Damas*. Once again, it was just the two of them in the world. He watched until she reached the ladies' room and went in.

"Life is funny," he said, mostly to himself. "Sometimes you have to go through the valley of the shadow to stand in the light."

"I guess," Ava said.

"I hope I have proven myself to you," he turned back to Ava and said. "I am a better man than the man I hired to make you think I was a good man."

"You don't have to prove anything to me."

"Of course, I do," he said. "California is about nothing except judging the rest of the country. And finding all of us out there unworthy, except maybe for people from New York."

He had a point.

"I'll never be like you people," Hadley said. "But I'll say this: my heart is tuned to her wavelength."

It was among the most Californian things Ava had ever heard, bless his heart.

Two things happened in quick succession.

Vivid came in with about a dozen people, blowing in like a gust of wind.

"Uh oh," Ava said.

Vivid stood just inside the door, waiting for everyone to spot her. In the last half hour, the room had filled, table by table, stool by stool at the bar. Now Ava knew why. Word must have gotten out that Vivid was on her way.

"Look at me, I'm so happy!" Vivid said to the room at large. Everyone laughed. Most of them were already on their comms, telling their friends what they were seeing: Vivid in the flesh.

The second thing that happened was Cali came out of the ladies' room.

She looked to the right and saw Vivid. Vivid didn't yet seem to see her. Cali glanced in the direction of Ava and Hadley at the table across the club—that's all it was, a glance—and then she started toward the empty stage through the grove of metal trees. A beeline, a straight course. She stepped up onto the stage, slowed just enough to make it seem she was going to take the mic and say something—or sing a song or introduce Vivid—but Cali kept going, moving faster. She continued on across the stage from front to back, headed as she was toward what was behind it: the open windows with the view of the ocean and the moon.

She jumped into the ocean—or so it seemed. There was a shattering sound. The ocean behind the open windows wasn't the ocean at all, just a wide screen; the moon wasn't the moon, wasn't even a projection of the real moon, the shimmering path to the unreal moon was just a pixel painting. The high drifting clouds weren't real. How could they be, so perfect? Hadn't anyone noticed the patterns repeating, noticed that the thirteenth high drifting cloud in the cycle had Vivid's face on it? Hadn't anyone figured out that the waves never broke, that the night sky was impossibly clear, that the constellations in the sky were from the Southern Hemisphere? With the shattering, the image went to black and jagged pieces fell.

Ava had seen every step from Cali's exit from the ladies' room on and she'd jumped to her feet. She knew what she was seeing. She knew this wasn't going to end on stage with a song or even a recitation of a poem from an amateur from Belleville, Illinois. She knew what was about to happen.

Hadley had his back to the club and wasn't seeing anything. Vivid saw, Vivid knew. She turned to a man who was part of her team and said something and he started in. "Cali!" Vivid said.

It was then that Hadley turned and saw what was happening. He sprang to his feet and went after Ava going after Cali, throwing people and tables and chairs out of his way. He and Ava both got to the back of the stage before Vivid's bodyguard did. They looked into the void behind the screen. Fake sea breeze propelled by oscillating fans blew in their faces. The air didn't at all smell like the sea—it smelled like the oil that lubricates electric fans.

"Oh, God no," Hadley said, looking down, stepping over the rail, over the shards of the screen. Cali was already halfway across PCH, the coast road, threading her way through the stalled traffic to the empty beach. Hadley ran after her. Ava followed.

Cali didn't look back once. She couldn't. She knew what was behind her, not just a man, not just who she had been—or tried to be—but mile after mile after mile of California. That was what was behind her, California. And beyond California was the desert and then Arizona and then New Mexico and the Texas Panhandle and then Oklahoma and Missouri…and Illinois. There was no chance of catching up to her. She ran like an animal, wild to live, driven by instinct that in the moment seemed to her infallible. The beach here was so wide, so groomed, she was thinking as she ran. They came through with rakes behind trucks in the hours just before dawn and raked it again in the afternoon. She ran past a red county lifeguard tower, tipped over on its side for the night. She could barely see the water from where she was, just the black-and-white stripes of the waves a hundred yards ahead. She'd pulled off her shoes as soon as she'd reached the sand. Now she tugged at the tie at the waist of her dress and it came undone and fell away.

Hadley had no chance of catching her. He was too fat and too old. He kept shouting her name into the wind. Her real name. She reached the water. She swam straight out and dove under the first wave that met her. Hadley was hopelessly behind her, but he followed her into the surf, shocked by how cold it was but not letting himself think about it. She was already fifty yards out, swimming with sure strokes, still not ever in any way looking back at him.

Someone at The Shinola had called the police and here they were already, four Crows.

Ava walked in the sand, carrying her shoes. She knew it made no sense to run after them—that she'd never catch Cali, never even catch up to Hadley—knew she couldn't stop either one of them if she did. Or wouldn't try.

She'd think about the philosophical questions some other night.

Ava reached the water's edge. The tide was coming in, each successive wave darkening more sand. Cali couldn't be seen anymore. She was out beyond the end of the pier already. Two of the Crows had gone with her but now—by the way they were flying—Ava knew they'd lost sight of her. The other two Crows split up to cruise just above the surf line, already looking for a body. Tourists and locals lined the railing on the pier, watching the show. Ava looked behind her. The window of The Shinola was filled with spectators, too.

Hadley flailed away in the black surf just fifty yards off the beach.

Cali knew his secret—that he didn't know how to swim—not that it meant she would turn back.

Ava looked up at the Crows as their NightSuns knifed through the night. In a perfect world, she thought, one of them would be Nate Cole. But it wasn't a perfect world. It was Los Angeles.

Chapter Forty-Four

Bodie opened the glove compartment, looked in, and closed it again.

"I listened to you on the radio the other night," he said. "That radio you gave me with the big black arrow drawn with Magic Marker at the frequency number, as if I was blind and senile on top."

Nate just drove. He felt so good in the moment—behind the wheel of the old pickup, the windows down, the engine humming—that he could barely contain himself. He was almost spilling out of himself. He hadn't felt that way in he couldn't remember how long.

"You can sure talk some bullshit, I'll tell you what," Bodie said. When Nate didn't say anything, he said, "Made me proud. The family tradition, bullshit. The Cole Man Way."

Bodie had his window down, too, had his arm out. Since air-conditioning had taken over the world, nobody rode that way anymore. How's a man going to get a respectable trucker tan sealed up in his car with processed air blowing in his face?

The sky was hard blue. "This thing still runs good, doesn't it?" Nate said.

"It does. I miss V-eights. Hell, I even miss straight-sixes." He looked over at Nate but Nate had his eyes on the road. Bodie seemed skittish. His leg was bouncing of its own accord.

It had taken some doing, but Nate had busted his father out of the Police Sunset Home in the middle of the night. He told the night guard it was Bodie's birthday the next day and that Nate and his sister were planning a big pool party. His nonexistent sister. The guard was just a guard and the duty nurse—who might have known about the new diagnosis—was over in the other wing. Nate rolled Bodie out in a wheelchair, picked him up, and stowed him in the second seat of the Crow, buckled him in, and blew up and out of there, leaving the wheelchair sitting in the parking lot, Exhibit A. Bodie hated to fly as much as anyone in the history of the world ever hated to fly, so there was a miniature bottle of emergency vodka in the seat. Bodie drained it as they flew over Dodger Stadium. They buzzed out to El Centro. Nate and Bodie had a car man, Galen— mechanic, painter, procurer of new/old parts, legal and otherwise—who maintained and stored the family wagons, keeping them road-ready. Nate had six cars with Galen, all but one of them illegal to drive now. Six cars, one truck, the '55 Chevy pickup Bodie'd dropped a 409 V-8 into. Nate had filled the truck's tank with Crow fuel, 101-octane leaded gasoline, and driven east. Once you were out of Los Angeles proper, the roads opened up, just electro slot cars and FedEx triple-rigs. Open road, what a concept.

Nate steered off onto the ramp for the overpass and Highway 62, heading north past Palm Desert toward Yucca Valley and Joshua Tree and Twentynine Palms.

"What happened with your crooked cop?' Bodie said, looking out his window at the spiky yuccas and organ pipe cacti. The desert liked the new dry world just fine, thank you very much.

Nate didn't seem to want to talk about it, but after another mile he said, "On Mondays, Wednesdays, and Fridays, I think everybody gets away with everything. On Tuesdays and Thursdays, I think nobody ever gets away with anything."

"What about the weekends?" Bodie said.

"I don't think about it either way," Nate said. "What was I saying, on the radio? I usually don't say much, believe it or not."

"You were talking about Mexico, constellations, dicking around when you were a kid."

"First time I ever went down there was with you."

"I don't remember," Bodie said. He didn't like the way that sounded. "I mean, I remember a dozen trips." He turned to look at Nate. "You didn't teach yourself to surf, you know. Or even how to drink tequila I don't think."

"You remember what I was playing, the song?"

"It's All right, Ma, I'm Only Bleeding..." Bodie grunted a laugh.

Wonder of wonders, the sky started getting dark, very dark. "Son of a bitch," Bodie said. "Smell that!" It wasn't raining yet—not where they were—but by God it was raining somewhere close by.

A half-hour later, they were in the middle of the town of Joshua Tree. JT had gotten itself back together again after becoming so fashionable and filled with rock stars and movie directors and actors and models that it was all but insufferable. Then the Big Quake came along, rolled the boulders, and realigned the chakras—whatever the hell they were—and the holy order of the pure desert was somewhat restored. Now you could buy a homesteader's shack without electricity or running water for less than a hundred grand.

Nate left 62 and went north, away from town and the National Monument. Bodie got quiet, hadn't said a word for ten minutes. As they drove farther and farther into the nothingness, the sky got darker and darker. It wasn't a sad or angry kind of quiet on Bodie's part. There was resignation in it. And what seemed like a little fear, which was always a surprise in a beat-up old man who talked a good game like Bodie.

"I sure miss the rain," he said, drawing in as much of the free air as his lungs would hold.

Ahead, there was a plateau. There were a half-dozen people there, desert people, Joshua Tree hippie leftovers and art lovers. There was an honest-to-God teepee, so honest you'd have to spell it *tipi*. Parked in a rough circle around it were a variety of mad homemade vehicles the beautiful oddballs had gotten themselves out there in or on: motorbikes and motorcycles and dune buggies and one vintage school bus with the back half of the top sawed off. And one powered unicycle painted purple.

Bodie looked across at Nate as he parked the pickup. "What is this?"

Nate tossed a screen to Bodie. On it was a map. "Something new, something they never needed before," Nate said. "It tells you where the closest rain is, where it's going to be. You want to just stay in the truck? Or I can lift you out, we'll sit on the tailgate. For as long as we want, at least until it rains."

Bodie laughed an odd laugh and shook his head. "Goddamn, I thought you were bringing me out here to shoot me."

"What?"

"You had some kind of weird look in your eye. You went to all that trouble. We're in the middle of nowhere. I heard you tell the guy it's my birthday and it's not. You're talking about how nobody gets away. You've got a forty-four Magnum in the glove compartment."

Nate said again, "Here or on the tailgate?"

Bodie pushed open his door and rested one bare blue foot on the running board. "I'm good here. Bring it on." Bodie handed Nate a scratched and scraped music cassette, Jurassic technology. "Stick this in," he said to his son. "It slid out from under the seat when you stopped back there. I can't even tell what it is."

Nate shoved the beat-up cassette into the player and punched the button.

"Walk this way!" the cocky singer demanded as the first heavy drops of redemptive rain fell onto the windshield from a great height.

THE END